Where There's a Will

Matt Beaumont is a feckless slacker who doesn't know the meaning of an honest day's work. How he managed to finish this, his *fifth* book, is, frankly, a mystery. Incredibly, he has a website – www.LetsTalkAboutMe.com – though that is due mostly to the hard work of others.

Praise for *Where There's a Will:*

'Beaumont's great gift is to make Alvin such a sensitive and believable character . . . the plot twists are marvellously ironic and compellingly drawn.'
Francis Gilbert, author of *I'm a Teacher, Get Me Out of Here!*

Visit www.AuthorTracker.co.uk for exclusive information about Matt Beaumont.

BY THE SAME AUTHOR

e

The e Before Christmas

The Book, the Film, the T-Shirt

Staying Alive

matt beaumont

Where There's a Will

HARPER

This novel is entirely a work of fiction.
The names, characters and incidents portrayed in it are the work of the author's imagination. Any resemblance to actual persons, living or dead, events or localities is entirely coincidental.

Harper
An imprint of HarperCollins*Publishers*
77–85 Fulham Palace Road,
Hammersmith, London W6 8JB

www.harpercollins.co.uk

A Paperback Original 2007
1

A catalogue record for this book is available from the British Library

ISBN: 978-0-00-733517-6

To Holly Beaumont,
my Mercedes.

Acknowledgements

I think everyone that works in a school deserves a peerage or a million pounds or something, but especially the ones who helped me with this book. They are Lynda Katzen at Fortismere, Christine Witham at Rhodes Avenue and Emine Salih and Hakkan Hakki at Park View Academy.

Thanks to John Saner and Mick Prichard, who gave me excellent advice on wills. I even followed some of it.

I'm grateful as ever to Special Agent Trevor. Also to Susan Opie and all her mates at HarperCollins for managing to print this the right way up.

A special mention for Jon at the Bottom of the Garden, a constant source of inspiration. In this age of personal mentors and gurus, he's my anti-life coach.

Finally, Maria. You're amazing, brilliant, sexy, clever, strong, sorted . . . Now, where's my fucking dinner?

Part one:

Kevan, Kelly, Louise

Of Mice and Men

'So why does George see ranch hands as the "the loneliest guys in the world"?'

Thirty-three blank faces. You couldn't quite hear a pin drop, but you could hear a schoolboy fart.

Yup, there it goes now . . . *fffffrrrrrrpp*. A schoolboy farting.

'Anyone . . . ?'

It's the teacher's first day. He's scared. Of *course* he's scared. No one tried to sell the school as Eton. He braced himself for the worst. Mayhem, basically. Shouting, cursing, that kind of thing. Maybe even a little violence. He wasn't looking forward to it, but he thinks he could have handled it.

Not this, though.

'C'mon, someone . . . *Anyone*. George. Ranch hands. Loneliness. *Why?*'

He looks out from his desk and no longer sees thirty-odd mute faces. No, he sees an arid, featureless prairie, empty save for the tumbleweed . . . And there on yon horizon, a skeleton, brittle and desiccated. It's him after just a few more periods of this malevolent silence. Lonesome cowboys? What about the poor bloody teachers?

Exasperated, he raises *Of Mice and Men* above his head. But what's he going to do with it? Throw it at someone? That would be illegal, wouldn't it?

'*Please* . . .' The word comes out as a faint rasp. He needs a drink. Water . . . Whisky . . . Hemlock.

Frantically he clears his throat. 'Anyone with any opinions

at all . . . ? On anything in this book . . . ? On *anything* . . . ?'

At last a hand goes up. At the back of the classroom. It's the boy who has had his face on his desk for the last thirty-five minutes, showing off the K freshly shaved into the back of his head.

'*Yes,*' the teacher says, way too eagerly, but sod it.

'Can I go for a slash?' the boy says.

The teacher now says something he will immediately regret because it sounds pompous and foolish. But you know, it's his first proper lesson and the words just spill out. This is what he says: 'And what's the magic word?'

A beat, then: 'Abracadabra, muthafucker.'

Now is the moment he should come down hard, force their respect. He knows that – they covered it in training. Or he should laugh.

There are two types of successful teacher – tough and cool – and he hasn't yet decided which he should be. And perhaps because he has been put on the spot, he freezes. Like a rabbit caught in the headlights of thirty-three oncoming trucks. Though the trucks aren't going anywhere.

They just wait.

For what? For him to faint? Implode?

He is saved by the bell, though not literally a bell. In this school it's a siren, as heard announcing air raids in shrapnel-scarred war zones. At its first note the room explodes into life. Desks scrape and chairs tumble as thirty-three mostly fifteen-year-olds stampede for the door.

A full minute after the classroom has vomited its children into the corridor, the teacher is still standing at the edge of the white-board. It's only now that he realises he is still holding up John Steinbeck.

K

As the boy with the K in his head zigs his way down one side of the packed corridor, another boy zags a path towards him from the other side. Inevitably their shoulders collide and they bump together against the flow of schoolchildren heading for fresh classrooms and fresh prey.

'Yo, Becker,' says K.

'Yo . . . So?'

'So what?'

'What's the new bloke like, then?'

'He's a fucking cock.'

'Got bastard-wanking-maths now. What about you?'

'Double-pissing-Alvin.'

Double-pissing-Alvin

What is Alvin Lee doing in a classroom where seven mostly fifteen-year-olds in various states of school uniform sit around a large table, work in front of them? Alvin sometimes wonders himself.

'What do I put here, sir?' mutters a girl whose face is hidden behind permanently drawn curtains of dark brown hair.

Notwithstanding the *sir*, Alvin Lee is not a schoolteacher.

'What's it say next to the box, Chenil?' he asks.

'Name, sir,' Chenil says, one eye peering through a slit in the curtains.

'Write your name, then.'

'Why?' says the boy with the K in his head.

'It's a form, Curtis.'

No one has yet told Curtis that his barber, a schoolmate, etched the wrong initial.

'So?' he says.

'Forms are kind of a deal. They ask for information. You give it.'

'That ain't a deal. If it was a deal you'd get something back, yeah?'

'I ain't getting nothing 'cept arm ache,' adds a boy with springy blond dreadlocks that bounce as he talks – Harpo Marx with working vocal cords.

'You usually do get something back, Roland,' Alvin explains. 'Like a bank loan or a holiday or housing benefit. You want any of those things, you have to fill in the form first. And put the cigarette away, please, Curtis.'

'It ain't lit, Alvin man.'

'Yes, but if Mr Chadwick visits us you'll get another exclusion and I'll get a bollocking.'

Roland laughs. 'Chadwick ain't never coming in a million years.'

'A *zillion* years,' adds a girl whose hair has been sculpted – laminated to her skull with about a pint of industrial-strength gel – with an attention to detail that could secure her a job as an icer of bespoke wedding cakes, but that never, ever will.

Mr Chadwick has not been to ILD since the day he invited the chairwoman of the governors to unveil the small plaque at the entrance of the newly built block. ILD, according to some professional educationalists, stands for I Love Delinquency. That's why Alvin never refers to it as ILD. He always calls it the Inclusive Learning Department. Inclusive Learning is a term that usefully embraces a number of things and accurately describes none of them.

The single-storey building that houses ILD looks like a shoe box. Not to Mr Chadwick, though. He sees it as a carpet, the corner of which has been lifted, allowing him to sweep many of his problems underneath. This is not Alvin's view. He is not yet that cynical – not even remotely. Alvin is fairly sure that any day now the pressure of high office will abate for long enough to allow the headmaster to make a fleeting, morale-boosting visit.

But probably not today. Today is a Tuesday and on Tuesdays Mr Chadwick keeps his hand in at the coalface, teaching a small group of Wood Hill School's sixth-formers applied maths. Alvin's year tens know little maths, let alone how to apply it. They don't even know how to fill in a simple form, which is why Alvin is teaching them, though, as has already been established, he isn't a teacher. He is a learning mentor, a title that covers a number of jobs. From personal life coach at the high end to mealtime supervisor (dinner lady if you prefer) at the low. Teaching his kids how to fill in a form places him somewhere between those two extremes.

'What are you doing, Chenil?' he asks.

'Putting my address, sir.'

'But you're sticking it in the box where you're supposed to write down your qualifications.'

'The address box weren't big enough and that.'

'And it don't matter 'cause she ain't got no qualifications,' adds Curtis.

Alvin ignores the slap that the girl with the sculpted hair gives Curtis on Chenil's behalf. At least Chenil is writing *something*. Alvin looks at the stunted boy at the end of the table. He has a selection of pens in front of him. He's using them to block out the boxes on the specimen form with colour. The boy is Dan. Three years ago he arrived with his family from Romania. He can't speak English – not a single word – nor can he write it. As far as Alvin knows, he can't write Romanian either. Every week he turns up and mutely decorates whatever piece of paper is put in front of him. At least, thinks Alvin, his colouring in has improved. A year ago he would have gone over the lines.

No one has ever taught Alvin to accentuate the positive; his mind is simply built that way.

Alvin turns around because there is a crash at the window behind him. He is too late to see anything, but the large sheet of toughened glass shudders tellingly. He turns back and scrutinises his students for a clue. They give him a collective shrug. The collective shrug is a genuine phenomenon, a telepathically coordinated movement that only small groups of teenagers, usually in a classroom setting, are capable of. It's worthy of scientific study, though the scientists probably have better things to do.

'What was it, guys?' Alvin asks, immediately before a second, louder crash. He doesn't turn this time, but looks at the smirks radiating dimly from his class. 'C'mon, what was it? A pigeon? Mr Chadwick?'

Chenil mumbles something into her hair curtains.

'What did you say?' he asks.

'It weren't nothing, Alvin,' Curtis snaps.

'It was Kevan, wasn't it?'

Alvin doesn't wait for confirmation, but turns round again to see the top half of Kevan Kennedy slam into the glass before dropping to the scrubby lawn below. Alvin picks up an orange plastic chair and takes it to the window. He stands on it and opens the narrow louvred panes at the top.

'Are you mad, Kevan?' he says through the gap.

He looks down at the boy, who appears to be winded. He's clutching a thin wad of paper and gazing up at Alvin with his big, black eyes; gorgeous, glacier-melting eyes, housed in a scary killer's face. Alvin believes those eyes could be Kevan's greatest asset, if only he had the faintest clue how to use them.

'If anyone sees you here, that's it, *finito*,' Alvin continues. 'You do know that, don't you?'

'I got that work you wanted,' Kevan says, flapping the paper.

'What work?' Alvin asks.

'You know, the map shite and that.'

Last week's assignment: Alvin asked his class to write road directions to Glasgow, an essential life skill according to the course book. And given how dog-eared their own bit of London's outer rim has become, escape to Scotland might one day be essential. Alvin often despairs for his charges. They are only eight or so miles from the Houses of Parliament, Tate Modern and Bond Street; from *London*, the Greatest City in the World. But here in the Land the Tube Forgot, all of that goes unnoticed. They are Londoners in name only.

All complied with the task, except for Dan, who instead handed in a beautifully rendered colouring of the photocopied map of Britain. And except for Kevan, who no doubt would have completed it had he not been excluded from school. Yesterday, the head of PE walked round a corner to find him with a gun. He'd seemed to be in the process of selling it to a boy in year seven. It was only an air pistol, but in twenty-first-century Britain, guns of any description are a zero-tolerance, one-strike-and-you're-out affair. He could have been caught towing an anti-tank howitzer through the school gates without making his situation appreciably worse. Whatever he pleads in mitigation, the likelihood is that his temporary exclusion will become permanent. Especially if he's caught on school property before his hearing.

'I think you should leave, Kevan. *Now,*' Alvin urges.

'Can't I give you the work?'

'OK, but then go.'

Kevan hauls himself to his feet and holds up the paper. Alvin feeds an arm through the window slats but he can't reach it.

'You'll have to climb on something,' he says to Kevan.

Kevan drags a wire litter bin up to the window. He clambers onto the rim and reaches up with the paper again. Alvin forces his arm through the thin gap, wondering if the pressure will shatter the narrow strips of glass, perhaps severing a major artery. The tips of his trembling fingers touch paper – just.

'Sir,' sculpted-hair girl calls out behind him.

'Just a sec, Debbie,' he gasps as he attempts to grasp the paper.

'*Sir.*' Debbie's voice again, this time more insistent.

'Hang on . . . Nearly . . . got –'

A sharp crack as a pane cleaves in two and slides free from the aluminium brackets that hold it in place. The two halves drop straight down like a twin-bladed guillotine, leaving Alvin's arm still attached at the shoulder, but also leaving a vertical scarlet gouge in Kevan's coffee-coloured cheek.

'Hello, Mr Chadwick,' Debbie says brightly.

Alvin looks away from the blood that is beginning to flow – make that *spume* – from Kevan's face and turns to look at his class, and at the now open doorway through which the headmaster has just stepped.

'It's OK, Mr Chadwick,' Curtis says. 'Alvin were just telling Kev to fuck off.'

Curtis still has the cigarette clamped between his lips.

But it's alright because it isn't lit.

What*s for tea?

'How many stitches?'

'Only six,' Alvin says, 'but you could see his cheekbone.'

Karen winces as she slides her head beneath the milky bath water. Alvin sits on the toilet and watches her hair. Thick, glossy blankets of black that loll to the surface like an oil slick, though an environmentally friendly one, *obviously* – Alvin loves Karen's hair.

After several seconds she surfaces. 'You're stuffed then, basically,' she says, wiping the water from her face.

'Well, headmaster witnessing staff member slash pupil doesn't look *ideal*, but actually it's Kevan I'm worried about.'

'He's a lost cause, isn't he?'

'That's just it; he isn't. He's been making real progress.'

'Selling guns? Shows entrepreneurial spirit, I suppose. That's what I love about you, angel: your perpetually positive spin.'

Alvin thinks about making the case for Kevan. But how do you defend a boy who has raped and pillaged his way through nearly twelve years of education? That is, when he has bothered to turn up at all. Usually when Kevan Kennedy has attended a lesson it has only been to stick around for long enough to thump the teacher. He started working them over at infant school, though only at groin level. With every growth spurt he has inched his way up their bodies. These days the experienced ones equip themselves with gum shields. Perhaps he suffers from a learning disability, but no psychologist has ever got close enough to make a diagnosis. From a safe distance, though, the shrinks have concluded that his entire incendiary demeanour constitutes a personality disorder that's not so much borderline as disappeared across the frontier and lost in the wilderness beyond.

So just how do you defend a record like that? Where there's a will . . .

'Do you know why Kevan came in today?' Alvin asks. 'He came to hand in an assignment. You know the last time he did that?'

Karen shakes her head.

'Never. Kevan has *never* handed in a piece of work.'

'*Wow*. Was it any good?'

'It was supposed to be directions to Glasgow, but if I'd followed them I'd have ended up in Somerset. Via northern France.'

'But you're going to tell me that that isn't the point, aren't you?'

'Exactly. He was *trying*. He was handing in *work*, for heaven's sake. It was a real breakthrough.'

'Who knows, maybe you'll make a Kelly of him yet.'

Alvin doubts it. Even he couldn't be so blindly optimistic as to believe that Kevan could emulate the success of Kelly Hendricks, his greatest triumph.

'Did Chadwick share your joy?' Karen asks.

'He was kind of preoccupied with the accident report.'

'What was he doing there anyway? I thought he left you lot alone.'

The headmaster was visiting with a community police liaison officer, a preamble to Wood Hill getting its own copper. Mr Chadwick hadn't been expecting Alvin and his charges to put on a fully dramatised demonstration (with real blood) of exactly why Wood Hill needed a constable-in-residence. Alvin is about to tell Karen this, but he's interrupted by a loud clump as a body hits the bathroom door. In some ways home is not so different from school.

'What's for tea?' a small voice shouts from the other side.

Alvin gives Karen a questioning look.

'I dunno. I need to shop. You'll have to improvise,' she says before sliding beneath the water again.

'What's this, Alvin?'

Mercedes recently celebrated her seventeenth birthday by turning vegetarian. This has added another layer of complexity to mealtimes *chez* Karen and Alvin. Though Annie and Sid eat anything that's put in front of them, they impose conditions. Food is only allowed on seven-year-old Annie's plate if it has first been cut into an amusing shape. In Sid's case, all solids must first be passed through a blender, even though the child-rearing textbooks agree that, at three and a half, he should have mastered the art of chewing. Actually, he did master it right on schedule, but after rapid consideration decided that really it wasn't for him. Then there is Shannon, the ten-year-old body that slammed into the bathroom door and asked, 'What's for tea?' A curiously pointless question because she lives on a diet of bread rolls, white, unbuttered. And in defiance of the nutritional know-alls, she appears to be in glowingly rude health.

'Well?' Mercedes prods, her question unanswered.

'It's a veggie burger,' Alvin says.

'No, it's not. It's a waffle in a burger bun.'

This is true. Although Alvin found a veggie burger carton in the freezer, it contained no veggie burgers. The potato waffle box, however, was burstingly full, and he was under instructions to improvise.

'You cooked it under the grill with the burgers, didn't you?' Mercedes says. She has adopted the tone of a prosecution barrister contending, 'I put it to you, sir, that you raped the victim brutally, nay, *satanically*, then left her for dead in the toxic waste skip.'

'Yes,' Alvin hazards, 'yes, but –'

'I'll eat out later,' she spits, shoving her plate to the middle of the table.

Veggie Mercedes is a fundamentalist. Meat is indeed murder, and to ram the point home she would gladly wage *jihad* on every last sonofabitch in the animal-killing industry. As Karen has pointed out, radical Muslims, Bible-Belt Christians, teenagers: irony is lost on them.

The meal is not a complete disaster. Shannon is tucking into a pair of burger buns (white, unbuttered and carefully denuded of sesame seeds), Annie is nibbling a Shrek-shaped burger and Sid is standing his spoon up in his burger, waffle and sweet corn purée, not seeming to mind that it is more or less the colour and consistency of cat sick.

Karen joins them, her hair glistening like wet slate.

'Not eating your dad's delicious tea, Mercedes?' she says. 'You want to be careful. A kid needed stitches after tangling with him today.'

'Been beating up your retards again, Alvin?' Mercedes asks.

'It was an accident,' Alvin protests. 'A window broke. Accidentally. And, please, they're not retards.'

'Sorry. What's the PC word? That's right: *losers*. Couldn't care less if you kill 'em all.'

'*Tsk*. And you a vegetarian,' Karen interrupts.

'You what?' says Mercedes, genuinely perplexed. Seventeen: post-puberty, pre-irony.

'We got a letter from the bank this morning, Alvin,' Karen says, picking up Mercedes's waffle and taking a bite.

Alvin wonders if, in an uncharacteristic fit of generosity, the bank wishes to reward their loyalty by wiping out not only their debts, but also those of a medium-sized Third World nation of his and Karen's choice.

'They'd like us to go in for a "budget review",' she continues.

'Fascist scum wanna take away your plastic,' Mercedes says bleakly.

The smaller children gaze up at Karen and Alvin as they exchange coded looks designed not to transmit alarm. Their finances *are* precarious. Not being a teacher, Alvin doesn't earn even a teacher's modest salary. Karen has recently managed to find Sid a free nursery place and has taken a part-time job as a receptionist at a veterinary clinic, but the money she brings home barely gets her past the bananas in Asda's fruit and veg section.

'Mum, I saw this advert on Fox Kids,' Annie says.

Karen and Alvin brace themselves. Karen contends that children's television is the supreme devil's pact. Satan supplies dozens of digital channels to give harassed parents much-needed breathing space, the corollary being that he crams the breaks with images of shiny objects that supply kids with the ammunition with which to further harass their parents.

'There was this man on a tightrope,' Annie explains, 'and he's holding all these great big boxes and he's going to fall off, but then he's lended some money and he buys a tiny little box and he puts all the big ones in it and then he crosses the rope all the way to the other side.'

'He should have falled off,' Sid says, too young to get a base-level metaphor for debt consolidation. No, man falling off rope does it for him.

'There was a phone number,' Annie says. 'Want me to remember it?'

'It's OK, sweetheart,' Alvin says, relieved that his daughter has not hit him with a request for another pricey pink toy, but unnerved that she understands so much of their financial hell.

'Jamie called this afternoon,' Karen says, moving the conversation on.

'Yeah? What's he want?' Alvin asks.

'Well, my guess is that he wants to tap you for another grand for a *can't-fail* theme pub venture or a *dead-cert* three-legged horse or whatever . . . But I didn't actually ask.'

Karen doesn't have a high opinion of Alvin's oldest, if not dearest, friend. Truthfully, Alvin doesn't have a high opinion of him either, but, being Alvin, he prefers to dwell on the roughly three per cent of Jamie that remains uncorrupted by either moral decadence or scabies.

'Maybe he just wants to chat about the old days,' Karen says.

'God, not the *old* days,' Mercedes gasps. 'Hey pop pickers, straight in at twenty-nine, *Top of the Pops*, Queen, Madonna backstage, blah, blah, *barf*!'

'You met the queen, Dad?' Shannon asks. 'What's she like? Is she a snot?'

'A different Queen, sweetheart,' Karen explains. 'Now, finish your bun.'

'*Bun*?' Shannon shrieks, throwing it back onto her plate.

'Sorry, *roll*,' Karen says, attempting to recover the situation, having momentarily forgotten that Shannon eats only rolls and never buns.

'I'll call Jamie after tea,' Alvin says.

'Cat sick!' Sid says.

Self-assembly

Tuesday: tomato soup day.

The woman sets the chipped mug on the desk in the spare room and lowers her body into the chair.

The desk came from Ikea.

Ikea assembly instructions represent a challenge to the nimble-fingered; for a woman with arthritis and someone else's bifocals (a long story) the folded A3 sheet might as well have been a map of a Royal Marine assault course. But she wasn't going to surrender.

The desk is a plinth for the sleek, white iMac, which has an Intel Core Duo 2GHz processor, but looks like an oversized Etch A Sketch.

She opens Safari, types in *talktalk.com* and heads for the message boards. Scrolling down the list, she plucks at the first thread that catches her eye.

Tommy Boy: Is it just me or is evrywere you go english is'nt the language you here being spoke. if you com to this country you should be made to speak the Queen english. whats happning to the bRitish way of life?

Von Krapp: go tomy!!! its getting like i cant buy petrol unles i ask for it in f*****g hindustanny. lern englih or eff of!!! and wile im at it wot hapened to galons????!!

Winston: By your own standards, you two Brits would be

	deported then, but who the hell would have you?! In two posts, you've managed at least 27(!) mistakes. Oh, and VK, what happened to the gallon is that it went the same way as the groat and the fathom – also sadly missed.
Von Krapp:	the libral is back! were you bin? making soop for bogus asylem seekers??!!
Tommy Boy:	LOL! HEy VK do you think WINSTON is one of our colourd friends?
Von Krapp:	Figurs! Innit funny how the name of the greatest englishman in history has been stollen by the . . . f***!!! wot am i alowed to call them?? afro-caribeans!!
Winston:	Having fought a war to protect our way of life, your Mr Churchill would find it *hilarious* that his country has been overrun by semi-educated chavs. If he'd seen the future, he'd have let the Nazis in!

Pricked, the woman types out a post.

Vera:	I believe Churchill would be sad that the freedoms the Allies shed blood for have been lost to the EU. Hitler never held the sway over us now enjoyed by Brussels.
Von Krapp:	hail vera! the voice of comon sense
Tommy Boy:	I rread that brusels is banning the queen from pub names. Like the QUeens' Head wil hav to be called just The Head.
Winston:	Whatever your views on the EU, do you think it's fair to compare it to the Nazi Party? The last time I looked, the Eurocrats weren't shipping Jews off to Buchenwald.
Vera:	They're worse than that. They're removing our

liberties by stealth. At least with the Nazis you knew what you were dealing with.

Winston: **Oo-er, paranoia levels are going critical!**

But at eighty-three, hasn't she earned the right to be a little paranoid?

So, what are *your* vectors like?

'I'll never forget your face, Alv,' Jamie says as Alvin sets down two glasses of beer on the table between them. 'Pure junxtaposition, man.'

Alvin met Jamie McGreevy twenty-three years ago. In all that time Jamie has made liberal use of the word *juxtaposition*, sprinkling it about as if it is malt vinegar to conversation's bag of chips. Two things to bear in mind: Alvin has never heard him – not even *once* – employ it in a correct context; secondly, there is that rogue N. Alvin, being Alvin, has never corrected his friend and he's not about to start, though the rogue N is setting his teeth on edge.

They're in the Three Roses, a pub half a mile from Alvin's house. Alvin would have asked him round to his place, except he knows that Jamie doesn't feel comfortable in the company of children. He also knows that his children are not entirely at ease in the company of Jamie. And Karen would have barricaded herself in the bedroom until he left.

'No, I'll *never* forget your face,' Jamie repeats after a slug of beer.

He's recalling the time that – No, let Jamie tell the story.

'Me and Lemmy, back of the tour bus, that Belgian groupie on my lap. We're bombing up the A1 and then *you* appear at the skylight –'

Stop. Time out. There is a kernel of truth in this account, just as there is a pip at the heart of an apple. In this case the pip is fiendishly small, while the fantastical Granny Smith that surrounds it is roughly the size of the dome of St Paul's. Something to consider as Jamie continues.

'What the fuck were you doing on the roof, Alv?'

'You know what I was doing. I was getting my trousers.'

'Getting your *strides*. Now, *that's* what you join a band for.'

Time to get a few things straight. True, Jamie and Alvin were in a band. And true, they toured with Motörhead. As for Jamie sharing the tour bus with Lemmy and a Belgian groupie, false and false. Lemmy went by plane and there were no groupies (Belgian or otherwise). It is true that Alvin climbed on top of a tour bus to retrieve his trousers (which Jamie had thrown up there), except it wasn't so much an air-cushioned motor coach, more of a Ford Transit. And it wasn't exactly bombing up the A1. Or even pootling. More parked in a side street behind Middlesbrough Town Hall.

Jamie McGreevy is a shameless liar, but Alvin thinks a strict definition of liar should exclude people who believe their own fallacies. Usually the only person Jamie fools with his cavalier retelling of history is Jamie.

Alvin hasn't seen his friend for months and he looks at him as he rolls a cigarette. Flabby, pallid and in need of a vigorous scrub, he has thinning grey-black hair that has been wrenched into an emaciated ponytail. It resembles something dredged from a plughole at the end of a salon's OAP day.

'You look well, Jamie,' he says. 'How's tricks?'

'Oh, you know, irons in fires, fingers in pies . . . As it happens, there's one particular pie. Very, very tasty.'

'What's that?' Alvin asks.

Jamie leans across the table and lowers his voice. 'I have seen the future: *ring tones*. Personalised ring tones. How about that? The junxtaposition of your own unique mobile ditty composed by a rock legend.'

Alvin's brow furrows.

'Composed by *me*, you twerp,' Jamie says.

'Right, yeah, that sounds –'

'Can't fail. Every kid's mobile has got rinky-dink top-forty crap on it. Which of 'em isn't gonna want his own little signature tune? You tell me. It *can't* fail. I warm up the Sinclavier, we stick ads in the teen mags and *ker-ching*.'

Alvin wonders who *we* is, but he suspects he knows.

'So, what do you think?'

'It sounds fantastic, Jamie. Good luck with it.'

'Hey, you think I'd leave my oldest mate out of the junxtaposition? You're in from the off. For a small up-front invest—'

'Jamie, I don't think . . . Karen and me, we're absolutely strapped.'

Alvin doesn't add that they might not be quite so strapped had he not given Jamie the only savings they ever possessed for the theme pub – the one that couldn't fail, but that somehow, against the odds, did.

'That's a shame,' Jamie sighs. 'You know, there's blokes in Seattle who were strapped the day Bill Gates came calling for some front money. Trouble is they're still a bit skint now. Bill seems to be doing OK, though.'

'I'm sorry, but we really are – Jesus, we're drowning in bills.'

'Yeah, yeah, aren't we all? Your loss,' Jamie says as he drains his glass. 'You fancy moving on after this one? You ever been to the Tropica?'

'What's that?' Alvin asks, thinking Tahiti-themed pub, one, perhaps, that couldn't fail and didn't.

'New massage place in All Saints Road. You know, just off the High Street. Bit low-rent, but they know how to relax the old musculature.'

'I've never had a massage in my life,' Alvin says.

'Funnily enough, neither have I,' Jamie replies with a leer. Jamie McGreevy is a man who has never had qualms about handing over money for sex – putting Jamie and the word scruples in the same sentence is a juxtaposition too far. 'I'll front you the cash, if that's what you're worried about,' he goes on, sensing his friend's unease.

'It's not that. I . . . I promised Mercedes I'd help with her homework.'

Alvin hops off his bike outside a forties-built terraced house that in Tardis-like defiance of the laws of three-dimensional space has three bedrooms plus a cowboy loft conversion squeezed into it. Alvin is home. As he slips his key into the lock a minicab pulls up and Mercedes climbs out. 'That's lucky,' she calls out. 'You couldn't lend us a fiver, could you?' Alvin fumbles in his pocket for a note. He hands it to her and she passes it through the window to the driver.

'We can't really afford cabs at the moment,' he says as he hefts his bike through the front door.

'Yeah, I know, but you wouldn't want me walking across Bennett Park at this time of night, would you? The place is crawling with muggers and dealers. Mostly from Wood Hill.'

Mercedes is doing her A-levels at East Park. Her attitude is born partly of inter-school snobbery, but mostly of the fact that the majority of the district's muggers and dealers have indeed learned their craft at Wood Hill.

Alvin sticks his head round the door to the front room and sees Karen dozing in front of the TV, Sid curled up on her lap. He joins Mercedes in the tiny kitchen and fills the kettle. He watches her fish her jewel-like mobile from her bag and key in a text. She's wearing a bulky orange parka over a pair of billowing black trousers and a tight white crop-top. Her red hair is gelled into spiky bunches that radiate from her head like antennae on a spy satellite. Her eyes are rimmed with heavy strokes of black liner and her impressive nose is splattered with freckles – which she hates and would have taken a blowtorch to, had she not grudgingly conceded that the scarring would probably look worse. To Alvin, at this moment, she looks exactly as her mother did eighteen years ago. And nothing like Karen. If that is confusing, it's because family life often is these days. Karen is not Mercedes's mother.

As she closes her phone, Alvin asks, 'Would you be interested in a personalised ring tone composed by a rock musician?'

'Yeah, sure, if you're talking *rock* musician. If you mean Jamie McSpaz . . .' She makes a noise that sounds like air escaping from an unenthusiastic whoopee cushion. 'Anyway, can't chat. Gotta bunch of maths stuff. Was supposed to hand it in, like, yesterday.'

'Want any help?'

'What are your vectors like?'

'Er . . .'

''Night, Alvin.'

The cyber-village people

That's the amazing thing about the Internet . . .

Vera:	There is a British way of life and it has stood us in good stead these past centuries. We toss it away at our peril.

. . . Where else could an eighty-three-year-old make herself heard?

Winston:	Press-ganging men into naval service used to be part of the British way of life. Don't hear anyone screaming to bring that back.
Tommy Boy:	youve had good idea at last Winston! Press gangs would clean the streets of muggers and rapists!
Von Krapp:	and queers!!!! in the navy you can sail the 7 seas!!!
Winston:	Quoting the Village People now, VK? Is there something you ain't telling us? My point, Vera, is that the British Way of Life changes all the time. Also, there is no single British Way of Life. If there are 60 million Brits, then there are 60 million ideas of what it should be.
Vera:	And my point is that tolerance is a basic part of the British way of life. I find it sad that we are now *tolerating* illiberal, repressive Muslim

	fundamentalists who threaten to undermine everything we have ever stood for.
Winston:	**Touché! You got me there. What we do with the mullahs has got us lefty-libs well baffled.**

Although the fact that no one knows she's eighty-three could be the one reason anyone is paying attention to her.

Von Krapp:	**bored now. if gollyw*g winston and vera is gona start agreeing its not worth hanging around.**
Tommy Boy:	**secrets of the nazi Death Camps is about to start on history channell.**
Von Krapp:	**c u there!**
Winston:	**So, it's just you, me and the night, Vera . . . I know that as far as politics go, we're like Itchy and Scratchy, but at least you can punctuate! Have to say I think you're cool.**

Can an eighty-three-year-old be cool?

Vera:	**Thank you. Tell me about yourself.**
Winston:	**Now that the Ku Klux Klan is safely logged off, I can reveal that I am . . . about as white as Winston Churchill. I'm 23, live in S Yorkshire, work as a facilitator in the cellulose-based communications business.**
Vera:	**Sounds fascinating.**
Winston:	**Means I'm a postman! But I'm sure greatness lies just around the corner. What about you? What are you? Catwalk model? Astronomer? Rock 'n' roll star?**

But she's not about to get into a truth session with a virtual stranger, not at this time of night. This being the Internet, she could lie, but she has never had the imagination to do that convincingly.

Vera: What I am is very tired. Until next time.

The shave, the shirt, the tie

It's eight forty-five as Alvin swings through the school gates and dismounts his bike, nearly bowling over a boy with a rucksack hooked over one arm and a heavy plaster cast wrapped around the other.

'Sorry, Finn, nearly broke your other arm then,' he says.

'S'OK, sir,' Finn replies.

'How's it mending?'

'S'OK, I s'pose.'

Finn claims to have broken it jumping off a wall. Finn, though, is the unofficial school barber and the accident happened at around the time Curtis discovered the K in his scalp. Of course, the two events may just have coincided, but as well as a shattered bone, Finn had KUNT felt-tipped across his forehead.

Alvin wheels his bike through the packs of kids, most of them cupping mobiles to their ears and probably talking to friends no more than a few feet away. If it's true that the microwaves generated by mobile phones pose a health risk, then by the time the school bell rings this lot will have brains the temperature and consistency of minestrone soup.

Alvin spots Lynette Moorhouse's blonde bob not far ahead. As the children in front of him part for his bike, he sees that she's sporting a shorter-than-usual skirt and higher-than-usual heels.

'Hi, Lynette,' he says as he falls into step beside her. 'Good weekend?'

He listens to her husky-voiced account of her church reading group, her dentist trauma and the unique hell of arm-waxing. He also listens to the wolf whistles directed at the shorter-than-usual skirt and higher-than-usual heels and decides that Lynette Moorhouse is the bravest woman he has ever met. Actually, anyone prepared to take on a room of teenagers, none of whom gives a stuff about, say, the Reform Bill of 1832, is – ipso facto – brave. But Lynette's courage is of a different order. She has been at Wood Hill for five years, but until last summer she was known as Andy.

Six months into her new life as a woman, the hormones are having a remarkable effect, one that at some primal level Alvin finds faintly unnerving. She has taken to her new wardrobe as if she was born to it – which, he supposes, she was. In the summer she'll travel to Holland, where she'll finally – and literally – cut all remaining ties with her nominally male past.

Her readiness to submit to irreversible surgery is brave enough in itself. What impresses Alvin more is her decision not to apply for a new job in a new town where nobody knows her as Andy, but to stay put and respond to the taunts by shortening her hemline and heightening her heels. For that she deserves an especially shiny medal. Maybe the queen could make her a dame.

On thing troubles him, though. Why, when she had fifty per cent of the world's names to choose from – everything from Jean and Carol to Cornelia, Copelia and Tallulah – did she pick Lynette?

'Ah, *Ms* Moorhouse, *Lynette,*' announces Tony Rowell as she and Alvin walk through the main doors, 'glad I caught you. Mr Worsnop is indisposed again, so I wonder if you'd look after 9G for him this afternoon. They're eager to hear your take on women's suffrage.'

Six foot two of towering superciliousness, Tony Rowell is the head of history, also the head of year eleven. His views on women's suffrage can probably be précised as 'a rather poor idea'. His views on women formerly known as Andrew can only be guessed at.

'I'd do it myself,' he continues, 'but I believe I'm dispensing justice to one of Alvin's tragic *mentees*.'

As a learning mentor, Alvin has mentees. The Inclusive Learning Department comprises special-needs teachers, the school counsellor (who does ten hours a week, more if a pupil dies) and mentors. Alvin is supposed to spend the bulk of his time mentoring, working one-on-one with his charges. And they need the work, these truants, delinquents and uncategorisable fuck-ups. It is his job to keep them in the system *by any means possible*. Actually, the *by any means possible* he added to the job description himself.

Alvin will tell anyone who'll listen – though not many will – that ILD has been a resounding success. He will point to the lowered truancy rates, the fall in classroom disruption and assaults on staff, the simple fact that teachers are now more able to teach. And though some of the statistics do bear him out, no one is much interested. Well, the difficult kids are now *over there* in ILD, a long-term sin bin that will keep them in check until age sixteen, when they can run along and get under some other government department's feet.

And besides, all the mentors in the world couldn't sort out Kevan Kennedy. Today Kevan is up before the headmaster, his year head and three governors. It is over two weeks since he was suspended for possession of the air pistol. Since then a committee of Wood Hill's senior management (the modern, corporate-friendly term for a bunch of teachers) has met and considered the evidence. They will almost certainly recommend his expulsion. It is up to the governors to decide, though clearly Rowell's mind is already made up.

'There's nothing *tragic* about Kevan, Mr Rowell,' Alvin says, beginning his defence early.

'Oh, I used the word in its *classical* sense,' Rowell responds, unable to pass up an opportunity to patronise. 'You might blame society for the way he's turned out, but, like Hippolytus, he's sown the seeds of his own destruction.'

'That's not fair,' Alvin argues, though he has no idea what Rowell is talking about.

'Who knows, perhaps he'll save himself with a Euripidean monologue, eh?' Rowell says, before sweeping off through a crowd of year sevens, scattering them like a swarm of midges.

'What the hell was that all about?' Alvin asks.

'His way of saying Kevan's shot himself in the foot. With an air gun,' Lynette explains. 'God, he can't wait to stick it to him. What're his chances?'

Alvin hasn't given up hope, but that's Alvin for you. If he had a football team (he doesn't; he's not a sporty bloke) and they were eight goals down in the eighty-ninth minute, with three players sent off and with the giant screens showing the referee pocketing a wad of cash from the opposition manager, Alvin would be the only supporter still in the stadium urging them on, the scent of victory in his nostrils. (Curiously, if he *did* have a team – say a not especially brilliant one, perennial strugglers – the experience might have knocked some of the senseless optimism out of him, and this might be an entirely different story. But he doesn't, and it isn't.)

'You know, Kelly Hendricks was in exactly the same situation at one point,' Alvin says, 'and look how she turned things around.'

'Oh, I think you turned things around for her, Alvin.'

'Whatever, I'll do my best for Kevan.'

'You'll need to. Is that why you've put on the tie?'

Any means necessary. Thus the shave, the shirt and the tie that he found buried beneath a bundle of socks. Alvin is hoping no one will notice that it is decorated with unseasonal Santas.

'You look gorgeous, but it's not you that's getting excluded today,' Lynette says. 'I think Kevan's the one that's supposed to scrub up.'

Alvin is sitting in the corridor outside the smaller of the school's two gyms. He's alone, but he shouldn't be. Kevan and, with any luck, his mother should be with him. The gym door opens a crack and Tony Rowell's astonishingly thin head slithers through the narrow gap.

'Any sign?' he asks.

Alvin shakes his head.

'This is intolerable.'

'I'm sure he'll be here any . . .'

Alvin trails off because Rowell has disappeared back into the gym. He cranes his neck and looks down the corridor towards the doors at the far end. He wills them to open and after only a few seconds they do. A woman crashes through them. She looks no older than thirty and she's tiny. Too small and too young, surely, to be managing something as big and feisty as Kevan Kennedy, but she appears to be making a fist of it because he's loping along in her wake. Alvin stands as they reach him.

'Hi . . . Mrs Kennedy?' he says.

'Nash,' she snaps. 'I haven't been Kennedy since his dad pissed off.'

'Right, yes . . . I'm Alvin Lee, Kevan's learning mentor. We'd best be going in. They're getting a bit antsy in there.'

'We late? We had to walk, didn't we? Didn't have the bus fare.'

Alvin smiles. 'That's good. I mean, maybe it's something we can bring up. Any financial hardship at home might work in Kevan's favour.'

'It's not that,' Kevan's mother snarls. 'The bloody driver wouldn't change a fifty, would he?'

She doesn't cut a sympathetic dash. But Alvin is looking on the bright side. She is really, really tiny, like a baby bird, one that hasn't had a juicy worm or a downy hug from its mother in days – no bad thing, surely, from the sympathy-vote perspective. Then he looks at Kevan. He's wearing school uniform. Of a sort. The shirt is white-ish, the baggy black jeans are dark enough to pass as trousers in the gloom of the gym and hopefully no one will pay too much attention to the non-regulation Reeboks. But he isn't wearing a tie.

'You're not wearing a tie, Kevan,' Alvin says.

'I told him,' his mother says. Her skin is paper-white. Alvin wonders if it's her natural colouring or if it's been bleached by the stress of the situation. Her son not only towers over her, but also throws her lack of pigmentation into sharper relief – he contains what Rowell would describe (but only in the safety of the staff room) as a large dollop of the tar brush.

'Lost it, didn't I?' Kevan says with a shrug.

'Wear mine,' Alvin says, reaching up and wrenching the happy Santas from his neck.

Any means necessary.

They are gathered at one end of the gym, away from the stacked mats, the benches and the horses. On two chairs sit Kevan and his mother, polar opposites that somehow swim in the same corner of the gene pool. Some ten feet away stands the long table set up for the occasion. Chadwick and Rowell sit at one end of it and in the middle are three of Wood Hill's governors. Alvin sits against the wall and studies them intently. He knows only one of them, the chairwoman, Allison Bird-Wright. She is rarely out of the *Gazette,* which might have something to do with the fact that she is a borough councillor, but could also be because her brother owns the *Gazette*. The Birds are the most prominent family in the area, mainly because they are the richest. Alvin doesn't begrudge Allison Bird-Wright her fortune, but he's beginning to resent the expression on her face. How dare she look as if she'd rather be someplace else, probably a Bermudan beach. Alvin wonders if she has children because she gives no impression that she might actually care about them. He could get angry at this point, but instead he tells himself that he doesn't really know the woman. Perhaps she has seven or eight little ones whom she clucks over like a Home Counties Ma Walton.

Anyway, a glance at Kevan tells him that he is more bored by the situation than anybody. Alvin wishes he would use his eyes on his judges. Those beautiful eyes, capable of puppy-dog pitifulness beyond the dreams of Walt Disney, are surely his only hope. But he is staring down at his Game Boy Advance in a studied act of dumb insolence. Mr Chadwick looks on. The slyest of smiles turns up the corners of his mouth, as if he is willing Kevan to switch it on and seal his fate.

Alan Chadwick doesn't look like Alvin's idea of a school head. When Alvin was at school his headmaster had a stoop, a shock of white hair that on windy days waved like pampas grass and cheeks crazed with tiny crimson capillaries. He was old. Alan Chadwick, by contrast, looks as if he has always been thirty-five and always will be. He resembles the CEO of a successful manufacturing company. Alvin likes to think this means he is dedicated to bringing the enlightened methods of progressive management to bear on the creaky process of education. He isn't exactly certain what the ramifications of that are, but he's keeping his fingers crossed. Anyway, Alvin will argue that progressive management has brought ILD to Wood Hill and, whatever anyone else says about it, that has been a *resounding* success.

Rowell finishes reading out the report from the head of PE, the man who caught Kevan with the gun.

'Perhaps Kevin would like to say something,' the headmaster suggests.

Kevan continues to stare at the Game Boy.

'Or Mrs Kennedy?' Chadwick prods.

'It's *Nash,*' Kevan's mother snaps as she stabs Kevan in the ribs with the stiletto point of her elbow.

'It weren't a real gun,' Kevan mumbles.

'It *looks* real,' Allison Bird-Wright exclaims, picking up exhibit A and cradling it in her hands. It's the first time Alvin has heard her speak. She has a voice that could read the BBC News – that is if the BBC wished to return to the days of haughty and unapproachable. 'Is it safe?' she adds, showing no appreciation of the difference between a weapon that can inflict a nasty bruise and one that can remove an entire face.

'It didn't even have no ammo,' Kevan continues in a slightly louder mumble than before.

'That's hardly the point, Kevin,' Chadwick says. 'Loaded or not, you must appreciate that we have to take the hardest line on firearms.'

Kevan shrugs.

'Could I say something?' Alvin asks.

'I'm not sure that would be appropriate,' Rowell mutters to Chadwick.

'I think Ke*van* has turned a corner recently,' Alvin announces, ignoring Rowell. He knows he doesn't have a speaking role at these proceedings, but someone has to say something positive – and there is *always* something positive to say. 'When he came into school a couple of weeks ago –'

'When he came into school a couple of weeks ago he was flouting the terms of his exclusion, Mr Lee,' Rowell spits.

'Yes, but he came to hand in some *work.*'

'Not to any member of the *teaching* staff.'

'No, to me.'

Rowell sits back and folds his arms, his case pretty much rested.

'Look,' Alvin continues, 'Kevan has . . . *struggled* to get to grips with the demands of Wood Hill' (which is one way of putting it) 'but I feel he's really turning a corner. His attitude has improved and the fact that he's handing in –'

'Have you seen the hour?' Rowell asks.

Alvin looks up at the clock on the wall – he hadn't realised they were on a fixed time limit.

'I refer to the *bigger picture,* Mr Lee,' Rowell explains in the tone he saves for his slower-witted pupils. 'In less than two months he would be leaving us anyway. Don't you think that perhaps it is a little *eleventh hour* for Kevin to be thinking of turning corners?'

'I thought education was about giving young people opportunities,' Alvin says, never one to give up in the face of mounting odds.

'Thank you, Alvin,' Chadwick says, 'your comments have been –'

'*Every* opportunity to make something of themselves,' Alvin continues. 'Kevan is taking the opportunity *now.* So it's a bit late, but if we reject him aren't we telling him it's not worth the bother? What kind of message is that?'

'I think the message is that he can only kick at the glass so many times before it shatters,' Rowell opines. 'I suspect Kevin understands that rather better than you appear to, Alvin.'

'It's Ke*van*!' Alvin snaps.

'Gentlemen, please,' the headmaster soothes before turning again to the governors. 'Mrs Bird-Wright, any questions?'

Allison Bird-Wright is leaning forward, peering at Kevan over the top of her glasses. 'There is something,' she says. 'Kevin's tie. Is that school issue?'

There's no chance for anyone to reply because something flies across the gym with a hiss of displaced air and Tony Rowell tips backwards abruptly, taking his chair with him. Alvin stands up and moves towards him, mentally reconstructing what has just occurred. It doesn't take him long. As Rowell lies dazed on his back, a patch of raw crimson bruising appears in the centre of his forehead. Fragments of Game Boy lie on the parquet floor around him.

Kevan follows up by flying across the room, diving over the table and flinging himself at Chadwick. His mother is close behind him. Alvin guesses she has no intention of holding her son back. No, they're in this together.

'Do something, for goodness' sake,' shrieks Allison Bird-Wright.

Alvin already is. As he moves towards them, he's wondering which of the Fighting Kennedys to tackle. Good sense tells him to go for Mum, though her arms are whirling like the blades on Boudicca's chariot wheels.

'Please, this isn't helping, Mrs Kennedy,' he says as he reaches her.

'It's *Nash,*' she yelps as her tiny granite fist smacks into his jaw.

Animal Farm

The teacher sits alone in the staff room, his head tipped back, a handkerchief pressed to his nose. He doesn't understand what happened. It was all so fast. He tries to reconstruct the incident, splice together the little scraps of film into an edited whole that he can replay in his mind.

He remembers sitting alone in the classroom after the siren had blared the end of the school day. That – sitting alone, waiting for the stampede of monstrous children to die away – has become his custom over the three weeks of his teaching career. When the noise had faded to a distant roar he ventured into the corridor. He gathered the stack of George Orwells from the desk and set off. After that the memory turns sketchy.

The staff room door opens and Colin Stanislavski walks in. 'What happened, matey?' he asks breezily. Despite the name and the thick Australian accent, he's a fellow English teacher.

'Nosebleed,' the teacher replies.

'I can see that. What *happened*? You didn't try taking on year eight, did you? I told you, body armour and baton rounds for those psychotic fuckers.'

The teacher shakes his head. He should tell Stanislavski what happened. As a battle-scarred pro, he's been assigned as his *buddy*, someone to keep a fatherly arm on his shoulder. The truth is, though, that he's scared of him – as much as he is of his psychotic year eights. There's something mocking and brutish about the guy. He may teach the language of Shelley and Shakespeare, but it's also the mother tongue of Ned Kelly and Russell bloody Crowe.

He decides he isn't going to tell him that when he stepped out of the classroom he heard footsteps behind him. He half turned, his view obscured by the stack of books he held in his arms. He saw a very big boy and a very small woman hurrying towards him. He stepped back to the side of the corridor and as he toyed with the notion of parroting a real teacher and shouting out, 'No running', he dropped the books. The woman stumbled and fell. As the teacher stooped to help her, the boy stopped and swung.

After that, blank.

All he remembers is sitting on the floor watching blood drip from his nose onto the textbooks. Big boy and little woman were nowhere to be seen.

No, he's not going to tell Stanislavski any of that. 'I just get nosebleeds sometimes,' he says.

'Well, just don't have one in the classroom. Those little bastards smell blood ... You ever seen footage of piranhas?' Stanislavski shudders. 'Anyway, you coming to the pub? There was a kerfuffle in the gym. Apparently Kennedy went for Rowell. Need to get to the boozer and get the lowdown.'

The teacher knows who Rowell is – another colleague who scares him, though for different reasons. He wonders who Kennedy might be. Another teacher? He shakes his head. He's not a pub person at the best of times.

'All righty, see you tomorrow,' Stanislavski says, moving towards the door. 'By the way, you know your hair's full of little bits of paper, don't you?'

Thank heaven for small mercies, the teacher thinks. At least his year eights are only pelting him with paper ... For now. Surely the day when they load their biros with poison darts can't be far away.

Pepsi + Shirley

'How far away was the lad sitting?' asks Hector Parr, licking the Murphy's moustache from his top lip.

'Not far,' Alvin says. 'Ten, maybe fifteen feet.'

'Not far? Rowell's head's no wider than a broom handle. Hitting a narrow moving target dead centre is marksmanship of the *highest* order.'

Parr teaches physics and has probably figured out both the trajectory and velocity required to hit a bobbing Rowell from ten feet, taking account of ambient temperature, relative humidity and Newton's first and third laws.

They're sitting in Minogue's, an Irish pub with a genuine Irish landlord who refused to change the name when Kylie came along and queered the pitch for Minogues everywhere. Lynette Moorhouse is with them. Beside her is Donna Hutton, a languages teacher, who belies her doll-like stature by bellowing at her class in foul-mouthed French or Spanish when the need arises – most of the time, then.

Lynette raises her glass. 'Anyway, here's to Kevan for managing to do what I've spent the last five years dreaming of, though usually it's with a brick.'

'To Kevan,' Hector echoes. 'Despite the fact that he once belted me with a retort stand.'

'Looks like he did for you today as well, Alvin,' Donna says. 'That's a nasty split on your lip.'

'That was his mum,' Alvin says despondently.

'The mums are the bloody worst,' she muses.

'Don't despair, Alvin,' Lynette says, patting him on the shoulder. 'You haven't had that many total write-offs this year, have you?'

'Bollocks!' barks a new voice. 'ILD is Wood Hill's very own junkyard, piled to the ceiling with mangled wrecks.'

They look up to see Colin Stanislavski. He stands on splayed rugby player's legs and slightly to the right of Heinrich Himmler. He lowers his broad backside onto a stool and slaps Alvin hard between the shoulder blades.

'Don't get me wrong, Alvin,' he says. 'I *love* ILD. It's great what you're doing with the little crims. Keeping 'em busy with the plastic scissors and wax crayons until they're old enough for the penal system proper.'

'It isn't like that,' Alvin says quietly.

'Sorry, mate, course it isn't. You have the technology; you can rebuild 'em. You're turning the gun-toting bludgers into future leaders. That's the power of the faded pop star. Imagine what we could achieve if we hired Toyah, Pepsi and Shirley, and Adam Ant to do a spot of *mentoring*. Take a reality check, Alv. ILD's just a holding pen for the unteachable. Look at Kennedy for one. The great cultural melting pot, eh? He's the scum floating at the top.'

'Kevan Kennedy is a nightmare, but leave his colour out of it, please,' Donna says. 'This isn't Alabama.'

'You telling me it's irrelevant?'

'Well, that's the problem with mixed-race kids,' Alvin says. 'You can't tell if the criminal streak comes from the black genes or the white ones, can you?'

'Ooh, I didn't know you did facetious, Alv,' Stanislavski chirps gleefully.

'I don't. Anyway, ILD *works*. Look at Kelly,' Alvin says, defiance returning to his voice.

'How could we forget *her*?' Stanislavski exclaims. 'Pretty thing. Skin white as a Klan hood.'

Kelly Hendricks: Alvin's great success story; from the girl who made Kevan Kennedy look like a boy scout to model citizenette in two years.

'Six GCSEs,' Alvin says. '*Six*.'

'Including an A in English,' Lynette adds.

'A C in French too,' Donna says, still as surprised as anyone.

'Who'd've believed, eh?' Colin says, a smirk lighting up his face. 'What's she doing now, then?'

'She's at college,' Alvin says. 'She wants to go into social work.'

'Oh, I think you'll find she already has,' Colin says, the smirk turning into a sixty-watt grin.

'What are you talking about?' Lynette says.

'Well, the clever girl must have graduated early. She's got herself a job.'

'Where?' Alvin asks.

'I haven't checked it out myself – not my kind of place, you understand – but some of my associates in the second fifteen scrum tell me they've seen her at the Tropica. They reckon she's got a mouth like the tube on a Dyson. See, she's keeping up with her French, Donna. You always had a pash on her, didn't you, Alvin? She might bung you a freebie. It'll be just like old times.'

As Alvin stands up and walks out, Lynette says, 'You know something, Colin? You really are a prick.'

'Come the summer we won't be able to say the same of you, will we, Andy, sweetheart?'

Jesus is on the telly. The telly is on a big truck

Alvin slumps onto the sofa beside Karen. Without looking away from the lurid images of torture on the TV, Karen says, 'Now, you might wonder why I, a fundamentalist atheist, am watching *The Passion of the Christ*.'

Alvin doesn't respond, though he is curious.

'*Ooph,* that hurt,' she says as the whip comes down again. 'Crap day at the clinic – they had to put down three dogs, a rabbit and a kitten with arrhythmia. I stopped off at Blockbuster on the way home. I fancied something soppy with Sandra Bullock. I don't know how I ended up with this. It's not a bad film though. And I'd forgotten he was a carpenter. He was quite good as well. Turned out a really nice . . . Oh, it was a sort of nest of tables thing. Mind you, that's just in the film. He was probably rubbish in real life. Bet he couldn't even stick a shelf up . . . Alvin, why don't you ever tell me to shut up when I'm talking rubbish?' She twists in her seat and looks at him. 'You look lousy. What happened to your lip?'

She strokes a soft finger across the swelling.

'Kevan's mum lost it,' he explains. 'Her darling little angel got expelled.'

'It could have been worse. If he'd been at the clinic he'd have got death by lethal injection . . . Poor Kevan.'

Karen's attention returns to the film, but Alvin tunes out and listens instead to the muffled sound of guitar drifting down the stairs. Annie has started lessons and practises devotedly. She strums disjointed, choppy chords, punctuating each one with an emphatic announcement: *Thrum* ... 'D!' ... *Thrum* ... 'D!' ... *Thrum* ... 'D!' ... *Thrum* ... 'E!'

'She's getting the hang of it, isn't she?' Alvin says.

'Uh-huh,' Karen agrees. 'Did you stop off for a drink on the way home?'

'I had a couple with Lynette. Then I went to the Tropica.'

'The what?'

'It's a massage place on All Saints Road.'

'You had a massage?' She's surprised.

'It's not that kind of massage place.'

'Oh.' She tenses. 'What are you telling me? I should warn you that just because Jesus is on the telly doesn't mean I'm going to come over all forgiving.'

'I didn't go in,' Alvin says.

'Cool, that's OK, so long as you only lurked *out*side ... Tell me, Alvin Lee, why are you hanging around knocking shops when you could be coming home to wonderful me?'

'Apparently Kelly's working there.'

'Kelly Hendricks?'

Alvin nods.

'You're kidding. How do you know?'

'Colin Stanislavski told me.'

'He sees everything through the bottom of a beer glass. You're going to believe an alkie like him?'

Alvin shrugs.

'Did you actually see her?' Karen asks.

Alvin didn't see anything much. He loitered across the street, trying to blend with the flyposters and trying to figure out why the place looked familiar. After a few minutes it clicked. It used to be Evans, a model shop, the plastic kind. When he'd been a kid, it had been a shrine. He'd spend Saturday mornings there, lusting after the stacked boxes of Heinkels, Messerschmitts and

Fokkers, never able to choose which to blow his pocket money on. Now, he supposed, the place was home to a different kind of Fokker entirely.

The window had been blacked out by the new owners, decorated only with a flickering neon sign: TROPICA – PERSONAL MASSAGE. Alvin wondered what sort of massage could not be described as personal. Was there an *im*personal variant where the masseuse operated on the client remotely, perhaps from another room? As he watched, he tried telling himself that perhaps it was a massage parlour in a fully non-euphemistic sense. Perhaps Kelly was in there, working the knots out of a client's spine, using therapeutic techniques recognised by accredited practitioners the world over.

Then a man in a suit, about Alvin's age, arrived outside. Before going in he paused to glance up and down the street. Alvin peered at him in search of any signs of an ailment – a cricked neck, say, or stiffness in the lumbar region – but he saw nothing except a shabby individual who would rather not be spotted outside a massage parlour. The man saw Alvin loitering and appeared to make the decision there and then that therapy of whatever sort could wait. At a brisk trot, he set off back the way he had come. A few moments later Alvin followed suit, cycling home to Karen and – not that he knew it at the time – to Jesus.

'No, I didn't see her,' he says.

'Well then, she probably doesn't even work there,' Karen assures him. 'And even if she does, your responsibility to her stopped when she left school. She's a big girl now, making her own way in the big world.'

'I know, but . . . Look, ILD gets a really hard time. It's only the successes like Kelly that keep us going. That sounds really selfish, but I'm thinking of her as well. She's bright, full of energy; she could be anything she wants. She shouldn't be working as a . . .'

He trails off – what is she working as?

Karen says it for him. 'Alvin, even if she's working as a hooker, at least she's working. She isn't dealing heroin or mugging old ladies.'

'She's the same age as Mercedes. What would you think if she dropped out of sixth form and got a job in a massage parlour?'

'I'm not sure I should say. You know how her mother feels about me having *views* on her development – even hypothetical ones. Anyway, that'd be completely different.'

'How? It'd be someone we care about screwing up her life.'

'Alvin, you're an amazing, *fantastic* bloke. God, you're practically a saint. If I had any clout with the Vatican, I'd get you on the fast track to canonisation. But you've got to learn when to back off. You can't help everybody. Kelly isn't your job any more. You've got a school full of screwed-up kids who are. Concentrate on them.'

'I should at least talk to her and find out why she quit college.'

'No, you shouldn't. Besides, I don't want you getting caught in a knocking shop. The old saving-fallen-women excuse doesn't wash any more. Especially not with the frump who's stuck at home with the children.'

'Come off it. You're the most gorgeous woman I've ever met.'

'See what I mean? A *fantastic* bloke.'

She snuggles up to him on the sofa and returns to the TV, where the Romans haven't quite finished flaying Jesus. Alvin looks down at her. At her wondrously glossy hair, which she practically treats as a part-time job, and at her mish-mash outfit – a washed-out lumberjack shirt, holed yellow harem pants, and socks, one black, one khaki. The garments could be a bold stab at art-student chic or the desperate, charity-shop purchases of a woman who's spent her last thirty pounds on Nikes for a three-year-old. Whatever, if Alvin were a fashion critic, he would describe the ensemble as 'a triumph'. That's

Alvin for you. As far as he's concerned, Karen is the most gorgeous woman he knows. It is a matter he is quite categorical on.

He met her nine years ago when she had just the one kid. Shannon was the tiny, dusky product of her relationship with a Canadian sound engineer who'd left the country the day after she'd told him she was pregnant. She worked as a receptionist in a recording studio when they met. At the time Alvin was still shuffling half-heartedly round London, trying to scare up work as a session player. They have Natalie Imbruglia to thank for their getting together. Alvin had been booked to play bass on 'Torn'. The sessions were held at Karen's place of work, a converted church in Willesden. As Alvin recalls it, the moment of their meeting was close to perfect, their eyes colliding beneath a framed gold disc for Baby D's 'Let Me Be Your Fantasy'. In reality the encounter took place by the water cooler. Karen brought him toilet paper to soak up a misconstruable spill on his trousers.

Karen made no mention of Shannon on their first few dates. It wasn't until Alvin showed her a photograph of eight-year-old Mercedes that she came clean. She saw fatherly devotion in his eyes and figured that perhaps he was worth taking a chance on. So far, her intuition has proved correct.

Annie comes into the living room dragging her guitar behind her. 'Why are they hitting that man?' she asks. 'Has he been bad?'

'Actually, they're hitting him because he's been good, sweetheart,' Karen says. 'But he's only a pretend person in a made-up story.'

'Like Legoland in *Lord of the Rings*?'

'Pretty much exactly like that, baby.'

Karen prods *stop* on the remote.

'*Aw*!' wails Annie.

'Sorry, I'd normally let you watch it,' Karen says, 'but I don't think it's suitable for your dad. It might un-lapse his Catholicism.'

Alvin often forgets that he's a Roman Catholic. His faith had atrophied through lack of exercise a few years before he met Karen. Even if it hadn't, it wouldn't have stood a chance with her in his life. Such is the force of reason she unleashes on superstitious dogma that she could probably persuade the Pope to renounce the Trinity and roll on a condom.

The doorbell rings and a moment later Shannon comes into the room. 'There's three men outside,' she announces.

'What do they want?' Alvin asks as he gets up.

'The telly,' Shannon says.

'I can't be*lieve* you two,' Mercedes screams. 'Why didn't you let them take the sofa or the cooker or something?'

'We weren't behind on the payments for the sofa or the cooker,' Alvin says, trying to keep his voice in check.

'The telly. The *telly*! *And* the video.' Mercedes gasps. 'How the hell could you miss the payments?'

'We have to prioritise, Mercedes,' Karen says. 'We're not a bottomless pit of money, your dad and I.'

We're not even an extremely shallow one, Alvin thinks, only slightly despondently, though. Being Alvin, he knows money isn't everything.

Sid comes into the room. He's been upstairs with his dinosaurs and Hot Wheels, but he is drawn to an argument like a wasp to a jar of jam. 'Where's the telly and video?' he asks, staring at the yawning void that has opened up in the corner, effectively doubling the size of the compact living room.

'Some men took them away in a big truck,' Karen says. 'To repair them.'

'Don't *lie* to him,' Mercedes snaps. She kneels down in front of him and says, 'They took them away, Sid, and they're not bringing them back BECAUSE YOUR MUM AND DAD FORGOT TO PAY FOR THEM!'

Sid starts to cry. 'I want to watch car*toooons*.'

Annie is crying now as well, and Shannon's lip is wobbling ominously.

'*Thanks*, Mercedes,' Karen says, sweeping Sid up into her arms and attempting to quieten him.

'Will everyone please calm down?' Alvin pleads. 'We'll get the TV back. Or we'll get another one.'

'How?' Mercedes screeches. '*How?*'

Karen stares at Alvin, her eyes asking the exact same question.

He isn't sure how to answer them because he doesn't, at this exact moment, have a serviceable plan. He could, he supposes, ram-raid the Comet in the retail park, except he lacks the requisite criminal disposition and also, more pertinently, the car.

'I'll get another job. In a pub or something,' he says.

'Maybe you could contribute, Mercedes,' Karen suggests. 'What about chipping in something from your Saturday job?'

'No *way*. I *need* that money. I get sweet fuck-all from you guys.'

'OK, I've had enough,' Karen says through gritted teeth. 'Alvin, you can discuss this with your daughter. I'm taking Sid for a bath. Annie, Shannon, upstairs too.'

'But, Mum, it's not even eight o'clock,' Shannon wails.

'Well, at least you won't be missing anything on the telly.'

As Karen shepherds the children from the room, Alvin looks at Mercedes apologetically.

'*What*?' she demands, misreading his expression as accusatory.

'Nothing,' he says. 'Just sorry. I will sort it out, you know.'

'Yeah, right.'

'Where are you going?' he asks as she stalks from the room.

'Janice's.'

Janice Sweeting is Mercedes's mother. She lives a couple of miles away on the literal edge of London, with a view of green fields from her six-bedroom home. A four-by-four (the size of Alvin's house) and an Audi TT (the size of Sid's box room) are parked on her drive. Tellingly, given the timing of Mercedes's migration, a 44-inch plasma TV (with DVD, Sky+ and cinema Surround sound) is parked in her living room.

Janice was a rock chick when Alvin went out with her – Chrissie Hynde meets the girl in T'Pau. These days she is married to John, the MD of a firm that distributes sound equipment – everything from tiny microphones that clip to a lapel to mountainous amps that can cause simultaneous bleeding in eighty thousand pairs of ears. Janice has maintained her ties with the rock biz more successfully than Alvin has. Having said that, he doesn't suppose, say, the girl in T'Pau is a member of the Women's Guild. Alvin has no idea what Janice does at her Guild get-togethers, but he doubts it involves swapping Zappa bootlegs and Courtney Love makeup tips.

Mercedes has done most of her growing up with Janice, John and her two half-brothers. For the last three years, however, she has commuted between her two parents, her hormones propelling her across the borough whenever the going in one home or the other becomes too tense. When she's with Karen and Alvin, she rails against the horror of Janice and John – their planet-warming cars, their mutant dogs, their chest freezer brimfull of animal parts. Alvin assumes that when she's with her mother, he and Karen are the targets.

Alvin listens to her slam the front door on her way out and collapses onto the sofa. He gazes dejectedly at the space where the TV used to be. And then he wonders how much a fish tank might cost. It would certainly fill the space neatly enough, but would Mercedes approve of captive fish?

* * *

'Don't worry, Alvin,' Karen says. 'They watched too much telly anyway.'

'It's not fair on them,' Alvin says, leaning back on his pillow and staring up at the bedroom ceiling.

'Neither is the fact that they have to live on no-logo fish fingers when all their friends get Birds Eye, but somehow they manage.'

'I'll get another job. The Three Roses is looking for part-time staff.'

'You'd do that for us, Alvin Lee? Pull pints and change barrels and listen to the dull, pointless ramblings of drunken people? You're a special man and you deserve a special treat.' As she slides down his body, she says, 'Just don't come on my hair, right?'

She tugs at his pyjama bottoms, but stops and exclaims, 'Bugger!'

'What?'

'I forgot to press eject. *The Passion of the* fucking *Christ* is still in the video player . . . No matter. It's not like I don't know how it ends.'

Penguins

What have they done with the Penguins?

Isn't Internet shopping supposed to make life easier?

Rubbish.

The virtual version is no better than the real thing. Supermarkets are supermarkets. No sooner have you found your way around, figured out where all your favourite things live, than they go and bloody move everything.

The Penguins. Where the hell are they?

The woman stares at the screen, feeling anger bubble up. Last week it was Lux. After hours of searching, she gave up. She had to make do with something called Dove. It cleans her hands well enough, but she doesn't like the smell.

She can't look at the screen any longer and forces herself to her feet. Slowly she shuffles across to the window and looks at the street below. Her flat is across the road from a convenience shop. They'll have Penguins, won't they?

Look at the traffic though. Everyone racing at a hundred miles an hour. How is she supposed to get across? Maybe someone will help . . .

But then she sees the board outside the shop. Beneath the *Evening Standard* logo, today's headline: VIOLENT CRIME SOARS.

She turns back to the computer. She'll find the Penguins if it kills her. Or perhaps she'll make do with Viscounts.

One-hit Wanda

'Tell us about *Top of the Pops,* sir,' says Debbie. Today her hair is gelled flat against her skull. A narrow strip is pulled down to make a kiss curl on her forehead – a tribute to Bill Haley, who she has never heard of.

'You're supposed to be finding an emergency plumber,' Alvin says.

Today's life-skills assignment: ascertain whereabouts of gas, electric and water mains at home; source numbers for appropriate emergency tradesmen.

'Can I put my dad down?' Debbie asks.

'Is he a plumber?'

'No, but he's who my mum always calls when stuff needs fixing. Go on, tell us about *Top of the Pops.*'

'Yeah, go on, tell us, Alvin,' Curtis urges.

Alvin is too tired to argue. Last night he started his new job. Not at the Three Roses – that one had gone by the time he called – but at Pizza Express. Alvin is a waiter. How hard can it be? he thought. The choice is pizza, pizza or pizza. But now he knows just how gruelling service with a fixed smile is. He has to stick it out, though, because the situation at home is becoming critical. A couple of days ago Karen managed to borrow a 14-inch portable from a neighbour, but the colour is off, giving everything a wonky green tinge. It will only keep the lid on the powder keg for so long.

'OK, five questions and that's it,' he says wearily.

Debbie kicks off: 'Who was on the show?'

'Well, us, obviously –'

'What were you called?' Roland asks. 'That weren't one of the five questions, right? You said *Top of the Pops*. That weren't about *Top of the Pops*.'

'We were called Living Saints.'

Only Dan the Romanian doesn't giggle, but only because he doesn't understand a word anybody is saying.

'Look, it was a good name back in eighty-six,' Alvin protests. 'It was the age of Kajagoogoo and Doug E. Fresh and the Get Fresh Crew. It could've been a lot worse. To answer your question, Debbie, we were on with the Bangles –'

'Who?' Chenil asks.

'They were a girl group.'

'Like Pussycat Dolls?'

'Nothing like Pussycat Dolls. There was Five Star. They were Britain's answer to the Jacksons, only slightly more spangly. Dodgy hair too . . . It was a difficult time for hair.'

He runs his hand across his scalp and recalls his own do – a power mullet that, when mixed with a can of lacquer, added up to six inches to his height.

'Pet Shop Boys – "Suburbia",' he says. 'You know them, yeah?'

'Batty men,' Roland mutters.

'Status Quo . . .'

Alvin surveys the blank faces. The history of a few years before they were born is as remote to them as events in pre-Christian Mesopotamia.

'Rockers,' he explains. 'They were old blokes even in eighty-six. There was Nick Berry. You know him from the telly. *Heartbeat* and stuff.'

Going through the list reminds him what a shiny, shoulder-padded decade the eighties was. What chance did surly, ascetic guitar groups have when ranged against Boy George, Bon Jovi and the awesome firepower of Wham!? Because even if they managed to be heard above that lot, they would still have to slug it out with Five Star, Swing Out Sister and Michael Bolton. And Duran Duran: Thatcherism with big hair and too much mascara. Duran *Duran*; so crap they named them twice.

Alvin has wondered if it was the Technicolored Duraniness of the eighties that prevented Living Saints from really making it. But in truth, with Jamie fronting them, they were never going to fly the flag for cool.

'Is that it?' Curtis asks, justifiably unimpressed.

'There was Madonna,' Alvin says. 'She was number one: "True Blue".'

'Never heard it,' Roland says. 'Anyway, she's shit.'

'The one in the stretch where she sucks off Ali G is cool,' Curtis says.

Roland titters.

'She does *not* suck him off,' Debbie says.

'Bet she did after the camera stopped and that,' Curtis says with a leer.

He and Roland slash the air with their hands, their fingers cracking like bullwhips, a move Alvin has always admired and never grasped the physics of.

'Shut up, man,' Debbie says. 'My mum's mad about Madonna. She's got that book where she's licking Naomi Campbell's – her *toe*, Curtis, you filthy fucker. Did you meet her, sir?'

'Er . . . kind of. Just before we taped our bit.'

'*Cool*. What was she like?'

'Yeah, did she suck you off?' Curtis says.

Roland is giggling helplessly now, his locks quivering.

'Shut up, Curtis,' Alvin says.

'Yeah, shut *up*, Cur*tis*,' Debbie says. 'What was she like, sir?'

'Very blonde. Quite scary,' Alvin says.

Quite scared is not the phrase to describe what Alvin felt when he first glimpsed Madonna through her protective ring of people, human razor wire. There she was, the world's most luminous pop star, and there he was, a hesitant bass player who'd earlier felt intimidated in the presence of Nick Berry – *Wicksy*! The sight of Madonna, therefore, left him more or less catatonic. Of course, he assumed that catatonia wasn't going to present a problem because, well, she wasn't going to hold a conversation with him, was she?

He was about to turn away and find the other three Living Saints when she spotted him through a gap. Their eyes met, Alvin froze like an extra in *The Day After Tomorrow* and she yelled, 'Hey, where did you get your shirt?'

In a panic, Alvin looked down – *was he wearing a shirt*? He was: black with a tapering rhomboid of fabric poppered to the front that gave it the look of a double-breasted military tunic. He'd bought it in Kensington Market. He'd hoped that, in tandem with his black PVC jeans, it would create a subtle but marked impression in the brief cutaway to the hesitant bass player hiding at the edge of the stage. He hadn't been anticipating impressing Madonna.

So in answer to her question he said, 'Er . . .' and then, 'Er . . .'

At that moment he couldn't remember where he'd bought the shirt. Madonna's chief of security could have produced a gun and pointed it at his head, and still he wouldn't have been able to elaborate beyond perhaps adding an 'Um'.

He was saved – is that the word? – by Jamie, who picked that moment to push him aside, barge through her entourage and thrust out a hand. 'Jamie McGreevy, vocals and guitar with Living Saints,' he announced with the undiluted confidence of the total imbecile. 'Gotta tell you I *love* "True Colors".'

As Madonna stalked off, Jamie turned to Alvin and growled, 'Rude fucking bitch. That's the last Kim Wilde record I buy.'

Afterwards, slightly drunk, Alvin rued an opportunity lost. If it hadn't been for Jamie, he was certain she'd have been his.

She would have tossed aside Sean Penn like an empty Big Mac carton and he, Alvin Lee, would have been the Englishman she settled down with till death did them part. Surely, he had her by the second 'Er'.

'What did you talk about?' Debbie asks.

'Shirts,' Alvin says. 'Now, let's do some work, yeah?'

'*Shirts*?' Curtis squeaks.

'You said five questions,' Debbie points out. 'We've only had three.'

'*Two*,' Roland protests.

'What did you look like, sir?' Debbie asks.

'About twenty years younger, I guess.'

'*No*, did you look like a *pop* star?'

The truth was that Alvin then looked much as he does now. The power mullet has long gone, of course. His mid-brown hair is left to do its own thing these days, which doesn't amount to much. But he hasn't aged appreciably. He's still thin, still relatively unlined, still OK-looking.

'You hang a bass round anyone's neck and they'll kind of look like a pop star,' Alvin generously tells Debbie.

With a bass round his neck, Alvin could and did pass himself off as a pop star, though he was never so gorgeous that the girls in the mosh pit targeted him with their knickers. But nor was he so ugly you'd have preferred him to hide behind the Marshall stack. A gig review in *Sounds* described him as having 'slightly less stage presence than his microphone stand', which was cruel, but not entirely inaccurate.

'What was your song called?' Debbie asks.

'"Wanda Lust". It was a pun on wander—' He realises he's losing them, so he says, 'It was about a girl called Wanda.'

'She your girlfriend?'

'No,' Alvin says, 'she was a figment of our songwriter's imagination.'

The figments of Jamie's imagination were many, but only one

led to anything truly marvellous. When he brought 'Wanda Lust' to his band mates, they wondered where on earth she'd come from. Most of his songs proved to be other people's. Alvin was convinced he didn't mean to steal. He'd simply wake up with a gorgeous melody in his head, bat-ishly blind to the fact that, actually, it was 'Waterloo Sunset' or 'Ride a White Swan' or 'Da Doo Ron Ron'.

But 'Wanda Lust' was different. Alvin, Gary and Kes couldn't recall having heard it before. They checked, of course – hours spent with their own and their friends' record collections, listening to tracks buried in the dustiest grooves of the obscurest albums. They couldn't find it anywhere, which was excellent news because it was easily the best tune Jamie had ever written – including all the ones he'd nicked from Lennon, McCartney and Stevie Wonder.

It needed some work. Jamie tinkered with the lyrics after Alvin put it to him that they could, perhaps, scan a little better. Thus Radio 1's audience was spared from hearing Jamie, Alvin and Kes perform a three-part harmony on the word junxtaposition (three times in each chorus, twelve times in total).

Soon after, Living Saints were a signed band. It was only a one-single deal. Their label was concerned that they didn't yet have enough songs to make an album – at least not enough that weren't actionable.

Bruno Brooks made 'Wanda Lust' his record of the week and it entered the chart at twenty-nine. The following week, after *Top of the Pops*, it climbed to fifteen. The week after, down to forty-three. Then nowhere.

'Did you have any other songs in the charts?' Debbie asks.

'No, that was it,' Alvin replies. 'We were one-hit wonders.'

The fact that their career went no further was not for want of trying. Jamie churned out tunes, sometimes half a dozen a day, only to discover that invariably someone else had churned them out already. Alvin felt sorry for him. Kes and Gary just felt like strangling him. The barrel-scraping nadir was reached when he turned up with a lyric about the miners' strike, set (to everyone's ears except his) to the melody of '(You Picked a Fine Time to Leave Me) Lucille'.

As the other three waited for Jamie at their next rehearsal, Alvin argued that at least he was *trying* – the rest of them weren't putting themselves on the line creatively, were they? But Kes and Gary walked anyway. Alvin stayed, sitting on his practice amp, mentally composing the ad they'd place in the *Melody Maker* for a new drummer and second guitarist. When Jamie showed up, two hours late, he announced that he was heading for LA, where he was going to write power ballads for Taylor Dayne and Jennifer Rush. He never got further west than W6, but it was the death of Living Saints.

'You gonna sing it for us?' Curtis asks.

'No,' Alvin says.

'Go on,' Debbie urges.

Alvin shakes his head.

'What did it sound like, then?'

Alvin isn't sure. Knowing how it goes and describing what it sounds like are two different matters. The thing was that 'Wanda Lust' didn't sound like anything else Alvin had ever heard.

'It was just a song, you know,' he explains lamely. 'Verse, chorus, verse, short guitar break in the middle, rock-pop sort of thing.'

'Guitars?' Debbie says. 'What, like Greenday?'

'I suppose. In a way.'

'Wankers,' Curtis says. 'Greenday, not you, Alvin.'

'Don't you feel sad?' Debbie asks. 'Just one hit. Like Junior Senior.'

Who? Alvin thinks.

'Who?' Chenil mumbles.

'You know.' Debbie starts to sing 'Move Your Feet' and Alvin vaguely recalls Annie shuffling her size-ones to it a couple of years ago.

Yes, he sometimes feels sad. He would have loved Living Saints to be big; to have stuck around long enough to have a back catalogue; to have played at the Freddie Mercury AIDS concert; to have supplied at least one song to a brat-pack movie soundtrack. But, being Alvin, he tells himself that one tiny hit is still one more than most people manage. And who else can claim that Madonna liked his shirt? Sean Penn and Guy Ritchie, obviously. And, when he really thinks about it, probably Warren Beatty, Antonio Banderas, Dennis Rodman . . . OK, so he isn't unique, but he's up there with some A-list shirt-wearers.

'No, I don't feel sad, Debbie,' he says. 'It was brilliant while it lasted. Now I've moved on. Like we're going to move on. Emergency numbers.'

He sits down at the small desk to one side of the room. He picks up a ring file and makes a pretence of studying its contents. This, he knows, is what real teachers do: sit at their desks and pretend to peruse paperwork while their students pretend to go about their assignments. Briefly, he wonders what the point is. But what matters is that they're here, putting themselves in danger of learning something, *anything*, even if it is only how to use the Yellow Pages. Without ILD, they probably wouldn't be at school at all.

And they respond to him. Why this should be so, he isn't sure, but they turn up, go through the motions and hand in work. Or, in Dan's case, some exquisite colouring in. Alvin has even got some of them doing the business for proper paid-up members of the NUT. He can fill, oh, at least two Post-its with the names of his successes. There was Daryl Smoker (*three* GCSEs), Robert Otifeh (*four*!), Helen Lysandrides (now making a decent fist of working motherhood) . . . And there was Kelly Hendricks.

Alvin hasn't thought about her for a couple of weeks, not

since the evening he lurked outside the Tropica. Karen was right: she's not his problem any longer; he has to let go.

He tunes in to the banter a few feet away. Curtis and Roland are texting one another across the table. He presumes they're not swapping numbers of plumbers and electricians.

'What you sending?' Debbie asks Curtis.

'Nothing, man,' he replies.

'It's 'bout me, innit?'

'Isn't.'

Roland starts to giggle again.

'Bet it is, fuck'ead,' Debbie says. 'Gimme it.'

She grabs Curtis's mobile, looks at the screen and shrieks, 'She will fucking not!'

'She fucking will,' Curtis says, his face lit up by a mile-wide smirk.

'Yeah, she fucking will,' Roland agrees. 'Ged's bruv, right, he's been there and she did him.'

'You're fucking liars,' Debbie yells. She turns to Alvin. 'Tell 'em, sir, they're fucking liars.'

Alvin is already standing, ready to calm a flammable situation. He takes the mobile from Debbie and reads Roland's message to Curtis:

keli wil suk u of 4 a 20

To Kill a Mockingbird

The teacher stares out of the classroom window. Across the patchy lawn he can see into the ILD block where Alvin is holding court. He has never spoken to him, but he knows who he is. Alvin Lee's reputation goes before him.

He spots the shaven-headed boy, the one who assassinated him that first day with 'Abracadabra, muthafucker', probably the longest two words in his vocabulary. As Alvin talks, a smile lights up the boy's usually murderous face.

How the hell does the man do it?

That's what they say about him: that he can *get* to the little bastards. Is it a special gift like lion taming or horse whispering?

Some of what they say about him is uncomplimentary – the teachers' staff room isn't the place to hear kindnesses. The word is that Alvin gets 'too close'. He's heard some gossip about a girl who left last year . . . But it's only gossip. Mostly it emanates from Stanislavski and mostly he's drunk.

As he looks on, he's aware of the thirty-five thirteen-year-olds behind him. How could he be *un*aware when every few seconds another spit-moistened bead of paper hits the back of his head? That has been the biggest shock of teaching – not the aerial bombardments, but the fact that he finds this physical proximity to children suffocating.

He wishes he could connect with them, even get 'too close' like Alvin Lee. But he has no idea where to start. He looks out over each class he teaches and feels he'd have more chance of engaging with a room full of Farsi-speaking, Semtex-wrapped suicide bombers.

'Can I go for a slash, sir?' a voice asks from behind him.

'Yes,' he replies, his lesson learned, his eyes not leaving the window because things across in ILD are taking an interesting turn.

Except for one boy who's bowed over a desk, his hand sorting through colouring pens, Alvin's charges are standing now. Alvin grabs a mobile phone from a hard-faced girl – God, they're *all* hard-faced. After a moment, she snatches it back, then flings it hard. The teacher can't see where it lands, but it can't be good for the little handset. The shaven-headed boy jumps at her – it must have been his phone. He slaps the girl. She retaliates with a plastic ruler, bringing it down edgewise on Shave Head's ear. Now there's a cry of pain – the teacher can hear it across the twenty-yard gap – and there's blood. Lots of blood, as if Shave Head's ear contains a major artery that has chosen a meandering detour through a peripheral organ or two. A boy with bouncy blond dreadlocks and a girl with hair like Cousin Itt's in *The Addams Family* both wade in. Others hover on the fringe, watching and waiting.

What will Alvin Lee do now? How will he handle this one without resorting to a) violence or b) flight?

What Alvin Lee does is to step smartly into the very *epicentre* of the storm – suicide, surely. But no, his arms shoot outwards, the palms of his hands are placed onto the foreheads of Hard Face and Shave Head. Slowly and firmly he pushes them apart. As they move backwards so do the others.

Incredible. It's like watching something spiritual – like the laying on of hands. Calm seems to have been restored, though the combatants still eye each other menacingly. In their midst, Alvin gesticulates. A girl bends down and picks up the fragments of mobile phone and places them on a desk and a boy runs from the room. After a moment he reappears with a thick wad of paper towels. These are held to Shave Head's bloody ear.

The children are all sitting now. Some of them even appear to be *working*. Meanwhile Alvin goes first to Hard Face and then to Shave Head. He bends to their level and talks to them. What is he saying? The teacher would love to know. Especially when, once Alvin has finished, they both stand and . . .

Just two or three minutes after he slapped her and she attempted to slice through the top of his skull.

. . . shake hands.

Truly awesome. Yet it looked so easy. As if anyone could do it.

He turns sharply to face his own class as a desk crashes over and two boys yell accusations at each other. The set reading task has been put aside – no more *To Kill a Mockingbird* because thirty-three children have turned their attention on the two who are about to act out *To Slaughter a Classmate.*

Small fists are already flying and sides are being taken.

I can do this, the teacher thinks, *anyone can do this,* and he strides purposefully, *confidently* towards the blossoming mêlée.

They don*t have a Kelly

Alvin looks at his watch: four forty. His shift starts at half five. Last night the manager's parting words were, 'Tomorrow Friday. Busy as anything. Don' be late.' Alvin didn't think he meant to be rude. English is his third language and even 'G'devening, smokingornonsmoking?' comes out as a grunted command.

Alvin is prepared to risk his anger because he hasn't been able to shift Kelly from his head. Ever since he read the text, ugly visions have been swimming around in there, like eels writhing in silted water: Kelly doing it for a twenty; pouring baby oil into the cupped palm of her hand; on her knees in front of half-naked strangers, fighting the gag reflex.

Instead of heading for Pizza Express, he stands across the street from the frontage that used to belong to Evans, the model man. He looks at his watch again. If he's going to do it, he'd better get on with it. He chains his bike to a lamppost, then steps into the road. He jumps back as a Domino's moped swerves to avoid him. Its rider looks back, yelling an obscenity that gets lost in the irritated buzz of his exhaust. Maybe that was an omen. Maybe he should leave right now, do as Karen says, let go.

He takes a breath and crosses the road. Without pause, he pulls at the Tropica's door handle. It doesn't budge. Then he remembers he used to do the same on his Saturday morning visits here as a kid: pull, when the eye-level sticker on the door unmistakably said *push*. The sticker has gone, along with Evans. He pushes and the door swings open.

It's not as he remembers it. Of *course* it isn't. He wasn't expecting walls lined with Airfix and Revell boxes. But he wasn't expecting the place to be so small either.

As the door closes behind him, he finds himself in a space no more than six or seven feet square. If this is supposed to imbue the client with a relaxed glow, a sensual starter ahead of the main course, it isn't working. Alvin feels trapped, as if the walls are closing in on him. He wonders if all the punters feel like this, or is it only the ones that would rather not be here at all?

A partition wall has gone up since Evans left, hurriedly erected sheets of unrendered plasterboard, thrown up, he assumes, to create new and private spaces. There's a door in the partition and another behind the small counter, at which sits a woman. An unshaded pink light bulb glows on the wall behind her, giving her brittle blonde hair a candyfloss halo.

'Therese is free right now,' the woman says without looking up from her flimsy TV magazine. 'Manda will be finished soon if you wanna wait.'

Alvin doesn't respond.

She looks at him and puts on a smile, remembering that this is a service business. She's in her fifties. Her face is over-made-up, but she's wearing a plain navy Umbro sweatshirt rather than some gossamer Ann Summers concoction. Alvin had imagined that Ann Summers would be the designer of choice here.

'Therese is our more mature lady, experienced, puts her gentlemen at ease,' she continues. 'Manda is nineteen, brunette, slim, very attractive, natural 36C –'

'Is Kelly free?' Alvin says.

The woman's smile drops. 'We don't have a Kelly.'

Oh, the relief! He wants to dance a jig, and probably would if the space allowed it. *They do not have a Kelly!* The woman stares at him, confused because customer joy upon failing to get what he asked for goes against the grain of her retail experience. But try as he might, Alvin can't contain his pleasure.

He's about to bid goodbye, rush off to sling pizzas, when the door behind the counter opens and a man steps through it. He's wearing a suit and tucking his lunch-stained shirt into his trousers. He gives Alvin the once-over and then a wink before pushing past and out into the street.

'Manda's free now,' the woman says. 'If you like.'

'No, it's OK, thanks. I'll just be –'

Alvin stops because the door has opened again. Only a crack, wide enough to allow a girl to poke her head through. She looks at the woman and says, 'We got any more kitchen roll, Roberta?'

Then she looks at the slack-jawed man, staring at her from the other side of the counter.

'I knew you'd find me,' she says, pulling her thin dressing gown round herself.

'Why Manda?' Alvin asks.

Kelly shrugs. 'It's the name the boss chose. Crap, innit?'

'And you're not nineteen.'

'I couldn't tell 'em my real age, could I? Gotta be eighteen, innit.'

'Glad to see you've found yourself a responsible employer. When she said there wasn't a Kelly, I really got my hopes up.'

'What, you didn't wanna see me again?'

'I didn't want to see you *here*.'

'I didn't wanna see you here neither,' she mutters. 'You shouldn't've come, Alvin.'

At this moment, he thinks so too. They are in a room upstairs. Alvin sits on a scuffed wooden chair. Kelly is on a narrow black massage couch, sitting with her knees pulled up to her chest. She has fishnets on beneath the gown and silly purple slippers on her feet. The last time he saw her – last August – she was wearing D&G jeans with bell-bottoms as big as two circus big tops. They billowed with her every strutting step. Her red crop-top showed off the stud in her flat stomach and around her neck hung half a dozen cheap gold chains that exuded bling way beyond their actual cost. She looked like a white Beyoncé, with jewellery from Argos. She swaggered through the school grounds, clutching the slip of paper that proclaimed her GCSE results and waving it at everyone she passed, a glorious, happy fuck-you.

'Debbie's pretty cut up,' Alvin says.

'Debbie Coates? She's just a kid.'

'Believe it or not, so are you, Kelly. Debbie looks up to you. A lot of the girls at Wood Hill do. You're a role model.'

Kelly snorts in response.

'What are you doing here? What happened to college?'

'College was shit, man.'

'You said the same about Wood Hill, but you stuck it out.'

Kelly shrugs. 'There was stuff going on at home.'

'You've always had stuff going on at home. That's nothing new.'

'I need money for a place of my own,' she says. 'I *had* to get a job.'

'There're other jobs.'

'Yeah, loads. I've been down the Job Centre. There's like B&Q, MFI, KFC, McDonald's, Burger King. It's all crap, *right*? Shit money, just . . . *shit*.'

Alvin looks at her, unsure what to say next. Should he tell her everyone has to grub for a living, tell her about Pizza Express?

'*What*?' she snaps defensively, sounding like Mercedes.

'Nothing,' he says. 'It's just that . . . I think . . . Look, is this really what you want for yourself?'

'The money's good,' she says with a shrug.

'It's not just about money. It's about what you want to do with your life, Kelly. If this is it, if this is what makes you happy, fine. I'll leave now.'

She looks away from him and gazes blankly at the dirty roller blind on the room's small window. It reminds Alvin of the first time he was alone with her. Nearly three years ago, the day she returned to school after a two-week exclusion for fighting. That time she was sullen and foetal as well. She said roughly three words to his several hundred. Everyone had told him she'd be a waste of his time. After their session was over, he was inclined to agree with them. But, being Alvin, he was also inclined to persist.

'Kelly,' he says, persisting again. 'I care about you. That's why I'm here.'

'You're here for the same reason every other bloke is,' she mumbles.

Alvin looks at her, shocked.

'Well, you've paid for it, haven't you?'

True. When Kelly saw him downstairs, she didn't wait for the answer on kitchen roll. She fled. The only way Alvin could get past the blonde was by paying her the minimum – 'Twenty-five for an aromatic back massage and manual relief.'

'I didn't come here for sex,' he says firmly.

'Don't you fancy me then? Everyone at Wood Hill reckoned you did. Most of 'em reckoned we done it.'

Alvin was aware of the gossip. It didn't bother him. He accepted that any staff member who formed a close bond with a pupil would be talked about. Since the only way he was going to be able to help Kelly was by forging a closer than usual bond, he decided to put up with the titters and get on with it. Besides, it was worth it in the end. The day Kelly showed up at school to flaunt her exam results, he felt as exultant as she did. When he saw Tony Rowell loom round a corner and head towards them, he wanted to grab the slip of paper from her and wave it under his nose – '*Six GCSEs. Fuck you.*'

'No, I don't fancy you,' Alvin says. 'I just care about you.'

There's a notice board in ILD covered with photos of the

mentors and their charges. Most of them were taken on trips – work-experience awaydays and Outward Bound weekends. That there's a budget for this is a source of resentment for some. Why, they argue, should the delinquents have money for rock climbing and white-water rafting? The pictures on the pin board do nothing to appease the critics. As Colin Stanislavski once put it, 'Just look at the little shit-rags, would you? We're struggling to buy enough *Macbeths* to go round and they're off acting out *Raiders of the Lost* fucking *Ark*.'

One picture stands out. It was taken a year ago and shows Alvin and Kelly sitting on a minibus bringing them home after a log-cabin weekend in Derbyshire. Kelly looks sleepily beautiful, a blinding beam of a smile radiating from her sunburned face. Alvin isn't looking at the camera, but at her. His expression could be one of pride. Or it could be lust. Which one depends on the viewer's perspective. Stanislavski again: 'Crikey, Alv, you look as if you wanna pork the little strumpet right there on the charabanc.'

When a moment ago he said, 'No, I don't fancy you,' he wasn't being entirely truthful.

Alvin hasn't always looked at Kelly in that way. It wasn't until she allowed him to get to know her that the thought occurred to him. He remembers the moment. He said something that made her laugh. It was the first time he'd seen her teeth engaged in anything other than a snarl. Used too liberally, he thought, that smile would make a potentially catastrophic contribution to global warming. Behind the gangsta swagger and the rock-hard face, Kelly is shockingly beautiful, and once Alvin had glimpsed it he couldn't escape it. Not that he ever did anything about it. Not even when she spent the log-cabin weekend glued to his side, her mind and body immersed in a hormone rush of flirting. There were plenty of reasons he didn't push it, not least the fact that he liked his job and wanted to keep it. And the discovery that at forty-something he was capable of stirrings for a sixteen-year-old was unsettling enough to make him hit a big red panic button in his psyche, the one marked SUPPRESS. But the biggest barriers to action were Karen and Kelly herself. He didn't want to betray the trust of either of them.

He looks at her now and doesn't feel even an inkling of desire. The shabby gown, the fishnets and the silly slippers don't become her. Neither does the subservience inherent in her job. He remembers the man who pushed past him a few minutes ago – Kelly's last client. He recalls the wink and feels an unwelcome bolt of anger, a sudden wish to charge out into the street, find the guy and do something violent to him.

'Look, it isn't bad, this job,' Kelly says, softening a little.

Alvin gives her a look. It says, 'Don't humour me.'

'It's *not*,' she protests. 'It's just, like, sex, you know. Not even that half the time. Hand jobs mostly. Quick rub, give 'em some moany shite about how turned on you are and it's over in a couple of minutes. I worked at McDonald's for a bit last summer – like, for a day. It took longer to stick a Big Mac and fries in a bag than it does to bring off most of the punters here.'

Alvin isn't buying it.

'*Work*,' she sneers. 'It's all prostitution, innit? So if I'm gonna have to tart myself, I'd rather not do it for minimum wage, right?'

Alvin wonders if that's a line she has heard from one of the other girls. Experienced Therese, perhaps, the one that puts her gentlemen at ease. It's not that Kelly isn't smart enough to have an intelligent insight, but something about it doesn't ring true. He remembers her going to see Pam Spottiswoode, the school counsellor. After three sessions she was talking about her life in glib therapese – about her needs to 'make friends with Me' and 'achieve closure' with her father. Only a few weeks previously she'd spoken of wanting to 'bash the fucker's brains out with a baseball bat'. She's like a lot of teenagers – Mercedes is the same – in her ability to absorb the language of those around her and replay it as unselfconsciously as a Dictaphone.

Now that Alvin remembers her therapy phase, he wonders exactly what kind of a friend Me is when Me is lying on her back, being fucked by a stranger.

'Look, I really think we should talk about this, Kelly,' he says.

'I'm not, like, your job no more.'

'I know, but . . . We should talk. College. Maybe it's not too late.'

'I don't wanna go back. I need money for a place.'

'I can ask around, see if I can get you into a hostel or something. Then you could go back to coll—'

'You're not listening, are you? *I don't fucking want to go back.*'

'OK, but please can we talk?'

'Go on then, talk.'

'Not now. I've got to go to work.'

She raises a curious eyebrow.

'Pizza Express,' he explains. 'I'm moonlighting. You're not the only one that's desperate for money.'

'And what, you paid, like, twenty-five for this?' she says guiltily.

'Forget it. Not important,' he says, getting up.

'Lemme give you a massage, then,' she says, smiling at last.

It's Alvin's turn for the curious eyebrow.

'It says massage on the door, dunnit? We even get blokes in sometimes and that's all they want. Hardly ever though. I've had, like, *one*. But I'm not bad at it, you know.'

'It's OK, thanks,' Alvin says, looking at his watch.

'Please,' she says, jumping off the couch. 'I *want* to.'

'Really, it's OK,' Alvin protests, blushing.

But she's tugging at his jacket, pulling it from his shoulders, and at the same time shoving him towards the couch. He feels himself giving in – because she's smiling now, because he feels sorry for her and because, actually, the idea of a massage is appealing.

'All right,' he says, 'but just a quick one.'

'Take your shirt off and lie down.'

'On the couch?'

'You seen the state of this carpet? Course on the couch,' she says, laying a greying towel over the black vinyl.

A moment later he's lying face down, wondering what he's doing in a massage parlour, waiting to be rubbed down by a fearsomely attractive seventeen-year-old prostitute. But she's not a prostitute, he tells himself. Well, she quite clearly is, but she's also *Kelly*, so that makes it different. Even though he has, technically, paid for it. But what exactly has he paid for? A *massage*. Forget the manual relief bit. That never was and never is going to happen.

He closes his eyes and listens to her smear oil on her hands. He can smell strawberries. Not strawberry strawberries, but the stuff that passes itself off as the real thing in cheap ice cream.

'Sorry, this smells shite, but it's, like, all we've got,' Kelly says.

She places her warm, slippery palms on his kidneys and he flinches.

'Jesus, you are *tense*, man. Relax. I have done this before.'

'Sorry, but I haven't,' he mumbles into the pillow.

She presses down and slides her hands along either side of his spine, all the way up to his shoulders and then down again. Up . . . Down . . . Up . . . Down. He feels his body melt slightly into the bench. She is undeniably good.

'Imagine if Rowell saw us now,' she says.

Alvin stiffens – a rigid length of telegraph pole on a couch.

'*Joking*. He's not gonna like *come* here, is he? But imagine if he did. That dickhead so wanted me expelled.'

'Don't you think that if he did see you here,' Alvin suggests, spotting a way in, 'he might feel vindicated?'

'What you on about? Anyway, shut up, I'm giving you a massage.'

She goes to work with fresh vigour, pushing her thumbs into his spine. It hurts a little, but it also releases tiny charges of something tinglingly pleasant. Alvin shuts up, relaxes, enjoys . . .

And as she changes pace, slithering the flats of her hands over the small of his back and along his flanks, he feels his cock harden. Which wasn't in the plan, but then, neither was a massage. Anyway, there's not much he can do about it, short of calling a halt, getting up and allowing her to see an erection pressing insistently at the front of his jeans. So he relaxes, enjoys . . .

Her body moves closer and he feels the front of her dressing gown brush his back. Then nipples. Unmistakably. Hard nipples through the thin towelling.

'Kelly,' he says, a hint of protest in his voice.

She kisses the back of his neck and, finally, he turns over to face her.

'Kelly, stop it,' he says firmishly.

He's looking at her intently, resolve in his eyes, which isn't easy because she has slipped the gown off her shoulders and let it fall to her waist.

Now he reaches out and yanks her towards him. They kiss and her oily hand slides down his bare stomach until it reaches his waistband. Deftly she pops the buttons and strokes him through his Y-fronts, which are a washed-out red and frayed at the edges – clearly not put on with the occasion in mind.

'I normally make blokes stick on a johnny for this,' she whispers.

Before he has a chance to ask 'For what?' she has swooped down his body and put him in her mouth.

Alvin knows he should stop this right now. Climb off the bed, pull up his trousers and go to work. It's not too late. The situation isn't yet irretrievable. But soon it will be. He hasn't known hair-trigger excitement like this since he was the same age as Kelly and, besides, she is good; she wasn't exaggerating with her Big Mac and fries claim. Alvin pushes himself up on his elbows and he's about to say something, really he is, but for a moment he's distracted by noise coming through the wall from the room next door. Rhythmic banging and the grunting of a man in the latter stages of gratification.

The grunts turn into words, just about discernible through the thin partition. 'Nnng . . . Uh-huh . . . Yeah . . . That's the one, babe . . . Right there . . . Right in the junxtaposition.'

Billy Liar

'That's quite a swelling,' the woman in the white coat says as she studies his groin. She sounds almost impressed. 'It'll be tender for a few days, I'm afraid. I suspect it's only bruising, but if you experience any more dizziness or fainting, you must come straight back in to see us.'

The teacher nods.

'OK, right, you can get dressed now if you like.'

Gingerly he hoists his underpants over the swollen testicle, now the size of a Christmas tangerine.

'How did it happen?' the doctor asks.

'Playing ... sport. *Rugby*,' the teacher replies.

'Rugby?'

'Yes.'

'Sorry ... No offence, but you don't seem the rugby type.'

'Well, it's become a much more universal game. Since England won the World Cup, really.'

'I see. That bruise ...'

She points at the mark on his inner thigh, a pink-turning-to-red patch, a near-perfect imprint of a size-six Caterpillar boot, chunky tread pattern and all.

'... Is that legal footwear in rugby these days?'

You taste of strawberries

'You smell of strawberries,' Karen announces as Alvin flops onto the sofa. He's still clutching his cycling helmet – it stops his hands from trembling.

'Do I?' he says, wondering just how much panic a man can infuse into two extremely short words and deciding that he's probably now the new world record holder.

'Well, it's mixed in with pepperoni and pomodoro and it's not exactly strawberries,' she says. 'Pretend strawberries, like in strawberry Starbursts.'

'There was an accident with the ice cream,' he explains. 'The strawberry ice cream.'

'What happened?'

'Oh, you don't want to know.'

Rather, Alvin doesn't want to tell her.

'I *do* want to know,' she says.

She looks away from the portable TV, which, even though it's tiny, is casting a sickly green light across the room.

'Sorry, I know it's only slinging pizzas, but I *need* to know,' she continues. 'I've spent an evening watching Will, Grace and Jonathan Ross being played by pea-green midgets. I need a dose of real life.'

'I'll tell you in a minute,' he says. 'I need to get my breath back. That bike ride. *Knackering*.'

He smears a hand across his brow, feeling the sweat, which has nothing to do with demented pedalling.

'You got a phone call earlier,' she says. 'Just after five thirty.'

'Oh, who from?' he asks, forcibly elbowing nonchalance into his voice.

'Foreign bloke. Sounded like Slobodan Milosevic. He said, "Where Alfie? 'E no' come tonight? 'E no' wan' job?"' She slips into a plausible East European accent for this – good enough to get her work as a Bond villain. 'I guess he's your boss, yeah?'

'I was a few minutes late. School shit. Debbie and Curtis fighting.' Alvin delivers this with a vague wave of his hand.

On an extremely narrow definition of the word *lie* – a definition the width of a tightrope, a tightrope in a flea circus (for extremely small fleas) – Alvin has not yet told one. Yes, he was a few minutes late for work, if twenty-five count as a few. And, yes, a waitress did drop a bowl of strawberry ice cream, though, given that Alvin was on the other side of the restaurant, that's hardly a reason to come home smelling of the stuff. And at school Debbie did attack Curtis. Alvin intervened, made peace and mopped up the blood, but, of course, this wasn't the reason he was late for work. Though, technically, on an extremely narrow definition et cetera, he didn't tell Karen that it *was*.

There is plenty of stuff that he hasn't told her, but is omission the same as lying? The best legal minds would surely argue not – provided they were arguing for rather than against Alvin. They'd contend that if to omit is to lie, then anyone who gives an edited account of his day – that doesn't include every minuscule tea-drinking, toilet-visiting, nose-picking detail – is therefore a liar.

So, the imaginary QCs on Alvin's hypothetical defence team would reason, he is not a liar. They might even win him an acquittal from a jury of twelve good pedants and true.

Nevertheless, he hates himself.

Alvin has never hated anybody. At least not since he was eight or nine and hate resulted from some other eight- or nine-year-old pulling his hair really hard. But now, sitting beside the woman he loves, he finally knows hatred.

He loathes himself for lying to her by any fair definition of the word. He hates himself for looking at her now and thinking – albeit momentarily – that on the un-level playing field of physical beauty she can't compete with a match-fit seventeen-year-old white Beyoncé. And he especially despises himself for getting into a situation whereby he could make that invidious comparison in the first place.

The barristers would argue that it was Kelly who made the running, that Alvin was the defenceless victim of a guileful temptress. But he doesn't buy that himself; why should anyone else? He didn't resist her. He didn't even say *no* so half-heartedly that it could be taken as meaning *yes* by anyone who believes one can ever mean the other. And didn't the fact that he was semi-naked in a place where sex is the only meaningful transaction indicate he *wanted* it to happen?

Actually, the lawyers will never get a chance to exercise their powers because Alvin will be yelling 'Guilty!' before the clerk even pops the question.

Guilty of betraying both Karen and Kelly.

Kelly didn't know what to make of his sudden flight and Alvin wasn't going to hang around to attempt an explanation. She'd have to settle for *sorry,* he decided, as he frantically buttoned his jeans, knowing that in the room next door Jamie McGreevy was doing the same thing.

'What's wrong? What did I do?' Kelly asked.

'Sorry, nothing, you didn't . . . This was a mistake, we shouldn't have . . .'

She didn't hear the rest because he was out of the door, throwing himself down the stairs four at a time, squeezing past the brittle blonde as she called out 'Everything O—', stumbling into the street heedless of traffic, fumbling with the lock on his bike, leaping into the saddle, looking back at the Tropica, praying that Jamie didn't exit, a sated grin on his chops.

He didn't.

As Alvin pedalled off he stole one last glance across All Saints Road and saw a blind roll up in a small first-floor window. Kelly looked at him through the dirty glass, perplexed and sad.

What had he done? he asked himself. *What had he done?* Well, he hadn't come. Was that a defence? Was not reaching ecstasy's peak – merely scaling its lower slopes – a lesser offence? Maybe, but Alvin suspected it was akin to the difference between murder and attempted murder. The would-be killer doesn't get life, but nor does he get away with a spot of community service.

He'd gone there wanting to help Kelly, he was still convinced of that, yet after only a few minutes he was just another grunting punter who wanted to come in her mouth. He couldn't see her again, that much was clear. How could he face her with any credibility?

Right now he has a bigger problem: facing Karen.

'You're amazing, you know,' she says.

He really has no response to that.

'I mean, after a day with a bunch of teenage psychos, you do a full shift in a pizza parlour – just to get our telly back. *Amazing,* man, I *love* you.'

No response whatsoever.

She nuzzles her body into his and turns her attention to the TV.

'This picture's unbearable,' she says after a moment. She hits *off* on the remote. 'There's nothing else for it, Alvin. We're gonna have to make our own entertainment.'

She leans into him hard and runs a hand up his thigh.

Oh bugger, he thinks, even as his cock stirs back to life. Which is understandable. It has been left hanging once today, so it's hardly going to pass up a second bite at the cherry. Body and mind at cross-purposes.

Not that Karen can tell because she says, '*Mmm,* that's nice,' as she nudges into his groin. She kisses his neck. 'You *taste* of strawberries. Shall we go upstairs or do you wanna take me like a groupie on the sofa?'

'*Mmmm,* that was *nice,*' Karen says, panting. 'I don't know what got into me downstairs. Must be the strawberry ice cream. Who needs oysters?'

Alvin, panting too, stares up at the bedroom ceiling. And as his breath comes back, he feels . . . a number of things, not least euphoric because the sex was about as good as it gets. But mostly he feels despicable. No doubt about it, he, Alvin Lee, is a common-or-garden cheating bastard.

'Sid'll be up at six,' Karen says. 'Best go to sleep.'

She's right, Alvin thinks, reaching for the light switch, best go to sleep.

He closes his eyes and sees a small dirty window, Kelly looking through it, sad and perplexed.

Something about a hatbox

It's late. Most sensible eighty-three-year-olds are tucked up now, mugs of herbal tea – the new Ovaltine – on their bedside tables. But this eighty-three-year-old is glued to a flat, wide screen that glows as if plutonium-dipped.

Winston: Love is a many splendoured thing . . . I've heard. Never tried it out myself – I've got Xbox. What about you? Loved up good?

She really doesn't know how they got onto *this*.

Vera: Loved and lost, Winston.
Winston: *Ahhhh*. Would you try again or are you of the once-bitten persuasion?
Vera: I'll make do with my memories. Plenty of those.
Winston: Tell me about them.
Vera: I keep them in a hatbox. The lid isn't coming off tonight.
Winston: Tell me something about yourself. *Anything.*
Vera: What would you like to know?
Winston: Er . . . How old are you?
Vera: The question one should never ask a lady.
Winston: We're on the net. Make it up. You think my real name is Winston?
Vera: OK . . . 22.
Winston: Next: student or working girl?

Vera: Neither. Lady of leisure.

Winston: *Leisure*! Who funds this idyllic existence? Mum and Dad? Tell me about 'family life' – I'm told by friends who have one that it can be quite wonderful.

She doesn't answer. Instead, she looks wistfully through the open door to the kitchen across the corridor and wonders if she has the stamina for the twenty-five-minute ordeal of *making a cup of tea*.

Winston: You still there? What did I say?

Some things simply upset her too much. Tea isn't the answer of course, but it's the best she's got. She logs off and begins the slow ascent from her chair.

All her sexual partners

Ah, time the healer.

Three weeks on Alvin feels better. Not great, but definitely better. He can put what happened at the Tropica down to a momentary lapse, file it away with the other incidents from his life that make him squirm with shame. Frankly, they don't amount to many.

He is sitting beside Lynette Moorhouse on a bench outside Minogue's enjoying the best that late May has to offer. The view isn't panoramic. A trunk road heaving with traffic in a rush to get into or out of the city proper, in a rush to pass through this apology of a London borough as quickly as possible.

Lynette lolls her head back, warming her neck in the traffic fumes and afternoon sun. It looks like a pose Lauren Bacall might once have struck in a publicity portrait. Except Lauren Bacall didn't have an Adam's apple.

'Did you ever find out what Kelly's up to?' she asks, plucking the question from nowhere as far as Alvin can tell.

He responds by choking, still-fizzing beer dribbling out of his nostrils.

'You OK?'

'Fine,' he says. 'Went down the wrong way . . . No, I never did find out.'

'I could ask round her college, if you like, find out how she's doing,' she says. 'I know some people there.'

'She's left college,' Alvin says because he can't continue the lie.

'I thought you said –'

'Colin was right. She's working at that massage place.'

'You've seen her?'

Alvin nods, hoping she doesn't ask *where*.

'And?'

'She claimed she's doing fine. She doesn't want help. I offered but . . .'

He trails off. He can't lie to Lynette, but he can't tell her the whole story either. She puts a consoling hand on his.

'From what I know of that girl, she'll be OK,' she says. 'She's got too much *feist* to get chewed up by the sex industry.'

She may be right. Alvin isn't sure. He only knows that he can never see Kelly again. He has thought about going back to the Tropica, trying again to talk to her or at least trying to apologise, but he suspects it would only make things worse. So it's goodbye Kelly Hendricks. He only wishes his final memory wasn't of her sad, puzzled face at the window.

Donna Hutton, the demure (unless provoked) languages teacher, joins them with fresh drinks. 'Can't wait for the summer hols,' she says as she hands out the glasses.

'Me too,' Alvin agrees, grateful for the change of subject. 'Going anywhere nice?'

'Me, Guy and the kids will be pitching our tent in the usual field in Brittany,' Donna says with resignation.

'Sounds lovely,' says Alvin, wishing that he and Karen could afford even a holiday under canvas.

'Oh, it would be, if it weren't for the Frogs. Weird, isn't it? I spend all year trying to beat the language into uninterested brats, then every summer I realise that, actually, it isn't worth the bother. When you can't understand them, at least you only *think* the French are being rude.'

'Where are you off to, Lynette?' Alvin asks.

'Only Holland.'

'God, I was forgetting. The *op*.'

Looking at Lynette's waxed and shimmering legs extending from her flowery mini and at her scarlet toenails gleaming like ten tiny car body panels, it's easy to forget that she is not yet the finished article.

'Aren't you scared?' he asks while making a mental memo not to stare at her legs so.

'*Excited*,' she replies.

'God, you're brave,' Donna says. 'I shit bricks at the thought of a filling.'

'Me too, darling, but a filling doesn't change your life, does it?'

'I've got to get off,' Alvin says, draining his glass.

'You working tonight?' Lynette asks.

'No, Mercedes has promised to babysit – it's a bit of a once-in-a-lifetime offer. Karen and I are going to the pictures.'

Alvin joins Karen in the queue and passes her a bucket of popcorn. She takes a handful. 'It's salty,' she says, screwing up her face.

'I asked you what you wanted and you said "Whatever".'

'Well, *whatever* meant *sweet*. I *hate* salty.'

'Sorry. I'll change it.'

'Don't bother. We'll miss the film.'

Silence for a moment as they wait in line.

'I can't stand Tom Cruise,' Karen mutters. 'I don't know why I let you drag me to this.'

'It was your choice. I wouldn't have minded seeing –'

'Alvin, I'd *never* willingly pick a Tom Cruise film,' she snarls. 'Why would I want to waste two hours of my life gazing at the vainest man on the planet?'

Karen has been cranky since Alvin met her. Far from revelling in a rare evening of self-indulgence, she has been taking issue with everything.

'What's wrong?' he asks her as the queue starts to shuffle forward.

'I told you. Tom Cruise is a twat.'

'No, it's not Tom Cruise. Or salty popcorn.'

'You're right, it isn't. But we're going to miss the trailers. You know I love the trailers.'

'Sod the trailers. What is it?'

She spins round to face him. 'Are you having an affair?'

The queue stops moving. Clearly learning the answer to this one promises more thrills than the trailers.

'*No*,' he says, brimfull of righteous indignation laced – it has to be said – with a generous dash of terror.

'*Good*. Let's see this film, then,' she says through ventriloquist's lips.

'No, not fine. I think we need to talk.'

'OK, let's talk, shall we?' She glares at him, her nostrils flaring.

'Here?' Alvin asks.

'Yes, here,' she spits.

Yes, here agrees the queue, albeit silently.

'Let's go get a drink,' Alvin says, taking her arm and marching her through the foyer.

'You can't eat that here,' the waitress says.

'No, of course,' Alvin says, dropping the popcorn back into the bucket.

'What can I get you?' she asks.

'Two coffees, please.'

'Black or white?'

'White, please,' says Alvin.

'Whatever,' says Karen.

Alvin glares at her.

'*White*,' says Karen.

Alvin watches the waitress walk across the empty Wimpy to the kitchen, then turns to Karen.

'We're going to miss the film now,' she says accusingly.

'Never mind that. Anyway, I thought you hated Tom Cruise.'

'So? Those tickets cost fifteen quid. In case you hadn't noticed, fifteen quids are thin on the ground.'

'Look, what's brought this on?' he asks.

'I went to the doctor yesterday.'

'You didn't say anything.'

'Well, pardon me, but at tea time the kids were too busy talking about play dates and school sports day for me to bring up vaginal discharge and a burning sensation when urinating.'

'Sorry. What did the doctor say?' he asks.

'Nothing much. She gave me a pelvic exam and took a urine sample. I didn't think much of it to be honest. I thought it'd just be thrush. Or cystitis. I got the results today: *chlamydia*.'

Alvin doesn't react. At least not outwardly.

'You know what chlamydia is, don't you?' she says.

Alvin hasn't sat through countless Wood Hill lectures from sexual health counsellors and picked up nothing. Chlamydia: the commonest sexually transmitted infection, the one you can catch from fucking, kissing and, yes, even from unfinished blowjobs . . . His heart sinks as his brain makes the connections.

'You know what she said to me?' Karen continues. 'She told me I should inform all my sexual partners. Those were her exact words – *all* my sexual partners. Well, I'm informing *all* of them right here, right now, Alvin. I've got chlamydia.' She folds her arms and stares at him, waiting.

'But I haven't got . . .'

He doesn't finish because, alongside a great deal of STI trivia (including how to roll a condom onto a candle using only one hand, an essential skill for anyone planning to have sex with an HIV-positive candle), he remembers that over fifty per cent of chlamydia sufferers don't show any symptoms.

'So who is she?' Karen asks as the waitress brings two milky coffees.

Alvin thinks about lying, but what's the point? He's done for.

Fucked by *Chlamydia trachomatis*, a bacterium that has inflicted him with not a single symptom. Unless being reduced to a snivelling sleaze-worm in the eyes of the woman he loves counts. It certainly feels like a symptom, though he doubts it rates a mention in the textbooks.

He has to tell her the truth now. He owes her that much and, perversely, it is the only thing that can possibly save him. He opens his mouth . . . But the words aren't quite ready to come out.

'So then,' Karen says, 'all *your* sexual partners.'

Alvin opens his mouth again and this time he tells her.

'You *bastard*,' she spits when he has finished.

'Sorry. I'm just so, so sorry,' he says.

She gives him a contemptuous look, which is fair enough. Even as it was forming in his mouth he knew that *sorry* was a cop-out. Sorry is demonstrably not up to the exacting task set by its definition. It is an *apology* of a word.

'It was a moment of insanity – no more than two minutes, I swear,' he says. 'I stopped it almost as soon as it started.'

'You not ejaculating, not getting your cheap bloody thrill, is supposed to be some kind of a comfort, is it? Jesus, what am I talking about? *Cheap* thrill! She's a *hooker*. You *paid* for it. And we're completely broke.'

'Sorry.' Alvin merely mouths it this time.

'You know, there is so much wrong with this,' Karen says. 'You having sex with a prostitute. Who less than a year ago was your *professional* responsibility. What is she? Seventeen? Younger than Mercedes? You're a hair's breadth from being a *paedophile*, Alvin.'

The waitress, who is alone at a table on the far side of the restaurant, looks up from her burger at the P-word.

'So much is wrong with this,' Karen repeats, shaking her head.

Her eyes are wet with tears now. Alvin wants to reach out and touch her hand but paralysis has set in. An inertia that arises from the certain knowledge that absolutely nothing he can say or do will be right.

'Haven't you got *anything* to say for yourself? Or does "sorry" cover it?'

'It was a mistake, Karen, I didn't mean it to happen, it wasn't why I went there.' He fires off the words rapidly, trying to make things right, but knowing he's only making them worse. '*It was a mistake*. It doesn't mean for one second that I don't love you.'

She picks up her coffee and stares at it with disdain.

'I didn't want milky,' she says quietly.

Then she tosses it at him.

It is *very* milky, though, and doesn't scald.

Wet and helpless – in so many ways – he watches her walk out.

The waitress reappears at Alvin's side. Her burger is unfinished, but she's the conscientious type.

'Do you want a cloth?' she says.

'Yes, please,' Alvin replies.

'Do you want anything else?' she asks, unable to prevent a smirk.

'No, thanks, just the bill, please.'

It is only as the waitress walks away that Alvin remembers it was Karen who was holding the money tonight. He has never done a runner from a restaurant before, but, just as he discovered at the Tropica three weeks ago, there's a first time for every crime.

Romeo + Juliet

The teacher closes the door behind him. He pauses in the hall. He can hear a voice in the front room. His mother is on the phone.

'... Oh, it's going fantastically well, thank you ...'

What is going fantastically well? Can't be anything to do with him.

'... Like a duck to water. He loves it ...'

She must be talking about his father. He's recently taken up tai chi. He's turned into a round-eyed version of Mr Miyagi in *The Karate Kid*.

'... That's right, it's a real vocation ...'

Tai *chi*?

'... teaching ...'

Oh.

'... His pupils love him. He's got a real flair ...'

He heads quietly upstairs before he hears any more and his grumbling depression ramps up to a raging death wish.

In his room he sits at his desk and pulls a sheaf of paper from his briefcase. He stares at the top sheet. It's covered with spiky scrawl that looks as if it caused actual pain to the writer. But at least it's covered. He checks the name at the top: Yasmin Oliver. He picks it up and reads.

Romeo and Julyet were a famous romantic couplet who shaklespears turned in to a famous play. It was acted in the days wen women was'nt alowed to act so a gay man acted julyet and the other girl parts to like the nurse and the mum and the sectary. mostly the story is about Romo. he wants to get of with julyet but his dad wo'nt let him becase he has to work in the famly shoe shop. In them days phones was'nt been invented so romeo has to go to Julyets balcony and shout out loud. In the end he does get of with her but shes' drinked poisin so she is dead wen he is doing her then he dies of the plaque. other storys like romeo and Julyet are taggert on ITV and lord of the ring becase its about olden people and allso its hard to undrstand what the people is saying in it allso nadia from BB becase shes' a man been a woman.

He gives it a C- on account of the fact that she at least got the *gist*. He picks up the next, an unpunctuated four-liner from Roland Goffe.

ROMIO AND JULIET IS LIKE TEXAS CHANE SAW MASSICER COS EVRYONE DIES ROMIOS GOT A CAR NAMED AFTER HIM BUT JULIET DOESNT SHAKSPEER ROTE THE STORY HE WAS A FAMOUSE

He awards this one an F and upgrades Yasmin to a B+.

The next sheet says Dan Ianculescu at the top. Dan, the quiet kid. Actually, the silent kid. He likes Dan. Wouldn't say boo to a goose, let alone to a teacher. He hasn't written an essay, but he's done a painstakingly coloured drawing of Romeo and Juliet sitting on a motorbike. It says Honda on the petrol tank, which apart from Dan and Ianculescu is the first word the teacher has ever seen him commit to paper.

Dan gets a C.

We cooked beans

Alvin doesn't want to open the bedroom door. Hell lies on the other side. But so too does a clean, dry T-shirt. He can hear Karen slamming drawers in the bedside cabinet, taking her anger out on defenceless items of underwear. Alvin has spent the last two hours trudging miserable circles. He was careful to avoid the Wimpy. He has promised himself to return as soon as possible with the price of two coffees.

He was hoping that Karen might have calmed down by now. She has never been this angry with him before, but then, he has never given her cause to be.

He slowly pushes the door open. Karen is sitting cross-legged on the bed. She has emptied a drawer of knickers onto the quilt and is sifting through the pile, tossing the more frayed and faded items in the rough direction of the wastebasket. He hopes the clear-out isn't symbolic. She doesn't look up.

'Do you want to talk?' he asks.

'I remembered this conversation I had in the pub last year,' she says, sounding calm but also deeply sad. 'Not a conversation really. Colin Stanislavski breathing beer fumes at me. Telling me I should keep you on a short leash, what with your following of panting groupies.'

'You're going to pay any attention to a thing he says? I know I've been a prick, but . . . Please.'

'That's just it. I *didn't* pay attention, did I? Especially to the bit where he told me Kelly Hendricks was at the head of the pack. Oh, how we end up laughing at ourselves, eh?'

'The thing with Kelly happened once, three weeks ago. Nothing before. Nothing since.'

'Why should I believe you? Why should I believe a word you've ever said to me? All those cosy camping trips you went on with her. You were just cooking beans and singing songs round the fire, were you?'

'It was one camping trip. And yes, we cooked beans. Nothing else. I'm telling you the truth. It's all I've ever told you.'

'Except for the one night you came home and *didn't* tell me what you'd been up to. Well, you're screwed now, aren't you? You may well be telling the truth, but I'll never believe anything you say to me ever again.'

She reaches down to the floor and picks up a cleanish T-shirt.

'You look a state. Put this on,' she says, throwing it at him. 'Mercedes has gone out clubbing. She won't be home till dawn. You can sleep in her bed.'

Shoes on

Time the healer, anyone?

Time the sticking plaster, perhaps. Antibiotics have cleared up the chlamydia. The other ailments are proving more intractable.

Another three weeks down the line, it's breakfast *chez* Karen and Alvin.

'What's going on?' Mercedes asks as she pours herself orange juice.

'As soon as we've finished breakfast,' Alvin says, 'I'll be walking Shannon and Annie to school –'

'I'm not talking about the stupid school run. I mean *what's going on?*' She nods her head towards the kitchen, where Karen is banging dishes.

Alvin looks at his daughter blankly.

'She means why aren't you and Mum talking,' Shannon explains, her mouth full of bread roll.

'We are,' Alvin says.

'Are not,' Shannon says.

'It's like Janice and John's round here these days,' Mercedes agrees.

According to Mercedes, her mother and stepfather converse via notes stuck to the Smeg – she reckons that if it weren't for fridge magnets, they wouldn't communicate at all. Alvin has no way of knowing if this is true, but he can't deny that he and Karen aren't exchanging words like they were, say, three and a half weeks ago.

'We're getting on fine,' he says.

'Yeah, *right*,' Mercedes snorts, 'and the Palestinians are throwing street parties for the Israelis.'

'*Party*!' Annie squeaks. 'Can I go?'

'*Duh*. I don't *think* so,' Mercedes says.

'Why not? The Zralies are going.'

'Who are the Zralies?' Sid asks.

'They're a people who've forfeited the world's *trust* and *respect* through their cavalier and *selfish* behaviour,' Karen says, appearing at the door with two pairs of trainers. 'Shannon, Annie, get your shoes on or you'll be late.'

'Don't wanna go to school,' Shannon pouts.

'There's some little girl in Guatemala telling her mum she doesn't want to sew shirts in the Gap factory for tuppence a day. *Get your shoes on*.'

I must be mad, Alvin thinks.

He chains his bike up to the lamppost in All Saints Road and steps off the pavement. He immediately jumps back, his ears assaulted by a scream of rubber on wet asphalt, his calf nudged by a bumper. He looks to his right at the blue estate car that very nearly killed him, at the electric window sliding into the door and at the head leaning through the opening.

'Are you mad?' the angry, shaken woman asks.

Evidently, thinks Alvin.

'Just look where you're bloody going,' the woman says.

Dazed, he steps back and watches the car drive on, giving his shoes a deserved splash from a puddle.

Stark raving bonkers, he thinks after a moment.

It is six weeks since he was last here. Six weeks since he pedalled away as if he was Lance Armstrong, swearing that he'd never come this way again, not even if the Tropica shut down and reopened as Evans the friendly model shop. Alvin being Alvin though . . .

He doesn't want to see Kelly again, but he needs to. To see that she's all right and to apologise. And to tell her that she's carrying a mild but highly infectious disease. She may only be passing it to a bunch of sleazy punters, but even the sleazy manage to acquire girlfriends and wives, very significant others who so don't deserve virulent infections – Alvin knows that better than anyone.

As his composure returns he recalls the last time he stepped off this pavement and was almost mown down by an angry moped. A line pops into his head: the one about those not paying attention in history never remembering which Richard had the lion heart and which the club foot; or is it those that don't heed history's mistakes are condemned to repeat them?

He steps off the pavement, but not before he has looked right, left, then right again.

'Yeah?' says the brittle blonde, not looking up from her *OK!*.

'Is Kell— Is *Manda* free?'

'Manda,' she says after a moment.

Alvin's hopes rise. Maybe Kelly doesn't work here any more. Maybe she's back at college. Or behind the counter at McDonald's. Whatever, maybe she's sorting things out.

'Sorry, I was miles away,' says the blonde, looking up at him at last. 'Yeah, she's free.'

Shit, Alvin thinks.

Shoes on 2
This time it*s personal

These days she doesn't go out much. Her Mac brings the world indoors, while her other mac stays on the peg. She shops, banks and entertains herself on the worldwide whatsit. And of course, the worldwide whatnot also provides her with a full and fully sedentary social life.

Why go out? *Outside,* where if the cars don't get you, the muggers will.

Today she has no option. She has letters to post.

She peels back the net curtain and looks through the dirty glass at the street below. She lives above a sweet shop. She can see a trickle of customers coming and going. She peers across the busy road at the T-junction. She can't see the postbox from her window – it stands a hundred yards or so along All Saints Road. It has stopped raining, but the pavements glimmer with greasy terror. Another danger to add to fast cars and street thugs.

She sits down and reaches for her shoes. Easing them onto her swollen feet takes the best part of ten minutes. Next she takes her tweed coat from the hook on the door. She struggles to feed her arms into the sleeves and feels her body weight double – it is a heavy coat. Finally she picks up her brown Chanel handbag, which as usual is empty. Not venturing out much, she has little use for it. She puts inside it her keys, her purse, which contains ten pounds and thirty-four pence in change, and the letters.

Ridiculous, she thinks. All this effort just to post a few letters.

Scum

'So, what d'you want this time? Just a wank or a proper shag?'

Kelly has her back to him. She's folding towels, not because she has to but because it allows her to keep her back to him.

'I owe you an apology, Kelly,' Alvin says.

'What for? You paid your money.'

'That's not the point. I didn't come here for that and I should never have let it happen. I'm sorry.'

''Pology 'cepted,' she says, spinning to face him. 'You can go now.'

She looks much as Karen did the night she found out: disappointed – after the anger, the only feeling left.

'I care about you, Kelly. That's why I should never have let it happen.'

'If you cared so bloody much you wouldn't have run away, would you? What the fuck got into you? I wasn't that rubbish, was I?'

'No . . . Of course not. I'm sorry . . . But the guy in the next room, I could hear him through the wall. I didn't want to bump into him . . . I know him.'

'Mick Jagger's mate?'

'Who?'

'The guy in the next room. He's mates with Mick Jagger.'

Alvin's heart sinks. She's talked to Jamie, which can only mean she's also had sex with him. He isn't sure why this bothers him. Why should putting faces to her clients make her situation seem worse? Maybe if it wasn't Jamie's face . . .

'I told him he should bring Mick down here some time,' she continues.

'He doesn't really know him. He's lying.'

'*Duh*! I know that.'

'Sorry.'

'You say sorry too much.' She smiles at him for the first time.

'Sorry.' Alvin shuffles awkwardly. 'Look, Kelly, I meant what I said before. If you need any help getting back on your feet –'

'I *am* on my feet, Alvin,' she snaps. 'For the first time in my life, right? I like the people here – well, I like the girls. I've got money . . . I'm moving into my own place next week. It's only a bedsit, but . . .'

'That's great. I mean it.' He feels himself edging backwards towards the door, ready to quit while he's slightly ahead, or at least not a thousand miles behind. 'If you ever want to call me, you know, to talk about things, you can.'

'OK,' she says.

'Maybe not at home though. But call me at Wood Hill. Any time.' He feels the door handle prod him in the back and remind him that there's one other thing he has to cover. 'There's something else, Kelly,' he says.

She looks at him expectantly and he feels his resolve shrivel.

'You've got . . . At least I think you might have chlamydia.'

'Kla-what?' she says.

Alvin wonders if he was the only one paying attention during the sexual health lectures.

'Chla*mydia*. It's an STI,' he explains. 'It's not life-threatening or anything, but you should get it treated.' He pulls a leaflet – plucked from a display rack in ILD – from his pocket and passes it to her.

'I haven't got anything,' she says, swiping the leaflet from his hand but not looking at it.

'Most people don't have any symptoms. They don't even

know they've caught it. I didn't.'

'If you didn't know you'd got it, how do you know you got it off me?'

'I passed it on to someone,' he mumbles.

'Shit . . . your wife,' she says quietly.

'Well, she's not actually my wife . . . But, yes.'

'Did you tell her what happened?'

'I didn't have a choice.'

'*Shit*. I'm sorry.'

'Don't be. It's not your fault.'

'Has she kicked you out?'

'No. It's not exactly peace and love, but we're still under the same roof.'

'You must be mad coming back here.'

'It had crossed my mind. Look, it's not your problem. Karen and me, we'll sort things out. But you should see a doctor. It clears up with antibiotics. You need to look after your health, Kelly. This is a dangerous job.'

'I always use johnnies,' she says.

Not when we did it, he doesn't say.

'They're not foolproof,' he does say. 'Remember those sex lectures?'

'Yeah, yeah, the only safe sex is no sex. Can't wait to try that one on the punters.'

Alvin laughs, then says, 'I'd better be going. I'm on my lunch hour.'

He reaches for the door.

'Alvin.'

'Yes?'

'Thanks for coming.'

She takes a step towards him and kisses him on the cheek.

'Thanks for not killing me,' he says. 'Take care, yeah?'

'Yeah. Give my love to Wood Hill.'

* * *

As he steps out into the light drizzle he feels better. Much, much better.

He takes a deep breath of damp air, but immediately gasps in alarm. All Saints Road is on the bus route that Karen takes to the veterinary clinic. He has no idea what time she's there today or even if she's there at all, but . . .

Mercedes was right. He and Karen have barely spoken for three weeks. He's tried to make things right, but clearly he has to try a damn sight harder. All Saints Road is hardly the place to start. He pictures Karen surrounded by sickly kittens and puppies, while he's *here,* in the sex quarter. He has to escape, get back to school and the blessed distraction of stroppy teenage screw-ups.

He checks the road for cars that might run him down and buses that might contain Karen, then crosses. He reaches his bike, smears the rain off the saddle and stoops to fiddle with the lock. But his eye catches movement a few feet away in a boarded-up doorway. He looks up and sees a man, more of a boy, but a big boy. His back is to Alvin and he seems to be struggling with something. Alvin decides to leave him to it and goes back to the lock. But the boy looks round at Alvin, big, Bambi eyes gazing from a dark, expressionless face.

'*Kevan,*' Alvin says.

Kevan Kennedy looks just as surprised to see Alvin. Terrified, actually. Alvin sees something move behind Kevan. A hairy tweed coat. Kevan is clutching something. So is the tweed coat. Whatever it is, Kevan yanks at it hard and the tweed coat comes with it, lurching out of the doorway and onto the wet pavement. Now Alvin can see the tiny old lady inside the coat and the brown handbag she's determined not to let go of. She doesn't look scared, not even of the short, gleaming knife that Kevan is grasping.

'What the hell are you doing?' Alvin says, taking a step towards him.

'Back off, Alvin, man.'

'No, this is *mad*. Put the knife down.'

Alvin isn't frightened. His heart is surging, but that's adrenaline, and his face is wet, but with drizzle rather than nervy sweat. He can deal with this. He's dealt with dozens of situations like this one, as often as not involving knives. He's not a big man – lean and five ten – but size is rarely the deciding factor. The winner is invariably the party with the greater knuckle-headed resolve.

'Gimme the fucking bag,' Kevan snaps at the old lady.

Yes, give him the fucking bag, Alvin thinks, *please*.

'I'm giving you *nothing*,' she snaps back.

She has a death wish, Alvin decides. She's very old, but surely this can't be her idea of assisted suicide. But perhaps she's demented enough to believe that her tiny meals-on-wheels-nourished body is a match for six foot plus of burger-fed Kevan Kennedy. Not wanting her to learn the truth the hard way, Alvin reaches forward and puts his hand on Kevan's arm.

'Give me the knife. Don't make things worse.'

Keven throws his hand back, bringing the point of the blade perilously close to Alvin's stomach. The old lady takes advantage of Kevan's momentary inattention by tugging at her handbag. Kevan reacts by whipping the knife to her face, steel resting against rosy cheek.

Alvin senses people behind him, passers-by drawn to the confrontation. He has no idea how many because he daren't take his eyes off the knife.

'Please, don't do anything stupid,' Alvin says, though he no longer holds out hope. Put Kevan under any kind of pressure and he's capable of being more spectacularly stupid than just about anyone.

Kevan doesn't respond, but says to the old woman, 'The *bag*.'

Still she doesn't let go – no longer gripped by defiance, but paralysed by terror. A white spot appears in the centre of her cheek, caused by pressure from the knife's tip. Alvin has to act before she dies, because he is certain that she will. He springs forward and brings his forearm down onto Kevan's, knocking the blade away from the woman's face. Momentum carries him into Kevan and the two of them stumble into the shop doorway. He presses Kevan back against the flyposters, gripping both his wrists tightly because he's fairly sure he hasn't dropped the knife. He glances over his shoulder and sees the old woman behind him. She is no longer clutching the precious handbag. Alvin can feel it sandwiched between his and Kevan's bodies. Kevan is pushing hard and Alvin knows he won't be able to keep him pinned back for long. He leans forward and speaks quietly into his ear: 'If you don't stop this now, you'll be scum your whole life. You're better than that, Kevan . . . Prove it to me . . . In a moment I'm going to stand back and let you go. If you've got any brains at all, you'll drop the knife and the bag . . . Do that for me, OK?'

Alvin eases his body off Kevan and looks at him. Kevan stares back. There's something in those beautiful eyes. Fear? Vulnerability?

Alvin feels they are sharing a moment . . .

Or perhaps the eyes merely express a desire to slit him with the knife.

Up this close Alvin really can't tell.

Finally Kevan nods. He may see the sense of Alvin's suggestion or he may be bluffing. Alvin has no way of knowing, but he stands back anyway.

Kevan lunges forward, bowling Alvin over. From the ground Alvin watches him sprint up the street, his long legs pumping like the back end of a thoroughbred. The handbag dangles incongruously from one hand. As it swings, its gold clasp gaily catches the light. Alvin knows enough about labels to recognise Chanel's interlocked Cs. He thinks about giving chase to retrieve it, but only for a moment – what could be in it beyond perhaps a couple of lottery tickets and a Mecca membership card? But then again, it is Chanel.

Once Kevan has travelled fifty yards or so, he disappears into a side alley that leads to the sprawling housing estate backing onto All Saints Road. Alvin looks up at the old woman. Even from ground level she seems tiny.

'Are you all right?' he asks her.

She nods her head uncertainly, then says, 'You saved my life,' which comes out as a wheeze. A posh wheeze, not the wheeze of a bingo gran.

Alvin hauls himself off the wet pavement. His legs are weak and barely able to support him. He looks at the people now moving in to help or merely to gawp. He recognises the brittle blonde from the Tropica who arrives at the old woman's side and puts an arm around her shoulders.

'I saw what you did,' she says to Alvin. She looks at him with a respect that wasn't there when he was just an annoying distraction from her *OK!*.

'I've called the police,' another voice says.

'He's got my bag,' the old lady gasps, realising now that she has lost the thing that she seemed prepared to give up her life for.

'Never mind that,' brittle blonde soothes.

'My letters,' the old lady whispers.

'Someone call an ambulance. She must be in shock.'

'Are you OK, mate?'

Alvin looks at the man who asked the question. A decorator in white overalls, his black skin spattered with magnolia emulsion.

'Yeah, I'm fine, thanks,' Alvin says.

The old woman is getting her voice back, telling a fresh batch of after-the-event witnesses, 'He saved my life, you know. The bastard was going to kill me. Give one of his kind a knife and –'

She pulls herself up, looking at the decorator, eyeing him warily.

'You're a hero, you know,' the decorator tells Alvin, 'a proper bloody hero. Well done, mate.'

He presses his hand onto Alvin's and as he shakes it vigorously, his words sink in. *A hero, a proper bloody hero.* One who should right now be someplace else because – quite apart from the fact that he's overrunning his lunch hour – don't proper bloody heroes get publicity? Write-ups and pictures in the *Gazette*? The *Gazette*, owned by the family of Allison Bird-Wright, chairwoman of the Wood Hill governors, Alvin's nominal employer, though why that should strike him at a time like this, he has no idea. Whatever; publicity of the HERO-FOILS-MUGGER-OUTSIDE-ALL-SAINTS-ROAD-BROTHEL type is the last thing Alvin needs right now.

'I've got to go,' he says, wrenching his hand free of the decorator's enthusiastic and Duluxy grasp.

'Hang on,' the man insists. 'The cops'll wanna talk to you.'

But Alvin is already on his bike, pedalling as if his life depends on it. Which it does. His relationship with Karen *is* his life.

An awful long way to fall

At school Alvin didn't try to control his charges. Only when Curtis and Roland played catch with Chenil's pencil case, causing Debbie to empty Curtis's rucksack out of the window, did he intervene. He spent the rest of the afternoon lost in thought.

By three thirty he'd reached a decision. He would tell Karen everything. Not because he believed she would find out anyway – though there was always that – but because he'd never hidden anything from her. Alvin has always been an open book, through which Karen has leafed at her leisure. And what had happened the one time he did conceal something from her? She'd rumbled him anyway, turning a page and finding it incriminatingly stuck to another.

Of course, telling her about lunch time risked inviting more anger and disappointment, but so be it. Honesty would see him through. Whatever he had done, he *honestly* loved Karen and he *would* make her see that.

That was the plan when the siren ended the school day.

It still is now that he's standing outside his house fumbling for his keys. He opens the door and wheels his bike into the hall. The place is desolately quiet. Alvin normally makes his entrance to a soundtrack of competing noises – the TV, Annie's guitar, Mercedes's music. Today, silence.

'Hi!' he calls out.

'I'm outside,' Karen calls back, her voice coming from the garden.

He makes his way to her, heartened. There have been several days over the last few weeks when she couldn't bring herself to return a greeting.

He finds her sunning herself outside the kitchen door. The rain stopped an hour ago and the garden smells of wet vegetation. It's tiny, but it's a magnet for the afternoon sun. They have privacy as well. The two gardens to either side are so untended that they've become as impenetrable as Madagascan rainforests. One muggy Saturday, Shannon swore she spotted a family of ring-tailed lemurs bounding through the canopy of weeds in number 24.

'Hi,' Alvin says again. 'Where are the kids?'

'Shannon and Annie are playing round at Cherry and Maisy's. Sid's gone to Clowntown with Freddie. I think Mercedes is back at Janice's. There're no knickers on the radiator in her room. That's usually a sure sign.'

'I'm glad we've got the place to ourselves,' Alvin says. 'We need to talk.'

'I know. Why do you think I got rid of the kids?'

'I've hated the last few weeks,' he says, sitting beside her on the grey, weathered garden bench.

'Me too . . . I'm sorry.'

'*You're* sorry? *I'm* sorry.'

'I know you are. I can read you like a book. You've got sorry printed in huge bold type on every page. I've been a bitch, haven't I?'

'I've deserved it. Karen, there's something –'

'In a moment. I've been rehearsing my speech all day and if I don't get it off my chest now, I think I never will.

'When I got that test result from the doctor I was so *gutted*. Right up until that moment I'd had you up there on a pedestal. I never thought you were capable of that. I'm telling you, you had an awful long way to fall.

'Paul used to do that screwing around shit all the time. He'd always say it was a one-off, it had *just happened*. By the time he buggered off back to Montreal his one-offs ran into double figures.'

Shannon's father, by Karen's accounts, set a new standard for infidelity – he raised the bar for bastards everywhere.

'Call me naïve, Alvin, but I expected better of you. Turns out you're merely mortal after all – just a bloke.'

'It was just a one-off, Karen. You've no reason to believe me, but –'

'I do believe you . . . I didn't when I was chucking coffee over you, but I've had a lot of time to think about it and I do now.'

He gives her a weak smile.

'You don't get off that easy. It was still a truly rotten thing you did.'

'I know. I'm sorr—'

'Stop it with the sorries. I was going to say that it was a rotten thing, but everyone should be allowed one fuck-up. Only one, mind. You ever do anything like that again, me and the kids will be out of your life faster than you can zip your trousers up.'

He nods.

'You can keep Mercedes though. She'll be your punishment.'

Her hand creeps along the bench until it's resting on his. He should tell her about lunch time now, but she's leaning towards him and he has yearned for this for the three longest weeks of his life.

And now it's happening.

They're kissing.

He should tell her. The longer he delays it, the harder it will be; he knows that. But he really doesn't want to kill the moment because this is the kiss he dreaded he might never have again – and as a consequence, it's the best kiss he's *ever* had.

He will tell her. But not right now.

He feels a shadow fall over them. So does Karen because she

pulls away. They look up and see Mercedes studying them. She couldn't look more disgusted if she were being given a tour of an abattoir.

'I wish you two would make up your bloody minds,' she says.

Exchange & Mart

The teacher sits at the front of the classroom and tries not to look up. There are only five kids in the room and all is quiet. Detention has fifteen minutes left to run . . . He's so nearly there, so near the weekend. Why risk triggering an incident with an ill-judged glance so close to the finish line?

But his peripheral vision catches something. Flesh. The girl at the desk ten feet from him is extending her long, skinny legs as if they're telescopic. The teacher can't help himself. His head rises inexorably from the pile of marking until his eyes meet first the limbs – still growing tentacularly – and then the gaze, which is fixed on him. A thin lollipop stick protrudes from her mouth and one cheek bulges outwards. She gives him the slightest of smiles.

He recognises her. She's the hard-faced one who triggered the fight he watched from afar. That was weeks ago, but the image of her slashing Shave Head's ear with a ruler is indelible.

Very slowly the legs move, swinging to the sides like the bow doors on a car ferry, like the mighty gates of Mordor in *Return of the King* . . . All the way out they go until the desk legs prevent them travelling any further. Like most contortionism, it's not a pretty sight, really it isn't. But like most contortionism, it's also compelling. Still staring at him, the girl switches the lollipop from one cheek to the other with a noisy clack.

'You looking up my skirt, sir?'

Well, didn't *that* get everyone's attention? He immediately lowers his head and tries to ignore the buzz that ricochets around the room.

'He was looking up my skirt,' the girl announces. '*Perv*.'

'Quiet,' he says without looking up, '*please*.'

'You was! You was *staring*.'

'Quiet!'

'I'm gonna tell Chadwick.'

'I said *quiet*!'

'You'll lose your job, you know.'

'Shut up. Just . . . fucking . . . SHUT UP!'

Silence for all of three seconds, then, 'You said *fuck*. You've had it now.'

The four younger detainees behind her stifle giggles. The teacher looks at his watch. Twelve minutes to go. He senses that of everyone in the room he's the most desperate for the detention to end. Why is *he* the one feeling punished?

'This your first job, sir?'

It's the girl again. Her tone is amiable now. Surely just another setup.

'Get on with your work,' he mumbles.

'Tell us. Is it?'

'*Yes*. Yes, it is. My first job.'

'I *knew* it. You like it here?'

He doesn't answer.

'I bet you don't, right? I bet you's only teaching 'cause you couldn't think of nothing else, right?'

I'm teaching because I like kids.

'I'm not having a go or nothing. I mean, I'm leaving next year and I ain't got a clue what I'm gonna do. It's really hard to choose, innit? When you can be, like, *any*thing in the world and that. What you wanna be, sir? I mean, apart from being a teacher which I don't reckon you wanna be, not really truly.'

Another look at his watch: eleven minutes.

'Fireman or something . . . Nah, you're too soft, innit. Working in an office. That'd be OK. Or a shop and that.'

'Driving instructor,' a new voice suggests.

'Nah, that's like teaching, innit.'

'Pilot.'

'Electrician.'

They're all chipping in now.

'Pop star.'

'Quiet, all of you,' the teacher yaps.

'Barman.'

'In a gay bar.'

'I wanna take you to a GAY bar!'

Oh, the hilarity.

'Weatherman.'

'*Gay* weatherman.'

'Window cleaner.'

'Wanker.'

'Shut up . . . SHUT UP! . . . Get out. Go. Leave me alone.'

The room clears in an instant, nine and a half minutes early.

After a moment he reaches under the desk and picks up his briefcase. He takes out the copy of *Exchange & Mart*. He was going to look for a car, but he turns to Jobs.

Part two:

One Debbie, two Karens

Save

It's quiet in the flat, but not quite silent. A saucepan sits on the electric hob. The heat is low, but soon the oxtail soup will have vaporised completely. In the spare room the computer glows with life. On the screen a window contains a letter, almost finished. The woman seems to be having trouble ending it, though. She sits in front of the Mac, staring straight ahead, her body motionless, her head at an insane angle. Is she asleep? If so it will require a team of chiropractors to remove the crick in her neck when she wakes. Soon, unless she feeds a fresh batch of coins into the meter, the computer will crash and most of the letter's content will be lost because she hasn't hit *save* since getting up to put the soup on.

But on closer inspection it's clear that she won't be moving again, at least not under her own steam.

Kelly Whatsit

In Alvin's *ideal* world – the one with peace, love and a healthy bank balance – that conversation in the garden would have been the end of it. But only in soaps do people stumble from one crisis – eviction, adultery, bereavement – to the next – bankruptcy, rape, murder – without accumulating baggage. Alvin, like anyone else, has spent his whole life acquiring a collection of emotional luggage, which, like anyone else, he drags behind him, trying as best he can to make light of it. The thing with Kelly takes up a space in his mental cargo hold the size of a small suitcase, the pull-along type favoured by aircrew. Most days, like a flight attendant gliding through the airport terminal, he's unaware of it, give or take the odd pang of regret – he never quite got round to mentioning the *second* visit to the Tropica. Occasionally, however, the wheels on his psychological Samsonite jam or, worse, run over Karen's toes.

As they are about to now, eight months on.

It's breakfast time. Shannon and Mercedes are arguing.

'It *was* him,' Shannon shrieks. 'Rubin won.'

'It was Ru*ben*, you doughnut, and he didn't win,' Mercedes replies.

This has been going on for a few minutes, oh-yes-it-was-oh-no-it-wasn't panto style. At issue is who won the first *American Idol*.

'I don't know what makes you such an authority, Mercedes,' Karen says. 'You don't even like pop music.'

She has a point. Mercedes isn't a pop girl. Today she's wearing the MAKE BONO HISTORY T-shirt and death-mask makeup, suggesting that, should she stumble into a position of authority come the revolution, then the entire top forty will be lined up against the wall alongside the vivisectionists and the Coca-Cola board of directors.

'Just 'cause I think pop's lame doesn't mean I don't *know* about it. I also know the dubya in George Dubya stands for Walker. Doesn't mean I wanna kill A-rabs and cook the planet,' Mercedes argues. 'It *wasn't* Ruben, OK? It was a girl that won. Brown hair, ordinary-looking. Can't remember her name.'

'Kelly Clarkson,' Alvin says automatically . . . And regrettably – he should have kept his trap shut. He risks a glance at Karen.

'How the hell did you remember that?' she says, her usually doe-like eyes narrowing until they resemble the slits in a concrete machine-gun emplacement.

'I dunno,' Alvin replies. 'The name just stuck in my head . . . for some reason.'

'Wasn't your star retard called Kelly, Alvin?' Mercedes says, oblivious to the subtext. 'You're probably just making the connection.'

Well, *obviously*.

The ensuing silence is broken by the clatter of the letterbox. Sid jumps up to fetch, reappearing a moment later with a stack of mail.

The envelopes are mostly brown, a fitting colour for those in the financial shit. Over the past eight months, he and Karen have been inching deeper into the mire. He takes no comfort from the fact that Britain is now a nation of debtors and by all accounts the entire national debt is on Visa. There's no sense of safety in numbers. Alvin stops at a slim white envelope branded *private and confidential*, words deliberately paired to strike fear into the insolvent's heart. On the letter within, Engle, Marks & Poll announce themselves in conservative type.

'Who's that from?' Karen asks.

'Someone called Trevor Poll. A solicitor.'

'Jesus, who wants our money now?'

'I have no idea. He wants me to get in touch with him.' He reads aloud. '"I would be obliged if you would contact my office at your earliest convenience on a matter of utmost importance."'

'Christ, we're being taken to court, aren't we?' Karen says.

'Who'd take us to court?' Alvin asks.

'The fascists who want your money,' Mercedes says with certainty.

'Wouldn't we get a writ or something first?'

'They don't bother with due process any more,' Mercedes explains. 'It's like *shock* tactics. Slam you in the dock, bang you up and repossess your house before you've had a chance to think.'

'They're going to arrest you?' Annie gasps.

'Na-naah, na-naah, na-naah!' Sid singsongs in the time-honoured impersonation of a cop car.

'Shush, Sid,' Karen says. 'No one's being arrested, Annie. Alvin, why don't you phone this Trevor Poll and see what he wants?'

'I should do, shouldn't I?' Alvin says, folding the letter and stuffing it into the back pocket of his jeans.

'Don't put it off, will you?'

'Would I?'

'Yes.'

'I'll call him. Today.'

He picks up the remaining letters. An electricity bill, a credit card bill and a postcard. A picture of a triangular white mountain against a blue sky. He turns it over. A French stamp. He reads the message.

Dear Alvin

Guess where I am!! I can ski. Et je peux parler le Français!!!

Working like a dog but not doing what you think! Tell you about it when I get back. Hope you're OK.

Love
Kelly
XXXX

Alvin looks at Karen. She's distracted with wiping butter off Sid's sweatshirt. He should mention the postcard. No harm in an itty-bitty postcard, is there?

'I've got a postcard from –'

'Annie, careful!' Karen wails.

Too late. Annie's cereal bowl slips off the breakfast table and onto her lap, covering her skirt with Coco Pops and chocolatey milk.

'It was an *accident*!' Annie shrieks.

As Alvin jumps up to grab a tea towel from the counter, he slips the postcard into his pocket. It can wait.

What*s the coypu doing?

'How have you been sleeping?'

'I'm still having the dream.'

'Tell me about it.'

'The animals are the same.'

'Describe them for me again.'

'Rats mostly. Some badgers, I think. And the weaselly things.'

'In our last session you described them as more like ferrets.'

'You know . . . weasels, ferrets . . .'

'The distinction could be significant.'

'Weasels. Very big teeth.'

'And they're wearing uniforms?'

'Yes, the blazers, white shirts, red and black ties.'

'And describe what they do.'

'I can't. Not again.'

'It will help.'

'They . . .'

'Take your time.'

'They climb onto my bed. The badgers. Then the others. Then they . . . God, I'm sorry, this is so . . .'

'Would you like a tissue?'

'No, I'm OK . . . They climb onto the bed. Under the duvet . . .'

'And they attack you?'

'Yes . . . Can I have a tissue?'

'Of course, here . . . Take all the time you need . . . Crying is an integral part of the process.'

'Yes.'

'Tell me, is anything different in the dream?'

'There's a new animal. Big, brown. It's like a . . . coypu? Why did I say that? Is there such a thing?'

'Yes, it's a large amphibious rodent, native to South America. It was brought into Britain for its fur. In the 1930s a number escaped into the wild and – I'm sorry. Please, continue.'

'This coypu, it has a letter shaved into its forehead. The letter K.'

'What do you suppose the significance of that is?'

'I don't know . . . I can see its pink skin . . . *exposed*.'

'How does that make you feel?'

'Scared . . . Disgusted . . .'

'What do you think the K signifies?'

'I don't know. My father.'

'Your father's name begins with K?'

'No, he's called Richard. But he's in the dream.'

'Is he an animal too?'

'No. In the dream he actually looks like Mr Miyagi from *The Karate Kid*.'

'Is that a TV show?'

'It's a film. About a boy. Who learns karate. Anyway, he looks like Mr Miyagi, but it's my father. He's wearing a white outfit, like for martial arts. My father does tai chi. He's very dedicated.'

'What's your father doing in the dream?'

'His tai chi.'

'Does he speak?'

'Sort of. In Japanese. These funny noises. It sounds kind of like . . . *Haaaaaiiiii-neeeeeeeee-ah*!'

'Anything else?'

'No, he just looks at what the coypu is doing . . .'

'And what is that?'

'I can't . . . It's very upsetting . . . OK, it's –'

'Actually, I'm afraid we're out of time. We should pick this up in our next session.'

'All right . . . Thanks . . . Next week, then.'

'Next week.'

'I might be a little late. I'm seeing a specialist about the, er . . . skin condition.'

'Good, that's good. It's been looking a little angrier lately.'

'Probably an allergic reaction.'

'Very probably.'

What*s for tea? (Again)

'You didn't call him, did you?' Karen says.

'Who?' Alvin asks.

'That solicitor.'

'Er . . . I lost the letter.'

'No, you didn't.'

She holds up Alvin's freshly washed jeans and the damp wad of paper she has just fished from the back pocket. It's the letter, illegible now, but Lenor-scented by way of compensation.

Alvin shrugs. 'If it's that important, I'm sure he'll write another one.'

'No, he won't. I already phoned.'

'Oh. How did you get the number?'

'Directory Enquiries. You don't easily forget a name like Engle, Marks & Poll. You're seeing the guy tomorrow at four thirty.'

Alvin has spent the week since the letter arrived fretting. Unable to figure out why a solicitor would want to see him on 'a matter of utmost importance', his imagination has filled the blank with horrific possibilities, most of them involving family accommodation in a Dickensian debtors' gaol.

'I'm working tomorrow night,' he says.

'I know. That's why I made it four thirty. Time for you to get there after school and wrap it up before work.'

She studies his face, smells his fear.

'Don't you think I don't know you by now?' she says. 'You've spent the last week going out of your head with worry, imagining the lot of us being carted off to Holloway's family wing and too scared to put yourself out of your misery by calling the guy. Go see him. I'm sure it'll be fine. And if it isn't ... Well, we'll deal with it. We always do, don't we?'

She takes a step towards him and slips her arms around his waist. Her way of telling him that they've always got each other – all they've ever had through much of their relationship. Alvin reciprocates the hug. Each-other has got them through some pretty shitty patches. He's sure it will get them through this one should it turn out poo-y.

'Did he tell you what it was about on the phone?' he asks.

'I spoke to his secretary. I did ask, but she wouldn't say. Snotty cow. Anyone would think she had a duty of confidentiality.'

'Will you come with me?'

'Trust me, you'll be fine, angel. Probably the rich aunt you never knew you had has died and left you her coronation mug. And even if it is bad, you're better off knowing, aren't you?'

She returns to the laundry, picking up Alvin's jeans. Something else is in the pocket. 'I wish you'd check before you chuck them in the basket,' she says. She reaches in and pulls out a soggy folded postcard. She peels it apart and looks at the picture – a triangular white mountain against a blue sky.

Alvin gulps inaudibly. He was going to mention it ...

'Who's this from?' she asks. She turns it over and squints at the blurred writing, all of it illegible except for *Love Kelly* XXXX.

'It's from Kelly Hendricks,' Alvin says pointlessly.

'I can see that.'

'I was going to show it to you. I just forgot about it.' This is the truth.

'Really?'

'Honestly. I *forgot*.'

'So what does Kelly X X X X have to say for herself?'

'She's in France. Learning to ski or something.'

Karen looks at him, her eyes narrowing ominously.

'I was going to tell you. I *started* to tell you. It came the same day as the solicitor's letter. I mentioned it, but Annie knocked her cereal over and –'

'Look . . . I'm sure you were. It doesn't matter.'

'Really?'

'It's cool, *really*. Do you want to keep this?' She waggles the damp postcard at him.

'No, it's all right.'

He watches her drop it into the bin.

'Are you sure you're OK about this?' he says. 'Maybe we should talk.'

'I'm fine. I *trust* you.' She kisses him on the lips to emphasise the point.

Shannon walks into the kitchen.

'What's for tea?' she asks.

'Rolls,' her mother says. 'What do you want on them?'

Eleven now, Shannon is growing up fast and expanding her horizons. These days she accepts both butter and any one of three different spreads on her bread rolls. Karen is working towards slipping a slice of cheese in there. Any day now.

'Eurgh! *Nothing,* man,' Shannon exclaims.

Some days, unfortunately, she regresses.

Fuck OFF

'Where you going, sir?'

As Alvin walks out of Wood Hill's heavy gates – wrought out of thick girders, as if Wood Hill were Porton Down and the children germ warfare experiments gone insanely wrong – Debbie and Chenil fall into step beside him.

'What's it to you, Debbie?' he asks.

'Well, you're going the wrong way for home, aren't you?' she says.

'How do you know where I live?'

Debbie giggles. Chenil blushes.

'Where's your bike?' Debbie asks.

'It needs new gears.'

He doesn't add that a set of derailleur gears is way out of his financial reach. Depressingly, it wasn't any particular green impulse that drove him to the two-wheel option, but the fact that he couldn't afford four. Well, now even a pushbike is beyond him.

'Fuck off . . . Fuck *off* . . . *Fuck* off . . .' Debbie is on her mobile now.

Alvin turns to her friend and asks, 'When's it due, Chenil?'

Chenil mumbles something – possibly 'Six weeks' – and automatically places a hand over the bump that is stretching her skinny red jumper to breaking point. Well off the fashion pace, the school outfitter has yet to launch a Wood Hill maternity line.

'Excited?' Alvin asks.

Chenil shrugs.

'What about Curtis? Is he going to be with you?'

She shrugs again.

'... Fuck OFF ... OK, laters, see ya,' Debbie chirps before snapping her phone shut and slipping her arm through Alvin's. 'She don't know if it's Curt's or Ro's, sir,' she says.

'Fuck off,' Chenil says.

'Can you let go of my arm please, Debbie?' Alvin asks.

'I reckon it's Ro's,' Debbie continues, ignoring him as well as her friend.

'Fuck OFF, will you?' Chenil yelps.

Alvin thinks it a shame that she couldn't have been this assertive when Curtis and/or Roland came calling, but he doesn't say so. Pots, kettles and so on – he has a less than perfect record when it comes to making no mean no.

As he attempts to shake Debbie's arm free from his, a car slows beside them. The passenger window winds down with a squeak and Tony Rowell leans across from the driver's seat.

'Hi, Mr Rowell,' Alvin says. 'Everything OK?'

'Far from it, Mr Lee.' He fixes his gaze on Debbie and says, 'Coates, if I see that skirt at school tomorrow, you'll be going straight home.'

The window squeaks back up and Rowell pulls away. Debbie finally unlinks her arm from Alvin's and jerks it upward. Alvin lunges reflexively to smother her hand before she can project a bolshy middle finger – Rowell doesn't have eyes in the back of his head, but he has a perfectly serviceable rear-view mirror. Alvin looks down at her skirt. It's the regulation black thing all right, but remodelled to a minimalist aesthetic. She has rolled the waistband into a fat sausage so that the hem barely covers her knickers. Which are yellow. Alvin can tell because she has unpicked the skirt's side seams, producing a pair of deep slits that expose the full length of her thin legs to the brisk March air.

'Fucking kerb crawler,' she mutters as the history teacher's car disappears round a corner.

'That's enough, Debbie,' Alvin says.

'What? You his mate now?'

'No, but I'm staff.'

'Nnnnnn, *staff*,' she squawks.

'He's right about your skirt.'

'It's a proper skirt, yeah? My mum got it from BHS, innit.'

Alvin laughs. 'Don't take the piss. Just sort it out.'

She shoots him a look that says *betrayal*. He isn't fazed. He's used to treading the tightrope that runs between pedagogue and pal. The occasional tumble goes with the job.

He stops outside a sweet shop. 'This is where I say goodbye, girls.'

Chenil mumbles something – possibly 'Goodbye.' Debbie, meanwhile, is busy on another call. He steps into the shop doorway and clocks the notice on the glass: NO MORE THAN 3 SCHOOLCHILDREN AT A TIME; a sign of the times. He remembers Hector Parr the physics teacher having the idea of placing a similar order on the school gates. He turns his head and watches the two girls walk on,
Debbie welded to her mobile, *fuck off* . . .

fuck off . . .

fuck OFF-ing

into the distance. When they have turned a corner he crosses the street. The sweet shop was a ruse. He didn't want the girls to see him head down All Saints Road.

Alvin stands outside another shop front and reads ENGLE MARKS & POLL SOLICITORS on the plate glass. An A4 sheet taped beneath it announces PHOTOCOPIES 10P EACH. He peers through the window into the unlit interior. The first thing he sees is a lumpy grey photocopier, an OUT OF ORDER sign tacked to its flank. He can also make out a couple of unattended desks with computers on them. He can see no sign of life, which means that perhaps he should turn right round and go . . . Except he thinks he can glimpse the mug on the nearest of the two desks giving off a reedy wisp of steam.

He holds off from going inside. Whatever awaits him in there, it can't be good. He is also unsettled by the fact that Engle Marks & Poll is situated in a stubby dead-end street off All Saints Road – something he hadn't realised until he looked up the address in the *A – Z*. He still feels queasy from having to run the gauntlet past the Tropica to get here. He hasn't been near the place for over eight months. At least according to the postcard Kelly is no longer there.

At last, he pushes the door and goes in. He steps over to the desk and peers into the mug. His eyes were deceiving him. It contains only an inch of coffee, so long past steaming that it is home to lily pads of furry blue mould.

'Hello,' he calls out.

He hears a lavatory flush and a door open. A man appears in the gloom at the back of the office.

'If you've come in for copies, it's out of order,' he says, looking at the cardboard wallet of schoolwork that Alvin is hugging to his chest.

'No, I'm Alvin Lee. I've come to see Trevor Poll.'

'Ah, my four thirty. You're a tad early,' the man – Trevor Poll evidently – says, stepping into the half-light.

He adjusts the waistband of his corduroys over a compact paunch before thrusting a hand at Alvin. He's a man in his fifties with a messy beard and a maroon tank top over a check shirt. Schoolteacher rather than lawyer.

'Step into my office,' Trevor Poll says, leading him into a small room furnished with a desk, a couple of chairs and more cardboard boxes. He clears a carton of dusty ring files from a chair and gestures to Alvin to sit. 'My apologies for the mess. My secretary rang in sick today.'

Alvin wonders where Engle and Marks are, never mind the help.

The solicitor sits and lights a cigarette. He looks like a kind man to Alvin. There is something uncle-ish about him, an air of shambling unprosperity – something that Alvin should feel entirely at home with. But, actually, he feels tense, nervous and – damn it, yes – he does have the first twinge of a headache. So he wishes that Trevor Poll would get to the point.

'You look worried, Mr Lee,' Poll says.

'Yes . . . Well. I'd just – Why am I here?'

'You must be curious. Fair dos. Nothing to worry about, though. Just the opposite. In fact, I think –'

Poll stops now.

To chuckle.

Just a few more flecks of white in that scraggy beard, a couple more pounds on that paunch, Alvin thinks, and he'd be Father bloody Christmas. He'd have to lose the fag, though.

'*Why* am I here?' he repeats uncharitably.

'Sorry. Not many opportunities for a giggle in this job. I was about to say that I think you're going to enjoy this.'

'Enjoy *what*?'

'The will I'm about to read to you. I certainly enjoyed drafting it. One of the more . . . *outré* ones I've worked up in my time. I like that word. *Outré*.'

Poll is scrabbling around amongst the rubbish on his desk now. 'Where the heck is it?' he mutters to himself.

What will? Alvin thinks. *Whose* will? He doesn't know any dead people. There was Sharona Pearcy whose heart stopped in geography just after Christmas. But she was in year nine. Fourteen-year-olds don't write wills. A last will and testament is something that a good many forty-two-year-olds haven't quite got round to, Alvin included.

'Got it,' Poll says, pulling a slim folder from a pile and knocking the rest of the stack of papers onto the floor, releasing a cloud of tobacco-scented dust.

'Can we hurry up?' Alvin prods. 'Only I've got to be at work soon.'

'Oh,' Poll says, looking at his watch. 'I thought you worked up at that school.' The way he inserts an almost imperceptible pause before *that school* makes it clear it isn't one he'd send any children of his own to.

'How do you know so much about me?' Alvin asks.

'Let's get on, shall we? Before I begin I should warn you about the language,' he says. 'Wills can be pretty impenetrable to the average Joe. Double Dutch to us professional half the time.' He opens the folder and lifts out a thin wad of stapled sheets. 'Now, brace yourself –'

'Whose will is this?' Alvin interrupts. 'It's just that I don't know anyone who's . . . passed away.'

'It's right here at the top of the page, Mr Lee. "This is the last will and testament of Louise Diana Mansell Bird." Now to business: "I Louise Diana Mansell Bird being of sound mind hereby request my family to FUCK OFF." – The expletive is capitalised, incidentally. Mrs Bird was insistent upon that.'

So come on, then, what is this coypu doing?

'Let's return to the dream, Jonathan. The coypu.'

'Do we have to?'

'Just for a moment. I think it's important.'

'Actually, I'm not sure it's a coypu. It's very big.'

'Coypus are among the larger rodents. They're quite common on the Norfolk Broads. From a distance, visitors often mistake them for beavers.'

'Perhaps it's a beaver.'

'Let's stick with calling it a coypu for now. It is after all merely symbolic.'

'Of what?'

'That depends what it's doing in the dream ... What is it doing?'

'It's ... It's ... Can I talk about my mother? She –'

'Let's stay with the coypu, shall we?'

'It's ... Have you changed your lighting? It seems brighter in here?'

'The coypu, Jonathan.'

'It's ... It's weeing on me.'

'I see.'

'*What*? What do you see?'

'Nothing as such. It's a figure of speech. What happens once it's urinated?'

'It looks at my father and says ... I'm not sure I can say.'

'Is it in Japanese?'

'No, it's . . . just horrible.'

'You need to tell me. Not today, if you're not ready, but –'

'It says, "Abracadabra, muthafucker."'

'Which is literally true.'

'Excuse me?'

'Your father literally fu— He had sexual relations with your mother.'

'I suppose . . . You know, it's getting so I don't want to go to sleep any more. Last night I stayed awake till four thirty just so I wouldn't dream of bloody rodents. I watched back-to-back repeats of *Rosemary & Thyme* on ITV3. Do you know how . . . *dispiriting* that is? I'm exhausted. What is it? What's wrong with me?'

'I wouldn't like to jump to a premature diagnosis.'

'I've been seeing you for seven months.'

'As I said, I don't want to be hasty, but the recurring dream, your general nerviness and your bouts of depression . . . I'm thinking along the lines of post-traumatic stress syndrome.'

'That's . . . *ridiculous.*'

'PTSS is usually associated with the military, victims of torture and violent crime and so on, but it occurs in many walks of life. I must say, though, it's the first instance I've come across in a teacher.'

'*Former* teacher.'

'Of course, former teacher. How's the new job going?'

'It's . . . er . . . I left a couple of days ago.'

'What happened?'

'The office had some schoolchildren in – for work experience.'

'I see.'

'They didn't do anything. They actually seemed quite nice – they weren't from Wood Hill. Even so, I couldn't face . . . May I have a tissue?'

'Of course, here you are . . . You know, flight is a valid

response in situations where we feel threatened, even when the perceived threat might not actually materialise . . . Perhaps, though, it might be best to look for a workplace where the ambient age is a little higher. Just for now.'

'I quite fancy working abroad. Saga Holidays are looking for reps.'

'The skin condition, though . . .'

'Yes, maybe the sun wouldn't be good . . . Or maybe it would be just what I need to clear it up. God, how do I make the right decision? It's so . . . *difficult*.'

'Perhaps that's a question for your dermatologist. What did he say, by the way? You saw him today, didn't you?'

'He said it was almost certainly stress-related. He said I should see a psychotherapist.'

'Ah.'

Everything's fine, Goran

'What's this?' the big man asks beerily.

'Your pizza, sir,' Alvin tells him.

'I know it's a pizza, Nigella. I mean the green stuff.'

'It's rocket.'

'If I'd wanted a salad, I'd have gone to a salad bar. I ordered pizza.'

'This is how the Soho comes, sir. It explains on the menu. The chef garnishes it with . . . Would you like me to bring you something else?'

'A burger. Plain. No green rubbish on it . . . *Please*.'

'I'm sorry, but we don't do burgers.'

'*Every*one does bloody burgers. What kind of a bloody restaurant is this?'

Alvin could tell the man at this point that, actually, it's a bloody pizza restaurant and the fact that it says Pizza bloody Express above the door is a bit of a giveaway. As it goes, there are so many things he could say – so much on his mind; so much that has nothing to do with pizzas or burgers or strips of wilted leaf – but he comes out with none of them. He makes do with, 'I'm sorry. Shall I get you the menu?'

'Chips. You must do chips.'

'I'll get you the menu.'

Alvin picks up the pizza and turns away, grateful to escape, but immediately slams into another wall of flesh.

'Watch where you're going, matey,' cries a voice saturated with Australian vowels and English ale.

Alvin takes a step back, looks up and winces visibly.

'What the hell are you doing here, Alv?' Colin Stanislavski whoops with undisguised delight.

'I work here.'

'Jeez, don't we pay you enough?' Stanislavski says, taking the seat opposite the big man. Alvin looks at them, a pair of prop forwards threatening to squash the small table that separates them.

'You're late, Stan,' the big man says to his friend.

'Got stuck in a staff meeting, Ellis,' Stanislavski says. 'Funnily enough, Alvin here wormed his way onto the agenda.'

Ellis – the big man – looks confused.

'By day he works up at Wood Hill,' Stanislavski explains.

'You a teacher?' Ellis cries gleefully. 'No wonder you can't tell the difference between a salad and a bloody pizza.'

'*Not* a teacher,' Stanislavski says. 'Alv works with the drongos. Keeps 'em out of mischief with basket weaving and suchlike.'

'I'll get you guys menus,' Alvin says in a sudden rush to escape. Alvin has never *got* sport, least of all rugby. For all its middle-class airs, it seems pretty much an excuse for big blokes to drink too much and gang up on the rest of the world. Right now, Colin and his mate are living proof.

'No rush,' Stanislavski says with a sly grin as he wraps a hand around Alvin's arm. 'You're getting yourself a proper little harem, aren't you?'

'Excuse me?'

'As I was saying, you were a topic of debate this arvo. Rowell's off on a morality drive. Says the place is turning into a hotbed of teenie fornication. Reckons your lot treats Inclusive Learning as their very own fuckpad –'

'Tony Rowell doesn't know what he's talking about,' Alvin says quietly.

'And that you're their personal pimp.'

'What the hell are you insinuating?'

'Don't shoot the messenger, matey. Rowell says he saw you sloping out of school with two of your prozzies today, one on each arm.' He turns to his friend and adds, 'One of 'em's preggers as well. Girl called Chenil *Shakespeare*, would you credit it? "Have you not heard it said full oft, A woman's nay doth stand for naught?" to quote her illustrious forebear.'

'You what, Stan?' Ellis asks.

'My point, Ell, is that the girl may have said no, but her body screamed *yes*. Result: she's about to squeeze out her contribution to the next generation of white trash. Or brown – fuck knows what colour it'll be.'

'You know, Colin,' Alvin says, hurt, 'if you've got so little respect for young people, you've no business calling yourself a teacher.'

'Thing about respect, Alv, is you've gotta *earn* it. You don't do that by spreading your legs and ovulating for England.'

'*Ovulating for England*. I love you, Stan,' Big Ellis hoots.

'Still, you must be proud,' Stanislavski continues. 'This'll be . . . what, ILD's eighth or ninth little un? You must think of 'em as your own. In a sense.'

'I don't have to listen to this,' Alvin says.

The manager appears at Alvin's shoulder. 'Ev'thing 'K?'

'Everything's fine, Goran. I'm just getting these gentlemen some menus.'

'He was not, maestro,' Ellis splutters. 'He was trying to palm me off with a salad disguised as a bloody pizza.'

'I'm mos' very sorry, sir,' the manager says, managing skilfully to flash a brown-toothed grin at his customer while simultaneously glowering at Alvin. 'We make mistake with order, we put right.'

'You're really not cut out for this lark, are you?' Stanislavski decides. 'You should stick to shepherding your bitches . . . Huggy Bear.'

This sets Ellis off giggling again and causes Alvin to snap. 'These men are drunk,' he says to his boss. 'I think you should ask them to leave.'

'Wha' you talk about?' the manager asks. 'We get 'em pizza.'

'Burgers,' Ellis mutters.

'Whatever, I'm bloody ravenous,' Stanislavski declares, shrugging his jacket from his shoulders and hunching over the table – *scrum down*.

'Either they go or I do,' Alvin says defiantly, wondering why he's having a face-off, wondering why he doesn't just walk. After what that solicitor told him, he doesn't need to be here. More than that, he *shouldn't* be here. He should be at home, telling Karen what the solicitor told him.

'Loosen up,' Stanislavski says. 'We're just having a laugh.'

Alvin glares at his boss, waiting for a decision.

'I wouldn't walk, Alv,' Stanislavski advises. 'I mean, if you're reduced to moonlighting here you obviously need the moolah.'

'You know something, Colin? I don't.' Alvin hands the pizza to his boss and strides for the door. He's in too much of a hurry to add, 'Because I've just inherited several million pounds and a twenty-five-room mansion, which I should really be telling Karen about rather than standing here soaking up abuse from a pair of drunks.'

Alvin stands in the kitchen doorway and says, 'Karen, we've got to talk.'

'In a minute, angel,' she replies. 'I'm busy.'

He can see that. She is standing on the worktop, a one-inch brush in her hand. Green paint is being worked downwards from the ceiling towards the cooker in an approximation of a straight line.

'What are you doing?' he asks.

'She's drawing a green line,' Sid says from the linoleum. His mouth is full of biscuit so he sprays the floor with a coarse dust of damp crumbs.

'Like the Green Line in Cyprus,' Karen adds helpfully.

'The what?'

'You know, Greeks on one side, Turks on the other.'

Alvin is none the wiser. 'Why?'

'She cooked my tea in Mercedes's olives,' Sid says.

'What's he on about, Karen?'

'There was some olive oil in a pan and I used it to cook the kids' chops,' Karen says wearily. 'I didn't know Mercedes was intending to fry her aubergines in it.'

Alvin sucks his breath noisily through his teeth.

'Look, I'd run out of Mazola, OK?' she adds defensively. 'Anyway, we had a bit of a row about it. I decided we need a demarcation line.'

'The green line,' Alvin says quietly, finally understanding.

'Carnivores on one side, veggies on the other.'

'But Mercedes only cooks for herself once or twice a week,' Alvin says.

'Look, it's just symbolic.'

'What's *symbolic*?' Sid asks.

'It means I'm having a laugh, sweetheart. Anyway, Alvin, we had some green paint left from doing the back door. It seemed a shame to waste it.'

She hops down from the worktop. She has reached the cooker, but she doesn't intend to stop there. She poises her brush, ready to bisect the four-ring hob with a line of sticky green gloss.

'Can you stop for a minute?' Alvin says. 'We really have to talk.'

Karen rests her brush on the paint can and wipes her hands on a square of kitchen paper. She steps over to Alvin and kisses him. Then she looks at him for the first time.

'It must be important. You've still got your apron on,' she says. 'And where's your jacket?'

Of course he realised as soon as the fresh air raised the hairs on his bare arms that he'd left his jacket inside Pizza Express. After his exit, he didn't think it would be too dignified to sidle back in to collect it. Besides, he can afford a new jacket now. He can probably afford the factory that makes the jackets.

'I left it at work,' he says.

'Have you been sacked?' Karen asks, mild concern creasing her face.

'No. But I don't think I'll be going back,' he replies, taking the order pad from his apron pocket. He sees that the couple on table six will still be waiting for their Gambero Piccantes, which is a shame because they seemed nice.

'It's that solicitor, isn't it?' Karen's creases deepen into anxious folds. 'What did he want?'

'Let's go sit down.'

She follows him into the living room. Shannon is sprawled on the sofa, chewing a pen and staring vacantly at a school worksheet – cowed into submission by sums.

'Why don't you take a break, sweetheart?' Karen suggests.

'*Yesss!*' Shannon flees the room before her mother can add a caveat.

Karen collapses onto the sofa and Alvin sits in the armchair opposite – the one that is oozing orange foam from the rips in its seams. Alvin wonders whether he could afford the armchair factory as well.

'Is it bad news?' Karen asks.

'The opposite of bad. I've been named in a will.'

'That's great.' She looks at his frown and tacks on, 'Isn't it? Whose?'

'Someone called Louise Bird.'

'*Who?*'

'She's – she *was* one of the Bird Birds.'

Karen still looks confused.

'You know, the family that owns the retail park. And the land that the old speedway stadium's on, the bit they're talking about building a multiplex on. And the Ford dealership next to Tesco. And all those houses on the other side of the Glenn Estate. And the *Gazette* . . .'

He could go on. Despite the name, the Birds are actually fish: very big ones in a small and amoebic pond.

'*Those* Birds,' Karen says.

If she wasn't from Manchester, but was, like Alvin, from round these parts, she wouldn't have needed the prompt. Alvin grew up being aware of the Bird family. They were as much a part of the landscape as the North Circular and the speedway stadium (which, of course, they owned). Douglas Bird, the late Louise's even later husband, made his fortune in mail order. Once upon a time, the Bluebird catalogue was as fat and ubiquitous as the Yellow Pages. In the days when the newsagent's top shelf was a distant dream, pubescent boys would leaf through it in search of *Ladies' Foundation Wear*. The matchbox-sized pictures of models in robust bras and strapping girdles really were the best a very young man could get. Their mums, on the other hand, would be far more interested in the photos of white nylon shirts and grey polyester trousers, which would ensure that (for a fraction of the prices at M&S and C&A) their little wankers would look exactly like every other mother's.

The Bluebird warehouse used to be the borough's biggest employer. Alvin worked there in the summer after his O levels, though by then things had already changed. In the early seventies Douglas Bird had sold up to a bigger and even more ubiquitous rival. The warehouse continued under a new name for a while, but by the slump of the eighties it had been rationalised out of existence. Perhaps Douglas Bird had seen it coming. In any case, he retired and watched the proceeds of the sale grow in the hands of his two children, who embarked on a buying spree, hoovering up chunks of land and property across the whole borough and beyond. They seemed to anticipate the day when London would be entirely belted by giant sheds selling cheap sofas, acres of carpet and everything a bloke needed to do it himself. They also own the Aviary, a tiled mall that is contributing to the death of the high street, as well as giving bored teenagers a place to mooch on rainy days.

Yes, they've done OK, the Birds, and they have fingers in just about every pie, including the stodgy, nutrition-free pasty called Wood Hill, where Louise Bird's daughter, Allison, presides over the governors.

'Why?' Karen says, stunned. 'Why is a woman like her naming you in her will?'

Alvin wasn't ready to answer this one when he walked out of Trevor Poll's office and that's why he headed straight for work – to give himself time to think. But thinking hasn't helped and he deflects the question with, 'She left me everything. She didn't get on with her family apparently.'

This is something of an understatement. By Trevor Poll's account, the Birds were a family at war. 'She was Ariel Sharon to her children's Hamas,' he told Alvin.

'*Every*thing?' Karen gasps.

Alvin nods, realising afresh just how outlandish this is.

'What exactly *is* everything?'

'Not sure *exactly*. A lot of money. And a big house. With a trout lake.'

Utterly outlandish.

Karen doesn't speak. She simply stares at him, wanting to look ecstatic, but not sure whether to let herself go. Finally she says, 'You're joking, aren't you? This is a wind-up, yeah?'

'Exactly what I said. No, it's for real. I spent an hour going over it with the guy. And he's a *lawyer*. They don't write to complete strangers to wind them up. Do they?'

'This is staggering, Alvin. *Amazing*. But ... *Jesus* ... *Why*?' Karen asks again, more insistently.

Alvin is unable to resist it this time. He takes a deep breath and says, 'A while ago she was being mugged and I stepped in and . . . Well, I sorted it out.'

'You what?'

Alvin tells her about the small lady in the big coat and Kevan Kennedy.

'You never said anything. When was this?'

'Eight months ago maybe.'

He explains how he left the scene, in a hurry to get back to school. And how – according to Trevor Poll – his elderly damsel in distress determined to discover the identity of her saviour and hired a private detective. And how she then decided to rewrite her will. Completely.

'*Eight* months ago? I know you've never been a glory hunter, but this is ridiculous. You didn't even tell *me*, Alvin.'

Alvin shrugs, delaying the moment.

'Where did it happen?'

This moment. The one that he has been dreading ever since Trevor Poll told him what was what. Having to tell Karen *where* it happened is the thing – the only thing – which has stopped him from leaping up and down with elation. It's why he's the only wealthy beneficiary in history to wear a frown.

'Outside a boarded-up shop,' he says. And after a long delay, 'On All Saints Road.'

Karen's face falls. 'It was when you visited that girl. I don't get why you didn't tell me.'

'Look, I know what you're thinking,' he says.

'Do you?'

'It's not how you imagine. Yes, I did go back to see her, but –'

'You went *back*,' she exclaims. 'After you promised?'

Something dawns on Alvin now, something that if he were a born liar – or at least a born wriggler-out-of-sticky-situations – would have dawned on him before he'd even walked through the front door. The born wriggler would have had the bright idea of merging the two visits to the Tropica into one. It's pretty obvious that Karen had assumed that there was only one trip anyway right up to the moment Alvin said the killer word *back*.

Now he is flustered, caught out by his own belated honesty, unsure whether to attempt a rapid rewind or plough on into the shit with the truth.

'Yes . . . No . . . Yes,' he stutters.

'You went back,' Karen repeats quietly.

'Not for what you think. Not for that,' he says hastily. 'I just went to tell her she had an infection.'

'If that's all it was, why didn't you tell me?'

'I was going to. It was the day we made up after – You know. I was honestly going to tell you, but . . . We started kissing and . . .'

He trails off, realising how lily-livered that sounds.

'Well, you know we finished kissing at some point for the purposes of breathing and whatnot,' she deadpans. 'You might have said something then.'

Alvin shrugs again. 'I didn't want to spoil things,' he says.

'Well, you've blown it now. Big time.'

He reaches across the space that separates them and takes her hand, but she pushes it away.

'Nothing happened, Karen. You've got to believe me.'

'*Why* have I got to believe you? To give you what every cheating shit wants when he gets caught – an easy ride?'

'I haven't been caught. I've told you about it.'

'Eight months after the event. And only because hiding a stack of money and a big house might have been a bit tricky. And what about the postcard she sent you? You only told me about that when I found it in your jeans. How many more love letters have you got stashed away? You're a slyer bastard than I ever imagined.'

Alvin can see Karen's anger building, spreading outwards

and upwards like the licking flames of a bonfire onto which he has only just tossed a match.

'Nothing's going on,' he pleads with an increasing sense of hopelessness. 'I swear on our kids' lives.'

'That's a cheap shot,' she snaps. 'You can do what you like with Mercedes, but you're not dragging my kids into this.'

'I'm not. I'm just trying to make you see that –'

'You're forgetting I've been here before. Over and over again. I lost count of the times I let Paul off the hook. Well, I warned you that if it ever happened again –'

'But it *hasn't* happened.'

The phone on the side table rings, like the bell in a boxing match. Karen picks it up. Alvin is glad of the chance to catch his breath.

'Hello,' she says.

He watches her face darken as she listens to the caller.

'Who the hell is this?' she demands. Then she slams the phone onto the rest and looks at him, tears in her eyes now.

'What's the matter? Who was it?' Alvin asks.

'It was for you,' she replies, an arctic chill in her voice. 'Colin Stanislavski. Doesn't want to stump up for Kelly Hendricks, so he says he'll give you a fiver for a blowjob off Debbie.'

'The bastard.'

'What the hell is going on?'

'Jesus, *nothing*. Colin was in Pizza Express. He was drunk, taking the piss, the usual crap. You're not going to take any notice of him, are you?'

'Why shouldn't I? He hardly seems any less reliable than you've been lately. Anyway, he's got nothing at stake in this fucking relationship so maybe he's just being honest.'

'*I'm* being honest, Karen.'

'Ha!'

'I am. I went back *once*. I saw Kelly, I told her she had that thing and I left. I swear.'

'Just fuck off, Alvin.'

'But –'

'Fuck off. Get out. Go drown in your trout lake.'

'But –'

'But *what*?'

'What about the money?' he asks – a last desperate resort in the complete absence of anything else that might persuade her to melt a little.

'It's your money. You *earned* it. Keep it.'

'It's *our* money. What about the kids?'

'Oh, I'll make sure they get what they're due, but I don't want a penny.'

'Karen . . . *please* . . . can we talk about this?'

'Nothing to talk about. Ever again. We're through. Just go.'

Alvin stands up and makes for the door. But he stops and looks at her. She has her head turned towards the muted TV. A presenter is unveiling a made-over room that presumably used to be something far less impressive – certainly far less *mauve*. Karen hates makeover shows, but she stares at the screen, determined not to watch her partner leave.

'Look, I'll go,' he says. 'But maybe in a couple of days, when things have cooled down, we can –'

She spits out a scornful little laugh. 'Things could not be any cooler between us. I hate you, Alvin. This is it: the end.'

It*s for my mum, sir

Alvin peers at the stack of doorbells. After a brief process of elimination he presses the only one that doesn't have a name beside it. Then he takes a step back and looks up at the flats that sit on top of the parade of small shops. The entrance is sandwiched between the Bina Korner Shop (which isn't on the korner of anything) and the Kurry Kabin. A glance to either side reveals Kwiks off-licence, Kandy's newsagent and a hair salon evidently owned by Kay and someone called Kompany. As he waits, he wonders whether this outbreak of Ks is somehow bacterial.

Like chlamydia – or is that klamydia?

Then – having made the link via the microscopic gobshite that started it all – he wonders if Karen (another K!) *meant* what she said; *really* meant it.

The entryphone crackles. '*Hoozah*?' asks a fur ball of distortion.

Alvin stoops to the intercom. 'It's me. Alvin. Can I come in?'

A dull buzz: his cue to push at the door. He heads up the stairs. He doesn't actually know Jamie McGreevy's flat number, but he doesn't need to. All he has to do is follow the sound: the theme from *Miami Vice*.

'So we're a team again, Alv. Richards and Jagger. Morrissey and Marr.'

'Look, it's just until I get things straightened out with Karen.'

'True love travels on a gravel road,' Jamie says gnomically.

All of his aphorisms are either the titles of country songs or sound as if they should be. Sitting on the sofa beside Alvin, he flips one hairy leg over the other. He is wearing a short dressing gown that shows too much thigh for Alvin's comfort. Alvin can't help noticing the nicotine patch stuck to his groin. Jamie has been Giving Up for well over three years. He has taken the instructions on the NiQuitin box at their word. They told him to vary the placement of the clear plastic squares and he has never put them in the same place twice. After three years he is like a junkie running out of usable veins – Alvin once saw him with a patch on his forehead.

'So why did she turf you out?' he asks. 'You been a scamp?'

Alvin tells him.

'You gave her the clap and she gave you the finger,' Jamie says ruefully – another mutilated nugget from the Nashville Book of Wisdom.

Alvin's head droops and Jamie gives him a hearty slap on the back. 'Stop it with the long face,' he says. 'You should be proud of yourself.'

'Really?'

'Too right. All of this . . . It just goes to show you haven't lost it.'

'What are you talking about? I never had it.'

'C'mon, this is me, *Jamie*. I *know* your work. Holiday Inn, Belfast, eighty-eight. You had the little love monkeys queuing down the corridor.'

'We'd broken up by 1988. And I don't think we ever stayed in a Holiday Inn. And we never played Belfast.'

'Whatever, we didn't call you the Anaconda for nothing.'

'For Christ's sake, Jamie,' Alvin snaps, 'you didn't call me that at all.'

'What's with you tonight?' Jamie asks.

'I told you. Karen hates me. Normally I'd love to spend an evening reminiscing about all the wild and crazy times we never actually had, but, you know, I'm not really in the mood.' He watches his friend deflate. 'Look, I'm sorry. It's good of you to put me up.'

'No problem, man.' Jamie licks the gum on a cigarette paper – the Giving Up isn't exactly working and the patches are less nicotine-replacement than nicotine-enhancement. 'You like the new place, then?'

In truth, the new place looks much like the old one and the one before that . . . Jamie moves with unsettling regularity: a combination of itchy feet and a succession of aggrieved landlords. Each home is a little more in need of fresh paint, shaded light bulbs and non-adhesive carpets than the last. None of which matters to Jamie since he simply papers over the decrepitude with his own mess. His keyboard is where it always is, in the centre of the room, draped with damp laundry. Since Jamie isn't likely to be composing the next 'Can't Get You Out of My Head' on it any time soon, it's good to see it being put to practical use.

'It's . . . nice,' Alvin says. 'Cosy. Where am I sleeping?'

'Sleep's for babies. Right now it's the bright lights, big city for us. Feeling single and drinking doubles.'

'That's a country song, isn't it?'

'Bollocks. It's a J McG original.'

Jamie and Alvin are in the bright lights, big city of across the street. A half-empty corner pub, the name of which Alvin didn't catch. More than likely it began with a K, though. They have been there for a couple of hours and Alvin is drunk. Not enough to climb on the table and burst into 'All by Myself', but sufficiently to believe that telling Jamie about the late Louise Bird's last will and testament is a most excellent idea.

'You want my advice?' Jamie asks, once over his thigh-slapping disbelief.

If followed, financial advice from Jamie is invariably the

as-the-crow-flies route to a county court judgment, but Alvin doesn't point this out.

'Pay the lot into an offshore account and build a big fucking fence around it,' Jamie says. 'If you don't protect it, the bitch will clean you out.'

'Snot a bitch,' Alvin slurs. 'And she doesn't want the money.'

'She *says* she doesn't want the money . . .'

'She *doesn't*.'

Jamie snorts scorn.

'Anyway, it's beside the point 'cause I haven't got the money.'

'You're in this will, yeah?' Jamie says. 'You got the money.'

'Yeah, but I didn't get a cheque there and then. There's something called . . .' Alvin dredges his beery head for the word Trevor Poll used a few hours ago. 'Dunno. Began with P. Or B. Whatever, it means no one can touch it.'

'No one *else* can touch it. QED it's as good as yours.'

'The s'licitor reckons her kids are gonna go ape. They'll claim the woman was mental leaving it all to me. Which she must've been.'

'You get yourself lawyered up and you'll be right as rain.'

'I'm never gonna see this money,' Alvin says, sinking his head into his hands, 'and Karen's not gonna have me back.'

'Alvin, mate, listen to me,' Jamie says, slamming the flats of his hands onto the table. 'Number one: fuck Kaz. And number two: I will personally see to it that you get every cent that's due to you.'

'Snot due to me. She had kids. A family . . . A *family*.'

'Bollocks. You saved the old cow's life. You're the Good Somalian.' He puts an arm around Alvin. 'Know what we're gonna do? Soon as the cheque's cleared we're gonna go out, buy some gear and re-form the band.'

'Brilliant idea,' says Alvin. He can just about manage irony when squiffy.

'Knew it wouldn't take much to cheer you up. Before you

know it we'll be gigging again. Hey, we can get on one of those retro tours. It'll be us, the Bananas, ABC, the Spands. No, scrub them. Wankers. Remember that time Tony Hadley came to see us at the T 'n' C . . .'

As Jamie veers off into a convincing yet entirely manufactured reminiscence, something strikes Alvin. He has been with his friend for several hours now and he hasn't once said –

'". . . that puts me in a very tricky junxtaposition, Tone," I told him straight up. That was the end for him and me.'

Still, *several* junxtaposition-free hours – surely a step forward.

'Fuck the Spands,' Jamie concludes, sitting back and folding his arms. 'No way am I sharing a tour bus with a bloke in a puffball skirt.'

'Knickerbockers,' Alvin says.

'You calling me a liar? The guy wore a fucking skirt.'

Alvin isn't about to argue. His attention is elsewhere. Jamie follows his gaze to the bar. '*Sweet*,' he coos, stretching the vowels to breaking point. 'Go for your life, Single Sid.'

Alvin stares at the girl leaning on the counter. Tall, angel-maned and –

'Up the duff,' Jamie bleats as she turns slightly towards them, revealing a stomach as round as a beach ball. 'You've been beaten to it.'

Alvin doesn't hear him because he is on his feet, lurching towards her. It is only now that he is upright, obliging his limbs into rudimentary coordinated movement, that he is able to make an accurate assessment of his condition: pissed, wankered, drunk as a skunk.

Alvin has always managed to get along all right with alcohol. He doesn't tend to exhibitionism, violence or teary mawkishness. Of course, he has a limit, where his body veers off the A-road and onto a dark and rutted dirt track signposted ATTENTION: NORMAL FUNCTIONS FUCKED BEYOND THIS POINT. The trouble is that his limit is set a little lower than the national average; at almost exactly three and a half pints if memory serves. And if memory serves, tonight he has had almost exactly one more than that.

Nevertheless, corner table to bar hardly represents a marathon. He should be OK. If only it weren't for the ripple in the baggy paisley carpet that ensnares his passing foot and sends the floor rushing upwards to meet his face.

As he pushes himself up she looks down at him, parting her hair curtains with both hands. 'Sir?'

'Chenil, we gotta talk 'bout this,' he says, grabbing the counter rim and hauling with all his might. 'You should *not* be drinking in your condition.'

'I'm not, sir,' Chenil protests as he finally reaches her level.

'Do *not* serve this young woman,' he commands the barmaid who has her back to them. 'She's with *child*.'

The barmaid turns now and hands a bottle of white wine to Chenil, sweetly but deliberately ignoring Alvin.

'You can't give her that,' Alvin almost shouts. 'She's und'rage.' He thrusts out his hand to grab the bottle, but sober Chenil gets there first.

'It's for my mum, sir,' she mumbles. Then to the barmaid, 'Ta.'

She turns and heads for the door. Alvin follows, taking exaggeratedly looping steps to avoid possible rucks in the flooring. Out on the street he grabs her arm. 'Lemme walk you home,' he slurs.

'Sawright. I only live round the corner.'

'No, you're having a baby. You shouldn't be out. Buying alc'hol. You're having a *baby*.'

'Sawright, sir,' she says pleadingly. If Alvin's nerve endings weren't so numbed by beer he would be able to feel the warmth of her embarrassment radiating across the space between them.

'You gotta think of the baby,' Alvin says. 'You're gonna be a mum. That's the most special, precious, sacred . . .'

He stops because he realises tears are streaming down his face.

'You OK?' Chenil asks, shivering from both the cold and the sheer bloody awkwardness of the situation.

'I've fucked up, Chenil,' he sobs. 'I've made such a mess . . . Oh, *shit*.'

He plunges forward, clawing at his knees on the way down and stopping himself from hitting the pavement. Chenil jumps back, but not fast enough to prevent the stream of thin vomit splashing onto her shoes. It looks and smells little different than it did when it left the glass not so long ago.

It's over as quickly as it started. Alvin forces himself upright and says, 'Jeez . . . that was – Feel awright now. Sorry, sorr—'

He stops to wipe his mouth with his sleeve and to look at the car that is passing them at a kerb crawler's pace. Drunkenness being what it is, he probably won't remember it in the morning.

Granny shagger

That is the wonder of alcohol: while it is triggering total disregard for regular standards of decency and restraint, it is simultaneously holding down a finger on an erase button in the brain's archive. It is wiping clean the slate, ensuring the absence of shaming memories that might prevent a repeat performance. By the morning after, the night before has been distilled into nothing more than a vile taste and a vindictive headache.

This particular morning after, Alvin's recall does not go much beyond the fourth or fifth sip of the first pint. His hangover, though, tells him that things must have progressed. He sits, body slumped, on a low wall that rims three sides of a playground marked out with basketball courts. On the far side stands a three-storey teaching block, built in the nineties during a flurry of New Labour spending, but already looking tired beyond its years. The playground is deserted apart from a lone boy taking half-hearted shots at a hoop. Alvin isn't sure who he is because his head is hidden beneath a hood big enough to wrap Ben Nevis. He hasn't the will to tell him to get to whatever class he is skipping. Besides, Alvin has work of his own that he's shirking.

The other effect of his alcoholic amnesia is that it makes him question the remarkable things his brain tells him happened *before* the visit to the pub. Did Karen really kick him out? The fact that he woke up on Jamie's couch suggests that, yes, she most probably did. And before that, did he walk out of his other job? He spent the best part of the evening boozing when he should have been serving pizzas. Asked and answered, then. But there is one memory that must surely be an implant. He cannot have spent a part of yesterday afternoon with a lawyer who told him he was a millionaire. That is simply insane.

He hears Lynette Moorhouse's signature: the *click-click-click* of heels on concrete. He raises his lead weight of a head and sees her walking towards him. She pauses as she draws alongside the NBA hopeful and says, 'Haven't you got a class to go to, Keifer?' He responds by upping gears and shooting a two-pointer. She carries on towards Alvin, sashaying like Angela Rippon in her prime; tailored, coiffed and *hot*.

Last summer's operation was a *total* success.

'Shouldn't you be busy as well?' she asks as she sits down beside him, crossing one long leg over the other.

'Gotta stack of paperwork. Can't face it,' he mumbles.

'You look as if you've been partying.'

'If that's what you call it. It's all going a bit shit-shaped if you want the truth.'

'This'll cheer you up, then. Some juicy goss that's doing the staff room. You know our esteemed chair of governors?'

Alvin's ears prick up despite the stupor permeating his body.

'Apparently her mother died a few weeks ago,' she continues, 'and it turns out she'd written a new will that no one had a clue about. She's disinherited her kids. She was loaded as well. Anyway, the word is that she left the lot to some virtual stranger.' She leans in close to him, though no one can hear a word she's saying. 'Now this is the best bit – and you will *not* believe this, Alvin: the virtual stranger is *one of us*.'

Alvin flinches and he feels nausea in the pit of his stomach. It has nothing to do with alcohol.

'How do you know?' he manages to ask.

'Who knows how these things get out? I guess Bird-Wright

mentioned it to someone else on the board who mentioned it to someone else, et cetera.'

'Maybe it's bollocks,' he mumbles. 'Sounds like bollocks.'

'I wouldn't count on it. Remember the Dogging Bob rumour that was doing the rounds for months? No one believed it until the kids Googled the mpeg in the IT lab. Poor Bob. Last teaching job he'll ever have.'

'Could still be bollocks.'

'No, too outrageous to be an invention. Hector Parr has started a book on the bloke's ID –'

'What makes you say it's a bloke?' Alvin asks.

'Don't know, to be honest. Just seems more likely. Anyway, when I left the staff room Stanislavski was arguing with the rest of English about the correct term for granny shagger. I told them it was gerontophile, but they wouldn't listen to me. I'm only History.'

'*Granny* shagger?' Alvin gasps as the penny drops.

'Well, whoever it is must've been screwing the old dear . . . That seems to be the consensus at least. Why, have you got a better theory?'

Alvin shakes his head – gently, because it really hurts.

'I put a fiver on Rowell,' Lynette says. 'I know he's uptight, but there's just something about him. The faintest whiff of sleaze.'

'It's me,' Alvin says quietly.

'Probably just wishful thinking, eh? You've got to admit that Rowell's fall from grace would be truly spectac— What did you just say, Alvin?'

'It's *me*, Lynette.'

'Come off it. Hector doesn't even have you down at a thousand to one.' She pauses and looks hard at him. 'You're not joking, are you?'

He shakes his head again.

'You were *shagging* her?' she gasps.

'For Christ's sake, *no.*'

'What, how, why, when?'

'You won't tell anyone about this, will you?'

'I've a feeling it won't stay secret for long . . . But, no, of course I won't.'

Alvin tells her the story. Or at least the edited highlights.

'That's fantastic,' she whoops – very quietly. 'Never was there a more deserving guy. Karen must be thrilled.'

'Not exactly.'

He tells her some of the bits he edited out of the first version.

'As *if,*' she says. 'You and Kelly? She really thinks you . . . did it with her?'

He didn't tell her *all* the bits.

'I . . . Yeah, she does,' he says.

'She'll come round, won't she? She's got to.'

'I hope so. Jesus, Lynette, this is a fucking nightmare. I woke up this morning thinking it was literally a bad dream . . . But seems it isn't.'

'You mad? You've never got two fifty pees to rub together and now you're drowning in dosh. It's *wonderful.*'

'It's not my money. I don't deserve it.'

'Of course you do. Who else would have stepped in and fought off a mugger? You can bet her own kids wouldn't have. Apparently they hadn't talked to her for years.'

A part of Alvin's brain – a small and dusty lobe that isn't taken up with shuddering hangover – dimly recalls his meeting with Trevor Poll. He remembers thinking it strange that a family as prominent as the Birds managed to keep their feud with their mother so quiet. By contrast, while he doesn't know the names of the elderly couple who live eight doors from Karen and him, he *does* know that they haven't seen their children for the past ten Christmases. Why then did he have no idea that the Birds – the nearest thing the neighbourhood has to nobility – were right up there with the Ewings and the Carringtons when it came to affluent dysfunction? Surely the fact that Mother Bird had left the palatial family home and moved into a down-at-heel flat should have been news.

But Alvin is too buggered to give all that any serious thought right now.

'Whatever,' he mutters, 'I'm never gonna see a penny anyway. Her kids'll have swanky lawyers crawling all over me.'

'Think *positive*, sweetheart. They have to *prove* you have no right to the money. Not as easy as you imagine . . . Oo-er, here comes trouble.'

Alvin looks up to see Tony Rowell striding across the playground, heading unswervingly for them. In passing and without pause he barks, 'Sutherland, class, *now*!' at which the hooded boy grabs his ball and sprints towards the teaching block. Rowell reaches Alvin and Lynette and judders to a halt. Swaying slightly like a tall and slender sapling, he peers down at them.

'That resource application was supposed to be in the post last night, Ms Moorhouse,' he booms.

'Yes . . . I . . . it . . . er . . . I . . .' Lynette splutters, like an eleven-year-old who has shown up without either her homework or an adequately thought out excuse.

But Rowell ignores her, turning his gaze on Alvin. 'Mr Lee, you make me sick. You're finished at this school, do you understand? I'll see to that.'

He spins on his heel and tosses out a parting 'The application, Ms Moorhouse, the application' as he strides back indoors.

Lynette is on her feet and grabbing Alvin by the arm, dragging him up. 'C'mon, let's walk and talk. What was *that* all about? He must know.'

Alvin struggles to keep up with her. After years of teacher-issue desert boots, it's hard to credit how readily she has taken to heels. She can keep pace with Olympic walkers without so much as a teeter.

'How would he know?' he asks her.

'I don't know, do I? How does he know I *didn't* post that application yesterday? He's like Christopher bloody Lee with his crystal ball in *Lord of the Rings*. He *knows* things.'

'Yeah, but ... Why would he want me out?'

'Good question. He reckons you were shagging her?'

Alvin struggles to think. Thinking, this morning, entails several more joules of energy than his body is prepared to release to his brain. His head crashes through the gears, attempting to engage, but missing grindingly. Then a tiny nugget of something comes to him.

'I was walking out of school with Debbie and Chenil yesterday,' he says. 'Rowell drove by us.'

'So?'

'He had problems with Debbie's skirt.'

'What skirt?'

'Exactly. There wasn't much of it.'

'He's not going to try to have you fired for *that*. He *knows*, Alvin.'

They have arrived at the door to the teaching block.

'I've got to get back to ILD,' Alvin says, remembering his imminent one-on-one with Dan, the hopeless Romanian colourist. He has been making real progress with him lately, sometimes cajoling as many as half a dozen words of English out of him in their half-hour sessions. Today, though, he thinks he'll try an approach that requires less effort on his part. Maybe bung the boy some crayons and get him to draw how he feels.

'See you at lunch, yeah?' Lynette says.

'Please don't tell anyone.'

'Of course I won't,' she calls out as she clicks her way indoors.

'That's very ... *powerful*, Dan.'

Alvin studies the angry swirl of reds on the lined paper, a maelstrom of colour with a small, angular figure caught in the centre of it. It is, perhaps, a rare window onto the damaged psyche of a displaced teenager.

'What is it?' he asks, looking earnestly at the picture. 'Is it your frustration at not being able to communicate?'

Dan stares at him uncommunicatively.

'You know,' Alvin prompts, 'not being able to make yourself understood must make you pretty mad at times. It'd drive me crazy too.'

Dan grabs the paper and holds it up to Alvin's face. 'Tony!' he yelps, pointing excitedly at the stickman in the centre of the whirlpool.

Alvin looks at the picture blankly.

'Tonee,' Dan repeats urgently.

Is it his father? Or his brother?

Alvin shakes his head apologetically.

'Tony *Adam*! Ars'nal legen'!'

He starts to sing.

Dan the mute refugee is singing.

'Tony Adam magic,
He have a magic knob,
And when he see Caprice,
He stick it in her –'

'OK, O-*Kay*,' Alvin says, getting the gist. 'That's . . . fantastic, Dan.'

The bell rings and so does his mobile. As Dan mooches from the room, Alvin pulls his phone from his pocket and puts it to his ear.

'The enemy's tanks are massing on the border, Mr Lee,' declares the voice at the other end of the line, 'and my spies have detected a major redeployment in their infantry positions.'

'Who is this?'

'The *Birds*. They're preparing for war.'

'No, who's *speaking*?'

'Trevor Poll. We need to meet up.'

'We only just met yesterday,' Alvin says.

'Yes, but we need to mobilise and –'

'Hang on. *Stop*. What are you talking about, Mr Poll?'

'Trevor.'

'*Trevor*. Look, I'm still very confused by all of this.'

'Yes, yes, of course you are. A lot to digest in one sitting. As I explained yesterday, although this is a doddle of a will – only the one beneficiary and so on – I didn't anticipate that it would be straightforward in the execution. Prophetic words indeed, Mr Lee.'

'*Alvin*, please.'

'*Alvin*. This morning I received a letter from Sandler Gonzalas –'

'Who?'

'Solicitors like me, Alvin. Only not a bit like me. They represent heirs to the throne, Tory luminaries and pop stars in their spats with the tabloids. They also represent the Birds. They inform me that they drew up Louise Bird's original will when she was still on nodding terms with her progeny.'

'Well, I s'pose that settles it then,' Alvin says, feeling strangely relaxed all of a sudden. 'I mean, if she already had a will.'

'Far from it. A new will nullifies any prior document. The law is crystal clear on that. However, they have no intention of making our lives easy. They mean to contest the matter. They cite the late Mrs Bird's dementia –'

'Her what?'

'They claim she was nutso.'

Well, thinks Alvin, she must have been.

'Utter poppycock,' Poll continues. 'In all of my dealings with her she was in possession of the full bag of marbles. And, frankly, I take the insinuation that she wasn't as a slur against me personally. I don't care if Messrs Sandler and Gonzalas have represented the Pope himself – and I say that as a committed left-footer – I will not have my integrity impugned.'

'Look, I really haven't got time for this now,' Alvin says.

Curtis and Roland have drifted into the room and they are waiting without a great deal of enthusiasm to find out how Alvin intends to keep them occupied until lunch time. Debbie is at the door, furiously punching a text into her mobile. Alvin can hear the foul-mouthed banter of others outside.

'We must meet up, Alvin,' Poll urges. 'You're going to need a lawyer.'

Alvin thinks he can actually *hear* the solicitor's chest puff up. If indeed he does need a lawyer, he wonders whether he really wants Father Christmas and his invisible partners.

'I don't know,' he says. 'I'm not sure about any of this, to be honest.'

'We'll talk again. In the meantime you mull things over. A good mull, Alvin. Therein lies the road to clarity.'

Alvin pockets his phone and surveys the room, struggling to focus. Clarity on this peasouper of a day seems an impossible dream.

'Who was that, Alvin?' Curtis asks.

'Personal,' he grunts. 'Let's get on, shall we?'

Now, why he said that he doesn't know. He hasn't given this session a moment's thought and he has no idea what he's going to do with the eight kids sprawled before him.

Make that seven.

'Where's Chenil?' he asks.

No reply, just a collective shrug. Alvin doesn't know why he's worried. Chenil will be leaving school any day now. Call it maternity leave, though it has less to do with the welfare of mother and baby than with the negative impact of a very visible pregnancy on the other children.

Roland and Curtis are sniggering.

'What's so funny, guys?' Alvin asks.

Debbie glares at him. 'You freaked her last night.'

'Last *night*?' he repeats, genuinely befuddled.

'Yeah, she thought you was . . .'

She trails off, but, ever helpful, Curtis chips in on her behalf. 'She thought you was coming on to her, innit.'

'But you was only puking on her,' Roland splutters before exploding into snotty chokes of laughter.

'What are you talking about?' Alvin asks, even as tiny memory-filled bubbles are popping to the surface.

'Shush!' Debbie shrieks. '*Shut up*!' She has her hand raised and her mobile pressed hard to her ear.

The room falls silent as the terror on the girl's face registers.

'It's Chenil, sir,' she says. 'She's fucking having it.'

'Where is she?'

Though there's no need to ask; it's a case of following the screams.

These things take hours

Alvin has discovered the perfect hangover cure; perfect because it is literally instantaneous. Anyone cursed with a head like an iron foundry, thinks Alvin, should forget the black coffee and Alka Seltzer. Instead, find a paralysed-with-fear-and-pain teenager in the desperate throes of childbirth. Then PANIC!

Actually, he doesn't think any of that. He is far too busy.

PANICKING!

Chenil has him by the hand. She is squeezing very hard and, *Jesus Christ*, it hurts. Right now, though, is probably not the most tactful moment to bring up his own discomfort. They are in the girls' toilet block on one side of the threadbare lawn outside ILD. Alvin had never visited it before and he was glad to find it a lot less pissy than the boys'. Chenil is on the floor, her skirt rucked up around her waist, her head resting on Alvin's rolled-up fleece. Alvin kneels beside her having the twenty-seven bones in his hand crushed into several more.

'Nnnnnnnnnnnnnnnggggggghhhhhhhhhfuck*uuuuuuugh*!' she screams, gripping him even tighter.

'That's it, Chenil, go with it,' Alvin says through the pain – hers and his.

'Please make it stop,' she pleads, panting hard, her face and hair drenched with sweat and tears.

He wishes he could. He has been here before. Twice. He wasn't around for Mercedes's arrival. He'd wanted to be, but he and Janice had only just split up and, well, she didn't call. But he was there when Annie and Sid popped blinking into daylight. He recalls witnessing the ordeal that must always remain an unfathomable mystery to anyone born without a functioning womb. Karen's labours were quick; huge and rapid contractions from the outset as if her body had opted for intense torture in order to *get the fucking nightmare over with*. He remembers feeling redundant, a spare part blathering half-remembered nuggets of antenatal crap. *'Breathe, baby, breathe.'* What was that all about? Let's face it, Alvin decided, hand-holding and brow-swabbing just weren't going to cut it; his useful role in the process had ended forty weeks earlier. Which led to a crushing guilt trip – *had he really started this?* It didn't lift until the moment it was over. (Which was also the moment – gazing wide-eyed and legless for the first time at Annie, then, four years later, at Sid – that it all *began*.)

Alvin doesn't feel guilt now – well, he didn't start this one – but he does feel utterly spare-part-ish as Chenil Shakespeare – reticence made flesh – screams like a metal singer and curses like a rapper. He's helpless in the face of contractions fierce enough to expel a baby elephant.

Here comes another one now.

'Nnnnnnnnnnnnnnnnnnnnnggggggggggghhhhhhhhhfuckfuckfuck*fuck*!'

Alvin listens to the wail and then to the sound of his own squelching joints as Chenil's grip on his hand tightens still more. He searches for some suitably encouraging words and comes up with, 'Breathe, Chenil, breathe.'

They are not alone. In the corner stands twelve-year-old Kylie Cotton, an unlit cigarette glued to her lip. Presumably she was about to enjoy it when Chenil's waters broke, and she has been almost literally petrified ever since. Alvin hopes that this compelling *live* performance promoting a significant downside to teenage sex is making a suitable impression on her. Debbie is also there, her back against the door, keeping at bay whatever audience may be outside. She has never looked more serious in her life and Alvin wonders what is going through her head. If it is something along the lines of *Childbirth? Whose rubbish idea was that?* he wouldn't blame her. It struck him when Annie was born that childbirth was a compelling argument against a creator. What empathetic god would have sat down with pencil and pad and *designed* such a system? *Hmm, how about – after nine months of debilitating gestation – we squeeze the seven-pound object down an inappropriately narrow tube, causing seismic pain, involuntary bowel evacuation, jagged rips in the flesh and, almost certainly, brain-scarring trauma? And how about we make the entire process drag on for as many as seventy-two hours? Yes, one of my better ideas. Think I'll have that cup of tea now.*

Debbie and Alvin were first into the toilet block. While Debbie called for an ambulance, Alvin sent Roland and Curtis – the *fathers* – to fetch grown-up help. Specifically a welfare officer, a staff member with emergency-aid training. Alvin isn't one of them. As a bloke, he feels uncomfortable being in a toilet with a teenage girl. As a bloke without any specialist skills . . .

'Do something, sir,' Debbie urges as Chenil visibly braces herself for another onslaught. 'It's gonna bloody come any second.'

'No, it'll be a while yet,' Alvin says, his voice quavering. 'These things take hours.'

This should be happening in a nice sanitary maternity wing, he thinks, with midwives, doctors and shiny equipment specifically designed for getting babies out of women. Instead they're in a toilet block. The place may not be as urine-soaked as the boys', but it's still a toilet. Six obscenity-decorated traps in a line, poor Chenil half in, half out of one of them; no equipment, because really you can't count bog paper, a wet, dirty roller towel and a slither of mushy soap; definitely no trained professionals.

'What the hell are Roland and Curtis doing?' he snaps.

90 free texts*

(*Terms and conditions apply)

'Gi's a light, Ro . . . Ta . . . Since when you been smoking lights?'

Roland shrugs.

'You is *so* gay.'

'F'k off.'

'You heard Sean Paul's new one?'

'Nah, how's it go?'

'Kinda dun, dun, dun, der-der, dun, *dun*, doof, *doof*.'

'Any good?'

'Sick, man. You done it with Becker's sis yet?'

'That sket? She is a *minger*, man.'

'You *wanna* though.'

'F'k off.'

Curtis drops his cigarette and grinds it beneath his foot.

'Shall we go get someone, then?'

Roland shrugs.

''Ere, you could just call an ambulance and that.'

'Get lost, man. I'm not wasting my phone . . . I could text, yeah? I get, like, ninety free texts a month or something.'

'Can you text 999?'

Roland shrugs.

'Gi's another light, then.'

Honestly, it can take hours and hours

'I think you're wrong, sir,' Debbie wails. 'It's bloody coming.'

'Honestly, Debbie, it's far too soon. I'm sure she's got ages yet.'

'No, sir, *look*.'

Alvin has done all he can to avoid *looking*. Carer looking at teenage client *down there* is an imprisonable offence. But he finally forces his eyes to move. A flushed and bloody disc of skin is visible between Chenil's legs.

'Shit, it's coming!' he yelps. 'It's the baby's head. She's nearly there . . . You're nearly there, Chenil!'

'*Told* you, sir,' Debbie says. She takes off her blazer and lays it between Chenil's legs. Then she crawls up to her friend's head and cradles it. 'C'mon, girl, we can see its head. You're *doing* it. You're nearly there. *Push*!'

'I can't,' Chenil gasps, wilting visibly, any further effort beyond her.

Alvin picks up her hand again. 'Yes, you can, Chenil,' he urges.

He remembers Karen reaching this exact moment with Annie. He can picture the bleached pallor of her face. Drained by the effort and shell-shocked from the pain, she couldn't go on. But the midwife – who up until that moment had been nothing but soothing – *commanded* her to make one last push. Alvin knew from her tone that there was no other option.

There is no midwife now, though. Just him and Debbie. And Kylie Cotton, the human freeze-frame.

'Yes, you *can,*' Alvin very nearly shouts. 'You've got to *push.*'

'C'mon, babe,' Debbie says, stroking her friend's face.

A sob catches in Chenil's throat. Slowly and seamlessly it mutates into a deep, guttural screech and her entire body goes into spasm.

The baby slides out. *Fast,* like a torpedo from a tube. Alvin lunges and only just catches it before it flops onto the blazer. He lifts it up and clutches it to himself as Chenil's body relaxes like it *never* has before. Alvin looks at the tiny, tiny thing, lifeless in his shaking hands. He wonders if he should dangle it by the ankles and smack its virtually nonexistent bottom – or is that just a myth? But all by itself it opens its mouth, splutters and utters a thin but authentic cry. Debbie shuffles towards Alvin and peers at it excitedly.

'What is it, sir?'

'It's a . . .' He looks down its body. 'It's a boy.'

'It's a little *boy,* Chenil,' Debbie says. 'It's – He's *gorgeous.*'

And he is, Alvin thinks.

'We need to keep this kid warm,' he says, marvelling that he has never seen anything so tiny, yet so defiantly alive.

Debbie is ahead of him, already unbuttoning her white school blouse and tearing it from her shoulders. She thrusts it at him and he manages to wrap it around the body of the crying baby whose eyes are now open. They are unfeasibly large . . . And uncannily like his father's. Who is at this moment somewhere in the school grounds, looking for a welfare officer. Or possibly not.

Chenil has hauled herself up onto her elbows and stares, dazed and incredulous, at her son. Debbie hugs her. 'Fucking *amazing,* babe.' Then she looks at Alvin. 'You were *wicked,* sir.'

'Me? What about you? You delivered a *baby,* Debbie.'

'I did . . . *We* did! We were well wicked, sir.'

Alvin hears a siren. The ambulance at last.

Then a rising commotion outside, adult voices joining the kids already gathered. The door is flung open and a woman in a paramedic's uniform stumbles through. Behind her are Stanislavski and Rowell.

Alvin might be worried how all this looks: a girl naked from the waist down; another girl naked from the waist up, apart from a gauzy black bra; a catatonic, fag-dropping twelve-year-old in the corner; a male staff member cradling a bundle of bloodied white cotton as he presides over the whole show.

He *might* be worried, if he weren't feeling completely, overwhelmingly elated.

His wife can*t tell which one*s the P.M.

Alvin is sitting, although it feels more as if he's floating, his bottom held an inch or so above the chair on a cushion of pure *elation*. He can't remember ever feeling this energised. Not after his first gig or on *Top of the Pops* or upon hearing 'Wanda Lust' on the radio. Not even, shockingly, after his own children were born. Of course he felt special then – as special as special could be – but the difference was that he hadn't *done* anything. This time, however . . .

As he was watching Chenil and her brand-new son being bundled into the ambulance, Debbie hugged him. And he hugged her right back.

They had done it.
They had delivered a baby.
To a terrified teenager.
On a toilet floor.

'How the hell did you know what was going on?' he said to Debbie, post-hug. She gave him a nonchalant shrug and said, 'I'm the oldest, ain't I? I was there for my three brothers. My mum couldn't get a sitter.'

Now he feels nothing is beyond him. Straighten things out with Karen? Pifflingly easy. Sort out the nonsense with the Birds? The doddle of all doddles. He is Alvin Lee, Deliverer of Premature Babies on Toilet Floors.

He is thinking these thoughts as he hovers slightly above his chair in Alan Chadwick's office, waiting. The head wants to see him. As he looks around, he realises that this is the first time he has been inside this room, at least since Alan Chadwick has occupied it. It seems bigger than it was in the days of his predecessor. Mr Wilkinson, literally old school, used to barricade himself behind stacked books and files, filling the room with them to the point of inducing claustrophobia. And if that failed to dissuade visitors, he possessed the ultimate deterrent: a pipe. (For younger readers, a pipe is a quaint briarwood contraption, the bowl of which is stuffed with odorous tobacco. It shouldn't be confused with the modern device used for smoking crack cocaine.)

Chadwick's new broom has shooed away Wilkinson's clutter. Now the room is the sleek, functional front office of Wood Hill PLC. What books there are have been consigned to a couple of shelves. A few certificates hang on a wall. A firm-looking sofa – clearly not designed for extended spells of loafing – squats beneath a window. A big desk takes centre stage. On its dustless surface sit a maroon diary, a beige phone and a purring laptop.

There is something else: a walnut picture frame. From his chair on the visitor's side of the desk, Alvin peers to see the photograph within, curious to know what Alan Chadwick's wife or children look like. But this isn't a family snap, unless he is married to Tony Blair. The two of them – Tone and Al – are locked in an extended handclasp. They seem to be wearing identical suits. And identical grins, as if they are the winner and runner-up in some national bridgework gala. But behind them a backdrop announces they're at the National Teachers' Awards. Alan Chadwick surfed into Wood Hill on a wave of acclaim. In his previous job he had single-handedly transformed a Moss Side comprehensive from a drop-in Borstal into an oasis of learning, competing in the league tables with Eton and Harrow. At least, that was how it read in the *Gazette* report. Alan Chadwick knows how to get good press.

The door opens behind Alvin. 'My wife is fond of saying it's hard to tell which one's the PM, but, well, I suppose she's biased,' Chadwick says. He sits down in the high-backed swivel chair opposite Alvin. 'Quite a morning you've had. I don't believe midwifery is in your job spec.'

'A lot of it was down to Debbie Coates. She was –'

'Not that it's something we want to broadcast. Teenage motherhood is a big issue and growing bigger. It'd hardly do us any credit to become a focus of national debate.' He smiles at Alvin, but there's nothing behind it. 'I'd appreciate you not taking this one to the media.'

Alvin is picking up a vibe. This isn't going to be the hearty pat on the back he'd been glibly expecting. Now he feels foolish.

'Going to the papers hadn't even crossed my –'

'Of course not.' Chadwick looks at his watch, then at Alvin. 'This is a troubling situation,' he says. 'Deeply troubling.'

'Well, yeah, the baby was very premature,' Alvin agrees.

'That's not what I mean. What on earth was going on in there?'

Alvin would have thought that – with four people going into the toilet block and five coming out and with Chadwick's teaching background being in maths – it should be pretty obvious what was going on.

'Why were you alone in a toilet with three girls?' Chadwick expands. 'Where was the welfare officer?'

'I sent Curtis and Roland to get someone,' Alvin replies, feeling sick at the barely disguised insinuation.

'Young and Goffe? Hardly our most responsible pupils. You should have gone for help yourself.'

'I thought I should be with Chenil until someone arrived. Curtis and Roland knew how urgent the situation was. They –'

'Mr Stanislavski found them sharing a cigarette behind the library.'

'Didn't they tell him what was happening?'

'They told him, but he didn't believe them.'

'Didn't he at least check it out?' Alvin asks.

'Why?' Chadwick shoots back, matching Alvin for incredulity. 'They were hardly infused with the *urgency* of the situation, were they?'

Alvin shrugs helplessly, his de-elated backside now firmly on the seat. 'There wasn't anyone else to send. I really thought I should stay with Chenil.'

'No, your first priority should have been ensuring she was looked after by an appropriately qualified *female* staff member.' Chadwick shakes his head. 'Have you any idea how this looks?'

'It was an emergency,' Alvin gasps, unable to digest the conversation's twist. 'To be honest, the last thing I cared about was how it *looked*.'

'Why was Coates half-naked?'

'She took off her blouse to – What exactly are you suggesting?'

'Well, when you put today's incident in the context of . . .' Chadwick halts for another dramatic hiatus. 'Of *other* events.'

'What other events?'

'Quite apart from the baby business, I was going to talk to you anyway. Tony Rowell says he saw you with Chenil yesterday.'

'What, outside school? That was –'

'No, outside a pub. At gone eleven.'

Alvin blinks, trying to focus on the still vague memory.

'He was in his car and he said he saw you walking out of the . . .' He pauses to look at a note in the front of the diary. '. . . The King's Head.'

'I was . . . She was . . .' Alvin fumbles for an explanation. Maybe Chenil can offer one. When she's out of hospital.

'What the hell were you doing in a pub with a sixteen-year-old girl from *this* school?'

Actually, Chenil is still fifteen, but Alvin doesn't point it out. Last night is suddenly regurgitating itself from his subconscious and he says, 'I'd had too much to drink, but –'

'That much was evident to Mr Rowell.'

'But I didn't go to the pub with Chenil. She came in after I'd got there and I was trying to get her home.'

'You were going *home* with her?'

'No, I just thought she should be at home. She shouldn't've been out.'

'That's not what it looked like to Mr Rowell.'

'How does he know what was going on?' Alvin says, irritated now. 'I mean, if he was in a car.'

Chadwick holds up a hand as he looks at his watch again. 'I'm going to have to cut this short. I've got someone waiting to see me,' he says.

'Hang on, you can't chuck out accusations and give me no chance to explain.'

'Don't worry, you'll have every opportunity to explain when this is properly investigated. In the meantime I suggest you take some time off.'

'Are you suspending me?'

'Put it this way: I don't think you should be anywhere near the children until this is cleared up. I'll have to talk to Basil Karadas about it, but as of now you're suspended pending an inquiry,' Chadwick says, making it official.

Basil Karadas is Alvin's line manager, the head of Inclusive Learning. He doesn't so much lead the department as shunt it in whatever direction Alan Chadwick chooses. At present he seems to be transforming Alvin and his colleagues into auxiliary dinner ladies, minus the smocks and trolleys. There seems to be less *mentoring* and more *supervising*. Alvin doesn't have a great deal of respect for his immediate boss. Being Alvin, he'd never condemn him as ferociously as Hector Parr did in one vitriolic outburst – 'He's a penpusher, a lackey, a lardy-arsed lickspittle' – and only partly because he isn't sure what a lick-spittle is. Even so, he doesn't suppose Basil will waste too much energy dissuading Chadwick from taking the severest possible line.

Chadwick is looking away now, focused on his computer screen, shuffling through emails. Alvin stands up, but he doesn't move from the spot.

'Anyway, you look as if you could do with some leave,' the head says. 'You don't look well.'

Alvin walks from the room without a word. The head was right. He doesn't feel at all well. He feels as if he has been gutted, as if his entrails are still on the chair he has just risen from.

In Chadwick's outer office, Gillian Duke, Wood Hill's senior administrative officer, looks at him over the top of her computer screen. So does the woman sitting on a chair next to a big, glossy-leafed cheese plant. She peers at him over the top of her *Daily Telegraph*. Alvin recognises her immediately, but Allison Bird-Wright returns his stunned stare blankly.

Mr Sugden

The unemployed former schoolteacher stops outside the gentlemen's outfitter: Sugden & Son. The window, which looks as if it hasn't had a makeover for decades, is populated by dusty, flaking mannequins that look like seventies footballers, though their suits might have been worn by the Preston North End team to the 1954 FA Cup Final. A discreet sign just below eye level announces ASSISTANT REQUIRED. He peers through the door. The place looks quiet and gloomy. And old. He can't see any customers. Just a man standing behind a counter – Mr Sugden? Or Son of Sugden? Whoever he is he's a throwback to an age of powdered eggs and Preston North End. Though the former teacher finds the view faintly depressing, he likes the fact that below the help wanted sign there *isn't* another that says NO MORE THAN TWO SCHOOLCHILDREN AT A TIME – no call for it, he supposes.

He needs the job and also the tranquillity. Before walking in, he checks his face in the window's reflection. The rash is looking bad today, like alien facial prosthetics on *Star Trek: Voyager*. But the shop interior is dingy. Maybe they won't notice.

You. Have. No. New. Messages

Alvin is hoping for peace and solitude, but Jamie's stereo is pumping out 'Should I Stay or Should I Go?' Good question. The volume is at a level that threatens to atomise the cheap speakers, but Jamie will yell at anyone not too deafened to hear him that this song was 'MADE LOUD TO PLAY LOUD!'

'Jamie?' Alvin calls out.

No response.

He kills the CD, but he isn't greeted by silence. Grunts and groaning springs penetrate the wall that separates him from Jamie's room. He should leave now; walk out the door and round the block. But he doesn't have the energy; his get-up-and-go got up and went in Chadwick's office. He flops onto the sofa and wraps a cushion around his face, forcing it over his ears to shut out the noise. But he can't breathe for the smell of kebab. *Shit*, he can *feel* kebab on the fabric. He flings it aside, wishing Jamie would discover crockery. And wishing his life hadn't come to this: sitting in squalor, waiting for his friend to ejaculate so he can have a moment's peace to stew in his own self-pity.

He looks at the clock on the video player. This time yesterday he was walking into a solicitor's office. He was nervous, but only because he thought he was going to be collared over some debt that he and Karen had no immediate prospect of repaying; nothing that he hadn't had to deal with before; nothing life-changing. The last twenty-four hours have seen an unimaginable transformation in his fortunes. Isn't there a song? 'Money Changes Everything' – an instrumental because it goes without saying. The irony is that he holds out no hope of getting his hands on the stuff that has rocked his world.

He thinks about Kevan Kennedy, wondering what he'd say if he knew what he'd set in train when he clapped eyes on the old lady. Kevan, though, wouldn't have much to say. Articulating stuff was never his strong point.

He reaches into a pocket for his mobile phone and stares at it, wondering if he should ring Karen. Not now, not unless her thinking he's calling from a payphone in a paper-walled Bangkok brothel would actually *improve* his situation. But hey, maybe she called already and left a message, a plea for him to rush home immediately and make tender, restorative love to her.

Well, you never know. Stranger things have happened. A lady he'd never even been formally introduced to left him several million British pounds. And a trout lake. Who the hell saw that one coming?

Index finger sprightly with optimism, he dials voicemail. Then he listens.

'You.

'Have.

'*No.*

'New.

'Messages,' comes the human-impersonating-a-robot voice.

'And.

'*One.*

'Com.

'Pletely.

'Fucked.

'Up.

'Relation.

'Ship,' it might as well add.

Alvin pockets the phone and winces as Jamie's grunts are suddenly swamped by the sounds of his partner. Triple-X squeals, which Jamie punctuates with a montage of soundbites from every porn movie he has ever seen, including (if Alvin's hearing isn't deceiving him) the German ones. He finishes with 'Cometodaddyyoudirtylittle . . . Ayyy-*yaaaaaaahhh*.'

Silence at last. A moment later Alvin hears the bedroom door open. He dares to open an eye, squinting at Jamie's silhouette.

'Thought I heard you get home,' he says, panting.

Jamie stands dressed in white socks, white-going-on-grey underpants and a nicotine patch on his knee. The last time Alvin saw him this naked was about eighteen years ago. He hasn't improved with age.

'You've gotta hand it to me, eh?' he says, firing up a half-smoked roll-up.

Alvin attempts to smile. 'Look, I'll go out if you want some privacy.'

'No need,' Jamie says, flopping onto the sofa beside him.

'Who is she?' he asks for the sake of something to say.

'New bargirl at the Ambassador . . . Danielle . . . Delia . . . Something.'

The Ambassador is where Jamie whiles away much of his time, playing aimless frames of snooker and hatching comeback tours to rival Aerosmith's.

'You could pop in for seconds, if you like,' Jamie leers. 'Reckon she's too knackered to complain.'

'Don't be disgusting.'

'I'm being serious.'

'Have you any idea what's happening in my life right now? And you want me to . . . ?' Although Alvin isn't shouting he feels anger rising.

'That's my point, mate. You've fallen off the horse. Thing to do is get straight back into the saddle.'

'Karen isn't just some shag, Jamie. She's . . . Why am I even trying to explain? You don't get it at all, do you?'

'Fuck, you can be a patronising cunt sometimes, you know,' Jamie snarls. 'If you loved Kaz so much, if what you had was so fucking perfect, what were you doing with a hooker? Take a good fucking look at yourself before you come round here and piss on my lifestyle.'

Alvin buries his face in his hands, accepting the point, but not wanting to concede it. He feels Jamie's hand pat him on the shoulder.

'Look, I don't mean to have a go, Alv,' he says. 'I'm just trying to say maybe we're not that different. It's the rock 'n' roll in us. You can't kill it just 'cause you hit forty. We're peas in a pod, you and me. Tweedle Dum and that other one. We're in the same junxtaposition.'

'JUXTAPOSITION!'

'You what?'

'It's *juxt*aposition, you moron!' Alvin is on his feet now. '*Juxtaposition*: the act of placing two or more items side by side, thereby creating drama, contrast or *tension*.' (Alvin is on solid ground here. He has looked it up in several dictionaries.) 'And it's J, U, X, T. No *N*. No fucking N.'

Jamie is stunned into silence. Alvin reaches behind the sofa and grabs the vinyl sports bag he turned up with yesterday.

'What are you doing?' Jamie says at last.

'I'm sorry, Jamie. I can't stay.'

'Course you can. This is just a hiccup. Musical differences sorta thing. We're mates.'

'Yeah, but . . . Sorry.' Alvin zips up the bag.

'C'mon, sit down, I'll get us a couple of beers,' Jamie says. 'I'll get my guitar out and we can play some of the old tunes. Or write some new ones.'

'Not now, OK? I've really got to go. I've got a lot to sort out. Look, thanks for putting me up. I'll give you a shout in a few days.'

Alvin closes the door very quietly behind him.

Enya Country

The house – a flat-faced fifties semi designed by an architect whose education stopped once he'd learned how to plonk a triangle on top of a cube – is the same as it always was. But it's different too. A year ago, a peek through the nets revealed an unadorned, uncherished beige living room. Now, though, there is no need to peek because the interior positively gushes, leaping through the window and assaulting the visitor as he steps through the gate. Pinkness radiates from the ruched curtains, the walls and what can be glimpsed of the furniture, all of it *accented* by flickers of candlelight.

This house hasn't just had the makeover; it has gone for the full sex change – or gender reassignment therapy, to put it correctly.

Alvin closes the gate behind him, but stops on the path, newly apprehensive. He didn't phone ahead. He couldn't. After a barrage of bilious nuisance calls, Lynette changed her number and Alvin never got her new one. He hates to descend uninvited, but he isn't quite ready for homelessness. He takes a fresh grip on his bag and heads for the front door. He presses the bell and listens to the soft *bing-bong* echo through the hall. As he waits he can hear music. A thousand decibels removed from the Berlin Wall of sound that confronted him at Jamie's, this is soft and lilting, and only a few bars in he knows that – like it or lump it – he is about to enter Enya Country.

After a moment he makes out a figure through the dimpled glass. The door opens and clunks against its security chain and a strip of Lynette's face appears in the narrow gap. 'Alvin!' she exclaims. She unhooks the chain and swings the door open. She is dressed in a diaphanous gown and negligée ensemble, the kind he didn't think existed outside *Confessions* movies.

'Bad time?' he asks because somehow it doesn't look as if she is about to settle down with only her TV remote and a tub of Häagen-Dazs for company.

'I have got someone round,' she says awkwardly. But then she takes a proper look at her visitor and says, 'No, it's fine. Come in.'

'Are you sure?'

'Of course. Come in. You look like you need a drink.'

As he walks into the hall, he sees bare legs and the bottom of a towelling dressing gown flash by at the top of the stairs before disappearing into a room.

'It's OK, Lynette,' he says, backing towards the door. 'I shouldn't have come unannounced.'

'No, you're here now,' she says, blushing slightly. 'It's only Donna. We did an aerobics class after school. I told her to come back here to shower.'

Only Donna Hutton, the demure (unless provoked) French teacher. Alvin is relieved. 'Right, *Donna,*' he says with a grin. 'I thought . . . You know, you had a bloke round or something.'

'Why would I have a bloke round? Coffee or something stronger?'

Jamie used to berate Alvin for his lack of interest in drugs. To Jamie, they were a career move, compulsory at that, and a sign of one's commitment. If you work in a bank, you put on a tie; if you want to be a rock star, you put it up your nose. Alvin wasn't anti as such. He'd tried most of the pills and powders going, but found that, all in all, he just didn't get along with them.

But now, in the bosom of middle age, he has discovered something as mind-altering as dope, but without the icky smell and the associated paranoia. Yes, he could develop a serious habit for soft furnishings.

He submerges his body in Lynette's overstuffed sofa, feeling her tasselled cushions nuzzle his cheeks like big, affectionate kittens. His nose takes in the vanilla scent of the candles, a relief after Jamie's aromatic *melange* of pizza, kebab and sock. Even Enya's swoons slosh over him like warm, milky bath water. At this moment, his brain rapidly losing focus, his senses really could lull him into the conviction that recent events represent a transitory blip; he hasn't lost his home and family and he isn't clinging to his job by his chewed fingernails. Normal service will shortly be resumed.

He looks at the photograph on the mantelpiece. A seven-year-old boy with a gap-toothed smile. He's ten now. The picture was taken not long before he left with his mother. 'Can't blame the woman for scarpering, can you?' Stanislavski said at the time. 'Why'd she wanna let her sprog watch his dad sprout bigger tits than hers?' Alvin thinks the kid would probably have coped. It was his mum who had the problem. Lynette doesn't blame her ex. After all, whoever wrote 'for better or for worse' into the marriage vows didn't live in an age that anticipated gender hopping. She hasn't been allowed to see her son for three years and the picture jerks Alvin back to reality: families disintegrate.

His hostess appears in the doorway with a tray of biscuits and coffee. Three cups, though there is no sign yet of Donna.

'You disappeared early today,' she says, setting down the tray. 'Thought you'd have stuck around to lap up the glory. Everyone's talking about the Baby of the Bog. Why did you run off?'

As his hand hovers uncertainly over the biscuits (they are a little exotic and he is more at home with ginger nuts), he tells her about his suspension.

'What were you supposed to do?' she says. 'Let her die on the toilet floor while you fetched *appropriate* help?'

Alvin shrugs.

'You know, the only thing you did wrong was sending Curtis and Roland to get someone. You should have known you couldn't rely on them.'

'Who else was there?'

'Anyone but Curtis Young,' spits a new voice. 'The fucking *shit*.'

Alvin looks up at Donna who is standing in the doorway. Dressed now, she is giving the damp ends of her hair a vigorous towelling.

'He's not that bad,' Alvin says. 'A bit in your face at times, but –'

'He's a total shitbag,' she says, sitting down on the sofa beside Alvin. '*Lovely* shower, Lynette. Anyway, are you going to tell him about Curtis?'

'No, it's OK, it's not important,' Lynette says.

'Come off it. It's disgusting.'

'What's disgusting?' Alvin asks.

'Nothing,' Lynette protests, 'just a few snidey comments.'

'*Pur*-lease! Look, if you're not going to tell him, I will,' Donna says. 'She's been getting porn sent to her email at school. Tranny, lady-boy stuff. Hardcore filth. It's been going on for weeks.'

Lynette has turned as pink as her salmon-pink wallpaper.

'That's horrible. *Curtis*?' Alvin says. 'Can he even switch a computer on? How do you know it's him? Does it have his address at the top?'

'Don't be daft,' Donna scoffs. 'It's some bollocks Hotmail account, but it's Curtis all right.'

'How do you know?'

'Something he said the other day,' Lynette mumbles.

'Just goes to show what a prat he is,' Donna says. 'For the first time in his life he does something that requires skill and ingenuity, but he can't resist blowing his cover by crowing about it.'

'Have you reported it?' Alvin asks.

'She's not going to report it, is she?' Donna says, her voice rising in indignation. 'Can't you see how difficult this is for her?'

Alvin looks at Lynette, whose eyes are damp now. 'Sorry,' he mutters.

He is shocked for a few reasons. At Curtis, because he didn't think he had it in him – the spite or the IT skills. At Lynette, because she has seemed impervious to abuse – and there has been a stack of it. And at Lynette again, because, well, why didn't she confide in him? He's better placed than most to deal with Curtis and, more to the point, he thought he was her friend. He knew that she and Donna got along, but he didn't have them down as confidantes.

But he looks at them now. Though they are separated by a rug and a coffee table, there's a vibe. He feels suddenly foolish. And gooseberry-ish.

'I'll talk to Curtis,' he says. 'I'll make sure it stops.'

'You'd better,' Donna says. She looks at her watch and drains her cup. 'I'd best get off. I'm late. I told Guy I'd be home by six.'

As Lynette gets up and walks Donna to the front door, he feels foolish all over again. Nothing is going on. Donna is married, isn't she? To Guy. They have kids and everything.

'I'm really sorry about Curtis,' he says when Lynette comes back.

'It's not your fault, is it?'

'Yeah, but . . . Why didn't you tell me about it? He has been known to listen to me. I could have sorted it.'

'I haven't told you about a lot of things, Alvin.'

'Like what?'

'I saw you looking at Donna and me.'

'I . . . No . . . I wasn't . . . Was I?'

Though it has been plucked to within a hair's breadth of its life, Lynette manages to raise an eyebrow.

'It hasn't been going on for long, you know. Just a few weeks,' she says. 'But it had been heading towards it for a while.'

Alvin flaps his mouth.

'Well, what did you think? That I'd change my sex *and* my sexuality?'

'No . . . I,' Alvin flaps.

The truth is that he hasn't really thought about it at all, but somewhere, somehow he'd made the assumption that that was exactly what she'd done.

'I'm a lesbian, Alvin. Always have been. I was a lesbian the day I got married. I just didn't have the body for it. Look, I'm only telling you because you'd have worked it out. She's round here a lot.' Alvin must look confused because she adds, 'You're staying, aren't you?' with a glance at his bag.

Of course, he had been hoping, but he doesn't like to say. 'Thanks, but it's OK. I'll find somewhere –'

'No, you're staying. Until you sort out this mess with Karen. It'll be nice to have the company. I get scared on my own at night. Such a bloody girl, eh?'

Find me one millionaire who toils harder than a street sweeper, a potato picker, one of those miserable Honduran girls earning slave wages and daily beatings peeling tiger prawns for Marks & bloody Spencer

Alvin is sitting on a bench in Bennett Park. Not much of a park. A stretch of grass bordered on three sides by tatty terraces and by a skip yard on the fourth. He once read that London has more parkland than any other European city. He wonders if the surveyors counted Bennett Park, because really they shouldn't have bothered. In one corner stands a statue of a ring doughnut. Henry Moore. Kind of. Unable to afford the real thing, the council poured concrete into a mould taken from a tractor inner tube and called it 'The Circle of Harmony' or something.

In another corner iron railings contain some rusty swings, a slide and a climbing frame. A couple of mums huddle, depressed penguins that have lost the rest of their flock. Their toddlers let rip on the equipment, apparently oblivious to the fact that the wind comes direct from Siberia. And it is a fact. Two separate weathermen tried to infect Alvin with their excitement about it. He pulls his jacket around him and speculates that there is probably a man sitting on a park bench in Tomsk who is feeling a mite warmer than he is. He glances at his watch. Twenty minutes he has been waiting.

He'll give it another two, not a second more.

Five minutes later he spots Trevor Poll, peeking from a corner of the graffiti-camouflaged toilet beside the playground. The mothers spot him as well – and if they're considering performing their civic duty by calling the cops, Alvin wouldn't blame them. He wonders how long the solicitor has been risking arrest by hanging around public loos in close proximity to small children. The two women jump back, startled, as Poll bursts into the open and makes a diagonal beeline for Alvin. Alvin's heart sinks because as soon as Poll sits down beside him he too will become a suspected pervert. All over again.

'Been waiting long?' Poll asks as he sits on the far end of the bench.

'Long enough,' Alvin replies, his jaw aching from the cold. 'Why here?'

'You don't seem to realise the seriousness of the situation. Who knows if they're bugging my office?'

'That's a bit unlikely, isn't it?'

'You think the Birds got to where they are by playing fair? They're quite ruthless, you know. I represented a couple of the families on the Glenn Estate when the Birds were putting in the access road for the new houses they were building. Utterly merciless bastards. The Birds – not my clients.'

Alvin has a recollection of desperate protesters lying down in front of bulldozers. The three dozen 'country-style executive homes' accessed by a stretch of fresh black tarmac which travels between several severely shrunken gardens now stand as a permanent memorial to the protesters' lack of success.

'They use the law to snuff out the little man,' Poll continues. 'Do not underestimate them, Alvin, because today you are that little man.'

'Look, I've been thinking about this. Maybe I should just let them have the money,' Alvin says, having no wish to be bull-dozed either literally or metaphorically. 'I didn't even know Mrs Bird, and they were her family.'

'You're a nice chap and I suspected you might take this line. You've got to disabuse yourself of the notion that the Birds deserve this money.'

'Well, I know I'd want my kids to get whatever I can leave them. This money is theirs. They do deserve it.'

'Why? Because they're smarter than the rest of us? Because they've worked harder? I remember Jeremy Bird giving evidence during the Glenn Estate case. He was being particularly high-handed and our side's barrister asked him if he thought that having money entitled him to ride roughshod over the lives of others. You know what he said?'

Alvin shakes his head.

'*Yes*. He said *yes*! Absolutely it did! He claimed he'd worked damn hard for that money, and that earned him rights beyond the rest of us . . .

'The memory makes me spit. Jeremy Bird is like all rich men; he might sit at a walnut desk eighteen hours a day, but he doesn't know the meaning of hard work. Find me a single millionaire who toils harder than a street sweeper, a potato picker, one of those miserable Honduran girls earning slave wages and daily beatings peeling tiger prawns for Marks & bloody Spencer.'

Poll is coming on like a Baader-Meinhof revivalist, not a family solicitor. 'You feel strongly about this, don't you?' Alvin says.

'Damn right I do. Remember this: before the rich get rich they get lucky. Douglas Bird was your classic capitalist chancer dealt a royal flush. As for his kids, they merely lucked out in life's great gene lottery.

'Anyway,' he continues, his fury subsiding a little, 'whether or not you think the Bird children deserve the money, the point is that Louise Bird was of the clear opinion they didn't.'

'Why?'

'I brought this along.'

Poll reaches into a carrier bag and pulls out a small leather-bound photo album. He shuffles along the bench and hands it to Alvin.

'What is it?' Alvin asks.

'It was Louise Bird's. According to her will – and until a judge tells me otherwise – it's now yours. I found it in a hatbox when I went round to her flat to try and make sense of her accounts. Take a look.'

Alvin opens the album and leafs through it with numb fingers. Black and white photos going back to the fifties, judging by the clothes. Pictures of a happy, frolicking family, one lucky enough to holiday beneath palm trees long before the age of universal air travel. Alvin recognises one of the two children. Allison Bird-Wright may no longer wear circular skirts and white ankle socks, but she hasn't changed her hairdo in over forty years.

'This just makes me feel even less deserving,' he says. 'This is Mrs Bird's family. It's *their* money.'

'You're missing the point,' Poll replies. 'Where is Louise Bird? I'll tell you: in not one picture. Plenty of Douglas Bird. Loads of Jeremy and Allison. Not a single one of their mum.' He grabs the album back from Alvin and turns the pages until he reaches the one he is looking for. He thrusts it at Alvin, who looks at a snap of the children sitting beside their father on a picnic blanket. 'See this?' he says, pointing at the hacked edge on one side of the picture. 'It's been cut. *Cut*! I'll bet you Louise was in this photograph. The woman has been hacked out of her family's history with a pair of blunt scissors.'

'You can't say that for sure,' Alvin says. 'She might have cut it herself. Or it might have been a complete stranger in the picture.'

'Well, it's not the only one that's been doctored. There are plenty more like that. We're not dealing with a *normal* family here. Louise told me she hadn't spoken to her children since 1975, the year her husband died.'

'Did she tell you why?'

Trevor Poll shakes his head. 'She wouldn't elaborate and it wasn't my place to pry. I have picked up one little snippet in the last few days, though. Sandler Gonzalas has been the Bird family lawyer since the year dot. An old university mucker of mine used to work there. He fled the legal rat race a few years back. Runs a lovely little hotel in the Lakes. Delightful view of –'

'Can you get to the point? It's bloody freezing.'

'Is it? Must say I don't feel it with the beard. Anyway, I gave my chum a bell, just to see if he could supply me with any intelligence. I was more interested in the partners and their methods than anything else. He had something much juicier for me, though. Of course, he could be disbarred for telling me, but waking up every morning to a perfect view of Ullswater, I don't suppose he's too bothered . . .'

Alvin shivers ostentatiously.

'Yes, yes, the point: my friend was a junior at Sandler Gonzalas in the seventies and he just happened to be sitting in when Douglas Bird turned up to draft a new will. He'd just been diagnosed with an inoperable brain tumour. He was given no more than a year to live.'

'I thought he died in a car crash,' Alvin says, remembering the pictures of a crumpled Mercedes that made even the national papers.

'He did indeed, and if he'd hung around and let the tumour

get him, you probably wouldn't be sitting here now catching frostbite. When Bird sold his mail-order business, he used most of the proceeds to set up trusts for his children. That still left a considerable fortune, as well as the house, that under the terms of his existing will was bequeathed to his wife. The new will would have changed all that. He planned to disinherit Louise entirely. Luckily for her, it remained nothing more than a draft. He wrapped his car round that tree before he'd had a chance to sign it.'

'What was going on?'

'Who knows? My friend wasn't privy to the whys and wherefores. He did tell me Gregory Gonzalas advised Douglas Bird that, being a dependant, his widow would have had compelling grounds to contest the new will, but he was determined to go through with it. Something had driven a mighty wedge between Louise and her family and I'd dearly love to know what it was.'

The solicitor pauses, his eyes going to the small gang of teenagers that has arrived at the playground. The two mothers gather up their toddlers and flee as the four teens take over the swings, their too-long legs dragging on the ground.

'Some of your lot?' Trevor Poll asks, recognising the uniform. 'Shouldn't they be getting to grips with the rigours of the national curriculum?'

'Probably,' Alvin says, identifying Curtis, Roland, Debbie and Aaliyah Pratt, a girl on course for decent GCSEs and someone he wouldn't normally associate with the other three.

'I represented that girl once,' Poll says, looking at Debbie. 'Woolies did her for nicking a dinner service. She was ingenious *and* persistent – she did it plate by plate. Twenty-four pieces. They got her on the twenty-second. Scary mother as I recall . . . Incidentally, why aren't you at school today?'

'I've . . . er . . . I've been suspended.'

'Good grief! Why?'

'Oh, it's nothing. Storm in a teacup sorta thing,' Alvin mutters. 'It'll be sorted out in a few days.'

'Are you sure? These things can gain a momentum all of their own, run out of control like –'

'Really, it'll be fine.'

'Mr Lee, Alvin, you must be open with me. If I'm not to be handicapped as your lawyer –'

'Are you my lawyer?'

'You jolly well need one.'

'I can't afford one.'

'Oh, I won't be billing you until this mess is sorted out. And when it is, well, my fees will come out of the estate. Drop in the ocean. You won't even notice it, not after the chancellor has raped you for his inheritance tax.'

'What if it isn't?'

'Isn't what? Sorted out? Take a look at the sculpture over there.' He points at the concrete inner tube. 'Do you see the doughnut or the hole?'

Alvin shrugs, not sure what Poll is getting at.

'I'm a doughnut fellow, Alvin. Always the doughnut, never the hole.'

Alvin too has always been a doughnut guy. Lately, though, he has felt his toes touch the bottom of his previously unplumbed reserves of optimism.

'It's not just blind faith. I know what I'm talking about,' Poll says. 'I haven't always worked out of a backstreet office, you know. I started my career at Kingsley Napley.'

Alvin gives him a blank look.

'Flashy solicitors, much like Sandler Gonzalas,' Poll explains. 'Sir David Napley was the most famous lawyer in the land in his day. I carried his bags at the Jeremy Thorpe trial. A far cry from legal aid work for shoplifters.'

'What happened?'

'You say that as if defending shoplifters is second-rate.'

'No, not at all –'

'Frankly, I'd had enough of the rich 'n' famous. I'd had enough of the *superior* justice their money bought them.'

'You left on principle?' Alvin asks, quietly impressed.

'I wish it were so noble. Sir David sacked me. Questioned my commitment when he saw me on the *Nine O'Clock News*. I was on a Rock Against Racism demo.'

'That doesn't sound fair. Your politics are your business.'

'I was supposed to be in Surrey taking an affidavit from Elton John.'

'Ah.'

'I sued for unfair dismissal. Lost, of course. He wasn't the most famous lawyer in the land for nothing. Anyway, enough of my CV. Suffice it to say, I've been around. I know the law and I know all the stunts that Sandler Gonzalas are apt to pull.'

'What do your partners say about the case?' Alvin asks.

'Messrs Engle and Marks? Oh, they'd be in full agreement. I'll be honest with you, Alvin. When I was a child, I had an imaginary friend. Frodo. I was a hobbit head for my sins. These days I have a brace of imaginary partners.'

Alvin questions the wisdom of being represented by a solicitor with a dodgy CV and imaginary partners; a solicitor who, after the Glenn Estate fiasco, is already one down to the Bird family.

Poll pulls a cigarette from a pack and struggles to light it in the genuine Siberian gale. 'We have common interests, Alvin,' he says, 'and trust me, you'll need a lawyer. Especially when the Birds start to play dirty. Think of it as an alliance, a coalition. They might outgun us with their legal panzer divisions, but with stubbornness and low cunning we can repel them.'

'You're enjoying this, aren't you?' Alvin says.

'I'll pin my colours to the mast. I'm loving it. I know my profession is supposed to espouse dispassion and objectivity, but . . . To hell with it. The Birds are truly loathsome. I'd like nothing better than to stick it to the bastards.'

'OK,' Alvin says with just a little hesitancy, 'you've got yourself a client.'

'Excellent, excellent. We'll have to go through things in detail, of course. You'll have to tell me about this suspension of yours.'

'Why? It's got nothing to do with Louise Bird and her will.'

'All the same, I need to know. The Birds will be trawling for anything they can get on you. Even your children's library fines will be used against you, so I shudder to think what they might make of this suspension. Yes, I need to know. I've just had a thought. Allison Bird-Wright, she's got school governor on her list of titles – not one of yours, is she?'

Alvin nods. 'She's the chairwoman.'

'Not good. She'll have access to your file. Please tell me there isn't any dirt in there.'

'*No*. No, there isn't,' Alvin says. 'Anyway, she's a fair-minded woman as far as I know. She wouldn't do any . . .' He trails off as Poll's eyebrow scoots up his forehead.

'She may have married a Wright, Alvin, but she never dropped the Bird. Remember that.' The solicitor stands up, making to go. 'I'll gather my thoughts and we'll meet up soon. I'll be in touch.'

'Can we do it indoors next time?'

'Fair enough, barring an unexpected heatwave.' Poll turns to leave, but stops. 'You know, there's a delicious twist to this drama. The tree that did for Douglas Bird was on his own land. One of the big oaks lining the drive up to Beresford House. Apparently he'd wanted to chop down the lot. Reckoned they buggered his view of the trout lake. But they were over two hundred years old and were covered by a preservation order. You should make that tree a shrine to your good fortune. Once you move yourself and your family into that place, of course.'

Poll says the last bit with the glibbest of smiles on his chops;

as if Alvin getting the keys to the big house is a foregone conclusion; as if he'll have an actual family to move into it when he does.

He watches his lawyer leave the park via his preferred route, the public toilets. As Alvin stands up to go, Debbie spots him from her seat on the swing and gives him a little wave. He trudges across the muddy grass towards the playground, studying Curtis. He and Roland are huddled over Aaliyah, the two of them vying for her attention like a pair of commission-starved salesmen. As well as being clever and relatively studious, she is a pretty girl. For them, sex with Aaliyah Pratt would be a major result; perhaps even worth having to endure the intelligent conversation afterwards.

'Hi, sir,' Debbie calls out as he reaches the railings.

'What are you guys doing here?' Alvin goes for an authoritative tone. He stares at Curtis, who has kept his back to him.

'Just hanging,' Debbie says. 'It ain't the same at that dump without you. When you coming back? You don't look too ill to me.'

'Ill?'

'Mr Karadas told us you've got glandular fever or something.'

Clearly Alvin's immediate boss is toeing the party line. The party line, as ever, doesn't involve taxing the kids with the truth.

'What's glandular fever?' Debbie asks.

'It's like VD, innit,' Curtis cracks. Aaliyah blushes, but Roland throws his head back, hooting.

'If I had glandular fever, I wouldn't be out on a day like today,' Alvin says, ignoring Curtis. 'I've been suspended, Debbie.'

'*Suspended*?' she gasps. 'Why?'

'I'm surprised you haven't been asked about it yet.' Alvin is annoyed that Chadwick hasn't begun his inquiry.

Debbie looks at him blankly.

'It's about yesterday. He thinks I behaved inappropriately.'

'*Bollocks*! What's that supposed to mean?' she screams. 'Chenil was *dying*, man. You were *brilliant*. I'm gonna go and tell Chadwick.'

'Don't worry, Debbie. I'm sure he'll be asking you about it himself.'

'Well, I'll fucking tell him. No one else came to help, did they?'

'They might have if Curtis and Roland hadn't stopped off for a fag,' Alvin observes. 'You let Chenil down badly, guys.'

'We were just smoking one on the way, man,' Curtis protests.

'And we told Fat Stan, but he didn't believe us,' Roland adds.

'Fat fucking wanker,' Curtis says.

Alvin doesn't disagree. 'How are Chenil and her baby doing?' he asks.

'He's called Kanye Pharrell, he weighs three pounds, eight ounces and you're not allowed to touch him 'cause he's got all these tubes and wires sticking out of him,' Debbie reels off, as if reading from a press release. 'He's *dead* cute, sir. I mean, titchy and that, but – You should see him.'

'Maybe I will. How's Chenil?'

'Still freaked. Dead quiet.'

Like she's normally the life and soul.

'Maybe she could do with some support, Roland,' Alvin suggests.

'You wha'?' Roland asks gormlessly, his eyes widening and his mouth lolling open, suddenly turning him into the spit of his tiny infant son.

'Curtis, can I have a word?' Alvin says.

'Whassup?' Curtis asks.

'Over here,' Alvin adds, nodding his head towards the concrete doughnut. He turns away and Curtis follows him, taking a backward glance, checking out Roland who has moved in on Aaliyah as if he has acquired sole rights. Alvin gets his attention with, 'What's with all the nasty shit you've been sending to Miss Moorhouse?'

'What you on about?' Curtis asks, his face a picture of innocence, one that he has spent the best part of sixteen years perfecting.

'Don't give me that. The emails.'

'Dunno what you're talking about, sir.' The *sir* is revealing. It is the first time Curtis has used it on Alvin.

Alvin simply glares at him.

'*Honest*, I don't know about no emails or nothing,' Curtis protests. 'Anyway, I'm shite at computers. I wouldn't know how to send her porn and that.'

'Did I mention anything about porn, Curtis?'

'It wasn't me,' Curtis says weakly, the façade crumbling. Then: 'Look, it was only for a laugh and that.'

'A *laugh*?' Alvin spits. 'You're making her life hell.'

Curtis shrugs. 'So? It's just a fucking freak,' he mumbles. The words only just make it to Alvin without being whipped away by the gale. He puts himself in Curtis's face and pushes him up against the doughnut, pressing hard on his chest with his forearm.

'*It* isn't just some teacher,' he snarls. '*It* is a friend of mine.'

'Get your fucking hands off me,' Curtis says, struggling. 'You're not allowed to fucking touch me.'

'We're not at school now, are we? Anyway, I've been suspended. Now listen to me. Little shits who send obscene, *illegal* emails, they're the *freaks*.'

'Illegal?' Curtis's body stiffens.

'It's called hate mail. There's a law against it. Miss Moorhouse has kept a copy of every one you've sent and all of them can be traced back to you.' This is a lie. Alvin knows for a fact that Lynette has trashed the lot, most of them unopened. 'It's gonna stop, OK?'

'OK.'

'And you're gonna apologise.'

'*Apologise*?'

To Curtis the concept couldn't be more alien if it had four eyes and two antennae and had just landed after a gruelling journey across interstellar space.

'Like you mean it,' Alvin adds.

'OK,' Curtis whispers.

'Don't let me down again,' Alvin says, lifting his weight off him.

Curtis stays put, still in shock.

'You're a dark horse, aren't you?' Alvin says, holding his anger in now.

Curtis looks at him blankly.

'I never had you down as an IT expert,' he explains. 'You could do something good with that.'

As he turns to leave, he glances at the swings. Debbie, Roland and Aaliyah are staring at him. Their shock is understandable. Apart from stepping in to break up fights, it is the first time he has ever got even remotely physical with any of them. It's not as if he is leaving Curtis in a pulped heap, but here and now in the third millennium, more or less any hand laid on a pupil – whether in violence or tenderness – is designated Inappropriate, a fact that Alvin is already painfully aware of.

'You lot better get back to school,' he calls out as he walks away.

Outside the park he keeps up a brisk pace, partly because he wants to walk off the anger, but mostly because it is *cold*. He passes a lamppost sprouting with flowers. Bouquets have been strapped to it, announcing that close to this spot someone – probably a child – died. He can see a photograph buried amongst the blooms, but he maintains his pace, not wanting to look at it and feel saddened.

His mobile rings. He stops and looks at the display: HOME.

Karen!

Hope.

He quickly presses *answer* and puts it to his ear.

'Karen?'

'What the hell have you been up to, Dad?' his eldest daughter replies. It's the first time she has used the D-word in more than a decade.

'It's complicated, Mercedes. A couple of days ago Karen found –'

'I'm not talking about Karen,' Mercedes says. 'I'm talking about the cops. They've just been round to knock for you.'

D for Duh

'What did the police say?' Alvin asks.

'Nothing much,' Mercedes says. 'They just wanna talk to you about this mugging.'

'That's it? Nothing else?'

'Nothing else. Don't look so worried. I mean, they'll just want a witness statement or something.'

They are sitting in a café, sipping tea. Alvin wonders why the police want to talk to him about the mugging after all this time. Maybe the Birds have been doing some digging. Have the dirty tricks that Poll predicted started already? Alvin can hardly complain, though, can he? If he'd been a fully upright citizen, he'd have reported Kevan to the police months ago.

'It's not the cops that should be bothering you,' Mercedes observes, apparently reading his mind. 'It's Karen you want to worry about.'

'She's talked to you?'

'She didn't want to, but I made her.'

'What did she tell you?'

'Not much. That you'd saved an old lady from being mugged . . . just after you'd been to a knocking shop. What the hell have you been playing at, Alvin?'

'Nothing. It happened *once*.'

'Not what Karen said.'

Alvin hasn't got the energy to argue with her. 'Was she home when the police called?'

'No . . . Her train'll be pulling into Manchester about now.'

Alvin's heart sinks. Karen has never fled to her mum's before.

'What about the kids?' he asks.

'Took 'em with her. Took 'em out of school and everything. Lucky gits. You should've seen Sid. Thinks a train ride is better than space travel.'

Yes, Alvin thinks, he should have seen Sid. And Annie. And – despite the lack of a biological connection – Shannon too. 'When's she back?' he asks.

She shrugs. 'You've really screwed up, haven't you?'

Until two days ago, Karen and Alvin had never fallen out so badly for her to feel the need to put two hundred miles and the protective barrier of her mother between them.

'Having an affair with one of your pupils,' Mercedes says with a curl of a nostril. 'That's *sick*, man.'

'It wasn't an affair. And she wasn't a pupil any more.'

'Whatever,' she says with a dismissive wave, her mind already made up.

Alvin is used to being viewed with contempt by Mercedes, but only because that is how she looks at anyone over twenty. 'She should come with a recorded announcement,' Karen once quipped. 'Mind the generation gap.' This, though, is different.

'It happened once, Mercedes. *Once*.'

'Once, twice, a hundred times. Makes no difference, does it? Anyway, hope it was worth it 'cause it's lost you the best thing in your life. She was brilliant, you know. Smart, funny, kind . . . And she *got* me. My own mum doesn't get me.'

Weird. Only a couple of days ago Karen was dividing the kitchen in half with green paint. Alvin has never been sure of her take-no-prisoners approach to Mercedes, thinking it safer to indulge her as he and her mother do. But obviously they've been getting it wrong. Karen's direct method has made the more positive impression. Until now Alvin has never heard her say anything remotely complimentary about Karen and here she is eulogising her. In the past tense, which of course is the only way to eulogise.

'It's not *over*,' he protests. 'We'll get through this.'

Mercedes snorts. 'I could use Janice's favourite line now.'

As you sow so shall ye reap? Alvin shoots her a glare.

'I only said I *could* use it . . . Sorry, Dad, but this is a mess.'

There she goes with the D-word again; D for Dad; D for Disaster, Devastation and Despair.

'Like, *duh* –'

Oh, and D for Duh.

'– Didn't you realise all this would catch up with you?'

'It was a *one*-off. And why should I have realised? I didn't know who the hell the old woman was, did I? I didn't know she was a millionairess –'

'Stop, stop! What did you just say?'

'She was a millionairess. Karen didn't tell you?'

Mercedes shakes her head.

'She was one of the Birds,' Alvin explains. 'She named me in her will. That's why all this came out.'

'Jesus. What did she leave you?'

'The lot. Everything.'

'What's everything?'

'I don't know exactly. A few million. And a big house. With a trout lake,' Alvin says, repeating the answer he gave Karen a couple of days ago.

'*Jesus* . . .' Mercedes gasps. 'A few *million* . . . ? Wow! Maybe Karen's not as smart as I thought. I'd've stuck around if I was her. So, we're rich now, are we?'

'*We*? I take it you're sticking around, then.'

'Where am I gonna go? I've got my As coming up, haven't I? Talking of which, I've gotta go.' Mercedes gathers up her bag, which is stuffed with textbooks and a ring file, and stands up. 'Tutorial,' she explains.

'I've got to head off as well. Better go and see the police.'

'Aren't you supposed to be at school?'

'I've . . . been . . . suspended.'

'Suspended? Fuck! What've you done?'

'Believe it or not, nothing. I tried to get a pupil out of a pub, then I delivered her baby on the toilet floor.'

Mercedes drops back into her seat. 'Tell me, then,' she urges.

'What about your tutorial?'

'It can wait. Come on, out with it.'

She rocks back in her seat when he's finished explaining.

'You believe me, don't you, Mercedes? You know I haven't done anything . . . *inappropriate*.'

'Yeah . . . Yeah, I believe you,' she says after a moment. 'But – *fuck* – you haven't half been naïve.'

'Thanks.'

'Well, what were you thinking? You can't get that close to schoolkids without the world going ape. Good job they don't know about the massage place or you'd be out of a job already.'

Something Alvin hadn't thought of. Something else to add to his woes.

'Look, I've really gotta go,' Mercedes says, standing up again. 'Go and get the cops out of the way, but, honest, they're the least of your worries. You've got to focus on getting Karen back.'

'I think I might have a problem with the police,' Alvin says quietly. 'I knew the mugger.'

'You *knew* him? Jesus, this just gets worse and worse. Why didn't you turn him in . . . ?' She looks at her father's face, reads the guilt. 'Oh, I get it. It was outside the knocking shop, wasn't it? Well, do the smart thing now, for Christ's sake. Give him up, yeah?'

'I don't think I can do that.'

'Why the fuck not? You got some sort of Mafia code of silence going on? He's a mugger. Of old ladies. *Scum*.'

She has a point, Alvin thinks. Maybe he'd be doing society a big fat favour by grassing Kevan Kennedy up. But he knows that when it comes to the moment, he almost certainly won't be able to do it.

'Please, Dad, don't make things any worse for yourself.'

'I'll think about it . . . Thanks for coming to meet me. It's been good to talk about things.'

'Has it?'

He notes the look on his daughter's face, a mix of pity and . . . Is that revulsion? Would she rather not be seen in public with her sex-junkie dad? But in a rush she reaches over and hugs him.

'It's gonna be OK, you know,' she says. 'And whatever happens, stuff the lot of 'em. You're gonna be minted, aren't you?'

As she walks out of the café she turns and calls out, 'Hey, you can buy me a gap year now.'

Flowers, chocolates and lingerie

It's four o'clock when Alvin gets to Lynette's. He finds her in the kitchen placing flowers in a vase. More blooms cover the worktop beside her.

'Who are those from?' he asks.

'Curtis Young.'

'Curtis?'

'The sod gave me *five* bouquets. He was ever so humble as well. I don't know what you said to him, Alvin, but it worked.'

'Big time.'

He picks up a bunch of gladioli still in its cellophane wrapper and spots a little white card nestling among the stems. He plucks it out and reads it.

Sara – so cruelly taken but remembered for ever.

Not exactly *Ms Moorhouse, I'm deeply sorry for the pain and suffering I caused you,* but it's the gesture that counts, Alvin supposes as he slips the card into his back pocket. Wrapped around the bouquet's base is a length of the nylon string that originally held it fast to the lamppost outside Bennett Park.

'How was your day?' Lynette asks.

'Oh . . . fine,' he lies. 'Met my solicitor. Met Mercedes. Mooched.'

He doesn't tell her about his visit to the police. He told them the truth. Everything bar the name of the mugger. He decided it would be much more honourable to *persuade* Kevan to do the decent thing and come forward.

Ha, ha.

Now, with the slightly behind schedule arrival of hindsight, the notion of Kevan Kennedy even knowing a decent thing, never mind *doing* it, can be seen for what it is: pea-brained.

'Fancy something to eat?' Lynette asks. 'I'm making ratatouille for Donna and me, but there'll be plenty to go round.'

Alvin wonders if Donna ever eats with Guy and the kids these days. She's round a *lot*.

'No, I'm not hungry, thanks,' he says. He has no appetite for anything. He feels hopeless. He's usually someone who can see the bright side of anything. He's the man who stood with his suitcase outside a half-built hotel in Torremolinos and saw not a ruined holiday but much-needed paid employment for poor Moroccan labourers. Now, though, Alvin the Optimist is gasping in a corner of the ring, spitting blood and teeth into a bucket, while Life – a steroid-inflated heavyweight – waits for the bell and the chance to finish him off.

But he's not out. Not quite.

As Lynette rips the wrapping off another bouquet, he catches the sweet, punchy whiff of lilies and it acts like smelling salts wafted under his nose by some invisible corner man. He *can* turn this around. If he is capable of wringing a grovelling, floral apology out of a thug with the social grace of a horsefly, then surely *any*thing can be turned around.

'Mind if I nip out?' he asks.

'You need permission? I'm not your mum,' she says.

'I'll see you later, then. Won't be long.'

The three tower blocks flaking with decay and bristling with satellite dishes are silhouetted against the rusty sky. The sight of them reminds Alvin how depressing this place is – and also how scary. The Glenn Estate is not somewhere he would visit in daylight with any enthusiasm. The towers are just the centrepieces. Laid out at their feet are several streets of low-rise living, a mixture of flat-roofed maisonettes and thin-walled terraced houses.

The estate is a virtual no-go zone. Those who have to visit – social workers, meter readers, doctors – arrive in pairs. The police come mob-handed in Transit vans with heavy steel grilles poised to descend at the drop of a brick. The only people who enter alone are those unfortunate enough to live here.

And pillocks like me, thinks Alvin.

He turns up his collar, hunches his shoulders and sets off towards the towers. Here on the fringe of the estate he can't see a soul, but he can hear noise. An aggressive buzz that swells and fades on the gusting wind. Soon he sees them: five lads, their knees almost level with their ears, their backsides just a foot or so clear of the tarmac. They glide towards him on comedy motorbikes built for monkeys. From a distance it looks as if the clowns ran away from the circus to join a biker gang. Hard to believe that this is the latest menace to Decent Society, keeping neighbourhoods awake till dawn with the two-stroke soundtrack of Chav Britain, the Fuk-U Mix.

Recently the *Evening Standard* reported that the Glenn has the highest concentration of antisocial behaviour orders in London. Or as the paper's anonymous police source put it, 'Welcome to Asbo Central.'

Warily he watches the stunted bikers. They wear caps, hoodies, hundred-pound trainers and baggy jeans that will hang off their arses the moment they stand up; the uniform of a culture they've never seen first-hand, but one that is beamed in from outer space. He wonders what has happened to home-grown cults? The skinheads and the punks. Even – God forgive him for thinking this – the frilly, feathered new romantics. What is it with global gangsta chic? Even as the world becomes more anti America, it grows to resemble it.

The boys drone past, heading towards a Volvo that is inching along the road a hundred yards behind him. The car doesn't belong. Not lending itself to spoilers, skirts and under-body neon lights that paint black tarmac the pulsating colours of a Dannii Minogue video, Volvo isn't the badge of choice on the Glenn. But the bikers leave it be – for now – and swing around. They draw alongside Alvin, their machines wobbling as they eye him from beneath pulled-down peaks.

'What you doing here?' shouts the nearest boy, a junior border guard.

Alvin hopes that the gathering gloom masks his nerves. 'Just come to see someone,' he says.

'Who?'

'Kevan Kennedy.'

'You a cop?'

Alvin shakes his head. 'A friend.'

'He ain't dealing no more.'

'That's OK. I'm not buying.'

Interrogation over, the boy accelerates to, oh, all of fifteen miles an hour, sucking his friends along with him. Alvin is close to the foot of the nearest tower now. Kevan lives on the eleventh floor. The lift won't be working so he heads straight for the stairs.

Alvin's jellied legs step onto the landing where he's greeted by a swoosh. To his right the lift door slides open and a small woman burdened with carrier bags steps out. She looks at him suspiciously, but more out of what-kind-of-idiot-climbs-the-stairs? than recognition. It is, after all, nearly ten months since she punched him in the mouth.

'Hello, Mzzz . . . Nash,' he says. 'Is Kevan home?'

'Who are you?' she says, going to her front door and stopping outside.

'I'm Alvin Lee. I was his learning mentor at Wood Hill. We met when –'

'Haven't you lot screwed him up enough? What do you want now?'

'It's not school stuff. There's just something I need to see him about.'

'What?'

'It's kind of private.'

She curls a nostril and slips her key into the lock. 'I left him looking after his sister. That doesn't mean he's home, though.'

She doesn't invite him in, but she doesn't slam the door in his face either. She disappears into the kitchen at the end of the corridor. Against a backdrop of crashing cupboards she yells out, 'Kevan, your teacher's here . . . *Kevan*!'

Alvin steps into the flat and peers through the first open door. A baby sits on the carpet surrounded by shiny toys and the powdered contents of a box of Ritz crackers. A Sony plasma TV big enough to grace a small cinema plays host to a paused PlayStation game. The room is a sanctuary for brand names: Toshiba, Technics, Moulinex (though it's debatable whether the Master Chef Delicio can function at its best on a burgundy leather pouf). Alvin marvels at the tiny Bose speakers on extra-terrestrial stalks and thinks that, were it not for baby and crumbs, he could be in any branch of Comet.

Kevan's mother sweeps past him into the room. She scoops the child from the floor and sweeps out again.

'*Kevan*!' Very shrill now. 'If you've gone out and left Kelis on her own I'll bloody kill you.'

Alvin hears a door opening followed a beat later by a scream. It's hard to tell if it was generated by outrage or terror, so he leaps out into the corridor to see for himself. Kevan's mother is rooted to the carpet, the now crying Kelis clutched tightly to her. They are both staring through an open doorway. Alvin moves quickly to their side and looks into the room. Kevan is sitting on a single bed, headphones the size and shape of soup ladles cradling his ears and an unlit spliff dropping from his mouth.

There are a number of reasons why any mother might be

outraged. The drugs go without saying. Then there are the headphones thrumming with bass, never an aid to effective babysitting. And what about the mess? It seems likely that Kevan has ignored several injunctions to *tidy his room*.

But his mum would tick none of the above. She is staring directly at her son's chest. Not at the T-shirt he is wearing, but at the pink bra he is holding up against it. Beside him on the bed, mixed up with the scattering of CD cases, are knickers, camisoles and more bras.

Kevan looks at his mother, his saucer eyes for once doing the puppy-dog thing. It's a lost cause, though. She thrusts her child at Alvin and charges into the room. 'You filthy, disgusting . . .' she screams, immediately running out of fitting adjectives. She slaps her son across the head, knocking the headphones and the joint to the bed. Then, staring with fresh disbelief at the pile of underwear, she yelps, 'That's *mine*!'

Alvin thinks that perhaps now is a good moment to retire – this is, after all, a *family* moment. He takes the baby into the living room, from where he listens wincingly. It's very one-sided. Big Kevan meets his diminutive mother's fury with mumbled incoherence. Alvin recalls the first time he saw the two of them together. It was clear then who wore the trousers, a thought that suddenly takes on a new and unsettling twist.

Baby Kelis is still crying. Alvin sits her on his lap and attempts to distract her. He's out of practice, though. Her cries don't let up even when her mother whirls into the room, the pink bra in her hand.

'Get your hands off her,' she yaps, snatching the child from him. Still in shock, but attempting to bounce her daughter soothingly on her arm, she stares at him. 'This is *you*, isn't it?'

Alvin can only flap his mouth in reply.

'You said it was private,' she continues. 'Is this what you wanted to see him about? To swap knickers?'

'*No*, please, I had no idea –'

'Get out, you fucking pervert.'

'Look, Mrs Kenn— *Nash*, you're upset, but you're getting this wrong.'

'Get out!'

She's coming at him now. She may be holding a baby, but her left hand is free and he *knows* the punch it packs.

'Teachers. You're all filth,' she screams at his departing back.

He has been waiting in the tower's small lobby for ten minutes when the lift door slides open and Kevan stumbles out, now, thankfully, wearing a beefy black puffa jacket. He clocks Alvin and freezes. The sight of those gorgeous eyes red-rimmed with tears is heart-stopping.

He recovers quickly and heads for the exit, pushing past Alvin.

'Kevan, wait,' Alvin calls, following him.

'Fuck off.'

'Let's talk.'

'Fuck *off*.'

Kevan increases his pace, but stops dead when he sees the mini biker gang cutting bored loops around a pair of lampposts a hundred yards ahead. Alvin catches up and says, 'You need to talk to someone . . . I only want to help.' Kevan looks at him, his usually blank face taut with stress.

A minute later, in the black shadow of the tower block, they have found a low wall to sit on.

'Your mum'll get over it, you know,' Alvin says after a moment.

Kevan doesn't respond.

'That's what mums do,' he continues. 'They find out . . . all sorts of . . . *stuff* about their kids and, however upset they are, they always realise they still love them. She'll get over it, I promise you . . . Maybe not today, though.'

Kevan still can't speak. Alvin looks at him pityingly, knowing that his body has been colonised by flesh-eating shame.

'Do you want to see someone about this?' he asks. 'I mean, like someone professional. I could ask . . . You remember Pam Spottiswoode? She's the counsellor at Wood –'

Kevan has sprung from his seat and has a hand round Alvin's throat.

'You ever tell *any*one and I'll fucking kill you, yeah?'

The fact that Alvin has just seen Kevan cooing over something pink and satiny doesn't detract from his terror. Right now Kevan Kennedy is one hundred per cent max-strength Psychotic Man.

His hand slackens slightly at the sound of a two-stroke engine. As Alvin struggles for breath, his peripheral vision catches one of the mini bikers on the street thirty or so feet from the wall.

'You wanna hand, Kev?' he shouts.

Kevan lets his hand fall and shouts out, 'S'OK, man.'

The questioner shrugs before revving his engine and setting off again.

Alvin rubs at his neck while Kevan glares at him with undiminished menace. 'I wasn't planning to tell anyone,' he says. 'I just want to help.'

'Don't need no fucking help, right?'

'OK, whatever . . .'

'Anyway, I wasn't doing nothing,' Kevan says. 'I was just helping, yeah? With the fucking washing . . . Sorting it out . . .' His voice peters out. The explanation is a bit late in the day to be plausible and he knows it. All the same, Alvin feels a certain amount of respect for him; from someone like Kevan even an admission of helping out with the household chores is quite a breakthrough.

'My mum just gets stressed out about everything,' he concludes, standing up. 'Stupid fucking cow.'

'There's something else I have to talk to you about,' Alvin announces.

Kevan doesn't sit back down, but he doesn't move off either.

'It's about that mugging,' Alvin explains. 'I need you to come forward.'

'You wha'?'

'The police have had me in. They know I know you.'

'So? It was ages ago,' Kevan says, as if last year's crimes don't count.

'They suspect we were in it together.'

This makes Kevan smirk.

'It isn't funny,' Alvin snarls, momentarily forgetting that he's talking to the guy that just tried to strangle him. 'I could go to prison for refusing to name you. I've covered your arse plenty in the past, but you know what? I'm not prepared to get banged up for you.'

Kevan shrugs. 'Grass me up then, yeah? I'll just deny it.'

'I wasn't the only witness, was I? You'd be helping yourself if you came forward.'

Kevan looks at him as if voluntarily entering a police station, wrists outstretched for the handcuffs, is about as mad a notion as confessing to a therapist his curiosity for ladies' underthings. It crosses Alvin's mind that he has something on Kevan now – a satin and lace lever. It's a high-risk strategy. Threatened with blackmail, Kevan could just, well, *kill* him. Alvin wonders what the boy's preference would be: a murder conviction or being outed as a transvestite? But the speculation is short-lived. He was never any good at figuring the odds. Besides, he's not a natural-born blackmailer.

'Put it this way,' he says. 'I don't want to give you up, but if they're gonna charge me with obstructing justice or whatever, I won't have a choice.'

It's a statement of fact and as close as he'll ever get to a threat.

Kevan gives him another shrug. 'Maybe they won't do you.'

'I wouldn't bank on it. At least think about going to see them. As a favour to me.'

Alvin is pretty sure that appealing to Kevan's humanity is a waste of breath, so he's surprised when he says, 'Maybe . . . I'll think about it, yeah?'

'Thanks.'

Kevan sits down, reaches into his puffa and pulls out a box of Milk Tray.

'I'm fucking starving,' he says, tearing off the cellophane. 'Want one?'

'Yeah, why not?' Alvin runs a finger over the chocolates and picks out what he hopes isn't an Orange Truffle. 'Remember the Milk Tray Man?'

'The wha'?'

'This guy in the adverts. Wore black and delivered chocolates to his girlfriend. *All because the lady –*' He stops himself, not wanting Kevan to see an insinuation where none was intended. 'You always carry a box in your jacket?'

'They're my mum's favourites. She gets 'em in with the shopping.'

He pushes the box towards Alvin again, who takes a Strawberry Kiss and knows that in his maddest dreams he has never imagined the day he'd sit in the shadow of a tower block sharing chocolates with Kevan Kennedy. The moment doesn't last. Kevan stands up and tosses the box to Alvin. 'Gonna see wha's going on,' he mumbles. He ambles off, shoulders hunched, towards the sound of tiny bike engines.

Alvin decides that the day is ending better than it began. Very much in the credit column – and ignoring the fresh crimson swellings on his neck – he has discovered a hitherto undetected shred of decency in Kevan Kennedy. Something like the supposed life on Mars, it is extremely rudimentary, but its mere presence is worth getting excited about. Admittedly, the lad isn't exactly rushing off to the police station like a born-again boy scout – more likely moseying off to burgle an OAP – but he's *thinking* about it. And he clearly has a sensitive side, as evidenced by his taste in underwear and his preference for the soft centres. When Alvin arrived at the Glenn Estate, whatever good sense he still possessed told him that he was pissing directly into the Siberian gale. To leave the place not only physically intact, but also with a (kind of) result is the stuff that champagne celebrations are made of.

And that's exactly what he should be doing now: leaving, quitting while he's marginally ahead. But you'll have figured by now that if he did that, he wouldn't be Alvin Lee.

He watches Kevan join his mates, who are basking in a pool of sodium-orange streetlight, before turning and making his way back to the entrance of the tower. As he rounds the building's corner, he spots the Volvo parked beside a muddy stretch of open ground. He smiles to himself because it's still in possession of four alloy wheels.

Perhaps the world is turning into a nicer place.

Back on the eleventh floor he stands at the door and listens . . .

He can hear the TV and the sound of his own damp breath.

He taps on the door. He hears shuffling footsteps and Kevan's mum: 'That you, Kevan?'

'It's me, Ms Nash,' he replies, 'Alvin Lee . . . from Kevan's old school.'

A pause and then the door is flung open. Kevan's mother stands on the other side, looking less angry than earlier – or maybe just tired. Alvin hands her the chocolate box.

'You saw Kev, then?' she deduces.

Alvin nods.

'Look . . .' she says hesitantly, 'I lost it a bit earlier. I probably shouldn't've laid into you.'

It sounds unnervingly close to an apology. This isn't how Alvin was expecting things to go.

'That's OK,' he says. 'You were . . . shocked, I guess.'

She gives him a snort, then says, 'I remembered you after

you'd gone. You were there when they kicked Kev out of that school, weren't you?'

Alvin nods again.

'You were the only one that had anything decent to say about him. I laid into you then as well, didn't I?'

'It's not important now.'

'That's me all over: lash out, regret it later . . . Sorry.'

Definitely an apology that time.

'Do you mind if we talk for a minute?' Alvin asks.

She gives him a shrug and he follows her into the living room. Baby Kelis is parked back on the floor and is gazing upwards at the television. Jeremy Paxman is bullying answers out of a politician, though it's much too early in the evening for *Newsnight*.

'It's a tape,' Kevan's mother explains. 'Only thing that keeps her quiet. She hates cartoons, *Fimbles*, all that. Loves this bloke. Don't ask me why.'

'My little boy used to like that gardening programme,' Alvin says. 'I think it was the brass band music.'

'How many have you got?'

'Four.'

'*Four*. I can hardly cope with two. Anyway, you want to talk about Kev.'

'Er, yeah. He was very upset when I saw him downstairs.'

'So he bloody should have been. That was . . .' She doesn't have the words and sags into silence. Then: 'I don't get him no more. One minute he thinks he's 50 Cent, the next he's coming on like . . . bloody Lily Savage. I don't know what's worse.'

'He's a bit mixed up about things.'

'He's not the only one. What the hell am I supposed to do with him?'

'Go easy on him . . . I think. He probably won't want to talk about it –'

'He's not the only one,' she says again.

'But it might do him good to.'

'Talk to who? Me? I wouldn't know where to bloody start.'

'Yeah, I know, but it'd be good if you could somehow let him know you don't think any worse of him . . . He's scared of you, you know.'

'Bollocks he is. He's scared of no one. That's his trouble.'

'He's scared of *you*. I could see it the day you came into school with him. And he was scared when you walked in on him in his room.'

She gives him the snort again and flops down onto the hard leather sofa. She pulls the baby up onto her lap.

'Kevan's been out of control since he was smaller than her,' she says. 'Truth is, I've always been scared of *him*. I've never told anyone this, but . . . there are times I hate him for ruining my life . . .'

They're both silent for a moment and, along with little Kelis, watch Paxman apply an intellectual knee to a cabinet minister's metaphorical groin.

'Look, you're not alone in finding him difficult,' Alvin says at last. 'Every teacher who ever had to deal with him gave up – they're trained professionals, remember.'

'That fucking school,' she spits. 'You know he never said a word about that place while he was there. I used to ask him when he came home. *How was school today?* He just blanked me. It was like the place didn't exist for him.'

'I think we let him down at Wood Hill in the end.'

'You didn't. He used to talk about you . . . Not a lot, but sometimes.'

'There's a good side to him. I could always see that. He really was turning a corner when he got kicked out. He just needs someone to have some faith in him.'

'I'm running out,' she says. 'I think I'd better concentrate on not screwing this one up.' She hugs her baby tightly into her body.

'She's a lovely little girl . . . I'd better be going,' Alvin says.

'Thanks for coming back. I appreciate it.'

Alvin turns to leave, but pauses. 'Look, you could talk to someone about this, if you want. I know a counsellor.'

'A what?'

'She's like a therapist, I suppose.'

'A *therapist*!'

'Kind of.'

'A *shrink*?'

She looks at him aghast and he readies himself for the tell-my-business-to-a-stranger?/you-calling-me-mental? onslaught.

'I'd . . . *love* to,' she says at last. 'Jesus, I'd *love* that.' Then: 'How am I supposed to afford a bloody therapist?'

You could sell the plasma screen, one of the two DVD players, the Bose speakers . . . Alvin thinks.

Alvin reaches into his pocket and pulls out his wallet. He finds Pam Spottiswoode's dog-eared card and gives it to her.

'Here's her number anyway,' he says. 'Just in case.'

She looks at it a little wistfully. 'I don't know why you give a damn,' she says. 'Kevan's left Wood Hill now. He's not your problem no more, is he?'

But of course she's wrong about that.

Dear Mr Lee

The following Monday Alvin is standing at a door beside a sweet shop just off All Saints Road. Next to him his solicitor fumbles with a bunch of keys.

'I shouldn't be letting you come here, you know,' Poll says.

'So why are you?' Alvin asks.

'Had that gleam of mischief in my eye ever since the Birds declared war.'

Within a minute they are in the damp gloom of a living room. Poll flicks at a light switch to no effect. 'Meter needs change,' he mutters. He jangles coins in his pocket and disappears into the hall. A moment later the lights come on and Alvin takes in his surroundings, a room furnished with castoffs from other homes. There's nothing of Louise Bird here. Nothing personal. No photos or any of the knick-knacks usually accumulated with age. There's no stamp of wealth either. But what was he expecting? Van Gogh's daffs on the wall?

'Doesn't the landlord want the place back?' Alvin asks Poll.

'I'm sure he'd love to have it back, but Mrs Bird had paid rent to the end of the year. Not something the old generally do – mindful of the odds of seeing out any given year, I suppose. But she didn't have the usual financial constraints . . . Talking of constraints, you should know that the Birds have lodged a Caveat with the Probate Registry.'

Alvin returns the statement with a blank stare.

'In effect, formal notice that they're disputing the new will . . .'

Alvin is glazing over already. Legalese has this effect on him. Fortunately Poll doesn't indulge too often.

'The next stage is that we lodge a Warning to the Caveat and . . . You're glazing over. I'd better get on.'

The solicitor has come to hunt for paperwork that might lead to any undiscovered bank accounts and investments.

'No time to waste,' he says. 'Whether or not you end up with the lucre, the Revenue wants its pound of flesh and it wants it now. Fiscal necrophilia, if you ask me. I'm a classic social democrat on most matters, but I'm monsterishly Tory when it comes to death duty.'

He starts with the pine chest against the wall, pulling out the drawers and tipping the contents onto the small dining table.

'Mrs Bird furnished me with an exhaustive schedule of her affairs,' he goes on. 'But when you've got millions squirrelled away, it's all too easy to forget the odd fifty grand here and there, isn't it?'

Alvin wouldn't know about that. 'Do you want a hand?' he asks.

'It wouldn't be advisable. Why don't you have a mooch; get to know your benefactor?'

Alvin sets off and finds himself in the tiny kitchen. He looks in the cupboards. A few cans, but no caviar or *foie gras*. Just soup, sardines and a half-eaten pack of Viscount biscuits. There are teabags in a tin caddy and he thinks about making himself a cup, but there's no milk.

Now that he's here he wonders – not for the first time – why someone rich enough to fill up a pool with ten-pound notes and swim in it chose to live like this; an old lady eking out her pension on no-label tins and thanking heaven for the winter fuel allowance. She had a home with twenty-five rooms and a driveway lined with protected (and lethal) oak trees. And let's not forget, *a trout lake*. Yet she walked away, giving Jeremy Bird and his family the freedom of Beresford House – though not, apparently, the deeds.

Did she leave voluntarily? Did her son throw her out? How can you be evicted from your own home? He can only come up with one plausible explanation: Louise Bird was bonkers. Ergo he isn't entitled to a penny of her money and he has no business rooting through the entrails of her life.

The thought doesn't prevent him from wandering across the corridor to have a root in the room opposite. It's unfurnished apart from a desk and a chair. The desk is new. Alvin decides she must have bought it herself. Well, she'd have wanted something smart to act as a plinth for her 20-inch iMac.

He is astounded. Old lady plus spacey information technology does not, well, compute. It's like seeing a mini-skirted blonde shopping in a Tehran bazaar – just plain *wrong*. Alvin only knows what the machine is – that it's a computer at all – because Mercedes once showed him a picture in a glossy Apple brochure, arguing with righteous conviction that the premium-priced rig was all she required to make her life complete.

He sits down in the chair and stares at it. Despite a layer of dust, the flat monitor still exudes Californian cool. What did Louise Bird *do* on it? Play patience perhaps – that's how old ladies fill their time, isn't it? Or did she surf the Net? . . . For what? He'd love to find out.

He isn't all that comfortable with computers – he hardly uses the one at home and struggles with the battered municipal models at Wood Hill – but he does know that, like most things that run on electricity, there's usually an on switch. At first, he's at a loss, but just as he's beginning to assume that this particular model must be powered by voodoo magic, he finds something that looks promising at the back of the monitor. He presses it tentatively, then starts as the the machine comes alive with a soothing *bong*.

A minute or so later he is staring – none the wiser – at a screen decorated with funky little icons. He wishes Mercedes or even Shannon was with him. Both of them would be unfazed now. They'd be up and running at full pelt, scooting around some uncharted digital universe, while he feels his age and wonders if he should pop a travel-sickness tablet.

'Ah, you got the damn thing switched on,' says Poll, who has arrived silently at his shoulder. 'More than I could manage.'

'What did she do on it?' Alvin asks.

'Write bodice-rippers for Mills & Boon? Your guess is as good as mine.'

Alvin rests a nervous hand on the mouse and moves the pointer aimlessly around the screen.

'Look at that!' Poll exclaims.

'What?'

'That.'

The solicitor points at a Word file in the corner of the screen. Alvin jumps in his seat, as if he's turned a corner and been confronted by his own reflection in an unexpected mirror. The caption beneath it reads *ALvin LEE.*

'Well, don't you want to take a look?' Poll suggests.

'I . . . suppose.'

Alvin presses down on the mouse. Nothing happens, so he repeats the action twice, quickly, at which a centre-screen banner makes the perfunctory announcement that Microsoft Word is starting up before making way for toolbars and a document window.

'It's a letter, by the looks of it,' Poll says.

Yes, a letter to me, Alvin thinks. He reads on:

Dear Mr Lee,

You will almost certainly have no idea who I am, but I wanted to write and express my thanks to you. I am

'She didn't get very far,' Poll says, leaning forward and peering hard at the screen. 'Look at the date. Jan. seventh.'

'Is that significant?'

'The day she died. Must have been what she was up to when she breathed her last. She passed away in that very chair . . .'

The solicitor looks at Alvin's whitening face.

'Didn't I tell you?'

'No!' Alvin yelps, on his feet now. 'No, you bloody didn't.'

'Her home help found her in here staring at the screen.'

'With that letter on it?'

'With nothing on it. The computer was off. The meter had run out. She'd been dead a couple of days.'

Alvin feels queasy and more than a little sad. He'd like to leave.

'Are you done with your paperwork?' he asks, edging towards the door.

'Another fifteen, twenty minutes. Why don't you make us a cup of tea?'

'There isn't any –'

'Milk? In my briefcase.'

Five minutes later Alvin is back in the living room with two steaming mugs. Poll is at the dining table, papers scattered before him.

'It's a mystery,' Poll says, looking up from a bank statement.

'How do you mean?'

'It's a matter of record that, apart from the house and furnishings, Douglas Bird left his wife thirty-three million in investments, equities and cash. Yet that seems to have dwindled to just over five million by the time she died.'

'He did die thirty years ago. She must have just blown it.'

'That's a lot of money for a single woman to get through, even in thirty years. Besides, do you see the signs of extravagant spending?'

He's got a point, Alvin thinks. The flat is hardly shimmering with bling.

'Maybe that's why she lived like this,' he suggests. 'You know, maybe she cut back because she'd been going so wild.'

'She was hardly destitute. The money she had left would have bought her a lot more comfort than this. No, I don't get it at all.'

'What about her bank statements? Don't they tell you what she was spending it on?'

'They might well do if I had them. She only kept her most recent ones and they tell me little more than that her pension was paid by direct credit and she was up to date on her gas bill . . . It's a mystery, Alvin. I suppose we should have a trawl around her computer. See if there's anything on there . . .'

Alvin is in no rush to return to the dead woman's chair.

Poll's attention returns to the statement. 'Do you fancy having a root round that machine of hers while I finish off?' he asks.

'Do I have to?'

'Well, it would make sense.'

But without warning the flat is plunged into darkness and Alvin feels salvation in the gloom.

'Damn the bloody meter,' Poll says. 'Used up the last of my coins. You don't have any spare, do you?'

'I'm afraid not,' Alvin says, grateful for once for being broke.

One of those things you get on the beach in hot places . . . You know, that you sit on and pedal out into the sea

Alvin hugs the phone to his ear, waiting for the words, 'Hello, Jackson residence,' which is how Karen's mother always answers. He has been ringing two or three times a day since Karen took the kids to Manchester a week ago. Frances Jackson has taken it upon herself to screen all calls. He spoke to her the first few times, but even plaintive begging didn't pierce her armour. If she'd told him once, she'd told him plenty: KAREN WAS NOT GOING TO SPEAK TO HIM. Now he hangs up when she answers.

Frances has always been sniffy about Alvin. At first it was a Music Biz Thing. She firmly believed that anyone who played a guitar that ran off the mains must be a sickening hybrid of Keith Richards and Axl Rose. The pisser is that if Alvin had enjoyed even a fraction of their success he could have lived with her disapproval. By the time he and Karen got together, his performing career was pretty much in a persistent vegetative state, waiting for someone to take pity and switch off the life support. When he finally cut his losses and moved into education, he thought things might improve, Frances having once been a primary school headmistress and all. But of course he's not a proper teacher – Karen might as well have taken up with a dinner lady.

He counts the rings – ten so far – and he's about to give up when it's answered. 'Hi, you have reached Granny Fran's house. How can I help?'

'Annie!'

'Dad!'

'*Annie*, how are you doing? I miss you.'

'We're playing in the garden. Sid fell off the birdbath.'

'Is he all right?'

'I think so. *Such* a crybaby. Are you coming to see us?'

'I don't know. I want to.'

'Guess what. I can play "Janie's Got a Gun"! . . . F . . . G . . . C . . . F . . .'

As she recites the chords, Alvin feels proud and desperately lonely all at once. Strangely amused as well – Frances must be seriously unnerved by the sight of her granddaughter turning into Aerosmith.

'That's fantastic, Annie, brilliant.'

'Daddy, what's a pedalo?'

'It's one of those things you get on the beach in hot places . . . you know, that you sit on and pedal out into the sea . . . Why?'

'Shannon phoned up Cherry and Cherry said her mum said you're a pedalo . . . I don't get it.'

But Alvin does and he feels panicky-sick. 'I don't know what she means,' he says. He can hear Sid whimpering and grown-up voices in the background. 'Annie, is Mum there?'

'Who's that, Annie sweetheart?' Frances's muffled voice asks.

'It's Daddy, Granny, it's *Dad*—'

'I want you to stop calling,' Frances's voice barks angrily into his ear.

'You can't stop me talking to my kids, Frances.'

'You shouldn't be allowed anywhere near your children. To think that someone like you can get a job in a school. It defies belief.'

'This is ridiculous. I haven't –'

'Don't bother phoning again. I'm having the number changed.'

After a click, all Alvin can hear is silence: a void big enough to contain every last one of his worst nightmares.

Puffy Dogg

'I'm very disappointed, Jonathan,' Mr Sugden says, sounding even more disappointed than his usual disappointed.

'I'm sorry,' Jonathan mumbles.

'What on earth came over you?'

'I thought she was going to hit me. It was self-defence.'

'She was *thirteen*, for goodness' sake. And she was only picking up your tape measure . . . And things had been going so well.'

He's right. Things have been going swimmingly. Jonathan Craig, former schoolteacher, has taken to the gentlemen's outfitting business like a born gentleman's outfitter. He has proved adept with the tape measure and his eyes have quickly attuned to the subtle variations of grey that form the Sugden palette. His assimilation into the world of (old) menswear has been eased by the shop's quietness. Sugden & Son sees an average of six customers a day, and rarely one younger than fifty. Jonathan doesn't exactly love the job, but he has stopped jumping every time the shop bell rings and at home he has managed to sleep two dreamless nights on the trot. Even the rash is receding. By that reckoning, Sugden & Son represents a sound career move.

Yes, things had been going just fine until the video started to beam down from the MTV satellite and the accompanying flyposters went up all over the borough. One of those rappers – Puff Doggy, Snoop Daddy, Jay-CB, whoever – surrounded by a platoon of gyrating women with globular backsides and jelly-mould breasts, dressed only in thongs and white string vests. That's right, suddenly string vests are back and who has the borough's widest selection? Why, Sugden & Son of course – at least until Topshop gets its act together. And like fruit flies homing in on a bucket of rotting apples, teenage girls have been zeroing in on the last shop in Britain still taking manual credit card imprints.

For Jonathan the last two days have been a return to the hell that was Wood Hill. A trip down Memory Lane – that being the street it's inadvisable to visit on account of its population of muggers, rapists and assorted psychos.

This morning things came to a head. Jonathan, twitchy as a Mexican jumping bean, found himself alone in the shop surrounded by half a dozen hormonal truants in search of that newly *buzzin'* foundation garment, the string vest. The one that approached him from behind proffering his dropped tape measure was only trying to help, but how was he to know that? She could have been holding anything in that outstretched hand.

Well, perhaps he was a bit hasty. Perhaps he shouldn't have spun round and slapped her.

'You made her cry,' Mr Sugden bleats. 'Her cheek came up crimson. I'll probably have her mother round here playing hell. Or the police.'

'I'm sorry, I'm truly sorry,' Jonathan murmurs. 'It won't happen again.'

'You're right about that, young man, it won't.'

Jonathan looks down at his feet.

'It's not going to work out,' Sugden continues. 'I think you'd better go.'

'But . . .' He trails off. Resistance is futile.

'There's one other thing,' Sugden says as Jonathan turns to leave. 'I really didn't want to say anything, but maybe you should get the doings on your face seen to. I think it's been putting off the customers.'

Don*t call me Baz

Alvin is back at Wood Hill for the first time in eight days. The nausea has grown worse since Karen's mother slammed the phone down. He has had a couple of hours to churn things up into a rich mix of calamities, which now sits in his stomach like a hunk of uncooked dough.

He walks through the school's deserted precincts. The kids are in lessons. Maybe it's his imagination. Maybe they're not staring at him through classroom windows and seeing a sleazebag. But he didn't imagine what Annie told him. He's a *pedalo*; Shannon's best friend Cherry says so. Cherry is in her first year at Wood Hill, a place where rumour spreads as easily as margarine, and in the process mutates as lethally as Chinese chicken flu (before travelling up the M6 and exiting at junction 20 for Granny Fran's house).

As he reaches the ILD block, his phone vibrates. He pulls it from his pocket and reads Mercedes's text.

GD LUK
C U L8R

It gives him his first smile of the day. He writes a reply.

thx

He's not good at the texting thing, but it's close enough to *thanks* to send.

In the staff office only the school counsellor is there, shuffling papers on a desk. Good old Pam I'm-here-to-listen-not-to-judge Spottiswoode.

'Hi, Pam.'

'Sorry, Alvin, I've got to get these pictograms copied pronto. Catch you later,' she says, grabbing the first binder that comes to hand and fleeing.

Yup, thinks Alvin, *I'm doomed.*

But how has he become such a pariah? he asks himself. He can explain everything that has happened. As Mercedes pointed out, his worst crime is naivety, which isn't even a crime.

He sees the answer on the desk that Pam has just fled. Part hidden beneath a stack of books, the *Gazette*. He pulls the paper free and reads the headline: MUGGED FOR HER MILLIONS? Beside it is a picture of Louise Bird, younger than she was when Alvin saved her life. Below her is a picture of him, the mugshot that appears on his laminated Wood Hill ID card. Taken in a photo booth, Alvin's attempted smile came out as a lopsided leer that showed off an elongated, fangy eyetooth. It never bothered him so long as the image remained tucked away in his wallet, but now that it's on page one of the local rag . . . Jesus, he looks like a low-rent vampire. How did the *Gazette* get it? Well, there's a file copy in the school admin office. And who might have access to his file? Allison Bird-Wright, as Trevor Poll pointed out. The caption below the picture reads 'Have-a-go hero?' The paper's subs appreciate the suggestive power of question marks.

He sits down and skims the story. It contains little fact and much supposition – enough to make sure he'll no longer have a job come lunch time. He feels sick and he's glad he set off without breakfast. Before he reaches the end, his phone vibrates again. It's a call this time.

'You seen the *Gazette*?' his lawyer asks. He doesn't sound too thrilled.

'Look, it's nothing like they've written it.'

'You *knew* the mugger?'

'Yes, but –'

'And you'd just come out of that seedy bloody cathouse?'

'Yes, but –'

'And why am I finding this out along with the rest of the borough?'

'It didn't seem . . . relevant.'

'*Every*thing's relevant,' Poll explodes. 'What did I tell you? Your parking tickets are relevant. Bird's an unscrupulous bastard. Worse, he's the unscrupulous bastard who owns the local paper. By the time he's through, he'll make you look like Ian Brady's evil twin.'

He's already made a pretty good start, Alvin thinks.

'As your lawyer, it's my job to give you the benefit of the doubt, Alvin,' Poll continues, calmer now. 'I'm presuming what this story implies isn't true.'

'What, that me and the mugger set her up? It's ridiculous.'

'But you knew him.'

'I had no idea who *she* was, though. We didn't pre-plan it.'

'Well, faking a mugging . . . It seems rather implausible. You'll have to talk to the police, you know.'

'I already have.'

'Of *course* you have,' Poll says, bubbling with fresh indignation. 'Why would you have mentioned it to *me*? After all, I'm only your *lawyer*.'

'Look . . . It just didn't seem –' He is about to say relevant, but he stops himself – *every*thing is relevant. 'Sorry . . .'

Basil Karadas comes into the room. He gives Alvin an abject look. He has a rolled-up copy of the *Gazette* sticking out of his jacket pocket.

'I have to go,' Alvin tells Poll, as he watches Karadas disappear into his small office. 'I'm at school. I've got things to sort out here.'

'You'd better call me later. We've got plenty to sort out ourselves. By the way, something else you didn't tell me about.'

'What's that?'

'Your lurid rock 'n' roll past. I'll talk to you later. *Phone* me.'

Perplexed, Alvin pockets his phone. He stands up and peers through the small window in the door of his boss's cubby. Basil Karadas's body is squeezed into the narrow gap between desk and wall. He's a fat man, but in mitigation his office is compact. Alvin opens the door and slips inside.

'Sit down, Alvin, make yourself . . .' Karadas trails off, not wishing to travel too far down the road of conversational niceties.

As Alvin flops onto a chair, Karadas pulls the *Gazette* from his pocket and lays it on the desk. 'Faking a mugging so you can charm an old lady out of her millions,' he says. 'It's un*real*.'

'It *is* unreal,' Alvin replies. 'It didn't happen.'

'It says it did here,' Karadas says, jabbing the story with his stubby finger.

'That's what it *implies*.'

'It says an eyewitness reckoned you knew the mugger. "He was talking to him as if he knew who he was." It says so here.'

'Yeah, but . . . Look, that doesn't mean we planned it. I can't believe this. I stopped an old lady from getting hurt. I did the right thing and now I'm being dragged through the shit for it.'

'What about the massage parlour? Kelly Hendricks worked there, didn't she?' Karadas shakes his head.

'It wasn't like that, Baz. I went to persuade her to go back to college.'

Karadas reads from the paper again. '"Roberta Nelson, receptionist at the Tropica and witness to the incident, said Lee was a *regular* customer."'

'I went *twice*. Just to talk to Kelly. I haven't done anything wrong.'

'Visiting a massage parlour isn't nothing. Going to the pub with Chenil Shakespeare isn't nothing.'

'I didn't *go* to the pub with her. She came in, I got her out of there . . . How many times do I have to explain?'

'Tony Rowell reckons you were all over her. And what about the massage place? What the hell were you thinking?'

'I went to talk to her.' The lie stings, but he repeats it. 'Just to *talk*.'

'You could've met on neutral turf. A café, a park bench . . . It's about how things *look*, isn't it?' Karadas says. He leans back in his chair. 'You've always been close to the kids,' he says.

'Your point being?'

'Distance is important.' Karadas tugs at the hairs in his little black goatee. 'A line has to be drawn. It's about behaving *appropriately*.'

'All these kids have ever had in their lives is *distance*. Their parents can't be bothered with them, their teachers hate them. If we don't get close to them . . . I thought this job was about forming relationships.'

'*Appropriate* relationships.'

Alvin tenses. If he hears that word – *appropriate* – one more time he'll . . .

'There's always been gossip, Alvin,' Karadas adds.

'Well, *yeah*. This is a *school*, fifteen hundred kids, a bunch of teachers with nothing better to do. You should hear what the kids say about you.'

'*What*?' His boss is worried. And so he should be; he's bone idle, lardy and permanently moist with sweat, and, well, kids can be so cruel.

'Just . . . *gossip*, Baz. That's the point. You can't convict on gossip.'

'Yes, but people were talking about you and Kelly Hendricks when she was here, and now it turns out you've been visiting her in a . . .' Karadas shrugs and holds his palms upwards, as if the court of Wood Hill opinion has already reached its verdict and there's nothing he can do about it.

'How long have we worked together?' Alvin asks. 'Seven years? You know me. You must know I wouldn't take advantage of the kids.'

He stares at Karadas, willing him to meet his gaze. He doesn't.

'It's about how things *look*, Alvin. And all this lairy rock star stuff . . .'

'What rock star stuff?'

'You haven't seen it?' Karadas slides the *Gazette* across his desk towards Alvin. 'They've really pushed the boat out on you today. Centre pages.'

He opens the paper. Across the spread a slab of type spells out MUGGER'S PAL IS THE ANACONDA. And should he, by chance, be in any doubt as to who this serpentine friend of street thugs could be, there's a fuzzy picture beneath. Two decades old, it shows Alvin in his mulleted prime, a chart-bound bass player. He isn't alone. Perched – *juxtaposed* if you will – on his lap is a girl with Chrissie Hynde cheekbones and big Carol Decker hair. The caption beneath reads 'Lee with teenage groupie'.

Alvin runs a trembling fingertip across the text, picking up nuggets as he goes. 'He was the wild man.' . . . 'You should have seen him in Belfast. He made those Irish chicks forget their "troubles".' . . . 'He had very high standards. I don't think any of them ever got more than a seven.' . . . 'After the Manchester gig even Hutchence couldn't keep up with him.' . . . 'Sure he liked them young.' . . . 'He always checked their ages, though. He was a proper gentleman like that.'

So nice of Jamie to add that last bit, Alvin manages to think between deafening palpitations, so fucking *considerate* of him merely to brand him a slobbering sex monster as opposed to a slavering paedophile.

'This is bullshit,' he gasps.

'C'mon, you were in a group. Sex, drugs, rock 'n' roll . . .'

'It's *bullshit*.'

'Why would they print it? No smoke without fire. And they've got a photo, a *teenage groupie*.' Karadas pulls the paper back across the desk and squints at the picture. 'Could just be the angle, but she looks pregnant as well.'

'She was,' Alvin confirms.

Karadas winces.

'She's not a *teenage groupie*, Baz. She was twenty-three.'

'Even so, she –'

'She's *Janice*, for Christ's sake, Mercedes's mum . . . We went out with each other for five bloody years.'

Karadas shrugs. 'But it all mounts up, paints a picture.' He checks his watch. 'We'd better get over there.' He's talking about the hearing that will shortly decide that, no, Alvin doesn't have a future in education.

'What about a union rep?' Alvin asks, panic rising. 'That's why I came in early: to talk things through with someone from –'

'Yeah, well, the thing is no one from Unison wants to touch it.'

'But I'm entitled to –'

'It's the nature of the allegations. No one wants to be associated with . . .' Karadas trails off.

'You can't even say it, can you?' Alvin shouts. 'It's not called *inappropriate* behaviour. It's child abuse. I can fucking say it because I haven't abused anyone.'

'That's exactly the kind of inappropriate outburst we're talking about,' Karadas says, suddenly sounding like a schoolteacher.

'I'm sorry . . . Look, I may have been naïve, but I haven't done anything wrong . . . You know that, don't you?'

His boss doesn't reply as he hauls himself to his feet, squeezes past Alvin and heads out of the room.

They walk in silence until, halfway across the basketball

courts, Karadas says, 'You're not the only one in trouble round here. Seems to be a rash of it.'

'What do you mean?' Alvin asks.

'Remember that pasty little English teacher we had last year? Crane or Craig or something, first-jobber, didn't last long.'

Alvin has a dim memory of a teacher walking out on the job mid-term, though he has no recollection of the man. 'What about him?' he asks.

'He's been working in some clothes shop off the High Street. A bunch of year eights were down there this morning. He assaulted one of them. Completely unprovoked, apparently. Anyway, her mum's gone mental. Should think the police will be having him.'

'Well, at least Wood Hill can't fire him for it,' Alvin says grimly.

'You'll get a fair hearing, you know,' Karadas says. 'Chadwick is nothing if not reasonable. And the chair of governors is turning up to ensure fair play.'

Fucking well doomed, thinks Alvin.

'Didn't know you gigged with INXS,' Karadas says after a moment.

'Neither did I, Baz,' Alvin replies. 'Must've been off my head on drugs.' As his boss's heavy eyebrows creep up his forehead like a pair of sidestepping caterpillars, he adds, 'I was *kidding*.'

'I just don't know any more, do I?' Karadas says. 'By the way, best to keep things formal in there. Best you don't call me Baz.'

As he heads for the school gates, Alvin is thankful that it's not quite three thirty and the buildings have yet to spew out fifteen hundred demob-happy children. If he keeps up a brisk pace, he should just about beat the bell. A figure is stomping across the grass towards him. Colin Stanislavski is possibly the last man he wants to talk to, but if he walks any faster he'll be jogging and how would that look? As Basil Karadas kept reminding him, isn't that what matters?

Stanislavski falls into step beside him and says, 'Just wanted to let you know I'm sorry, Alv.'

'Get lost, Colin.'

'Seriously, mate, I know I've joshed you a fair bit in the past, but I've always thought you were trying to do your best with the drongos.'

'So is that why you were in there speaking up for me just now?' Alvin snaps. 'Oh no, silly me. You weren't there, were you?'

'Hardly my place, was it? But look, a load of us were rooting for you. Us male teachers are stuffed these days. You can't stick a friendly arm round a pupil without the PC mob running you out of town.'

This is rich. Stanislavski isn't famous for friendly gestures – tactile or otherwise – towards schoolchildren. Alvin doesn't respond.

'You'll be OK, Alv,' Stanislavski says, sounding sincere enough. 'A bloke of your talents, you'll bounce right back. I mean that. Keep the faith, yeah?'

'Cheers, Colin,' Alvin says, softening.

'Yeah, the Anaconda no less. You kept that one hidden, so to speak. Bigger than Hutchence, eh? The Wanger of Oz himself.'

'Oh, for fuck's sake . . .'

'And you've got one over on Bird-Wright. Walking out of here with her birthright in your pocket must feel pretty sweet.'

'You just can't stop yourself, can you?'

'One thing we're dying to know in the staff room: did you or did you not pork her old mum?'

Alvin spins to face Stanislavski. 'You lot had better make your minds up. Either I'm a paedophile or a granny shagger. You can't have it both ways.'

'The word is *gerontophile.*'

'You're the expert,' Alvin says, walking away.

'That's why I'm the teacher, matey,' Stanislavski yells, 'and you're an unemployed KIDDY FIDDLER!'

Paediatric

'I'm amazed you're prepared to be seen out in public with me,' Alvin says.

'Don't be stupid,' Mercedes replies, even as she looks around her nervously, aware what anyone looking their way might be thinking.

They're in the café where they met a few days ago. It's close to East Park and it heaves with Mercedes's schoolmates. Normally she wouldn't be seen dead so close to school with a parent.

'Janice is gonna kill you,' she says with a grin. 'That photo makes her look like . . . It's *sad*, man.'

'I didn't give it to the *Gazette*. She can thank Jamie for that.'

'Whatever. She's gonna *kill* you.'

'Well, she'd probably be doing me a favour.'

'You gotta get a grip, Alvin,' she says, reverting to Alvin after the brief outburst of Dad the other day. 'I dunno why you're so bothered about that stupid job. You should've jacked it in years ago.'

'I loved that stupid job,' he says bleakly.

'I know you did. I never got that.'

'Anyway, what am I going to do now?'

'Play bass . . . ? Look, you'll find something.'

Three men in Transco overalls sit on the next table drinking sweet tea and eating all-day breakfasts. One of them looks up at Alvin – it's only a glance, but it doesn't seem friendly.

'What will I find?' he asks. 'I'm the local bloody pervert now. My reputation's trashed.'

His daughter smiles.

'What's so funny?'

'Nothing . . . It's just that I never thought of you as having a *reputation.*' She uses her fingers to give the word airborne inverted commas.

Now he thinks about it, Alvin has never had any concept of his own reputation. Reputations are for doctors, judges, members of parliament. Well, he has one now: con man cum sex hound.

Mercedes reaches her hand across the table and squeezes his. 'It'll be OK,' she says. 'It'll blow over in a few days.'

The gas worker looks up again, spots Mercedes's hand on her father's. The distaste on his face is unmistakable this time. And on the table in front of him is a copy of the *Gazette*.

'Maybe it will,' Alvin says, attempting to smile. 'Whatever, I wish Karen was here.'

'You tried phoning?'

'Repeatedly. I keep getting her mum.'

'That's one scary bitch.'

Alvin doesn't disagree.

'I'd better be off, Alvin,' Mercedes says, finishing her coffee.

'Me too. I'm going to get my stuff from Lynette's and move back home.'

Alvin made the decision as he left Wood Hill for the last time. He has been feeling increasingly uncomfortable at Lynette's, a spare prick at a wedding – worse than that, at a lesbian one. Lynette has been nothing less than hospitable, but Donna has been oozing a subtle fragrance – *Eau de Piss-off*. Frankly, it has surprised him how much time the two of them have been spending together. If they do many more aerobics classes, they'll soon be little more than hardened sinew and swollen joints held loosely together by pink Lycra. And what about Guy Hutton? Is he too busy marvelling at his newly buff wife to wonder what's going on? Alvin has felt himself growing uncharacteristically judgemental and thinks it best that he packs his bag.

He has no intention of returning to Jamie's, certainly not after today's kiss 'n' tell, so home it is. Karen may have chucked him out, but it doesn't look as if she's coming back any time soon.

'Where are you staying at the moment?' he asks Mercedes as they leave.

'At Janice's,' she says. 'But I'll come to yours if you want the company.'

Alvin stops on the pavement outside the café and looks at his daughter. He hasn't felt this close to her in years. But now he thinks about it, her warmth is entirely in keeping. As he's plummeted in the estimation of everyone else, of course he's risen in the eyes of Mercedes the contrarian. He reaches out and wraps his arms around her. She returns his hug with interest. Tears sting his eyes, but he blinks hard, stopping them at source. He hears footsteps, feels a rough hand grab his shoulder, feels his body spin round.

Now he's facing the gas man whose fists are balled and ready.

'Get your filthy hands off her, you sick bastard,' he snarls as his two mates arrive behind him.

Alvin raises his hands peaceably. 'She's my –'

'You're that paediatric from Wood Hill.' Gas man turns to his friends. 'I told you it's him. The whole fucking school's talking about him. He's taught my Shelley. If he's laid a finger on her, I'll fucking kill him.'

But not waiting to find out, he moves towards Alvin menacingly. Schoolkids pour out of the café now, alerted to the ruckus. A couple of elderly women at the bus stop look on nervously.

'Leave him alone!' Mercedes shrieks. 'He's my –'

Too late. Gas man has swung a fat fist, hitting Alvin hard in the stomach. Alvin collapses to his knees, clutching his gut, gasping for air.

One of the old women screams.

'It's all right, love,' one of gas man's mates soothes, 'he's that paediatric.'

Gas man moves forward again, but Mercedes steps across Alvin's doubled-up body. 'Leave him alone, you fucking moron,' she yells at him. 'He's my father!'

It works. Gas man backs off now, returning to the café with his workmates. Mercedes bends down and wraps an arm around Alvin's shoulder. One of the old women steps across the pavement, her wrinkled face lined with concern. 'He's your *father*?' she asks.

Mercedes nods, her face streaked with tears.

'God, that just makes it even sicker.'

Ugly is as ugly does

Alvin is back in his own front room.

In his own house.

Alone.

Mercedes brought him back and again offered to stay, but he insisted she went – 'I want to be alone,' he told her, even though he didn't.

'It's not safe here,' she said, looking at the fresh graffiti on the downstairs bay window, amazed and frightened at how fast the local vigilantes had got to work.

'I'll be fine,' he replied uncertainly. 'Anyway, it's my home.'

When she finally left, he plonked himself down on the sofa, his bag at his feet. He hasn't moved since, watching the room slump into darkness, staring at the black paint on the other side of the glass:

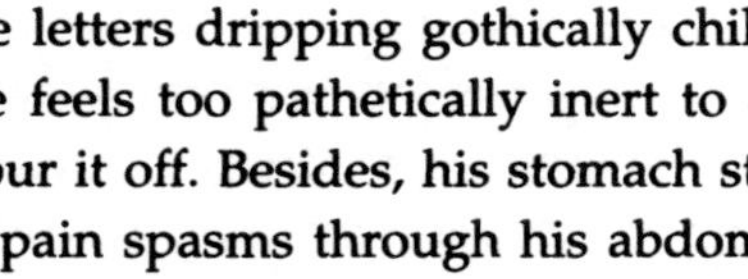

The sight of the letters dripping gothically chills him – he's a *trevrep* – but he feels too pathetically inert to do anything as proactive as scour it off. Besides, his stomach still hurts. Every time he moves pain spasms through his abdomen. He'll clean up in the morning. In the meantime he can't even stir himself to switch on the light. He closes his eyes and tries to replay the sounds the house made just ten days ago. Back then the place never struck him as particularly noisy (though Karen used to tell him – shouting above the din – that it was). Now it feels as silent as a sensory deprivation tank.

If he concentrates really hard he can hear Annie slowly chugging out the chords of a song that, if she knew it in its entirety, would take her a full working week to finish, leaving her the weekend free for an improvised solo.

Thrum . . . 'F!' . . . *Thrum* . . . 'C!' . . . *Thrum* . . . 'F!' . . . *Thrum* . . . 'C!'

And again.

Thrum . . . 'F!' . . . *Thrum* . . . 'C!' . . . *Thrum* . . . 'F!' . . .

The phone breaks the sequence. Alvin thinks about ignoring it – it's probably for Mercedes – but decides that only getting up to answer it will save him from dying on the sofa. Melancholia, the first reported case since 1878.

'Yeah,' he says into the receiver.

'Alvin, *mate*, been trying to reach you all day. Why haven't you rung? I mean, a call to say thanks would've been nice.'

'*Thanks*? I should kill you, Jamie. What the hell were you playing at?'

'Doing what mates do, bigging you up. This hack got in touch with me, said he was doing a piece on local celebs, so I took him through the photo albums, told him some tales. Anyway, I'm glad I did. When I saw what the scum journos had written on page one . . . The bastards. This place needs to know the real Alvin Lee.'

'That's not *me*. The only thing you got right was my name.'

'C'mon, I was there, remember?'

'Jesus, I thought you were too, but obviously your brain was on another planet. Jamming with Michael Hutchence, swapping makeup with Simon Le Bon, shooting up with Boy bloody George for all I know.'

'Don't be stupid. Share a needle with that gaylord?'

'What's the point?' Alvin asks of no one in particular because arguing with Jamie – trying to persuade him that his memory might be having a laugh – is futile. How Jamie McGreevy remembers it is EXACTLY HOW IT WAS.

More than once Alvin has envied him. Jamie's eighties were so much better than anyone else's were. How wonderful, he has thought, to reach forty utterly assured that during your quarter-hour in the spotlight you redefined popular music, helped Bowie beat his mid-career block, were the uncredited genius behind both 'Relax' and Band Aid, and still somehow found the time to fit in two cold turkeys and lashings of rock-star sex.

Now, though, envy is the last thing he feels.

'I thought you'd be pleased,' Jamie sniffs, hurt.

'Have you any idea what happened to me today, Jamie?'

'Apart from getting more press than you've had since the *NME* stuck us on their cover?'

'They never stuck us –' *What's the point, remember?* 'Apart from that, yeah. I lost my job. I got fired.'

'You telling me that was my fault?'

'No, it wasn't, but you didn't help.'

As Alvin sat in his disciplinary hearing, he looked at the *Gazette* on the desk in front of Alan Chadwick, Allison Bird-Wright and the other two governors. Jamie's testimony was never submitted as evidence, but it never needed to be. Its work had already been done.

'Trust me, you're well out of it, Alv,' Jamie says. 'Rubbish job. Anyway, now you've got some time on your hands you can help me out. I'm recruiting.'

'What for?'

'My boy band. I haven't told you about it? *Killer* concept – Westlife meets Led Zep. Written a bunch of songs already, but I thought we'd launch 'em with a cover of Judas Priest's "Genocide".'

'Sounds perfect for the pre-teen market.'

'I *knew* you'd get it, man. We are gonna go all the way with this one.'

'I've got to go, Jamie. There's someone at the door.' He's not lying. The bell has rung. 'We'll talk about it, yeah?' he says, safe in the knowledge that the next time they speak, Jamie will be consumed by a fresh scheme – re-forming the Fab Four, perhaps, and having them sing live with Buddy Holly.

He hangs up and goes to the window. He peers through the nets at the man standing on the path. The bald patch at the back of his head glimmers with reflected streetlight. He's too smartly dressed to be a debt collector and too old to be a date for Mercedes. Too ugly as well. She preaches the politics of inclusiveness but doesn't live them. None of her boyfriends has had so much as a misplaced dimple; getting the male lead opposite Cameron Diaz is generally easier than getting a back-row snog out of Alvin's daughter.

He thinks about ignoring the visitor, but the man jabs again at the doorbell, keeping his gloved finger pressed down insistently. He isn't going to take no for an answer. Alvin goes into the hall and opens the door.

'Have you had your electricity cut off?' the man asks. 'Your neighbours' lights are on so it can't be a power cut.'

Alvin reaches for the switch, flooding the hall with light, and he immediately takes an involuntary step backwards. *God*, is this guy ugly! His face is a car crash – ghastly but utterly compelling. His forehead bulges Elmer Fuddishly and the scrunched features below it are so compressed they'd slip into a wallet. What does he do? Sleep with his head in a vice?

It's a face that only a mother could love.

She'd have to be blind, though.

'Sorry,' Alvin says – for the lack of a welcoming light and, unconsciously, for the ludicrously short straw this poor man drew when looks were being dished out. 'Can I help you?'

'Alvin Lee?'

Alvin nods.

'Not that I had any problem finding your house.' The man gestures towards the graffiti. 'You've got your sign out.'

'Who are you?' Alvin asks.

'I'm Jeremy Bird. I think we should talk.'

The two men stand in the living room eyeing each other. Alvin feels a host's urge to break the silence, but with what? An offer of tea? He doesn't even know if there is any.

'Your mother,' he says haltingly. 'She was a very brave woman . . .'

Jeremy Bird just looks at him.

'. . . I'm sorry for your loss.'

'Of my mother or of my inheritance?'

Is that a smile or a sneer? Jeremy Bird's face hasn't been constructed to transmit a range of expressions.

'Your mother,' Alvin says.

'Interesting question, though, isn't it? It must be hard for you to feel sadness for a woman you claim hardly to have known. Just the one meeting, wasn't it? Under rather stressful conditions as well.'

'It was just once,' Alvin blurts. 'What you wrote in your paper wasn't fair. You should've given me a chance to put my side.'

'*I* didn't write anything. The editor states it as he sees it.'

The remark is as unbelievable as it is pompous.

'Why are you here?' Alvin asks.

'Another interesting question.' Jeremy Bird's voice *projects*, as if it's RADA-trained. Or perhaps its ring of self-importance is genetic. 'My lawyer has told me I shouldn't touch you with a barge pole, but he also said that if and when this matter reaches court, we – you and I – will need to demonstrate that we made sincere attempts to reach a settlement. That's lawyers for you. Their advice is never clear cut, is it?'

'So why are you here?' Alvin repeats.

'To have a stab at a settlement. I haven't time for a court battle. You have time aplenty now, but, frankly, I suspect you haven't the appetite.'

'Look, Mr Bird, I was stunned when I was named in your mum's will, honestly . . .' Alvin knows that if Trevor Poll were with him now, he'd be climbing all over him, smothering his mouth with a cushion to prevent the words from coming out, but he can't stop himself. '. . . And I must admit that I felt . . . *bad* . . . You know, what right did I have?'

'What right indeed?'

'But . . .' But what? '. . . She must have had her reasons and shouldn't we respect that?'

'There was no *reason* to anything my mother did. If she was in the least bit rational, why did she choose to live in squalor? She was sick in the head. *Ill*.'

'How can you be so sure? You hadn't seen her for years.'

'I *knew* her. I knew her a damn sight better than you did,' Jeremy Bird booms in a momentary explosion. 'She was my *mother* . . . And what about respect for my father? He worked bloody hard for what he achieved. He sacrificed everything to give my sister and me a future.'

Alvin could point out that Douglas Bird apparently assured his children's futures when he set them up with trusts. He could also ask what, exactly, did he sacrifice. Certainly not a standard of living way beyond the reach of most.

'My father didn't kill himself working eighty-hour weeks . . .'

Yes, and shouldn't Alvin point out that, actually, the old guy killed himself by driving his car into a sturdy English oak tree?

'. . . so that my mother in her madness could give it away on a whim. The lucky recipient could have been a cats' home or a tramp. It happened to be you.'

Well, neither a tramp nor a cats' home nor, for that matter, *you* saved your poor mum from a backstreet mugging, Alvin thinks.

'What do you want?' he says wearily – it has been a tough day.

'I want what my father intended me to have; what's *mine*. The question is, what do you want?'

'I don't know what you mean.'

'*Money*. Let's be honest, it looks as if you need it.' Clearly Jeremy Bird hasn't learned to compensate for dud looks with sugary charm.

'I don't need a penny.' Alvin is bristling now.

'Oh, come on,' Bird says impatiently. 'Today you lost your job and in a month or two you'll lose this place too.'

'Excuse me?'

'How are you going to make the next repayment on your mortgage? You're four months in arrears already.'

Alvin goes from bristling to outraged. 'How the hell do you know my –'

'Do you think I'd walk into a situation like this without having done my homework? I also know your girlfriend has left you. A saying about rats and sinking ships springs to mind, but far be it from me to moralise.'

Alvin can't speak. His brain has turned into a mush of fear and anger. What *doesn't* this man know about him? And – given that, actually, he's only *three* months behind with his mortgage – what fact isn't he prepared to distort for the benefit of the *Gazette*'s readers or, if it comes to it, a High Court judge?

'I'll make you an offer,' Jeremy Bird says, 'one you'd be ill advised to refuse. One hundred and fifty thousand pounds, if you'll agree to drop all claims on my father's estate.'

His *father's* estate. The distinction would strike Alvin as instructive if he weren't in such a state.

'It'll clear your debts,' Bird continues, 'and leave you with enough to tide you over until you find yourself a job. One that doesn't require police vetting.'

'You're treating me like an extortionist,' Alvin manages to say.

'Well, aren't you?'

'*No*. I helped your mother. I saw her in trouble, I helped her out, I walked away. That's it.'

Jeremy Bird utters a brief, brittle laugh. 'I've got to admire your front. You'd better enjoy the pretence while you can because the truth *will* come out.'

'What truth?'

'That you and your mugger friend set my mother up, of course.'

'That's rubbish.'

'Fair enough, I'll humour you. Let's say you're the Good Samaritan. A hundred and fifty grand is a fair reward, wouldn't you say? A damn sight more than you'd get from Crimestoppers.'

'My solicitor told me what you were like,' Alvin says. Being Alvin, of course, he hadn't wanted to believe him.

'Ah, your solicitor. We've had dealings in the past. I wouldn't trust his advice, you know. He's too wrapped up in his dislike of me to be objective. Besides, he shouldn't even be representing you. Since he drew up this bogus will and is also its executor, there's a clear conflict of interest if he continues to act for you . . . Still, that's not my problem, is it? Think about it, Mr Lee. If you decide to let this continue, the court case will end your life – I'll make sure of that. No, this is the best offer you'll get, and an improvement on bankruptcy.'

'I don't need to think about it. I don't want your money.'

'That's rich. Every penny my mother left you is *my* money.'

'She didn't seem to think so. I'd like you to go now.'

'If you see sense and decide to accept, have your lawyer inform mine,' Jeremy Bird says as he turns to leave. 'The offer expires on Monday morning, so you have the weekend to think on it.'

Alvin remains rooted to the spot as he listens to the front door open, then close. He goes to the window and angrily pulls the curtains shut, almost ripping the track from the wall. Then he sees him again through the gap where the curtains have never quite met. Sitting in his car, staring at him from across the street. Alvin knows now that it's not a smile, but definitely a sneer. He sees her too. She presided over his hearing today and now she's sitting in the passenger seat beside her brother. She doesn't look at him, just as she didn't at his hearing. Before he can turn away, the car pulls off.

A great big bloody Mercedes, wouldn't you know it?

Alvin wishes he'd called his daughter something else – Sarah, Cathy, Vauxhall, anything.

He sits on the sofa and attempts to force something sweet into his head. Annie returns.

Thrum . . . 'F!' . . . *Thrum* . . . 'C!' . . . *Thrum* . . . 'F!' . . . *Thrum* . . . 'C!'

'Paint It Black', which is about right for the occasion. But instead of letting her rummage through his old sheet music, why didn't he go out and buy her something fresher and chirpier? Green Day, the Darkness, Busted for Beginners, *anything*.

Jumper

'Just popping out, Mum,' Jonathan Craig calls out from the hall.

'Will you be long?' his mother replies from the kitchen.

'I don't know. A couple of hours maybe. Why?'

'I wanted you to run me to the Aviary after lunch. I've got some things to get and I can nip into Boots while I'm there, get you some aqueous cream for that rash. It's looking a bit livid today.'

'Can't Dad take you?'

'He's tai chi-ing all day.'

'OK . . . I'll be back by lunch.'

'Thanks, love. Bye then. Take a jumper. It's nippy out there.'

'Got one, thanks . . . Bye.'

Jonathan Craig, ex-teacher, former gentlemen's outfitter, pulls the cable-knit sweater over his head and opens the front door for what he has decided will definitely be the last time.

All those moments will be lost in time, like tears in the rain

Alvin sits down and tries to remember how this goes. It has been a long time. But it'll be like riding a bike, won't it? He leans forward, bows his head and mumbles, 'Forgive me, Father, for I have sinned.' Yes, just like riding a bike.

On the other side of the grille a throat is cleared. 'How long has it been since your last confession?'

He was thirteen and he fessed up to copying a friend's homework. Well, he wasn't going to tell a priest with the voice of a hanging judge the dark stuff, the how-many-times-in-a-single-day-can-a-boy-beat-off? stuff. It turned out to be an astute move. Condemned to eternal hellfire for tracing a pal's cross-sectional diagram of a fjord, Alvin (teenagerishly oblivious to the irony) thanked God that he hadn't opened with the wanks.

'A long time,' he replies. 'About thirty years.'

'That is a while,' the priest says gently. 'Where do you want to start?'

Now that he's trapped in the little box, Alvin wonders why he came. Ave Marias and the promise of better things in the hereafter aren't going to dig him out of his hole in the here and now.

He needs counselling. For his lost job, dignity, lover, children . . .

But all of that loss can be traced back to the single sin.

That, then, would be why he's here in search of absolution.

Or it's simply the act of a desperate man with no one else to talk to.

God and his earthly spokesman may be his last remaining friends, but now that Alvin is with them, he finds himself under-prepared.

'C'mon,' the priest nudges as the silence starts to drag. 'I've heard it all in this little box ... I've *seen* things you people wouldn't believe ... Attack ships on fire off the shoulder of Orion. I watched C-beams glitter in the dark near the Tannhauser Gate. All those moments will be lost in time, like tears in the rain ... That's a line, by the way. *Blade Runner*. A wonderful film and very moral in its own fashion. Very ... *redemptive*. Look, I'm just filling the silence here ... Until you're good and ready. If you want me to shut up –'

'My wife – Actually, she's not my wife. She's left me.'

'She had cause?' the priest asks.

Once again Alvin finds himself shamed into silence.

'You know, everything goes through this church,' the priest says, setting off on another void-filling ramble. 'Literally everything. The steeple, seventy-six feet of it, built in 1864 to reach out to God. A conduit for our prayers. It's a different kind of conduit these days. The diocese, in its ineffable wisdom, has rented it out to Vodafone and they've put one of their little aerials up there. So when I say everything goes through here I mean it. No doubt a lot of it is as dull as ditchwater; *I'll be late for the meeting* and *Don't forget the milk on the way home* and so on. But some of it ... *Phew*. It's a literal Tower of Babel up there, even as we speak. The promiscuity, the perversion, the deception and lies ... All human vice is pinging off this very building. Humanity is confessing and it doesn't even know it. And because it doesn't know it, it doesn't dress it up, edit out the horror, soften it with spin.'

Alvin wonders if he's listening to the rehearsal for tomorrow's sermon.

'So you see,' the priest concludes, 'surely nothing you tell me could be any worse than some of the vile stuff that God is already obliged to listen to.'

'I had . . . sex . . . with a prostitute. It was just once, but . . .'

'There's usually a but.'

'It's not that sort of but,' Alvin says. 'She – Karen doesn't believe me. She thinks there was more to it.'

'And was there?'

'No, honestly.'

'Frankly, once would be more than many relationships could bear, but I suspect that you believe this one is worth saving.'

'Of course.'

'Then talk to her, prove your worth. And keep on talking until she relents. You'll waltz out of here with the Lord's forgiveness, but you're going to have to work a damn sight harder to earn hers.'

'I want to talk to her, but she's left. Gone away.'

'To her mother's?'

'How did you know?'

'I'd like to say it was divine guidance, but it was an educated guess. Mothers can be tricky. She'll be giving you short shrift, I imagine.'

Alvin doesn't have to imagine. It is a measure of how defeated Karen must be feeling that she has swallowed her pride and gone home to a diet of reheated I-told-you-sos.

'Still, you've got to face the fury,' the priest says. 'I'll give you some Hail Marys, but the Mother of Karen will be your real penance.'

Face the fury.

The priest is right.

He should go there now.

It's Saturday morning. He could be in Manchester for tea.

'Thank you, Father,' he says.

'Is that it? Thirty years without confession and that's my lot?'

'Yes, well, I –'

'No, it's fine, really. You go. Talk to Karen.'

Has God worked his magic or is it just good to talk?

Either way, Alvin feels a little better as he leaves the church. He stops at the top of the steps. Across the road is a Transco van. Beside it a man sets up cones around a colleague who is battering the tarmac with a pneumatic drill. He recognises them from the café yesterday. His attacker is the one with the drill.

He decides he can do without another confrontation – he has a train to catch. Instead of heading down the steps, he makes his way along the alley at the side of the church. He used to come this way as a kid, sneaking out of mass to leap over the wall at the rear and into the allotments on the other side where he and his mates would share cigarettes. Was that a sin – should he have mentioned it just now? Whatever – and perhaps this was God's will – he never took up the habit full time. He was never able to jump the pain barrier between allowing the smoke to loll pointlessly around his mouth and full-on nico-junkie inhalation.

He scales the wall and trudges across the squishy allotments. Though it's Saturday, they're practically deserted. An old man leaning on a fork follows his progress. He eyes him suspiciously and Alvin wonders if he sees him as a paedophile or merely as a trespasser.

Twenty yards away from the man, a pair of boys sit smoking on a rusting roller. Despite their hoodies, Alvin recognises them. He doesn't suppose Curtis and Roland are here to dig potatoes. In the old days – which ended only a week or so ago – he would have stopped for a chat. But he doesn't feel like facing them today. He pulls his head down into his shoulders, ignores them, hurries on – he has a train to catch.

On the other side of the allotments he joins the footpath leading to the road home. He climbs the steps of the footbridge that spans the railway line. He used to come here as a kid, too, and look at the trains. Just to look – he was never one of those who lobbed paving slabs onto passing Intercities. Not that they're doing it any more. British Rail – or whatever it is these days – has taken measures. A ten-foot fence of close-knit steel mesh has been mounted on top of the bridge's parapet, making slab-hurling a kamikaze hobby.

Alvin stops in the middle of the bridge and leans on the iron parapet. He gazes through the mesh at the glistening tracks stretching away from London. No sign of any trains, and he supposes the chances of seeing one any time soon are slim. This is the weekend, time for track maintenance and general public-transport crappiness. He wonders how hard it will be to find a train that will get him to Manchester before, say, Tuesday.

As he ponders, he's aware of something above him. His eyes travel up the lamppost beside him. It runs up the full height of the fence and two or three feet above bends at a right angle to illuminate the bridge below. At the top, clinging to the angle, is a hunched figure, perched on the fence like a vulture and wearing a chunky cable-knit jumper. Alvin stares, not quite believing what his eyes are telling him. The effort required to shin up the lamppost must have been considerable. The figure doesn't appear to be clutching a paving slab, so Alvin decides that the only thing it intends to throw at a train is itself. *It*, he concludes after further scrutiny, is a man, though he can't see his face.

'Excuse me,' Alvin says quietly – he doesn't want to startle the guy off his perch.

The figure doesn't respond.

'Excuse me,' Alvin repeats a little louder. 'Are you OK?'

Still he doesn't respond. He seems calm, Alvin decides. Perhaps he's a trainspotter. His crouch atop the fence looks like something he might have learned in a yoga class. A Buddhist trainspotter?

'Are you OK?' Alvin shouts it this time.

At last the man turns to look at him. Harsh discoloration covers one side of his face, thrusting out from the neck of his sweater and extending up his cheek. The man has the rash from hell, but surely nothing bad enough to prompt suicide.

'Leave me alone,' he says. 'Go away.'

'I think you should come down,' Alvin suggests. 'It's not safe up there.'

The man ignores him, choosing to stare straight ahead.

'You're not thinking of jumping, are you?'

When the man blanks him again, Alvin studies the drop. He estimates that the man would fall about thirty feet, that is if he didn't first get caught in – and possibly sautéed by – the overhead power lines that run between the bridge and the railway track. Thirty feet isn't enough to guarantee death. The man must be waiting for the next train. If he gets his timing right, several hundred tons of London-bound express will ensure success as well as further disruption to the skeletal weekend timetable.

'I'm going to climb up,' Alvin says. 'Just so I can talk to you properly.'

The man doesn't move.

'Don't do anything silly, OK? I only want to talk.'

Still no movement, so Alvin uses the lamppost to climb onto the parapet. The man is only four feet above him now. 'I said leave me alone,' he whines, sensing Alvin below him.

'What's the matter?' Alvin asks amiably. 'What's so bad that you want to jump in front of a train.' He looks up, waiting.

'Everything,' the man says at last. 'Life. *Everything*.'

'Really? You know, I bet my life's crappier than yours.' He didn't really think about that line, but now that it's out, he reckons he might have a point. Today, if the Samaritans organised an impromptu competition – the Prozac-sponsored Miserable Sod World Masters, say – Alvin reckons he'd trounce all comers. Actually, low as he is, he's possibly the worst person to talk a would-be jumper down from the precipice. Then again, maybe his own depression gives him a unique qualification. He looks to his left and right. Not a soul in sight. No one else is going to save this guy. He might as well get on with it . . .

The view from the roller

Another blast of wind sweeps across the allotment.

'Can we go?' Roland whimpers.

Curtis looks down at him from his spot on top of the roller, where he is throwing his body into Kung Fu shapes. 'Give him another ten minutes, yeah?'

'I'm fucking freezing. He's not gonna show, man. Let's go.'

'Tell you what. We'll give him ten, then we'll go round his gaff.'

'Why didn't we just go there in the first place, man?'

''Cause he don't like dealing from home. His dad's in on Saturdays.'

'Call him, see where he is.'

'Can't. His dad took his mobile off him.'

'Mr fucking Big or what. You need to find us another dealer, Curt.'

'Yeah, whatever . . .' Kung Fu Curtis has frozen. He's peering with Buddha-like stillness towards the railway line. '*Fuck*, man, what's that?'

'Wha's what?' Roland asks without looking up.

'Over there. That geezer.'

'*What* geezer?' says Roland, still without raising his head.

'On the bridge. Top of the lamppost. What the fuck's he doing?'

'Fixing the fucking lamppost. How the fuck should I know?'

'Just *look*, man,' Curtis says. 'I think the cunt's gonna jump.'

Roland finally stands up and joins his friend on the roller.

He's shorter than Curtis, but if he stands on tippy-toes and cranes his neck, he can just about see the footbridge. '*Fuck*,' he agrees. 'Stupid cunt'll kill himself.'

'That's the whole point, you spaz.'

'You wha'?'

'He *wants* to fucking kill himself.'

'Reckon we should do something?'

'Like what?'

'I dunno. Call the cops or something.'

'Nah . . . Let's just see if he jumps, yeah?'

They stand and look. But Roland can't really see without losing his balance so he drops to the flats of his feet and relies on Curtis for a commentary.

'*Shit!*' Curtis commentates.

'*What?* Has he jumped?'

'There's another geezer.'

'Where?'

'Climbing up. What the fuck's going on? It's like a queue or something . . . Fucking hell, you won't believe *this*.'

'*What?*' Roland squeaks, hopping up and down on the roller.

'It's Alvin.'

'Where?'

'On the fucking bridge. Climbing up. What the fuck's he doing?'

'Is he jumping an' all?'

'Dunno . . . He must've gone a bit Frank Bruno since he got fired.'

'Shall we go over there?'

'Dunno. If we go we might miss Ajab and if we miss him we won't have no gear for tonight.'

'We should go, though, shouldn't we? Just to see if he's OK, yeah?'

'S'pose . . . We'll give it another five, then go.'

Meanwhile, back at the bridge

Alvin, trying to ignore the pain in his hands as they cling to the frigid metal lamppost, looks up at the man. 'I've lost my job, my girlfriend, my kids,' he begins, mentally ticking boxes as he goes. 'I'm about to lose my house and the whole district thinks I'm a con man. I've got *pervert* sprayed across my bay window and some gas engineers across the way want to beat me up and they don't even know me. Oh, and my bike doesn't work.' *Top that, matey,* he wants to say, but he resists the temptation. Instead he asks, 'What about you?'

The man doesn't speak for the longest time. But he looks no closer to jumping either. Eventually he says, 'I know you . . . I know who you are.'

Oh God, thinks Alvin, *wouldn't you just know it?* Even suicidal depressives, neck-deep in self-pity, are taking the time to check out the name of the latest local paedo.

'I worked at Wood Hill,' the man explains, turning to face him now.

'Really . . . ?' Alvin peers at him, tries to see past the rash, but draws a blank. 'I'm sorry, but I don't –'

'Oh, you won't remember me. It was my first job. I was pretty anonymous. I quit after a term and a half.'

'Wood Hill's a tough place to start a teaching career,' Alvin says.

'You seemed to handle it.'

'Well, I'm not – I *wasn't* a teacher.'

'Whatever, I used to watch you with the kids. You were good.'

'Not any more. Like I told you, I lost my job yesterday.'

'Snap . . . So did I,' the man says.

'Which school had you moved to?'

'I hadn't. I gave that up after Wood Hill. I was working in a shop. I slapped a customer.'

'Well, perhaps he deserved it,' Alvin suggests.

'*She*. She didn't deserve it. She was only thirteen.'

Alvin clicks now. He remembers Karadas telling him about it, though he still doesn't recognise the man from his time at Wood Hill.

'Look, mate,' he says, 'slapping a girl isn't good, but there're worse things you could have done. And jumping off the bridge won't make it better, will it?'

'The police came to see me. They'll probably charge me with assault,' the man says. 'I'll never be able to teach again.'

'I thought you'd given that up. It's not the greatest career anyway. You're young. There must be loads of things you'd like to do.'

The man doesn't respond.

'C'mon, what else do you fancy doing?' Alvin asks, mostly because he can't think what else to say.

'I started out as a traffic-flow analyst,' the man says. 'Before teaching.'

'*Wow* . . . That sounds . . . very . . . high-powered,' Alvin says.

'You don't even know what one of those is, do you?'

'No . . . Sorry.'

The man doesn't speak.

'Well, aren't you going to tell me about it?' Alvin asks.

'Why? So you can have a laugh?'

'I won't laugh, I promise. I'm interested.'

Silence.

'I'm *fascinated*,' Alvin says. 'Tell me.'

'I coordinated traffic lights,' the man says testily. '*Optimised* the *sequencing*. Made sure you can drive down Oxford Street in less than six hours. That kind of thing. I was the complete anorak. There, I've told you.'

'Honestly, that sounds amazing,' Alvin says, and he *is* genuinely amazed. 'I mean, *traffic* lights. You just take them for granted, don't you? Well, I do. I'm sure most people do. But someone's got to make them work, haven't they? You *sequenced* traffic lights!'

'I was very good at gyratory systems. My section head said I had an excellent analytical mind and a superb grasp of detail,' the man says.

'You'd have needed all that, I should think,' Alvin says. 'Why don't you go back to that?'

'Because I hated it. Staring at computer monitors all day. I got migraines. And depression ... My therapist says I'm suffering from post-traumatic stress syndrome.'

'From traffic light ... er ... sequencing?' Alvin is surprised. It doesn't sound like the Somme, though what does he know?

'From *teaching*,' the man says. 'From Wood ...'

He trails off and Alvin knows why. Though he can't yet see it, he can hear the train. He doesn't have long.

'Look, come down. We can talk properly. We've got a lot in common ... School, being sacked ... Come down.'

The man doesn't move. Alvin can see the train now, a sleek, aeroplane-nosed express moving towards them at speed.

'Please, climb down ... You really don't want to do this.'

The man shifts his grip on the top of the lamppost and his body rocks forward. Talking isn't working. Alvin stretches an arm upwards, but he can't reach him – he's at least a foot short. The train is only a few hundred yards away now. Alvin grips the lamppost with both hands and pulls. He hooks his knees up beneath him and wraps his legs as best he can around the post, gripping onto the metal with the insteps of his trainers. He remembers climbing a rope in PE. He was good at that, the best in his class, but it has been a long time. The train is almost on them. He slides his hands up again and *heaves*, getting closer to the top. Tentatively he takes a hand off the post and grabs hold of the top of the fence. 'Take my hand,' he shouts, 'I'll help you down.' But the man can't hear him over the sound of the train, which seems to be getting faster as it draws nearer. He leans forward again, getting close to the point of no return. With one last effort Alvin uses his grip on the top of the fence to haul himself up. He takes his other hand off the lamppost and stretches up as the man teeters and the train reaches the bridge. He grabs, taking a handful of jumper, and he grips more tightly than he's gripped anything in his life. Closing his eyes, he *clings*, feels the man's weight pull against him, listens to the train thunder beneath, carriage after carriage after carriage after carriage . . . How long is this bloody train?

At last it has gone, charging on to central London.

Now the man falls.

But backwards.

Still holding his sweater, Alvin goes with him, the man's momentum ripping his legs from the lamppost. Although the man started out the higher, he hits the footbridge first. Alvin lands on top of him, the man's thighs cushioning the worst of the impact. He pushes himself up onto his knees and looks down at him. His eyes are closed and he doesn't move. But his chest rises slowly – he's still breathing. Gradually, blood pools on the tarmac at the back of his head.

Alvin reaches into his jacket and takes out his phone. It seems to be in one piece. He switches it on and calls for an ambulance.

Sunday

Alvin sits as he has sat for the past two hours: watching the Southeast turn seamlessly into the Midlands and now into the Northwest. He likes trains for this very reason: big windows out of which he can stare.

He has been practising the speech he'll deliver to Karen. If she's in . . . If she's in *and* she agrees to talk to him. He didn't phone ahead – he didn't dare.

It's Sunday. He's making the trip a day later than planned because much of yesterday was spent in hospital. He travelled there in the ambulance with the man. His name is Jonathan Craig. Alvin found that much out by going through his wallet as he waited for the ambulance. Oddly, his hadn't been the first emergency call. He was told that help was already on its way, though Alvin had no idea who could have rung for it. The engine driver?

Once at A & E, Alvin waited while the doctors attended to Jonathan. They wouldn't tell him what the damage was – he wasn't a relative. He was still there when Jonathan's parents arrived – a small, frightened woman and a much older man dressed incongruously in judo pyjamas. Reluctantly he told them what had happened – there are nicer things to do than telling parents that their child wants to kill himself. They were too shocked to take it in; also too shocked to appreciate what Alvin had done. Jonathan regained consciousness before he left. It turned out he had a fractured skull and a broken hip. Hopefully no brain damage, though – at least none beyond the mental turmoil that had made him contemplate suicide in the first place. The police arrived then and a constable took his statement. He knew who Alvin was and was eager to pick holes in his story, sensing another crime he could pin on the local con man cum sex hound. Alvin wasn't too worried, though. With characteristic optimism, he presumed that when Jonathan was well enough to talk he'd bear out his account.

He got home late afternoon, exhausted. He spent the evening alone, feeling guilty. He hadn't even noticed Jonathan Craig when he'd been at Wood Hill. Maybe if he had, he could have helped him.

When he woke up this morning his mind was once again consumed with Karen. He was terrified at the prospect of seeing her – and her mother – but excited because he was *doing* something. And here he is now, sitting on a train, rehearsing his speech.

Actually, mental oratory isn't the only thing that's keeping his gaze fixed on the damp fields, chilly Friesians and electricity pylons. It's also the young man in the seat opposite. It's as if the guard announced as the journey began that it is no longer rude to stare – *official!* The guy has been making the most of a brand-new freedom by staring at Alvin across the narrow width of the table. He's been keeping it up since the train left Euston.

Feeling increasingly freaked, Alvin has thought about getting up and moving, but – typical Alvin – he doesn't want to offend the man.

Who's about halfway through his twenties and wears a mustard jacket, a pea-green T-shirt, maroon cords and faded red Converse All Stars. Perhaps he's colour blind, Alvin speculated as the train cruised through Birmingham New Street, and it all looks brown to him. Brown would be just fine.

He must be a student.

Reading weirdness. You can get a BA in that these days, can't you?

Alvin's neck has frozen – probably the vertebrae are fusing together as he sits – because he has held his position for so long, not daring to turn his head and meet the young man's gaze. But now he has to do something because the pain is becoming intense. He is going to have to . . . *move.*

Slowly he turns and finds his view filled with the yellow-toothed rictus of the young man's smile.

'I got it!' he exclaims loud enough to make Alvin jump.

'What?'

'It's been bugging me, but I just worked it out. *I know who you are.*'

He knows who I am. Alvin now knows that his level of freaked-out-ness just a moment ago was *nothing*.

'You were in a band,' the man continues. 'Don't tell me the name. Tip of my tongue . . .' He screws up his face in concentration. '*Da-daa!* Living Saints. 'Wanda Lust'. Number sixteen in eighty-six.'

'Number fifteen, as it goes, but . . . Wow!' Alvin says, feeling both relief and a big thrill swirl through him. Talk about mood swings; from unsettled to overjoyed in an instant. This – being *recognised* – hasn't happened in . . . Actually, it never used to happen when he was still *in* the band. 'You must have been in nappies back then,' he continues. 'How the hell did you know that?'

'Bit embarrassing really . . . Bit anoraky,' the man explains only a little sheepishly. 'I've got this thing about one-hit wonders. I had this fantasy: it was gonna be my specialist subject on *Mastermind*, but then they went and canned it . . . *Bastards*. Go on, ask me anything you like about the Crazy World of Arthur Brown, Spiller, the Jags, M/A/R/R/S . . . Or Saint Winifred's School Choir. Sad, eh?'

'No, it's amazing.'

'"Wanda Lust". Pretty good song. Your singer was a bit of a prat, though.'

Putting it mildly, but Alvin doesn't say. He sits back, relaxed now, and basks in a tiny rock pool of glory – just big enough to paddle his feet in, but lovely all the same – as his travel companion peppers him with questions.

He's glad of the distraction; happy to be a pop star again.

Though of course such nonsense will have to stop the moment he reaches Frances Jackson's front door.

Frances Jackson still lives in the house that Karen grew up in, a wide pebble-dashed semi buried amongst hundreds of similar houses. The house is in Cheadle, a suburb to the south of Manchester.

Alvin doesn't like Cheadle, but it is only now on his walk from the bus stop that he realises why. It has nothing to do with the place itself or even with Karen's schoolma'am mother. He realises that he could be in any suburb of any city in England, and that's his problem. Cheadle is at once totally anonymous and utterly familiar. Frances Jackson lives in the type of house in the type of street that takes him back thirty years to frozen mixed vegetables, log-effect electric fires and *Alias Smith & Jones* on the telly; Sunday visits to uninterested aunts and uncles who made the stack of schoolwork waiting at home seem enticing.

And of course it's Sunday today.

He stands on the pavement side of Frances's garden gate . . .

Hesitating.

It's a long way to have come only to turn round and head straight back to London, but he's seriously thinking of doing just that. But no, he hasn't spent money he can't afford and five hours on a grubby train with a slightly stalkerish pop fan to bottle out now.

He pushes at the wrought-iron gate. It opens with a squeak and he freezes. Not because of the gate, but because at the same moment the front door swings open and Frances Jackson stands framed by the porch. She is holding a black bin liner swollen with rubbish.

'Hello, Frances,' Alvin says.

She stares at him with the expression she has been saving for the day she is on the jury handing down a guilty verdict to a kiddy-porn baron – her moment has arrived sooner than hoped for. Something brown and viscous seeps from a hole in the bottom of the bin bag. It forms a pool on the welcome mat, but she seems not to notice.

Alvin dares to take a step onto the garden path – Jackson land – and that triggers something in her. The attack-dog instinct, plainly, because she throws the bin bag aside and comes at him like a Rhodesian ridgeback. 'How dare you?' the ridgeback barks. 'How *dare* you? On a *Sunday*, as well.'

As if she'd be any happier to see him on a Monday.

'Frances, please, I just want to see Karen, talk to her.'

'Well, she doesn't want to talk to you.'

She has reached him now and is pushing him towards the street. He feels his bum nudge the gate closed, but she doesn't stop shoving him. Soon he finds himself bending over backwards, not out of accommodation – though he'd do more or less anything right now to accommodate Frances – but because unless he is prepared to engage her *mano a mano*, he has no choice other than to do an arthritic limbo over the gate.

The physical attack takes him by surprise. She is a former headmistress, after all, a comfily upholstered pillar of respectability. Mind you, if he had a leisurely moment to consider it, he would remember that she took retirement soon after it was made illegal to beat small children with canes, plimsolls and the sharp edges of rulers, and he would draw the appropriate conclusion.

'Frances, please, I just want to . . .' he says, his head swinging dangerously close to the pavement.

As quickly as she was on him she backs off, leaving Alvin

folded over the gate. He manages to heave himself to a position where his spine is only cricked at a ninety-degree angle and he sees Karen pulling at her mother's shoulder.

'What the hell are you doing, Mum?' she says. 'What's got into you?'

'What do you think I'm doing? I'm keeping this . . . *man* away from you.'

'*Jesus*, I'm not fifteen any more . . .'

Alvin breathes again. Karen, it seems, is prepared to be reasonable.

'. . . Don't you think I can take care of the bastard myself?'

Karen and Alvin sit in the conservatory. Frances calls it the sun lounge, as if the eight-by-twelve room is located on an upper deck of the *Canberra* and spends the bulk of the year in the South Seas. Alvin can't see her, but he can hear her crashing about the kitchen, serving notice that she's ready to grab the first heavy and/or sharp utensil and finish what she started on her garden path.

'You shouldn't have come, Alvin,' Karen says. 'Not without warning. I mean, what were you expecting? Sunday lunch?'

'You wouldn't take my calls. I didn't have a choice . . . I miss you. I miss the kids like mad.'

She doesn't say anything; just stares out at the fussed-over garden. Frances tends her little patch as if it's an English Heritage project with coachloads of Japanese tourists treading its turf in the peak summer months. Alvin is surprised that she hasn't yet turned her shed into a tea room and souvenir shop.

'Where are they?' Alvin asks. He's hoping she'll tell him the children are out someplace because the only alternative is that they've been locked away in an upstairs closet until the Child Catcher is back on the Euston-bound train.

'Janet's taken them to Southport,' Karen replies.

Janet is Karen's sister. Born Janet Jackson and, though she's married, still Janet Jackson – her husband is a Jackson, first name Michael. What are the odds? Alvin has occasionally wondered. Probably not that high. There are plenty of Michaels, Janets and Jacksons kicking around. Besides, he read somewhere that people have a subconscious tendency to find partners with similar surnames. This is a Proper Theory developed by psychologists with too much time on their hands. Janet, Michael and their three kids (not, blessedly, called Marlon, Tito and La Toya) live a few miles away in Wythenshaw.

'They OK?' says Alvin.

'They're fine. Having fun. It's a holiday for them, isn't it? They've even gone to the seaside today.'

He wants to ask if they've missed him, but doesn't dare. Instead he says, 'I can't believe you took off like that. Took them out of school and everything.'

'And I can't believe you turned out to be just your average sexual predator, so there you go: one all.'

'I'm not a . . . sexual . . . *predator*.'

Karen produces a snort that Alvin hasn't heard before.

'I'm *not*,' he protests. 'It was one time. One sorry, stupid bloody time.'

'Why did you get the sack then? For giving your girls Polo Mints?'

'You know I lost my job? It was only on Friday.'

'Oh, I get all the gossip up here. Shannon phones her mates and lucky me gets to talk to their mums who can't wait to tell me how sorry they feel for me.'

'That's all it is, Karen. *Gossip*.'

There goes that snort again, a little angrier this time.

'Please believe me,' Alvin begs.

'Why? Because you've asked me to – *nicely*? Tell me, why should I give an ounce of credence to a guy who visits brothels, is on first-name terms with muggers and loses his job on account of his *inappropriate behaviour* with adolescent girls? Oh, and one who has his trophy shots of groupie girlfriends plastered across the local paper?'

And Alvin tells her why she should. He gives her the speech he practised on the journey. It's not stirring or impassioned, but it's heartfelt and entirely honest. 'Keep on talking to her until she relents,' the priest told him, and he does. And though he sees no sign of her relenting any time before his return ticket expires, he talks and talks and talks until he realises that he's giving her the true identity of the groupie for the second time. 'I don't know what else to say,' he says because he doesn't think she needs to hear it a third time.

He looks at her, but she doesn't speak. But at least she doesn't snort.

'Well?' he says after a while.

'That was very good. Very . . . *plausible*. But you've had a week to get it right, haven't you?'

'It's the *truth*, Karen.'

'I'm sure some of it is. That's the thing with good liars. They manage to weave truth in with the fiction so you can't tell one from the other and it all looks the same. Paul used to do it, but he only fooled me for a couple of years. You're much better at it than him.'

'I'm not fucking Paul,' Alvin snaps, frustrated now, looking for a brick wall to smash his head against. 'I'm not . . . *him*.'

He stops because Frances has appeared in the opening that leads to the kitchen. Her white-knuckled hand is gripping an eight-inch Kitchen Devil. Its blade is decorated with vermilion slivers of chilli, which could be there because she's rustling up something spicy for the kids or simply because she wants the wound to smart that extra bit.

'Please, Mum,' Karen says without looking round.

Frances backs off without taking her eyes off Alvin.

'No, you're not Paul,' Karen continues. 'You're a lot more complicated. A lot more screwed up, to be honest. You need help, Alvin.'

'I need *you* . . . Come back home. We don't have to live together, but at least we can . . . work on things.'

'I can't. I can't be with someone I basically don't trust . . . Don't look at me like that. All . . . *wounded*. I'm not going to apologise for it.'

'You're staying up here?' Alvin asks, incredulous. In the past Karen has had little good to say about her birthplace. 'Where are you going to live?'

'We'll stay here until we get something sorted out.'

'*We?*'

'You think I'm gonna leave the kids in London? We're fine here. It's not so crowded without my dad.'

Karen's father hasn't been seen for a decade. He ran off with his dentist's receptionist, a woman fifteen years his junior. This partly explains Frances's grip on the knife handle.

'What are you going to do?' Alvin asks.

'I met someone last week –'

'*Already*? Jesus.'

'Not that kind of someone. Who do you think I am? You? She's a vet at the Blue Cross in Gatley. They need a manager. It's a full-time job. Permanent.'

Permanent. The word shocks Alvin into silence.

'What happened to your wrist?' Karen asks after a moment. 'It wasn't my mother, was it?'

Alvin looks down at the graze on the joint and the purplish swelling around it. 'No, it wasn't your mother. I fell over yesterday.' He doesn't feel up to telling her about his adventure on the footbridge.

She reaches over and brushes the bruise lightly with her fingertip. 'You should get it seen to. It could be a sprain.'

Her touch brings tears to his eyes.

'Look, I'm not going to stop you seeing the kids or anything,' she says, reading him like a book.

'*Supervised!*' Frances has reappeared, her mouth set in a thin and geometrically perfect straight line that cuts her face in two.

'Mum, butt out, *please*.'

'You can't let him near those children unsupervised.'

'You think I'd lay a finger on my kids?' Alvin is on his feet now, angry.

'Enough, the pair of you.' Karen is on her feet as well, her hands held up like a policewoman's at a congested junction.

They both pause because Karen has told them to and because the front door has opened and small children are tearing through the house.

'Mummy, I got rock, I got ROCK with my NAME!'

Sid appears in the opening with Kieran, his slightly smaller cousin, in tow. He freezes when he sees his father. Karen immediately rushes to him and smothers him with a hug. 'What's wrong, Sid?' she says. 'Why are you crying?'

'Because Daddy is,' he replies.

Positions of trust, abuses thereof

As far as Alvin Lee is concerned, his life pretty much ended that Sunday afternoon in Cheadle. The fact that ten days later he is sitting in the windowless interview room at his local police station is neither here nor there. He is alone, waiting for a detective to come and talk to him. About what, he doesn't know – more questions about Louise Bird's mugging, he supposes – and he doesn't care. Let them throw fifty years of unsolved crimes at him – the Lucan nanny murder? He'll cop for that – because things can't get any worse. He's at the very bottom with nowhere left to sink.

You might say he's depressed.

He should have phoned Trevor Poll when the police called at the house to bring him in, but he didn't see the point. He's beyond help, isn't he? Let Poll look after his shoplifters. Or his sideline in photocopies.

The detective who's questioning him now isn't the one who did it the last time. This one is older and less enthusiastic.

'The mugger's knife: how big?' the policeman asks, wearily going over old ground. Alvin wonders if the man would notice if he gave him a fresh set of answers. Made the knife six inches long, say, instead of four. Or made it a gun . . . or a light sabre, which – *obviously* – Kevan had stolen from an umbrella stand at the dentist while Luke Skywalker was seeing the hygienist. But he sticks to the truth as best he can remember it.

'I dunno. About four inches or something.'

'And when he threatened you with it, you reckon he meant business?'

'Well, yes . . . I think . . . I dunno . . . Maybe he wouldn't have done anything, but the knife was real and I wasn't going to take the chance.'

'So you definitely weren't playing out a script –'

'No.'

'You and the mugger hadn't got together beforehand and choreographed yourselves a little fight scene –'

'*No* . . . Look, I've already told you all this stuff. Yes, I knew the mugger, no, it wasn't pre-planned, and no, I'm not going to give you his name. Nothing's changed.'

'Something's changed, sir,' the detective says. 'We've got the mugger.'

'You've arrested him?'

'He saved us the bother. He came forward.'

Alvin rocks back in his seat, astonished. And delighted.

Kevan Kennedy has done the Right Thing!

Contrary to cynical rumour, wonders have *not* ceased. All that remains is for whales to evolve a harpoon-proof blubber layer and malaria-carrying mosquitoes to go off the taste of the human race. Oh, and for Karen to come home. Preferably with a smile on her face, but a scowling Karen would be sufficiently miraculous.

'He gave himself up,' Alvin says quietly, unable to believe the words.

'Bit of a first for these here parts,' the detective says, livening up now.

'So, why all the questions?'

'Thing is, his version of events and yours . . . well, there are discrepancies.'

Alvin nods, unconcerned – a slight misting over of respective memories, nothing more.

'Have a listen to this.'

The detective produces a cassette and feeds it into the machine that sits on the desk. He presses *play* and sits back in his chair, his eyes settling on Alvin.

And Alvin listens to the taped voice of the detective . . .

'Tell me again, Kevin . . . Sorry, it's Kevan, isn't it? When did Alvin Lee come and talk to you?'

. . . and then to Kevan Kennedy.

'Dunno. Three or four days before . . . Yeah, four days before we did her over.'

'That's bollocks,' Alvin protests as the penny drops, 'absolute –'

The detective raises his finger. 'Best shush and pay attention, eh?'

'Did he tell you why he wanted you to mug her?'

'He just said she was minted and that. You know, he'd, like, save her and then she'd bung him a load of money or something.'

'And what was in it for you?'

'He said he'd give me five grand, but he never fucking paid up, did he?'

'Is that why you're coming forward now? Because he cheated you?'

'I s'pose . . . Sort of . . . But also 'cause what he did weren't right, yeah?'

'How do you mean?'

'Well, I was like a kid and that, and he was like a teacher. He was, you know, abusing his position of trust and that.'

The policeman presses *stop* without taking his eyes off Alvin, who can only shake his head. His mouth is parched, all the moisture in his body seemingly going to his palms, which are slick with sweat.

'You don't actually believe that, do you?' he manages to say at last, though it comes out as a husky whisper.

'Why shouldn't I?'

'Well . . . 'cause it's bollocks from start to finish, that's why.'

'There's a lot more on the tape, you know. A lot more *detail*: how you briefed him on where the old lady lived, filled him in on her routines; how you worked out a plan where he jumped her while you waited in the massage place; how he wasn't supposed to hurt her, just scare the living Jesus out of her. He told it all to me and then again, word for word, to another detective. And it tallies with what the eyewitnesses have told us. How the two of you talked to each other during the, er, *struggle* and how you then let him get away.'

'I didn't let him get away. He knocked me over and ran off like Ben Johnson. And he had a bloody knife. I wasn't going to chase him, was I? And, and . . .' Alvin's mouth flaps wildly while Kevan's confession replays in his head. '. . . What did he say at the end?'

The detective shrugs. 'Something about you not giving him his wedge.'

'No, after that. That I was *abusing my position of trust*. Are you telling me he wasn't working from a script? Does he honestly seem like the sort of kid who'd use words like that?'

'Who knows?' the policeman says. 'Kids are like sponges, aren't they? Sounds like the sort of teacher-speak he'd pick up from someone like you.'

'I'm not a teacher,' Alvin mumbles.

'No, definitely not after this goes down. I'd say you're pretty much fucked.'

The two men stare at each other, silent for the moment. Who knows what the detective is thinking, but Alvin is waiting for him to hit him with the Lucan nanny murder.

A ham-fisted sergeant squashes Alvin's fingertips into the inkpad and then rolls each one onto its designated box on the form. The detective looks on, bored again, his shoulders slouched, his hands in his pockets.

'I've been set up, you know,' Alvin says, not for the first time.

'If I had a pound for every time . . .' the sergeant responds – probably not for the first time. He looks up at the detective and says, 'You know this one used to be a bit of a rock star, don't you, Brian?'

'Uh-huh, I read the *Gazette,*' the detective replies. 'There was me hoping my career high would be nicking Keith Richards with a suitcase full of scag . . . or Sir Elton lurking in the gents. Looks like I'm going to have to settle for the one-hit wonder. Wasn't even the bloody lead singer.'

Now Alvin knows where rock bottom is. It's precisely where he's lying: on a metal bench in a bare cell, which, aptly enough, is in the police station's basement. The deep, dark dungeon, then . . . Though its walls are constructed of whitewashed breeze blocks. And actually, given that he's lying about eighteen inches off the floor, he supposes that technically he could sink a little lower.

It is his possibly unique ability to clutch at such subatomic particles of hope that makes Alvin the man he is.

He hasn't been charged yet – with conspiring to rob and defraud or with the Lucan nanny murder – but it's only a matter of time. He's made his phone call. It wasn't the one he dearly wished to make. That would have been to Karen – a drawn-out scream along the lines of *'Heeeeeeeeelp meeeeeeeeeeeee!'* – but he didn't think it would bear fruit. He made do with Trevor Poll, who is cutting short whatever he's been up to in order to rush to his aid.

As it happens, there doesn't appear to be any rushing going on. Alvin has been locked up for three hours now. Though he doesn't have a watch, he knows how long it has been because every hour on the hour the little hatch in the door slides open and part of a face peers through, checking that he hasn't hanged himself with a trouser leg.

Poll had better get a move on. Alvin is supposed to start his new job at the weekend. Miserable as he is, he remains Alvin Lee and he hasn't spent *all* of his time since Manchester wallowing in grief on his sofa. He made himself a to-do list. It included cleaning the graffiti off the window, visiting Jonathan Craig in hospital (so heavily sedated that Alvin couldn't tell if he was glad or gutted to be alive) and catching up with Lynette, the one person at Wood Hill who's prepared to be seen with him (a point she emphasised by insisting on meeting in a very busy pub). The priority item, though, was Find Job, so Tebbitishly he got on his bike (a metaphorical one – his real one still needs new gears).

He was successful at his first interview. It's only Homebase, where he'll feign knowledge of everything from bedding plants and coach bolts to that white stuff you wrap around pipe joints, the name of which he can never remember. But at least it will pay some bills and, hopefully, provide a distraction.

Which he could do with right now. He thought he had run the gamut of emotions with regard to Kevan Kennedy over the past four years, but betrayal is a new one. He wonders what's in it for Kevan. How much is Jeremy Bird paying him? Money is the only thing that could have propelled him into a police station. And it must be sufficient to make it worth the time he'll surely have to serve. Or perhaps Jeremy Bird was smooth enough to convince him that he could walk away from a violent robbery charge with a spell on probation – if only he did the *right thing* and fessed up. If only Alvin had called on Kevan that day with his chequebook and pen, he might have left with more than a vague promise and a couple of chocolates.

He has also wondered how Bird fingered Kevan for the crime against his mother, but not for very long. Jeremy Bird is a man with no shortage of flunkies. Alvin presumes now that the incongruous Volvo he spotted on his visit to the Glenn contained one of them. And to think he fretted over the car's welfare.

Bastard sneaky Volvo driver.

No, that's not fair. He – or she – was only doing his – or her – job.

Bastard Jeremy bastard Bird.

That's more like it.

And so Alvin grows to hate Jeremy Bird as much as his solicitor already does (and by the way, where the hell is *he*?), but his seething is interrupted by an argument making its way along the corridor outside his cell.

'You've got no right to bang me up. I'm only a kid.'

'A *kid*? You're a bloody psycho.'

'You can't say that. That's racist. You'll lose your job for that.'

'What are you talking about? You're white.'

'Yeah, and you're a Pa— *Asian*. So it's racist, innit?'

The policeman responds by slamming shut the cell door. As he returns the way he came the girl yells out, *'Wanker!'*

In the ensuing silence her panting is audible through the wall that separates Alvin's cell from hers and once again he can't believe his ears.

'Debbie?' he calls out. 'Debbie Coates?'

'Who's that?'

'Alvin.'

'Alvin! *Sir*? What the hell are you doing here?'

'I could ask the same of you. What have you done?'

'Nothing, man.'

'C'mon, it's me you're talking to.'

'Shoplifting,' she admits, her mumble barely making it through the wall.

'Jesus, not again.'

'Look, it was only one tiny thing, right? And I'd've paid if it hadn't been so fucking expensive.'

'Where?'

'Baby Gap . . .'

The label-conscious shoplifter now. She's come on – last time it was the Pound Shop. Perhaps he should be pleased.

'. . . It was for Kanye Pharrell . . .'

Kanye Pharrell. He'd forgotten about him.

'. . . This dead cute all-in-one with little turtles on it . . . And some little tracky bottoms to go with it . . . And the top that goes with the tracky bottoms 'cause you can't not get both, innit?'

'I thought you said one thing.'

'One *outfit*, yeah . . . ? If you count the hat and the bootees. It was gonna be Kanye Pharrell's coming-home present. But it came to, like, over *fifty* quid. Rip-off, man. You can get the same stuff for, like, fifteen down the market.'

'Why didn't you go down the market, then?'

'*Duh*. Down the market they don't wrap it all up in tissue and stick it in a box with Baby Gap on it, do they?'

Funny, Alvin thinks, but beneath the brassy exterior Debbie is just a typical girl with a typically girly love of shopping and baby things and pretty packaging. She has all the right attributes. She just lacks the necessary finances.

But something else strikes him as well, this on a more practical level. 'Hang on,' he says. 'If you took it to the counter for them to gift-wrap, you must have been going to pay for it.'

'*No*, you take it to the counter, get 'em to stick it in the box, say thanks, then run like fuck,' she explains breezily. 'There was a big twat on the door though, a fucking psycho bouncer. What the fuck's he doing in a *baby* shop?'

'Probably there to stop thieving oiks like you. What have they locked you up for?' A fair question because even recidivist teen shoplifters don't usually warrant custody.

'For my own safety, they said.'

'Your own safety?'

'I slapped one of 'em.'

'Jesus, Debbie.'

'Well, he was really bending my arm back, yeah? Twat could've broken it. Anyway, they won't do me for that. He's like ten foot tall and that. He'd look like a right gay testifying. They'll let me out when my mum gets here.'

Her confidence isn't misplaced. She speaks from experience. She should worry, though. Alvin has met her mum and she's scarier than any copper.

Talking to her again, albeit in a raised voice through a wall, makes Alvin realise how much he misses her. Not just her, but Curtis, Roland, Chenil . . . all of them. Even Desolate Dan and his colouring pens. He misses Wood Hill; normal life, which was never actually that normal, but which was at least free of vertiginous changes of fortune.

'Anyway, what about you?' Debbie says. 'What've they done you for?'

'You wouldn't believe it if I told you.'

'Try me.'

'You don't want to hear about it, Debbie, really.'

'Why not? I ain't got nothing better to do. Go on . . . Hey, it hasn't got nothing to do with you losing your job and that, has it? 'Cause they can't do you for that 'cause you didn't do nothing wrong and you shouldn't've even lost your job and – bloody hell – Chenil'd probably be dead if you hadn't been there so if they do you for that . . . That is *bang* out of order . . .' She has worked herself into a lather of rage. Alvin listens to her stand up and pace her cell angrily. '. . . I'm gonna tell 'em. I'm gonna fucking tell 'em.'

'Calm down, Debbie,' he says. 'It's got nothing to do with school.'

'What is it then? *Tell* me.'

So he does. He tells her everything, starting with the mugging and ending with Kevan's confected statement. He even tells her about the visits to Kelly Hendricks. It's like confession all over again – even down to the fact that his confessor is on the other side of a divide – and like confession it feels cathartic.

'I don't fucking believe it,' she says when he's finished – the same words with which she has been punctuating the entire story.

'Well, don't say I didn't warn you.'

'No, I don't believe what that bastard is doing to you.'

'It seems rich people aren't the same as us, Debbie. They didn't get that way by being nice to people.'

'I'm not talking about him. I mean Kev. The . . . the *cunt*. Sorry about that, but you've gotta admit he's pulled a right cunt's trick, yeah? I mean, after all the stuff you did for him.'

'I didn't stop him getting kicked out of school, did I? He's just surviving as best he can. He was probably offered a load of money. It's not easy to turn –'

'Shut up, will you? Stop being so bloody *nice*. That's your trouble, you know. He's a cunt. End of.'

'Yeah, you're right,' he says because he supposes – at last – that she is.

Kevan Kennedy is a cunt.

'What does your missus say?' Debbie asks. 'You getting sacked and now this. She must be going mental.'

'She doesn't know about it – not about the Kevan thing anyway. She's left. Gone to Manchester.'

'*Manchester*,' she squeals as if it's another planet, which it might as well be. 'That's so not fair. She's out of order buggering off.'

'You can hardly blame her. Look at the rumours flying about.'

'But they're not true, are they?'

'Well, after Kelly . . . Why should she believe me?'

''Cause she just *should*. 'Cause you're a good bloke. You're kind. And honest.'

'Thanks, Debbie. It's sweet of you to say so.'

'Well, it's true, innit? She won't find another one like you in a hurry – not in bloody *Manchester* anyway.'

Alvin doesn't disagree.

After a moment she says, 'We've gotta do something about this.'

'Thanks, but it's my mess. You've got problems of your own.'

'Shoplifting? That ain't a problem. Not like yours. No, I'm gonna talk to Curtis, get him to round up some guys to have a word with –'

'Don't even think about seeing Kevan. Someone will get hurt – probably seriously, knowing him. Please leave things be.'

'I've gotta do *some*thing, man.'

'No, you don't. Just stay out of trouble . . . *please*.'

Debbie is incapable of staying out of trouble, but he hopes that at least she won't get herself into the shit on his account.

'You got a brief?' she asks. 'You'll need a top brief.'

He is prevented from answering by the clank of the lock in his cell door. 'Your solicitor's here,' the constable says once he has opened it. 'Says sorry he's late. Had to wait for a bloke to repair the copier.'

Oh yes, thinks Alvin, a *top* brief.

The gnat in the Savlon

Actually, two days later, Alvin has much to thank Trevor Poll for: five thousand pounds' worth of gratitude. It is possible to be that precise.

'Thank you,' he says, making a start. 'You didn't have to do that. I can't imagine many solicitors do it for their clients.'

'Oh, neither can I, but as I keep saying, Alvin, this is personal. I'm not going to give Jeremy Bird the satisfaction of seeing you remanded in custody.'

'I just don't know how I can repay you.'

'So long as you don't abscond before your trial, you won't have to. Just don't tell Mrs Poll about it. She's earmarked that money for a new porch.'

They are standing outside the magistrates' court, where Alvin has just been committed for trial having pleaded not guilty to two charges of criminal conspiracy, each one carrying the certain threat of a jail sentence. The magistrate set bail at five thousand pounds. That he is standing here and not being driven away to a remand centre is entirely down to Trevor Poll's generosity.

'Well, thanks,' Alvin says again, 'five *thousand* thanks. And don't worry. I'm not planning to do a runner.'

'I'm sure Ronnie Biggs once told his minders something similar, but I trust you. Anyway, I felt obliged to bail you out after keeping you dangling at the police station the other day.'

The other day: Poll's excuse of hanging on for the repairman wasn't a case of skewed priorities, but a matter of physical necessity. In an attempt to fix his chronically sick copier, he'd whipped out his Swiss Army knife and opened the machine up. However, he only succeeded in getting his wrist irretrievably wedged between the rubber rollers of a paper feed. If he hadn't been able to lean over to a desk and reach the phone he might still be there.

'What now?' Poll asks as they walk down the wide court steps.

'Well, I'm starting my new job tomorrow –'

'I meant now as in right now. You fancy repairing to a saloon for an ale and a bite? Fear not, my shout.'

As Poll scrapes up the last of the pie gravy with the edge of his fork, Alvin mentions something that has been on his mind for a while.

'Trevor, when Jeremy Bird came to see me he said you shouldn't be representing me. It's a conflict of interest or something.'

'Technically, Alvin, *technically* . . .' Poll says slowly '. . . he's right. However, the only person in a position to sue me for malpractice is you, seeing as you are both the sole beneficiary of the will and the man whom I'm defending on a charge of inspiring its very existence.'

Alvin looks at him, feeling a little lost.

'Frankly, I'm the best hope you've got, Alvin, and I'm prepared to take a chance on your goodwill lasting the course. Yes, I know, it's all a bit wing and prayer . . . Anyway, you don't want to pay too much attention to anything Bird says. The man is desperate. That is the truly good news. This whole business shows how utterly desperate he has become.'

'How do you figure that?' Alvin is perfectly happy to dwell on the good-news side of the track, but, frankly, he's having trouble finding his way there.

'Given there's no medical evidence that his mother was demented, his only hope of getting the will overturned is to prove she was put under improper pressure when making it,' Poll explains. '*Id est* you conned her.'

'Yes,' Alvin says, with it so far.

'And since he has no legitimate evidence of that, he's had to concoct some. See how low the truly desperate stoop? What foetid barrel did he have to scrape to find Kennedy?'

'Yeah, but he found him, didn't he? And if a jury believes him, I'm –'

'Buggered? That is indeed the potential gnat in the Savlon. You go to jail; JB gets his mitts on the moolah . . . But don't look so bleak. Kennedy hardly sounds the brightest spark. A good barrister will wipe the floor with his story.'

'Kevan's impulsive, violent . . . I wouldn't call him stupid, though. You know, I think I'm going to go and see him again, have another –'

'Stop! Let me stop you right there. You will do no such thing, not unless you want to have perverting the course of justice added to the charge sheet. Anyway, it'd be a waste of time. Any shred of conscience he had the last time you tried has been bought by Bird. And while I'm at it, don't go anywhere near that bastard either. He's never possessed an ounce of better nature to appeal to.'

Until now Alvin hadn't thought of approaching Jeremy Bird. It's probably a lousy idea, but . . .

Doesn't everyone have a better nature somewhere? If Alvin didn't believe in the fundamental redeemability of even the most recalcitrant motherfucker, he would never have taken the job . . .

No, not Homebase but the job he doesn't have any more.

Ultraviolet happiness

'Are you trying to tell me this is Happy Violet?' the flat-capped man demands.

'It's Sugared Lilac.'

'More like Desire.'

'Soft Aubergine?'

'No, too light.'

'Whatever, it isn't Happy Violet.'

Flat Cap has prised open a five-litre can of Rich Matt and holds it up in front of Alvin. The small crowd gathered around them seems to have such an assured grasp of the spectrum (and the correct names for every colour therein) that it might have assembled for a fringe debate on violets, lilacs and mauves at the Dulux annual conference.

It being only his second day on the job, Alvin should really defer to their expertise, but he can't help pointing out, 'It says Happy Violet here,' as he squints at the side of the can.

'Well, it's not, is it? It's nothing like the swatch. What are you going to do about it?' Flat Cap is looking directly at Alvin's *Can I help?* badge, which does suggest that he might indeed be the man for this particular crisis.

'I'm sorry, but it's only my second day,' Alvin says. 'I'll try to find someone on Paints.'

'Who? *Who*?' Flat Cap waves frustrated arms at the store's aircraft hangar interior. 'There's never anyone here.'

Alvin understands his pain. When he used to come here to buy screws and drill bits, he would wonder if the staff hid when they saw a confused-looking punter trolleying towards them. Now he's an employee, he knows that is exactly what they do. Along with the jolly green uniform comes a sixth sense. The first whiff of a customer with questions has staff disappearing into the store's maze of aisles like timid woodland creatures melting into the forest.

'I can't stand this place,' Flat Cap snarls. 'It's like the *Marie* bloody *Celeste* with power tools.' He slaps the lid back onto the pot and walks away muttering. The crowd of colour experts disperses as well, all except for one couple and their small son. The woman looks at Alvin intently.

'Can I help?' he asks, hoping she says no because unless it's 'Do you know where the checkout is?' Alvin won't know the answer to any question she might have.

'It *is* him,' she says to her bloke. 'He's just like his picture.'

Alvin suddenly feels like a zoo exhibit – not the graceful flamingo or the awesome tiger, but one of the viler creatures, perhaps a flea-ridden monkey that likes to repel visitors by masturbating in front of them.

'Take Fenton to the car,' the woman says. 'I'm going to find a manager.'

The man grabs the little boy's hand and whisks him towards the exit. The woman makes a move to pass Alvin, but he stops her by saying, 'Look, madam, I don't know what you're thinking, but –'

'I don't know how they let you work here,' she spits. 'Don't your kind have to be vetted these days? This is a *family* store. The place is full of kiddies.'

She pushes past him and heads down the aisle, but another woman wheeling an empty trolley stops her progress. 'You should take the trouble to get informed before you open your silly mouth,' Lynette Moorhouse says to her. 'This man has never done anything to harm a child.'

She pushes her trolley to Alvin and stands squarely beside him, staring down the woman, defying her to take up the challenge.

'Are you his *wife*?' the woman asks, the disgust in her voice palpable.

'No, I'm not,' Lynette replies, slipping her arm through Alvin's, 'but if I were, nothing could make me prouder.'

'You're *both* sick,' the woman says as she stalks off in search of a manager – though, for the reasons already covered, she'll be lucky to find one.

'You couldn't have timed that better, Lynette,' Alvin says. 'Thanks.'

'My pleasure. That sort of rubbish happen a lot?'

'Only the third time.'

'This is only your second day, isn't it? I thought the abuse I got at Wood Hill was bad, but this is appalling.'

'Oh, I'll survive,' Alvin says, raising a smile. 'Sticks and stones and all that bollocks . . . Anyway, what are you doing here?'

'Just stopped by to look in on you, but I might hang about and do some shopping. You didn't tell me there was a Laura Ashley concession.'

'I didn't tell you there's twenty per cent off Bosch hammer drills either. You interested?'

'What do you think? When's your lunch hour?'

Alvin looks at his watch. 'Five minutes. I'll take it now, though. I reckon I deserve it.'

'Where do you go to eat round here?'

'We could try the burger stand in the car park. Only the one case of botulism this year apparently. Best to steer clear of the fried chicken, though.'

They walk and talk.

'How's all your legal stuff going?' Lynette asks.

'Grinding on. My lawyer's still chirpy, but I don't share his optimism.'

'That's not like you, Alvin. What about Kevan? Any cracks in his story?'

Alvin shakes his head. It strikes him for the first time that his friend and Kevan the psycho actually have something in common. He briefly wonders if he should tell her about Kevan's fetish, but decides against it. 'What's new at school, then?' he asks her.

'You know Rowell's retiring at the end of the year. I thought I might go for his job.'

'Head of history? Brilliant.'

'It's bigger than that. Chadwick's taking the opportunity for one of his management restructures. It's going to be head of humanities.'

'You what?'

'A new *uber*-department. English, drama, languages, history . . . All the arts and social sciences basically. Chadwick's way of making a crappy old comp's crappy old departments seem like *faculties*.'

'You'd be running English? You'd be Stanislavski's boss. He'd love that.'

'Wouldn't he just?'

'What does Donna think? She isn't going for it, is she?'

'That'd be tricky. No, she's not. She thinks I should, though.'

'She's right. You'd be fantastic. Want me to write you a reference?'

Lynette laughs. 'You know your mate Bird-Wright will have a bit of a say in the appointment, don't you?'

'Well, you shouldn't get caught hanging round with me, then.'

'You reckon she comes down Homebase on a Sunday?'

Alvin doesn't answer. He has pulled up thirty feet short of the burger stand.

'What's up?' Lynette asks.

'You seen who's manning the grill?' Alvin says.

The last time Alvin saw Curtis Young, he was pressing him up against a concrete doughnut. Actually, no. He saw him on the allotment on suicide Saturday. He never imagined he would see him here, wearing grease-spattered overalls and a white paper hat. But stranger sightings have occurred lately – Kevan Kennedy plus pink bra springs all too readily to mind.

'Unbelievable,' Lynette says. 'He's actually doing an honest day's work.'

'You still up for the burger?' Alvin asks.

'Why not? Curtis and I have been like *that* since the flowers.'

They walk up to the stand and watch Curtis through the hatch. Oblivious to his new customers, he attempts to pour frozen chips from a plastic sack into the fryer. The chips have melded together in icy clumps and would prefer not to go anywhere. 'Fucking things,' he curses.

'Bash the bag on the counter,' Alvin suggests. 'That should loosen them.'

'You wha— *Jesus*, Alvin, what the fuck are you doing here?' Curtis stares at him open-mouthed, never having imagined he'd one day see his former mentor in Homebase green; like Robin Hood without the redistribution mandate. Then he sees Lynette standing at Alvin's shoulder. 'Hello, Miss Moorhouse,' he adds with pitch-perfect humility.

'Hi, Curtis,' she replies. 'How long have you been working here?'

'It's my auntie's van,' he says a little sheepishly – too cool for school, he's also way too groovy to be seen slumming it in the family catering business. 'I just work Sundays, yeah? Here, you're not gonna tell no one, right?'

'Not if you don't want us to,' Alvin says.

Alvin seems to be accumulating secrets from Wood Hill kids. This one, though, lacks the *News of the World* resonance of cross-dressing Kevan.

'You want something, then?' Curtis asks. 'The chicken's well safe.'

'Just two burgers,' Alvin says. Best not to trust *safe* in either of its senses.

Curtis picks up a spatula, scoops a couple of too-pink-to-be-true patties out of a box and slaps them onto the hotplate. 'You get fresh ones,' he says. 'Not warmed up like the other twats . . . Sorry, Miss Moorhouse.'

'It's OK, you *can* swear,' Lynette says. 'I'm off duty.'

Curtis grins inanely at Alvin. The doughnut incident, it seems, is forgotten, but Curtis has always had a short attention span – just one of his problems according to the educationalists.

'I saw Debbie the other day, Curtis,' Alvin says.

Though with her being in a locked cell, technically he didn't *see* her.

'She told me, man.' The corner of Curtis's mouth curls in a smirk. He's clearly itching to say something, but doesn't want to be the first to mention police cells and criminal charges.

'Is she OK?' Alvin asks.

Curtis shrugs. 'Saw her at Becker's party last night. Seemed cool, man.'

'She hasn't done anything stupid?'

Curtis is grinning now. 'She was snogging Mark Shakespeare . . .' Chenil's big brother, not long out of prison: indecent assault. '. . . I'd call that pretty fucking stupid.' He flips the burgers. 'Onions?'

'Please,' Alvin and Lynette say in unison.

They watch him throw pre-fried slivers of onion onto the griddle and then press down on the burgers with his spatula, causing them to spit testily. 'You're good at this,' Alvin says. 'Multi-talented: grill chef, computer geek . . .'

'You taking the piss?'

'No, seriously, what else can you do that I don't know about?'

'You're taking the piss,' Curtis decides, deftly splitting a bun and putting it on the edge of the hotplate to warm through.

Within a minute the burgers are sitting before them in open

Styrofoam containers and Curtis is offering a choice of condiments in colour-coded bottles.

'How much?' Alvin asks, reaching into his pocket.

'No, I'll pay,' Lynette says, putting her hand on Alvin's arm.

'Forget it, man,' Curtis says. 'They're free.'

Alvin thinks about putting up a fight, but given mounting debt and the fact that he won't see a Homebase pay cheque for a while yet, he can't afford to win. 'Thanks, Curtis. We owe you.'

'You owe my auntie,' he says, grinning again.

Alvin bites into the burger, which isn't at all bad and might even contain a modicum of beef. 'Debbie told you everything, then?' he says.

'Uh-huh. Told us last night. Fucking Kev. Fucking cunt, eh?' That would seem to be the consensus. 'Sorry, Miss,' he adds for Lynette's benefit, 'but he's a right one of them.'

'There really is no other word for him,' Lynette agrees.

'You know the cops pulled him over last night?' Curtis continues.

Alvin shakes his head.

'On the North Circ, yeah? No licence, no insurance . . . He's doing, like, ninety an' all. He's in this totally bitchin' custom Astra: teal blue, Reiger body kit, super-fat tailpipe, UV ground kit . . .'

All of which means less than nothing to Alvin.

'. . . blinging ICE.'

Alvin looks at Lynette, his brow furrowed.

'In-car entertainment,' she explains – as a man she used to know a thing or two about cars. 'Sounds impressive, Curtis. Who did he nick it off?'

'That's the thing, yeah, Miss,' Curtis tells her. 'He *didn't*. It was his, yeah? He got it off a geezer in Edmonton. Paid for and everything. Cops couldn't believe it when he showed 'em the log book.'

Lynette looks at Alvin in alarm, but he has already started to back away from the burger stand. 'Don't do it, Alvin,' she says. 'Talk to your lawyer, call the cops. Don't go there.'

But Alvin has set off across the car park, back towards the superstore.

'Alvin!' she calls out pointlessly to his receding back.

Alvin can spot him clean across the estate. The luminous rectangle of ultraviolet tarmac moving at speed gives him away. In the late-afternoon gloom, it's harder to make out the teal-blue Astra immediately above it, but he can hear it as it spins wheel-locked circles on the approach road to the tower blocks, marking out its territory as clearly and deliberately as a pissing tom cat. A small crowd looks on, individuals jumping back onto the muddy wasteland whenever the car comes too close.

Alvin has no business being here, but the news of a car bought with blood money stunned him and he set off for the Glenn, having pleaded nausea to his boss. It's Sunday, so he couldn't have taken Lynette's advice and called Trevor Poll for guidance. But he wouldn't have done so even if it were Monday.

Outrage propelled him here, but now he has arrived, the boiling indignation is being swamped by nerves. What does he hope to achieve? And how, exactly, does he hope to achieve it? Kevan is on his own turf, his homies around him, and he's wearing a teal-blue suit of armour.

Perhaps Alvin simply wants to look him in the eye.

Whatever, he keeps walking until he's on the outer edge of the circle of admirers – kids and teenagers, mostly boys. No one looks at him. All eyes are on the car. Alvin glances to his left and sees a familiar face. Like him, she looks on helplessly, not part of the group of spectators, but with an interest far less passing than theirs. After a moment he makes his way to her.

'Hi, Ms Nash,' he says.

'It's Karen,' she says, raising her voice above the tyres' screams.

'*Karen*,' he repeats, feeling a little stab.

'He's gone fucking mad, hasn't he?' she says almost inaudibly. 'Look at him. *Mad*. I daren't think how he paid for that thing.'

'Have you asked him?'

'Like he'd tell me. He's always coming home with . . . *stuff*. But *this*? He's loaded at the moment. God knows what he's done.'

God knows he's made a pact with the devil, Alvin thinks.

'I'm seeing that shrink,' Karen Nash tells him. 'Kevan gave me the money. Not that I told him what it was for.'

'Is it helping?' Alvin asks.

'It's *fantastic*. You know how nice it is just to talk about . . . *yourself*?'

'I can imagine,' Alvin says as his mind wades through the soupy irony.

Who suggested therapy? Alvin Lee did.

And who's paying for it? The devil.

'Just dumping my shit on someone . . .' she says, her eyes rolling in an unspoken *wow*. 'And it's giving me coping strategies . . . You know. To deal with my anger and stuff.'

'Great,' Alvin says, weirdly pleased that someone is benefiting. If an ugly fight over money inadvertently leads to one seriously stressed individual developing useful coping strategies, well, that must be a perverse consolation.

'Why are you here?' she asks.

He wonders whether he should tell her, drag her into this thing between Kevan and him. But what could she do? And why should she even care? About Kevan, sure – that he doesn't end up in jail, that he doesn't kill himself in his new toy. But about Alvin?

'He was going to help me out,' he says vaguely, 'but he let me down.'

'What are you talking about?'

'You should ask him yourself.'

'You something to do with this?' she demands.

'Not in the way you think.'

'What the fuck are you talking about? *Tell* me!'

'You should ask Kevan.'

'I'm asking *you*.' She steps towards him menacingly, the coping strategies forgotten for the time being. 'You're behind this, aren't you? What the fuck have you done to him?'

'I haven't done anything, Ms Nash,' Alvin snarls, responding for once in kind, 'and that's my trouble. If I'd done something, if I'd turned your boy in the first bloody chance I got, maybe I wouldn't be here now.'

Before she can come at him again, the car slews to a stop. The engine cuts, leaving only the hammering, deafening stomp of dancehall coming from within – blinging ICE indeed. The driver's door opens and out climbs the Monarch of the Glenn.

Alvin and Karen Nash hang back as wannabes throng around Kevan. Alvin can't speak for Kevan's mother, but he feels his own anger subside because, well, he has never seen the boy look so *happy*. How can he spoil it for him? So what if his joy comes at the cost of, for Alvin at least, a jail sentence?

Funny thing, empathy. Even as Alvin is experiencing an unwanted but tangible sense of it, so it appears in Kevan's eyes as he sees him with his mother.

Empathy in the form of guilt.

And so, Alvin supposes, he has what he came here for.

Kevan has a conscience and those bush baby eyes of his can do nothing but advertise the fact.

Karen Nash looks at her son, then at Alvin. Her mind is perhaps figuring that if she presumed Alvin was here on account of some unpaid criminal debt, then she'll have to rethink. But probably not.

Kevan's eyes flicker suddenly from guilty to fearful. Without looking about him, Alvin immediately knows why. Pulsating violet-blue light bounces off both the jostling faces and the Astra's body panels, and Alvin knows it doesn't come from another car's under-body neon. The crowd knows it too because it disperses like a herd of gazelle getting a whiff of lion.

Kevan jumps back into his car, fires up the engine and exits north, leaving behind only the stench of burnt rubber. The patrol car sends the runtish remains of the crowd fleeing with a brief whoop of its siren as it sweeps past in pursuit of the Astra.

Alvin should leave, but he remains rooted as the scene takes on a surreal twist. Out of the shadow of a tower block comes a supermarket trolley, manned by two smallish boys, one hanging onto the bar at the back and the other huddled in the basket like a week's groceries. It rolls down the slope towards the speeding Astra. The boys didn't see *this* coming, but now that they do they seem frozen, locked on course like trolley-borne rabbits.

It's time for Kevan's conscience to be put to a real test and to Alvin's ineffable relief he does the right thing. Literally, because he veers hard to the right, bouncing the car over a high kerb. Its front wheels are still airborne when it slams into the lamppost on the other side.

The trolley glides on, but judders, then heels over onto its side as its corner clips the wing mirror of the belatedly braking police car.

Karen Nash, until now immobile beside Alvin, rushes forward to the wrecked car with a scream of 'Kevan!' Alvin starts forward too, but stops as he sees the two boys crawl from their own tiny wreck, shaken but apparently unbroken. He then watches the Astra's window slide open and Kevan's hulking body squeeze through the hole. He lands in a heap on the pavement, but jumps to his feet and, pushing his mother aside, sets off without pause on legs built for getaways. Two policemen, stiff with body armour, emerge from the patrol car. While one checks the welfare of the trolley riders, the other sets off after Kevan. Alvin watches the shadows of the towers swallow up both of them.

Now it really is time to go and he turns and trudges purposefully back the way he came.

But not before he has taken one last look at the trophy car. Its bent grille envelops the base of the lamppost, embracing it in a big, mechanical hug. Steam hisses from its ruptured radiator. Black oil glistens in the streetlight as it forms a fresh pool around a tyre, now ultra-low-profile on account of being flat.

Justice of a sort has been served; Alvin can presume that since he was nicked last night, Kevan won't have been out to buy a fully comprehensive insurance policy – not on a Sunday.

Double-C and other letters

Alvin sits on his sofa gazing at the handbag.

He has the police to thank for the fact that he found it – literally stumbled across it, as it happened. As he neared the point where he rejoined the main road on the edge of the Glenn Estate, a second patrol car careened around the corner as if auditioning for reality TV. Feeling suddenly like a fugitive himself, Alvin decided to leave the pavement and set off on a jog across the wasteland. Too busy looking over his shoulder for pursuing coppers, he didn't see the looming pile of dumped rubbish until he was face down in it.

The dirty brown handbag was the first thing he spotted as he pulled himself upright. There it was at the base of the sign that read NO FLY-TIPPING. It wasn't fully visible, but there was just about enough gilt left on the bag's interlocked Cs to wink at him in the moonlight. Don't see many of those round here, he thought, as he peeled back a slimy polythene sack, lifted a broken paving slab and freed the bag beneath.

As he walked home with it, he wondered why Kevan had dumped it, a valuable and perfectly fence-able item of swag.

Now it sits damply on his lap. Despite months in the open, it isn't sodden. Alvin guesses the builders' sacks that lay roughly on top of it formed a crude but effective umbrella. He pops the magnetic catch and opens the flap. Inside there is a purse. Any money it contained is long gone, but it isn't completely empty. A pensioner's travel card is inside. He looks at the mugshot in the corner. It's the same Louise Bird he saved from Kevan.

Alvin replaces the card in the purse and sets it on the sofa beside him. Then he looks inside the bag. At the bottom are a set of keys and a tube of lip salve. In a side pocket is a wad of five envelopes. He pulls them out and leafs through them. The paper is cool with moisture, but the writing hasn't been blurred. The addresses, written in carefully sloped italics, prick his curiosity. He slips a fingertip under the flap of the first envelope and holds it there. He's desperate to open it . . .

But he knows he shouldn't.

The doorbell puts the debate on hold. Alvin tenses. He's been a nervous resident since the graffiti, keeping the curtains closed even during the day. He returns the letters to the handbag and puts the bag under the sofa. Then he goes into the hall and sees the shape of a heavyset man through the frosted glass. 'Who is it?' he calls out, sensing trouble.

'It's me . . . *Col,*' Stanislavski slurs.

Trouble all right, but not the kind he expected.

'What do you want?' Alvin asks.

'Just a chat, matey. C'mon, open up.'

'Go home, Colin. You're pissed.'

'No, I'm not. Need to talk. Just bumped into a pal of yours.'

'Who's that?'

'Jamie McSomethingorother. Great bloke. Sends his love.'

Telling himself he'll regret it, Alvin opens the door and Stanislavski stumbles into the hall. He heads straight for the front room and collapses onto the sofa. 'Get us a tube of something, Alv,' he yells. 'I'm dry as a witch's fanny.'

Alvin goes to the fridge and gets a couple of lagers. He returns to the front room, hands one to his former colleague and sits in the armchair. He watches Stanislavski drink, grin at him foolishly, then drink some more.

'If you've just come to take the piss, Colin, you can drink up and go,' he says. 'I haven't got time for it any more.'

'Matey, matey, you do me a disservice. I've come to pick your brain. That friend of yours . . . Jimmy –'

'Jamie.'

'That's what I said. Great bloke. Great, great bloke. Met him down the Four Kings . . . Three Feathers . . . Seven Dwarves . . . Wherever the fuck. Spent a *highly* entertaining afternoon in his company. Mind if I smoke? Course you don't. He regaled me and my rugger cohorts with some storming tales of your rock 'n' roll years. You were a one, weren't you, Mr Lee?'

'Apparently. He tell you about the time we jammed with Springsteen?'

'You never did!'

'No, we didn't.'

'*Wow*, you jammed with the *Boss*. *A*-mazing. You got an ashtray? No matter, I'll use my tin. Fetch us another, matey.'

Knowing he'll regret it, Alvin gets Stanislavski another beer.

'You said you wanted to pick my brain, Colin,' he says on his return.

'Did I? That's right. Your mate Jamie. Great bloke. Met him in the Two Princes. Anyway, he took me aside and hit me with a little proposal. Strictly between him and me because it is *dyn*amite.'

'Well, if it's hush-hush, you'd better not tell me,' Alvin says, ready to knock this on the head now.

'No, I've *gotta* tell you, Alv. Gotta pick your brain. Mind if I smoke? Did I already ask you that? This idea. Brilliant. A-fucking-*mazing*.'

'What is it? A heavy metal boy band?'

'You what? No, it's ring tones. You know, those little fellas you get on your mobile. You got an ashtray? False alarm. Got an empty tube right here.'

'Ring tones,' Alvin says quietly, remembering.

'*Customised* ring tones, matey. That's the beauty of it. *Customised*. Tailor-made little tunes, written by a real fucking rock star. Is that not fantastic?'

'Yes . . . It's a good idea. He mentioned it to me a few months ago.' Alvin is surprised that the concept is still alive. Given his fish-like memory, Jamie's schemes usually last no longer than a single circuit of the goldfish bowl.

'He's *told* you about it?' Stanislavski gasps, as if they're sharing the whereabouts of the Holy Grail. 'You investing?'

'Er . . . No plans at the moment.'

'You've *gotta*, Alv. All those Bird millions must be making a big old bump under the mattress. Put some of that little lot in.'

'Well, I won't be seeing a penny of that for a while. Probably never.'

'You gotta do it *now*. While it's hot. Before some other bugger nips in.'

'What about you, Colin? Did Jamie ask you for a few quid?'

'Didn't need to ask, matey. I *jumped* in with an offer. An idea *that* good . . . Got a few quid put aside and this ISA bollocks that's going nowhere. That's what I wanted to ask you. This Jimmy fella, he's straight, yeah?'

'How do you mean?'

'You'd vouch for him, right? Got his head screwed on? Wouldn't scarper with my hard-earned?'

Alvin doesn't know what to say. He just looks at Stanislavski, whose eyelids are drooping.

'That's what I like about you, Alv,' Stanislavski slurs. 'You always *think* before you speak. *Always* liked that about you. Too many buggers at Wood Hill shoot their fucking mouths off. Miss you at the old place, you know. Those horny little pre-pubes miss you as well, you *scallywag*.'

Alvin has an answer ready now. 'You know what, Colin, I'd invest whatever you can in this scheme. If I had the readies myself, I'd hand them straight over. Jamie is as honest as the day is long and he's got the business brain of Richard Branson. Ring tones. Brilliant idea. Can't fail.'

'That's what I told myself, Alv. Good to hear it confirmed by a scholar like yourself. *Good* to hear it. You wanna smoke? You don't, do you? Very sensible. So Wood fucking Hill. You missing it?'

'Yes, I am as it goes.'

'Don't waste your energy, matey. It's a shit hole. Mind you, it's all change up there. You know Rowell's retiring in the not too distant?'

'I'd heard.'

'Well, there's a job up for grabs and it's a biggy. Head of humanities, whatever the fuck that means. Between you and me, Chadwick's been nodding and winking in my direction. Reckon I'm in with a serious shout.'

Somehow this doesn't surprise Alvin. Something he's learned about Colin Stanislavski: he may come across as an invariably sozzled prick to most of the world, but in the company of authority he knows how to hide both his beer breath and his prickishness. The likes of Rowell, Chadwick and the board of governors don't see an abusive, idle bigot, but a no-nonsense, hardworking English teacher who speaks fluent national curriculum. Alvin doesn't know how he does it. Maybe it's instinctive. Maybe he can submerge his baser traits without thought, drunk or sober. Whatever, it's shocking but very possibly true – Stanislavski could well be in with a chance of the big new job.

'Your mate Andy – Pardon me, *Lynette*. She's angling for it,' Stanislavski continues. 'Reckon she's gonna be disappointed. Mind you, I won't be able to rip the piss when I'm her boss. Bitch'll have me up for sexual harassment. Couldn't've done that when she had a dick, eh? Only teasing, Alv. She's your mate, isn't she? You know me. A terrible old tease. Where're you off to?'

Alvin is standing up, desperate to get out of the room. 'I'm going to make a cup of tea,' he says.

'Tea! Thought you'd never ask. I'm dry as a witch's whatever. Milk, no sugar, if you don't mind.'

Alvin heads gratefully for the kitchen. He stands over the kettle and wishes Stanislavski would stay drunk for long enough to sign over every penny he has to Jamie's ring tones. Right now he'd like nothing better than to see him bankrupted.

'Ring tones!' Stanislavski cries out, reading Alvin's mind. '*Storming* idea. As the bard of Avon said . . . *Fuck*, I need a piss. Where's your dunny?'

'Top of the stairs,' Alvin replies.

He takes his time making the tea. He listens to Stanislavski stagger up the staircase . . . Then stumble back down. He's in no hurry to return to the front room. He sips at his own mug in peace, waiting for his guest to yell out something obnoxious . . . But he doesn't.

And when Alvin eventually goes back to him he finds him flat on his back on the sofa, snoring loudly. An empty beer can lies across his chest and a burnt-out cigarette droops from his lips. Ash decorates his shirtfront. And his trousers are still round his ankles. That he made it back downstairs without breaking his neck is both a mystery and a crying shame.

Alvin has an idea – one that only a few weeks ago, when he was still relatively uncorrupted, would never have crossed his mind. He goes upstairs and into the bedroom that Shannon and Annie used to share. Most of their belongings are still in there. It's a mess, but it doesn't take him too long to find the Polaroid camera that he and Karen bought for Shannon last Christmas. He takes it downstairs and lines up Stanislavski in the viewfinder. He clicks the shutter, then waits for the image to fade up . . .

Excellent – Stanislavski looks like shit. Better still, his penis is just visible, peeping pinkly from beneath his shirt-tail like a baby Australian possum.

He finds a pen and on the white strip below the picture he writes THE NEW HEAD OF HUMANITIES. Then he puts it in an envelope. He addresses it to Alan Chadwick, care of Wood Hill

School, seals it up and makes a mental note to buy a stamp in the morning.

Job done, he wakes Stanislavski up, tells him it's Monday morning and gets him the hell out of his house.

Alone at last, he reaches beneath the sofa and retrieves the handbag. He takes out the letters and – sod the ethics – he opens the top one. Straight away he knows that Louise Bird was a woman after his own heart.

138 big ones

A pair of heavy iron gates hung between thick limestone pillars topped with carved stone acorns as big as the eggs in *Alien*. On the other side of the gates, what looks like a quarter-mile of winding, gravel drive. At the end, a winged and turreted gothic pile. It's the sort of place to which the Addams family might relocate and not feel as if they'd moved an inch.

Alvin counts the chimneys. It seems to have more than his entire street.

Beresford House.

Home.

What a bizarre thought, and it's the first time he has entertained it.

Home?

Louise Bird – a woman for whom he has fresh respect – decided so.

But no, all that space ... It would take a week to vacuum the carpets, a month to mow the bloody lawn ... And the sight of it gives rise to a sudden rush of agoraphobia, which surely tells him something.

It's not for him.

Even though in an ideally fair world it would be.

But not in this one.

A metal box is fixed to one of the pillars. The usual thing with a button, a speaker grille and a tiny wide-angle lens. Alvin thinks about doing this the legal way, but knows that if he rings the bell, this is as far as he will get. So he climbs, hauling himself up the gate's black-painted rails, looking at the spiked tops and thinking he'll worry about those when he gets there.

As it happens, it isn't the spikes he should have been concerned about, but the drop to the other side. He sits on the gravel where he landed, pain in his hip and his left ankle, hoping the latter isn't sprained. Gingerly, he gets to his feet and puts his weight on his trainer . . . Just twisted.

As he sets off up the drive, limping only slightly, his mobile rings. He thinks about ignoring it – he's a man with a mission, after all – but he has a long enough walk to the house in which to take the call.

'Hello.'

'Alvin, you're there,' Trevor Poll says, though with Alvin being on a mobile, he will have no idea where *there* is. 'We've got to talk.'

'I'm kind of busy at the minute.'

'What are you doing?'

'I'm . . . having a walk.'

This is true. Pausing only to post a letter to Alan Chadwick, Alvin has walked the nearly six miles from his house to – depending whose side you take – his *other* house. He got out of bed this morning, threw back the curtains, saw an unseasonably cloudless sky and knew exactly what he had to do.

Walking was the only option. His bike doesn't work and the bus doesn't come this far out of town.

'Having a *walk*,' Poll splutters. 'I thought you had a job now.'

'I called in sick.'

'Listen, something's come up. The police have been in touch.'

'What now?' Alvin asks, thinking back to yesterday and the Glenn.

'You know a girl called Deborah Coates?' Poll asks nervously.

'Debbie, yes. What the hell's she done?'

'Ah . . . What she's done is gone missing.'

'*Jesus*. When?'

'Went to a party Saturday night, left early Sunday, not been seen since.'

Alvin's mind spools back to his conversation with Curtis yesterday. 'Have they talked to Mark Shakespeare?'

'Who?'

'The cops. Have they talked to Mark Shakespeare? A guy she was with at the party. He's got a record. He's on the bloody sex offenders' register.'

'How do you know all this? Please tell me you weren't at this party.'

'No, of course I wasn't. I bumped into a mate of hers yesterday. He told me . . .' Alvin's head is swirling as he pictures Debbie, her clothes torn, her face cut and bruised, her body on a fly-tip. 'Poor bloody kid.'

'Look, I'm sure the police, as is their wont, are exploring every avenue,' Poll says, 'but they want to talk to you.'

'Why?'

'Seems you and this girl have a . . . history.'

'Christ, I worked with her at Wood Hill; spent three years trying to keep her out of bloody trouble. That's a *history* now? Anyway, you have a history with her as well.'

'Do I?'

'You defended her when she was caught shoplifting – Woolies.'

'Is that her? I thought the name rang a bell. Tough little thing, isn't she? She's got a scary mother too. Look, come and meet me, we'll go to the station and get this cleared up.'

'I can't. Not now. There's something I have to do.'

'Well, I'm sorry to spoil your fun, but I'd say that whatever you're up to, removing your name as a suspect in a teenager's disappearance takes priority.'

'This is important. I think I know how Louise Bird blew all her money.'

'What the heck – *Explain*.'

'Later, Trevor.'

Alvin switches off the phone and returns it to his pocket.

He stops walking, trying to clear his head of sickening images of Debbie. The optimist in him breezily insists that she's one of the brightest girls he knows, certainly one of the most resourceful; she'll be OK. Won't she?

But despite the sunshine, optimism isn't working any more.

God help Debbie Coates.

God help Alvin Lee.

He's going down. That much is certain. In the short time he has left, he might as well try to prick as many consciences as possible.

He is about three-quarters of the way up the drive now. He looks about him . . . At the oak trees that line both sides of his walk. He wonders which one killed Douglas Bird. Some hundred yards off down a gentle, grassed slope he can see the edge of the trout lake.

What the fuck would he do with a trout lake?

The question, though, is moot and he knows it.

He sets off again and doesn't stop until he reaches Beresford House. Out front, three Simonised cars fan out on the raked gravel like an arrangement in a glossy brochure: Jeremy Bird's Mercedes panzer, a Freelander and a tiny, sparkling Peugeot. People are home, then. And, given the absence of slavering hounds and game keepers with shotguns, they haven't seen him coming.

To the left of the heavy wooden door is a large antique bell push. He presses it, then stands back as he listens to the quiet tinkle from within.

A long pause, but Alvin supposes that the walk from wherever to the front door takes a lot longer than in the average family home.

In the wait, he can only gaze at the door. It has *presence*; the kind of door that in an ideal world would be opened with a menacing creak by Bela Lugosi . . .

But not in this one because when it swings noiselessly off its latch, a petite and jewel-eyed teenager stands on the other side. She's wearing clothes that could have been stolen from Mercedes's wardrobe. She stares at his leg and it's only now that he realises his trousers are torn at the ankle – his tumble from the gate.

'Hi,' Alvin says, 'is –'

But she turns her head and yells, *'Mum,* door!' before brushing past him and heading for the Peugeot – a young woman with places to go and, unlike Mercedes, the wheels to get her there.

As the car takes off, spitting gravel behind it, a woman appears at the door. Mum, surely. She has her daughter's gemstone eyes. She also has a model's deportment – every pavement a catwalk, every casual encounter a casting call – and Alvin wouldn't be surprised if she once sashayed down runways. Given her age, she would have been wearing something with shoulder pads big enough to upholster a sofa. The years haven't diminished her, though. She's a credit to her skincare regime, her personal trainer and, very possibly, her cosmetic surgeon.

Alvin feels as he always does in the presence of opulently maintained beauty; how he felt when he briefly shared airspace with Madonna: knock-kneed and intimidated, and on this occasion, wishing his trousers weren't ripped. But he manages to say, 'Hello, I'm –'

'I know who you are,' she snaps. 'Jerry! You'd better come here . . . *Jerry*!'

She stares at him, her face placed somewhere between vexed and frightened. In response, Alvin finds himself smiling, probably rather inanely.

But he reels back when Jeremy Bird appears at her shoulder, his head seeming to sprout from the graceful curve of his wife's neck like a large, psychotic boil. Somehow Alvin had forgotten what a gloriously, comically ugly twat this man was – and in the unforgiving light of a sunny day, still is.

'Call the police, darling,' he barks.

Darling, Mum, Mrs Bird recedes into the gloom of the hall, not for an instant taking her eyes off Alvin. As she fades to black, he can't help wondering the obvious: how did she end up with him? Or how about this: maybe he used to be quite the handsome cove, but like a vampire, she sucked it out of him in order to nourish her own perfection. Well, it would fit the gothic setting.

But he pulls himself up. Why, at a time like this, is his mind prattling?

'What the hell are you doing here?' Jeremy Bird demands. 'Don't you think you're deep enough in the shit already?'

'I don't think it matters any more,' Alvin says. 'I should've listened to you when you came to see me. What was it you said? Something about ending my life, wasn't it? Well, you managed it without even taking me to court.'

'I want you to leave. I have nothing to say to you.'

'Oh, I've got plenty to say to you, you bastard. *Plenty*. I never had you down as the type to go slumming it on the Glenn Estate. You and Kevan Kennedy. A lot in common, have you? God, how do you sleep at night?'

'Get off my property.'

'Your property?' Alvin laughs. 'It was your mother's. You're only here because she didn't have the nous to chuck you out when she was alive.'

'You've got a bloody nerve.' Bird takes a step towards him, but stops as he sees his torn trouser leg, as if that somehow makes Alvin more dangerous.

'I didn't come here to fight,' Alvin says, much as he'd love to kick the living crap out of him. 'I came to show you something.'

'What could you possibly have that would interest me?'

The woman, his wife, has reappeared at his side. 'They're on their way,' she says quietly. Alvin sees that she's holding something at her side . . . A poker partially hidden in the folds of her skirt.

He needs to get on with this, though he figures the police will take a good half-hour to get all the way out here.

'I found something,' he says. 'Letters. Cheques your mother was going to post the day she got mugged by your new friend.'

'You ended up with my mother's bag?' Bird gasps. 'If that isn't proof you were in on the whole thing – I told you, darling. I said they were in cahoots.'

Darling, Alvin guesses, hasn't been party to the truth. 'I did end up with the bag, but not how your husband has told you,' he says for her benefit. 'I found it yesterday . . . Your mother was a good woman, Mr Bird –'

'She was mentally unstable, *suffering*, and you took advantage of the fact.'

'She was a *good* woman.'

He reaches into his jacket pocket and pulls out the five cheques that he spent the best part of yesterday evening staring at as they lay on the coffee table like the final pieces of a jigsaw puzzle.

'Look at these . . . The RSPCA: thirty-five thousand . . . The Parkinson's Disease Society: twenty thousand . . . Macmillan Nurses: twenty-eight thousand . . . Mencap: fifteen thousand . . . The Children's Society: *forty* thousand. That's a hundred and thirty-eight grand she was giving away to help sick people, the disabled, the *deprived*.'

He thrusts the cheques at Jeremy Bird, who takes them and looks at them blankly, but somehow not surprised.

'Tell me, what are you going to spend the money on when you get it?' Alvin continues. 'Another Merc? An extension for this place? I mean, you must need the space.'

'I'd say that's none of your business, though it's good to hear you accept that the estate belongs to me.'

'My solicitor told me your mother had got through the bulk of it over the last few years,' Alvin says, ignoring Bird, needing to finish. 'She didn't exactly live the high life. My guess is she gave most of it to charity.'

Jeremy Bird's face darkens, telling Alvin that he's not far from the truth.

'That's why you fell out, isn't it? You couldn't stand her generosity with your father's –'

'My father was a great man,' Bird explodes. 'How do you think it made him feel to see all he'd worked for . . . *pissed* away? In his own lifetime it started. She couldn't even wait till he was dead before she tried to save the bloody world, one lost cause at a time.'

'That's enough, Jerry,' his wife says pleadingly, but he bats her concern away with a flap of his hand.

'She wanted to give this place away,' he rasps. 'To a charity for *junkies*!'

'That's why he tried to change his will, isn't it?' Alvin says, only now realising it.

Jeremy Bird, his face flushed purple now, lurches towards Alvin, but his wife grabs his shoulders and forces him to stop. 'How the hell did you find that out?' he wheezes. 'How the hell . . . ?'

His wife eases him back into the hall and presses his now breathless frame into a chair. Alvin watches as she reaches into his shirt pocket, takes out an inhaler and forces it into his mouth. As her husband recovers, she returns to the front door, no longer concealing the poker in her skirt's folds, but brandishing it openly.

'My mother-in-law was . . .' she starts. 'She was *mad*, Mr Lee. She'd lost all proportion, all sight of what mattered. She did everything she could to tear this family apart while she was still alive. I'm not going to let a piece of filth like you finish what she started.'

'Oh, I'm done with you lot, believe me,' Alvin says. 'You can go to hell all by yourselves.'

She moves towards him, the poker pointed towards his stomach. Alvin looks over her shoulder at Jeremy Bird, blanched and breathless in the hall. Bird looks back at him, too ill to speak but hate burning in his eyes. A desperate wheeze stops his wife in her tracks and she turns to tend him. Alvin looks on as she presses the inhaler into his mouth again, wondering if the man is taking his last few breaths, and wondering why he doesn't feel any guilt or pity.

Then he turns and heads back towards the gate, listening to the thick gravel crunch beneath his feet.

4x2

It's just after four o'clock. Alvin sits on his sofa feeling doomed.

But vindicated, if only in the court of Alvin Lee.

Not that vindication is much of a comfort. The pain and suffering – even death – that he wished on Jeremy Bird just a few hours ago, well, that was a new one. Before today he had never so much as wished a mild dose of flu on even his worst enemy. Hatred isn't an emotion he's used to, but he supposes he'll have to learn to accommodate it.

He's surprised the police haven't shown up yet. He saw them on his walk home from Beresford House, a patrol car rushing towards him, flashing blue despite the empty road. Five minutes later he heard a car approaching from behind. Assuming it was the police again, he stuck out an ironic thumb. A van passed him, then pulled up and he found himself riding into town with a bunch of cement-spattered builders. Very grateful he was too – his ankle was swelling and his feet were blistered. He felt uncomfortable when one of the builders described in detail exactly what he'd like to do to paedophiles. (It involved a length of chain and a nail-studded hunk of four-by-two.) Alvin thought he'd been made, but it turned out the guy was simply reacting to a story in the *Sun*.

When he got home there were a couple of messages on his machine from Trevor Poll. Since he's been here, his solicitor has called again, but he ignored it. He's not running away. He's sure the police will come and get him when they're ready.

He's been trying to put thoughts of Jeremy Bird out of his

head. If he dwells for too long on that man with his magnificent home and immaculate family he could grow truly bitter. No, the Bird chapter of his life is over. Though, of course, he has yet to serve his punishment for so recklessly saving the old lady in the first place.

Clearing his head of Bird has left space for Debbie Coates and, frankly, he's bothered. He called her mobile, but only got through to her gobby voicemail announcement. That's her only hope: her gob. It's what usually gets her into trouble, but it has also proved pretty useful in getting her out of it.

He hears a tap at the front door. Too polite to be the police – he's not expecting them to respect niceties such as knockers and hinges. In the hall, he looks at the blurred shape through the frosted glass: female and vaguely familiar. Even so, when he opens the door, he's stunned.

'Kelly.'

'Hi, Alvin.'

'Kelly, Jesus, what the hell are you doing here?'

'Hello, good to see you would've been nice, but you know . . .'

'Sorry, it's just . . . You'd better come in.'

And as he ushers her in, he gives himself a sharp mental kick on the shins for his shameful glance up the street, on the lookout for twitching nets.

'You heard about Debbie?' Alvin asks as they stand uncomfortably in the front room. The awkwardness of their last parting is still in the air.

'Debbie, yeah, I'm really worried,' Kelly replies.

'Me too.'

'I saw her –'

'When?'

'Saturday, at Becker's party.'

'Oh.'

Kelly looks different. She's wearing tight blue jeans tucked into brown cowboy boots and a short turquoise satin puffa. Her hair is piled on top of her head, held aloft by a broad white Alice band. Overall, it's an improvement on the scraggy dressing gown she was wearing the last time Alvin saw her, but then so would be a loosely belted bin liner. But he decides that it's not the wardrobe that's rung the change; it's the tan. Her perennially sugar-white skin is still sugar-coloured, but now it's a rich demerara. It suits her, he concludes.

'Debs told me,' she says, 'you know, about what happened at school and that, and about the cops and what Kevan did. Such a *cunt*, man . . .'

Pretty much carried unanimously, then.

'. . . And about your wife –'

'We weren't married, but, yeah . . . *C'est la vie*, I suppose.'

'I feel really bad about it. Like it's all my fault, right? I knew about the mugging, but I didn't know it was you who was like the *hero*. I mean, Roberta told me it was one of the punters, but I just thought – No, I *didn't* think 'cause if I had I'd've fucking *known* it *had* to be you. Every other bloke I know would've crossed the road if they'd seen an old woman getting knifed. Anyway, if I'd known about it, I'd have come to see you sooner, tell your missus she'd be mad to dump you and that, but right after the last time I saw you I went to the clinic and had that thing checked out and they made me have an AIDS test – Well, they didn't *make* me, but they said I should and I did. It's OK, I wasn't positive or nothing, but you know, it really scared me, man. Anyway, I jacked in the, you know, massage place after that.'

'Can't say I'm disappointed. What have you been doing since?'

'I've been away. This guy I met – one of the punters – works for this tour company and he said he could get me a job in France . . . *Chamonix*. It's like in the Alps, right?'

'I know. I got your postcard.'

'Anyway, I was cooking and cleaning in this chalet for these posh tossers on skiing holidays. I've been doing that till last week. Was supposed to be there till the end of the season, but I'd had enough. I mean, it's just skivvying, basically, and all the other girls were a bit stuck up, but I learned to ski and everything. Black runs!'

'You look good on it,' Alvin says. 'Tanned.'

'Yeah, just my face though. Anyway, I see Debbie Saturday and she tells me everything and I couldn't believe the shit that's been going on . . . I'm really sorry, Alvin. I feel really bad.'

'Well, don't. None of this is your –'

'Yeah, but if I hadn't given you that thing and you hadn't come back to see me, you wouldn't have met that old woman and you'd still have your job and your missus wouldn't have left, would she?'

Though she has taken several hundred words to do it, Kelly has, as she usually does, got to the crux of the matter. Even so, Alvin says, 'It's not your fault, Kelly. You didn't make me do anything. I'm a grown-up. I did it all by myself. Anyway, it could have turned out differently. I could have ended up with the old lady's money and I might be thanking you now.'

'You're not gonna get it, then?'

He shakes his head. 'To be honest, I've never once felt I had any right to it . . . Not that her family deserves it any more than I do.'

'Have the cops charged you 'cause of what Kevan told 'em?'

''Fraid so.'

'*Cunt*. Can't believe he'd shit on you like that. Debbie was, like, *steaming* about it when she told me. She really wanted to sort him out.'

'What the hell's happened to her, Kelly? I saw Curtis yesterday. He said she was with Chenil's brother at the party. Do you think he could have –'

'That sleazebag? No. He was trying to cop off with everyone.

Tried it on with me, but I told him where to get off. He got a snog off Debbie, but she left ages before him. He was totally mashed by the end. His mates had to carry him out. He didn't do nothing to her. You know what I think might've happened?'

'What?'

'She was going on at Ro and Curt and that lot to sort Kevan.'

'I told her to leave it alone.'

'You know what Deb's like. Anyway, they didn't wanna know.'

'Thank God.'

'Yeah, but I think she might've gone up to the Glenn on her own and maybe she saw him and maybe he did something to her.'

'*Shit*. I saw him yesterday as well.'

'Did he say anything?'

'No, I didn't talk to him. He was too busy wrapping his car round a lamppost. Have you told the police this?'

She shakes her head. 'Thought I should see you first . . . Look, there's something else I need to tell you.' She looks fearful now. 'Deb's mum thinks you've done something to her. You know, after what they said in the papers and everything that happened at school and that . . .'

'*Jesus*. Is that what you think?'

'Come off it,' she scoffs. 'You think I'd come round here on my own if I thought you was Fred West or something? No, I heard it off Deb's uncle who lives next door to my mum and I told him it was like the most stupid thing ever. I told him you weren't no pervert and you wouldn't even hurt a fly.'

'Thanks,' Alvin says quietly.

He feels utterly beleaguered now. Misjudged, misunderstood and totally friendless, apart from a couple of teenage girls who, sadly, won't be sitting on any jury he's likely to face in the coming weeks.

'Know what? I could murder a tea,' Kelly says.

* * *

When Alvin walks back into the front room with two fresh mugs, Kelly is staring out of the bay window into the growing gloom outside.

'Debbie's mum isn't the only one who thinks I've done something,' he says. 'The police want to talk to me about her.'

'Well, they'd better get a move on.'

Alvin joins her at the window and looks out . . .

At the mob that has gathered on the other side of the low brick wall separating his property from the pavement. Not a mob exactly. Half a dozen people, four women and two men. The gathering lacks scale, but he can feel its anger simmering through the glass. They seem to be arguing with one another, though, as if they can't agree which house to firebomb – it would figure, because Alvin's door lacks a number. They haven't quite reached the stage where they're so stoked with rage that they don't give a shit who they lynch.

The light isn't yet on in the front room, so as hard as they peer, they can't see inside . . . So long as Alvin and Kelly stand *very* still. That's what they do now. It's an instinctive thing, as seen on nature programmes where the fawn cowers statue-still in the undergrowth while the wolves patrol a few feet away.

Alvin recognises Debbie's mother. She has been to Wood Hill a couple of times. She has her daughter's coal-black eyes and chiselled cheekbones. But her Debbie didn't inherit the Biffa Bacon jaw line. Nor did she get her mum's bulk, though perhaps she has that to look forward to – that's assuming the girl will be in a position to look forward when the dust settles.

'What the hell are they doing out there?' Alvin whispers.

'You fancy hanging around to find out?'

'Well, what else do you suggest?'

'Dunno. You got a back way?'

'I'm not running away. It's my bloody house.'

'Could be your coffin if you stick around. See that bloke?' She must mean the one built like an Acme safe. He has a home-made tattoo circling his twenty-inch neck. 'His twin brother's doing life,' she explains. 'I reckon he's feeling left out.'

Now Alvin finds himself thinking about the back door, wondering if a sprint across his neighbours' gardens would get him clear, then thinking that perhaps the jungle next door might provide refuge for weeks if only he could find enough roots and berries to live on . . .

But *no*. This is home. More to the point, he hasn't done anything. To Debbie or to anyone else.

'I'm going to deal with this –'

'You mad?'

'You go out the back way. I don't want you getting hurt.'

'If you're staying, so am I.'

The mini mob comes alive. One of the women has spotted Alvin's house number painted on the side of his wheelie bin. Debbie's mother pushes open the gate and leads the others in an assault on the front door.

'*Go*, Kelly, please,' Alvin urges.

He pushes her into the hallway and hard towards the kitchen.

'The back door's open,' he gabbles. 'Go over the gardens and knock for a neighbour. Get them to call the police.'

He watches her disappear and then turns to face them. Through the glass they look like a single monstrous mass. He's heard of studies on crowd behaviour; how a kind of collective thought process takes over, explaining how mobs appear to act with a single mind. Does it kick in with just six people?

They're banging on the door.

'You in there?'

'He's in there.'

'You in there, you fucking pervert?'

'He's in there. I can see him.'

'Come out here and talk to us!'

'We only wanna talk.'

They only want to talk.

Alvin takes deep breaths . . .

I'll tell them.

I haven't done anything.

I don't know where Debbie is.

. . . Trying to smother the terror that's attempting to rip its way out of his chest and flee with Kelly.

I'm as worried about her as they are.

I'll tell them.

Right now, just as soon as I open the –

The frosted glass shatters and Alvin stares at the half-brick that has landed at his feet. Probably from the skip across the street, though quite why he's worrying about the provenance of a brick at a time like this . . .

He remains frozen as a thick forearm reaches through the jagged hole and fumbles for the catch. The door flies open and Debbie's mother – Alvin can't recall her first name – falls through. Her friends are right behind her, holding her back, though she doesn't appear to want to kill him just yet.

'What have you done with her?' she barks.

'Mrs Coates, I haven't done –'

'What the fuck've you done with her, you evil bastard?'

She's moving towards him now.

'I swear, I don't know wh—'

He's stumbling backwards, winded, and all that stops him falling over is the newel post at the foot of the stairs. The sharp corners of its wooden cap dig into his back as she presses into him with her fleshy forearm, all of her considerable weight behind it. They're all yelling at him now, a torrent of bile that he can't withstand. But there's another voice, coming from behind him . . .

'Get off him, you idiots!'

. . . Kelly . . .

'He hasn't done nothing!'

... Returning from the garden, which, probably, she never went into.

'You've got the wrong bloke!' she concludes with absolute certainty.

Debbie's mother eases some of her bulk off Alvin and looks at Kelly.

'He's the wrong guy, Maddie.'

Maddie Coates – that fits.

'He wouldn't hurt no one.'

'Why'd he get sacked, then?' Maddie demands, unconvinced.

'Yeah, he was touching her up at school, weren't he?' another woman adds. '*Grooming* her.'

'Debbie and who else?' adds another.

'What's he fucking done with her?'

The mob looms, filling Alvin's face again. But they're pushed aside by Acme Safe, who has plunged himself through the front door and into the narrow hall, a three-foot length of four-by-two held above his head – a second trip to the skip, then.

Instinctively, Alvin slams his eyes shut.

When he reopens them, he's on his back on the staircase, clutching his forehead with wet hands, feeling blood run down his face and, after a moment's delay, an intense burn of pain.

Acme Safe stands over him. 'What've you done with her, *pervert*?' he snarls. He grips the wood tightly, limbering up for another whack.

'What's he done with who?'

A new voice, and one that can't be real. It can only be a figment, an auditory hallucination caused by the impact of timber on delicate skull. That must be it, because it cannot be Karen saying, 'What the hell's going on? Alvin, what've you done?' Alvin lets his bleeding head loll backwards, assured in the knowledge that Karen hasn't come home; the voice is simply a first glimpse of the interior world of a coma, the one he's about to slip into.

But now he can see her. Pushing her way between Acme Safe and Maddie Coates. Not exactly an angelic vision – too fretful, and she's wearing an anorak – but the best he can hope for.

'Karen?'

He blinks, trying to get the blood from his eyes and bring her into focus.

'Jesus, Alvin, your *head*.'

She drops to her knees and puts her hand out tentatively, and although her touch hurts like hell, he rejoices because he can *feel* her.

'You his wife?' Maddie Coates demands.

'No, I'm not, but this is my house. What are you doing here?' Karen responds, as feisty as ever.

'Trying to find out what he's done with my daughter.'

'What's she talking about, Alvin?'

He opens his mouth, but he can't speak.

Kelly does it for him. 'They reckon he's killed her or something, but it's bollocks,' she says.

Karen looks at her for the first time. It takes a moment for the recognition to click, but when it does, her eyes narrow.

'He's done *some*thing to her,' Maddie Coates says confidently. 'Where's my Debbie, you bastard?'

'*Debbie*?' Karen says. 'Debbie Coates?'

'You know her?' Maddie Coates says, turning her venom on Karen now.

'I know she isn't dead.'

'You're in this together?'

'They're in this together!'

'She's another Myra Hindley!'

'Maxine fucking Carr!'

Acme Safe has raised his four-by-two again. Now it's poised above Karen's head. Alvin pushes against the stairs with both hands and forces himself up onto wobbly legs.

'Where is she?' Maddie Coates yells at Karen. 'What've you done to her?'

'*Nothing*. She's probably home by now. I only just said goodbye to –'

The wood comes down with sufficient force to split Karen's head in two. Fortunately for her, it has to get through Alvin first. The last thing he sees before slumping into blessed unconsciousness is her face. It's close enough to kiss as his body flops onto hers.

How the electoral roll and government pension records can save a relationship

'I always wondered if you'd stop a bullet for me. Now I know,' Karen says. 'Well, you'd stop a lump of wood, anyway. How's the arm feel?'

'Broken. Actually, it doesn't feel like anything much. I think the painkillers are working.'

Alvin, sutured, plastered and painkillered to the gills, is propped up on pillows on a hospital bed. Five stitches hold together the vertical cut on his forehead. A sixth has been applied to the nick at the top of his right ear. Luckily for the rest of his head, his right forearm took the brunt of the blow intended for Karen. Now it's in a fresh white cast that runs from hand to elbow. He wants to go home, but the doctors, as is their way with head injuries, would like to keep an eye on him overnight.

'It was very brave,' Karen says. 'Thank you.'

Alvin gives her a weak smile.

What with the mob, then the police, the ambulance crew and various doctors and nurses, this is their first moment alone. They are in a small ward – the other three beds are empty. To Alvin's left, windows run the width of the wall, opening the view to the bustle in the corridor outside.

'Why did you come home?' he asks. It's the obvious question, the one he has been gagging to ask since he first saw her.

'Because your friend Debbie told me to.'

'She phoned you?'

'She came to see me.'

'To *Manchester*?'

'She caught a train up yesterday. She nicked the fare from her mum's boyfriend – he's the psycho with the timber, by the way. She put up a strong case for you and she wasn't going to come back to London without me.'

Alvin shakes his incredulous head, but stops because the sudden movement hurts.

'You know, I was amazed by the sheer . . . *dedication* you've inspired in that girl,' Karen says. 'At first I thought it was . . . I thought the worst. But she couldn't have faced me with such a complete lack of shame if you two had – Whatever. I figured that if she was prepared to come two hundred miles to fight your corner, then maybe I should at least give you a fair hearing.'

'Thanks.'

'I got a shock when I saw *her* at the house, though.'

'Kelly?'

'I thought, *shit*, he's moved her in *already*.'

Alvin panics. 'Look,' he splutters, 'let me explain –'

'No need to,' she interrupts. 'She already did. We talked while they were fixing you up. She defended you even more passionately than Debbie did. She was very straight with me – about the massage place and all that. She seems like a nice girl – God, I never thought I'd say that.'

'She is a nice girl,' Alvin says nervously.

'It's OK, you're allowed to think that.'

'I'm sorry about what's happened,' he says.

'Please, stop apologising, Alvin.'

'No, I'm sorry for the total bloody mess I've made of things. I'm probably going to end up in prison. I think I can handle that – I'm not pretty enough to be some twenty-stone gangster's bitch. And I can handle everyone round here thinking I'm scum – which they do. I couldn't care less, honestly . . . But you not believing me . . . Karen, I swear I'd die rather than see you hurt.'

She looks at the plaster cast, the swellings and the stitches: evidence that his words actually mean something.

'The only reason I came back is because I want to believe you,' she says.

'I need you to . . .'

She doesn't answer, but only because a mobile phone is ringing. It comes from Alvin's trousers, which are folded over the back of the chair that Karen is sitting on. 'Shall I get it for you?' she asks. Alvin shrugs. She reaches behind her and fumbles for the phone.

'Hi,' she says after a moment. Then, 'Oh hello, Jamie . . .' Alvin gives her a look. She knows what to say. '. . . No, he can't talk right now . . . No, he's *busy*, Jamie . . . Yes, I'm back . . . Yes, maybe for good . . . I don't know. Look, it's really none of your business . . .' She's irritated now. '. . . I'll tell him you called . . . OK, I'll tell him that . . . Bye.'

'What does he want?' Alvin asks as she returns the phone to his pocket.

'He wanted to say thanks for the reference.'

'You what?'

'Says some Aussie bloke's just given him a cheque for twelve grand. What's that all about, then?'

Alvin can't help smiling. The day is certainly ending better than it began.

Visiting hours are over, but Karen is still there, lying on the bed by Alvin's side, her head on his shoulder, her arm nestling underneath his sling.

She's back . . .

Maybe for good.

A nurse appears at the bedside, coming to check Alvin's wounds. 'You shouldn't be here really,' she says to Karen.

'I'll lie very quietly,' Karen whispers.

'And I'll pretend I haven't seen you.'

'Do you know if there's a bloke called Jonathan Craig on this floor?' Alvin asks her.

'The name rings a bell,' she replies.

'Broken hip and fractured skull,' he prompts.

'Yes, he's a couple of wards down.'

'How's he doing?'

'Oh, he'll be here a while, I'm afraid. Now go to sleep. You need to rest.'

'Who's Jonathan Craig?' Karen asks when the nurse has left.

'A guy who used to teach at Wood Hill.'

'You never talked about him.'

'I never noticed him. I don't think anyone did.'

'How did he get in here?'

'He had a fall a couple of weeks ago.'

Alvin considers telling her about it, but he's too weary. Later, then. They lie without speaking for a while. They've been talking a lot, so the silence is comfortable rather than fraught.

'How did Debbie find you?' Alvin asks eventually because the question has been baffling him.

'With a great deal of ingenuity. She got my name from the electoral register. She looked up who was listed to vote at the same address as you.'

'But all I told her was that you'd gone to Manchester.'

'She also remembered you once mentioned your girlfriend's mother was a retired headmistress –'

'Did I?'

'She obviously paid more attention to your classes than you did. She assumed I'd gone to my mum's and found her address in the pension records.'

'What pension records?'

'The Department of Education's. She got a mate to hack into some scary government mainframe and found two retired headmistresses called Jackson living in Manchester. My mum's address was the first one she tried.'

'*Curtis*,' Alvin whispers.

'Curtis the thug?'

'Uh-huh. Turns out he's a closet IT geek. I saw him yesterday. He didn't say a word.'

'You should be proud of yourself, Alvin.'

'Really?'

'Everyone gave up on those kids years ago, but you never did. They've proved you right in the end.'

All those life-skills classes weren't a complete waste, then. Though while he was getting Debbie and Curtis to find emergency numbers, he was oblivious to the fact that at least one of them could have sourced not only a plumber, but also his tax records and, more than likely, his complete medical history.

'I was wrong about Kevan Kennedy,' he says.

'He'll never keep it up. His story will collapse in court.'

'I wouldn't be so sure. He's not stupid and he'll have the best coaching.'

'Have faith . . . And go to sleep. You must be knackered.'

Alvin drifts off, turning his mind from Kevan to Karen. Though his body is racked with pain and an inaccessible itch has developed under his cast, he feels happier than he has for months.

'Karen?' he whispers.

'Go to sleep.'

'One more thing.'

'What?'

'Are you back? I mean for good.'

'You know something? I've missed you.'

'Me too.'

'No, what I mean is that once all the shit hit the fan and I thought I didn't know you any more, I really missed the bloke that I *had* thought you were. Now, I'm thinking that, actually, you were that bloke all along, as in the bloke I fell in love with and not the one I thought you'd become . . . And since you *are* that bloke, well, I'm back. That answer your question?'

But Alvin is asleep already.

Bird shit

'You promise?'

'I promise.'

'You're not going to let your mother talk you out of it?'

'The last time Mum successfully talked me out of anything I believe I wasn't quite thirteen and she could still lock me in my room. Don't worry. I'll see you the day after tomorrow.'

'Promise?'

'*Promise*. You going to be OK feeding yourself?'

'That's the genius of the Big Mac. You can do it one-handed.'

'What about the police?'

'I can cope with them . . . As long as I know you're coming back.'

'I've promised, haven't I? I'd stay on here an extra day, but if I leave the kids alone with Mum for much longer, there'll be blood. Did I tell you she thinks Sid needs boarding school?'

'He's *four*.'

'You know my mum. Spare the thumbscrew, spoil the child.'

'Give them my love.'

'You can give it to them yourself the day after tomorrow. They've really missed you, you know.'

'Not half as much as I've missed them.'

'OK then, I'd better be off.'

'Call me.'

'Soon as I get there.'

'I love you, Karen.'

'I love you too, angel.'

She kisses him gently and climbs into the minicab. She'll be back on Thursday. With children! She has promised.

But he misses her already.

Actually, Alvin was wrong. Try eating a Big Mac with one hand. It's just too, well, *big*. Bun slides against burger slides against cheese slides against tomato slides against burger slides against bun, the whole towering lot lubricated by ketchup and mayonnaise. Alvin watched helplessly as each component part of his brunch slithered in every direction but that of his mouth. It was like watching a model of shifting tectonic plates. Scale this up by a factor of ten thousand and he really could picture a city the size of Los Angeles disintegrating in an earthquake. That scrap of lettuce tumbling through the gap between his thighs? MacArthur Park disappearing into a gaping fissure.

Now he's a walking paradox: his stomach nags insistently for sustenance, while his spattered sling announces to the world that its wearer has pigged out.

'Bit of a palaver on your sling,' the detective says, waving a chubby finger at the smears of mayo and ketchup. 'Looks like haemorrhagic pigeon shit.'

That's the other thing that Alvin was wrong about. The police. He can't handle them on his own. He thought he was coming to see them to offer a statement on yesterday's assault and maybe to apologise for trespassing on Bird land (which technically is his anyway). Oh, that it were so simple.

Same interview room as the last time, different cop. This detective is well fed and verbose and he seems to take pleasure in Alvin's wounds. 'Under the circumstances, the guy showed commendable restraint,' he concludes.

'*Restraint*? I hadn't done anything.'

'Sending his slip of a daughter haring off to Manchester? *Manchester!*' He shakes his head, for once lost for words.

Alvin thinks about setting him straight – Debbie could never be described as a *slip* of anything, the man with the plank is not her father and Alvin sent her nowhere – but he decides that he's had enough of protesting his innocence. He'll save it for a judge.

'So you're not going to charge him?' he says.

'Oh, we'll have to charge him. It's the *law*,' the detective says, spitting out that last word as if it's a pubic hair he's found in his soup. 'These days it's pretty much set up for the convenience of you paedophiles.'

'I'm not a paedophile,' Alvin protests, stung now.

'Save it for the judge. Anyway, that's not what I want to talk about. Witness intimidation is a very serious offence, you know.'

'I haven't intimidated anyone.'

'You were popping round the Birds' for tea and a chat? C'mon, I'm a fat bastard, but I'm not stupid.'

'I was taking Jeremy Bird some letters his mother wrote before she died.'

'Ever seen those round red things in the street?' the detective asks. 'You slide an envelope through the slot and – *shazam!* – the next day it's someplace else. Amazing. It's called the post, should you ever wish to avail yourself.'

'Do you guys get off on being smartarses? Is it a contest?' Alvin has had it with being amenable. 'You listen to the tapes and the loser buys the curries?'

'Don't kid yourself you can take on the CID, Mr Lee. Sarcasm is our stock in trade. Drummed into us at Hendon. Now, why did you feel it necessary to *hand*-deliver those letters?'

'I want to see my lawyer.'

'You caused Mr Bird to have a serious asthma attack. You're lucky he didn't die or you'd be looking at a murder charge.'

'I'm not saying anything until I've seen my lawyer.'

'You do realise you've screwed yourself for bail now?'

Alvin's eyes widen.

'That's right. I'll have to check the small print, but I doubt your bail conditions include the right to harass witnesses. My guess is you'll be on remand for the foreseeable.'

'I didn't do anything . . .' His head fills with a vision of his reunion with Shannon, Annie and Sid and he can't see them properly for the prison bars. '. . . I didn't threaten him. I gave him some letters; that's all.'

'Not what Mr and Mrs Bird have told us. What have you done with the old lady's handbag?'

'It's –'

'And the baseball bat? Where's that now?'

'What baseball bat?'

'The one you used to smash the windscreen on Mr Bird's Merc.'

Alvin rocks back in his chair, this new accusation hitting him like another lump of four-by-two.

'I didn't smash his car up,' he says after a moment.

'You suggesting he vandalised his own S-Class Mercedes?'

'His wife. She was waving a poker at me when I left.'

'Can't say I blame her, what with you wielding a baseball bat.'

'I didn't have a bloody baseball bat.'

'Mrs Bird says you nearly decapitated her with it. She's a former Miss United Kingdom, you know. Came seventh in Miss World.'

'And that makes her incapable of lying?'

'Well, I like to listen to both sides and draw my own conclusions,' the policeman says with a smile. 'As will a jury.'

'I want my lawyer,' Alvin grouches.

'You can call him right after I've charged you.'

'I've been charged already –'

'Not with criminal damage, threatening –'

He stops because the door to the interview room has opened. A cop in uniform pops her head through the gap.

'I'm in the middle of something here,' the detective snaps.

'There's been a development, sir,' the policewoman says.

'Can't it wait?'

'To do with him.' She nods her head at Alvin.

'What have you done now, eh?' the detective asks Alvin with a smirk.

'Rape, murder,' Alvin mutters. 'Bring it on.'

'Don't move a muscle,' the detective says, rising to his feet. 'I'll be back.'

Alvin doesn't know how long he has been on his own. There isn't a clock in the room. Maybe that's a psychological trick. Disorientate suspects by removing access to time – as seen in Guantanamo. Of course, this theory doesn't allow for the many suspects who, unlike Alvin, must wear watches. But psych-game or not, it's working. What has probably been just twenty minutes has stretched in his mind to several hours . . .

Possibly days.

And he finds himself projecting to the weeks, months, years ahead, first on remand and then in prison proper. He wonders how long he'll get for conspiracy to rob and defraud, criminal damage, threatening behaviour, the Lucan nanny murder. He wonders if Karen will stick by him, hold things together at home, bring the kids in for monthly visits. And he wonders – *very* idly, it must be stressed – if he should save her the bother of a tough decision by killing himself. He'll bust out of whatever remand centre they take him to, head back to Beresford House, commandeer a Mercedes (with or without windscreen) and drive it into an oak tree. First, though, he will have to find a way of securing Jeremy Bird to the bonnet. Why give that sick bastard the satisfaction of dying even a second after him? No, if Alvin can spend his final earthly moment watching a great big oak tree force Jeremy Bird's freak-show head into his chest cavity, then he'll die happy.

The detective reappears. He stands in the doorway, arms

folded over the flab that circles his waist like a rubber ring, and stares at Alvin. Alvin can't work out his expression. Annoyance? Bafflement? Constipation? All three?

'What am I supposed to have done, then?' he asks.

The detective ignores the question. 'My colleague was right,' he says. 'There's been a development.'

'What?'

'Something we need to look into. In the meantime, you might as well . . . *go*.' The word seems to catch in his throat.

'Go?'

'Yes, *go* . . . Skedaddle . . . Piss off.'

'What's happening?'

'Not sure at the moment. Like I said, there's something we need to check out. We aren't through with you, though. You're still going to end up in court. Just if certain lines of inquiry pan out, it might be as a witness for the crown.'

Alvin, of course, is confused.

He doesn't have to wait long for the answer. As he checks out of the police station, he sees her sitting on the other side of the wired glass in the anteroom. He pushes the button to release the lock, leans on the door and joins her.

'Hi Karen,' he says.

Karen Nash doesn't look at him. She is too busy cooing desperately at baby Kelis, who is struggling against her buggy harness, as if she can sense that this place is all about confinement and she wants no part of it.

'Didn't know you were here,' she says as she finally unclips the buckle on the harness.

'Didn't know you were either,' Alvin says. 'What's going on?'

She frees her baby and pulls her onto her lap. Then she looks at Alvin for the first time. 'Jesus, what happened? You in a car crash or something?'

'No . . . This guy thought I'd . . . He thought I'd done something I hadn't.'

'Story of your life, innit?' Karen Nash says. She pops open a bag of Quavers and feeds one to Kelis, who sucks on it quietly.

'What's going on?' Alvin repeats.

'Look, he'll probably never say it to you. It's not his *thing*, right? And you probably wouldn't forgive him anyway. Why should you . . . ?' She trails off, embarrassed and nervy – she wasn't expecting to see Alvin here and she's having to wing this little speech. She clears her throat and carries on. 'But I know him, right? I can tell . . . He's sorry.' She nods towards the innards of the police station. 'He's in there now.'

'What made him do it?' Alvin asks.

'What? Drop you in the shit in the first place or come back here?'

'Come back.'

'I did.'

'Thank you.'

'I went fucking mental when I got the truth out of him. When you were at the estate Sunday I knew something was up. I mean, you told me it was. I thought it was like . . . I dunno, a drug deal or whatever. I know he's dealt a bit of pot and E before. All that money, though. I knew this was something big.'

Baby Kelis is crying again. Her mother has taken the Quavers away.

'Do us a favour,' she says. 'There's a jar of Heinz and a spoon in my bag.'

Alvin sits down on the bench and fumbles one-handed in the bag on the floor. It's bloated with nappies, wipes, cream, milk measured into bottles and more than one jar of baby food – Karen has come prepared for an extended vigil. He chooses a pot of broccoli and cheese casserole and hands it over. Karen loads Kelis back into her buggy and starts spooning the goo into her mouth.

'He didn't come home till last night,' she continues. 'I made him tell me what was going on. He didn't want to, but I made him.'

'I told you he was scared of you.'

She huffs dismissively. 'I couldn't believe it. Couldn't fucking *believe* what he'd done, the little bastard. He got ten grand for dropping you in it. He was gonna get another ten when they put you away.'

'*Twenty* grand.'

'Could've been twenty million. He still shouldn't've done that. I haven't been much of a mum. I've let him get away with murder . . . Not actual *murder*.'

'Of course.'

'But not this. You don't stitch up your mates, especially when you've got as few as he has.'

She poises the loaded spoon in front of her baby's clamped mouth. 'C'mon, Kel,' she pleads. 'You like this, sweetheart.' Kelis is stretching out her arm towards the half-eaten bag of Quavers on the bench. Karen gives up. She twists the lid back onto the jar and hands Kelis the bag.

'Apart from me, you're the only person who ever gave a damn about him,' she says. 'And he does *that* to you. I'm ashamed.'

'Don't be,' Alvin says. 'Anyway, he's making it right now.'

'He'd *better* be.'

'They wouldn't have let me go if he wasn't. What did you say to him to make him turn himself in? I can't imagine he was too keen.'

'He wasn't,' she says with a harsh laugh. 'I mean, when it all came out he felt really bad and all that – he really did – but he didn't wanna come back here. He was giving me all this crap about it being too late, the bloke who gave him the money'd kill him and that.'

Alvin wonders if Jeremy Bird would kill and decides he'd put nothing past him. 'So what swung it?' he asks.

'Not sure I wanna tell you,' she says quietly.

'It's OK. You don't have to.'

'After you came to see him . . . You know, the first time, when you saw him, *you know* . . .'

Alvin nods.

'After that, I searched his room. Ripped it apart. Dunno what I was looking for. More of my stuff, I suppose. Anyway, I found some photos. He'd hid them under the carpet . . . *Sick*. He'd taken pictures of himself in my . . .' Her face tightens into a wince. 'You *know*.'

Alvin nods again, feeling for her as well as for Kevan.

'Kev didn't know I'd found them, but I told him last night. And I told him that if he didn't come down here and sort it out, I'd give 'em to one of his idiot mates on the estate. He's tough, but he wouldn't've lasted five minutes if those had got out.'

Alvin can imagine. 'And you'd have done it?' he asks.

'If it had come down to it . . . ?' She shakes her head. 'Anyway, I couldn't even if I'd wanted to. I burnt the sick fucking things as soon as I found them. But he wasn't to know that, was he?'

'You're brave,' Alvin says, remembering how Kevan half strangled him when he tried to talk to him about underwear. 'He might've gone for you.'

'He wouldn't've done that,' she says with a mother's certainty. 'If he kills me, who the hell's gonna give a toss about him? He knows that.'

Alvin sits back and rests his head against the wall as relief washes over him. In the space of less than twenty-four hours his life has been saved by a pair of Karens. And a Debbie – he can't forget her.

'I owe you,' he says. 'I *really* fucking owe you.'

'I'm sorry for what he did. And I know Kevan is. Honest he is.'

'No, I owe you. They were about to cart me off to jail in there.'

'That's where Kev's off to now. But he'd've done time whichever way he played this. The bloke who bunged him told him he wouldn't go down for the mugging. Said he knew someone on the council who's got an in with the cops.'

Allison Bird-Wright, Alvin thinks. She must be on the police committee as well as everything else.

'Pillock,' Karen Nash decides. 'You don't walk for mugging old ladies.'

But now he'll be doing time at least ten thousand pounds poorer, Alvin thinks. That's a lot of sacrifice.

'You know what really pisses me off?' Karen says. 'I won't be able to afford to see that woman no more . . . You know, the therapist. I've been getting on brilliant with that. I've always felt like a rubbish parent, but you don't half feel good when you can blame it all on your own mum.'

'Why don't you try and do it through your GP?' Alvin suggests.

'Tell my doctor my personal business? You mad?'

Alvin stands up. 'I'd better be going . . . Do you fancy getting a coffee?'

She shakes her head. 'I'd better wait. Kevan might ask for me.'

He reaches out and clasps her hand with his. 'Thank you, Karen.'

She turns away, blushing. 'Forget it,' she mumbles. 'I'm just sorry that's how he paid you back for everything you tried to do for him.'

Tried being the operative word, Alvin thinks.

On the police station steps, Alvin sucks in a fat lungful of fresh air and kids himself that it tastes different. But it doesn't. It's the same London air as ever, stale and past its breathe-by date.

But he feels different.

In a word, *free*.

He bounds down the steps two at a time, not caring that the movement jogs his cast hard against his ribcage, and sets off home at a brisk trot.

But he stops because he feels a sudden warmth on his face. He looks up at the sky to where the sun has punched a small hole in the thick cloud and, in a moment apparently designed by Hollywood, is shining a narrow beam of hot, white light on him and only him.

Or so it seems.

As he basks in his personal solar spotlight he feels something slap wetly onto his forehead. He spots the culprit flapping a getaway across the terrace roofs. And he can't help laughing out loud, like the madman we all cross the street to avoid. After all the threats and intimidation, after the libels, slanders and the sheer bloody-minded spite, this – a small splodge of slightly warm, slightly dribbly poo – is the absolute worst a bird can do to him.

Part three:

Kelis,
Kanye Pharrell
and Sid

Gravy trains and stains

Alvin raises the sledgehammer and lets it fall for the last time on the wooden post. Then he stands back and reads the hand-painted sign nailed to the top: NO FISHING

He looks at the lake beyond.

The trout lake.

His trout lake.

'Is there *really* fish?' Sid asks.

Their trout lake.

'I guess,' Alvin says, though he hasn't actually seen any.

'Why can't I catch them?'

'Your sisters don't want us to.'

'My sisters are *mad*.'

'No, they're not. They just think it's cruel.'

Alvin had never thought about the cruelty or otherwise of angling until Mercedes and Shannon mounted their campaign. Mercedes's stand on the issue went without saying. At almost twelve, Shannon has decided to march in her stepsister's footsteps.

'Shall we go back, Sid?'

'OK, Dad.'

Sid climbs onto his first ever new bike and they set off back to the house.

Their house.

It looks big from here, a quarter of a mile away, at the top of the slope.

You should see it up close.

They moved in six weeks ago. They're in the east wing. Several times a day Alvin marvels at the fact: he lives in a house that has *wings*.

And of course a garden, though with its lake, woodland and lawns, its miles of paths winding between beds of entrenched shrubbery and its avenue lined with protected oaks, it goes way beyond *garden*; it's an entire ecosystem.

'Can we build my castle there?' Sid asks, pointing at an inviting knoll.

'We could,' his dad replies. We could also elect our own government, draft a constitution and declare independence, he thinks.

'I just had a call from Mr Salter,' Karen says as she pulls Sid's wellies off.

They are in the kitchen . . .

'Who's he?' Alvin asks, as he tugs off his own.

. . . Which contains an Aga and two microwaves, as well as a cooker that looks like a cooker (to the relief of Karen and Alvin who after six weeks are still fazed by the Aga and two microwaves).

'You don't know Mr Salter?' Karen scoffs, though until the phone call she had no idea either. 'The Salters have been tending the grounds for centuries. Since before the Norman Conquest, I think he said. Anyway, it's mentioned in the Domesday Book. He wants to know if we want to keep them on.'

'Them?'

'Him and Young Mr Salter. They come as an item.'

'What do you think? Do we want to keep them on?'

'It's either that or we do the gardening ourselves. Or let it revert to its natural state. I shouldn't think it'd be long before we see the return of wolves and wild boar.'

'Boars!' Sid squeals. 'Can we hunt them?'

'Let's keep them on,' Alvin says, preferring for now to ignore his son's alarming outbreak of bloodlust. 'I mean, they've been part of the place much longer than we have. It wouldn't be fair to turf them out.'

'That's what I thought,' Karen says. 'Anyway, they're coming on Monday to clean the koi ponds.'

'We have koi ponds?'

Alvin expects the surprises to continue for some time yet.

'What's koi?' Sid asks.

'Giant goldfish from Japan, Sid,' Karen explains. 'Mr Salter said some of the bigger ones are worth thousands, Alvin.'

'Can I catch them?' Sid asks.

'No, sweetheart,' Karen says. 'It wouldn't be nice and they're a bit like the Salters. They've been here a lot longer than we have.'

Alvin holds the suit jacket against his body. There is a brownish, crusty stain on the lapel. He scratches at it with a thumbnail, but it doesn't want to know – it seems to have gone through some sort of petrification process.

'Gravy,' Karen announces as she walks into the dressing room.

That's another cause of spasmodic bouts of stupefaction in both of them: *they have a dressing room*; a room just for *clothing*; not for *people*. Their old house didn't even have a room just for brooms, as in a broom cupboard. The dressing room has an entire wall fitted with wooden cubbies *solely for the storage of footwear*. Karen has managed to fill six of them, Alvin another three.

'Gravy?' Alvin echoes.

'Beef gravy,' she says with certainty. 'The last time you wore it was at Faye's wedding . . .'

The suit only comes out for wedding and funerals.

'. . . She served up roast beef and Yorkshire pudding.'

'How do you remember these things? That was five years ago.'

'Seven. She's divorced now. You want to wear it tomorrow?'

'I thought I should. What do you think?'

She peers at the stain. 'Well, the judge might not be able to see it. Depends how far away you are and how old and blind he is.'

The suit comes out for weddings and funerals and also for criminal trials.

Alvin is due in court tomorrow. Not – to his continuing astonishment – on his own account. He's to be a character witness for Kevan Kennedy.

Six months ago, when Kevan confessed, the police didn't believe him right away. They presumed Alvin must have got to him with a better offer. However, they grudgingly got off their arses and checked out his claim that he'd been paid his bribe in the multi-storey car park at the Aviary Shopping City. The CCTV tape bore him out, showing him taking a package from a man in a Volvo. The car turned out to belong to a private investigator, previously seen crawling around the Glenn. Both he and Kevan are on trial, alongside a third defendant. The irony is that he owns the Aviary. Alvin has wondered how Jeremy Bird feels, knowing that he was fingered by his own security system.

Unlike the other two, Kevan pleaded guilty.

Now guilty verdicts are in on Bird and his detective. The three of them will be sentenced tomorrow and Alvin will be there to do what he can for Kevan. That's the other irony of the case: the one person prepared to put a positive spin on Kevan's character happens to be the victim of the conspiracy he's on trial for.

It's not the first time he has been to court recently. A couple of months ago Kevan was tried for the mugging. Alvin was called as a prosecution witness. Being Alvin, he kept his tone as unaccusatory as possible, something that delighted Kevan's barrister, but annoyed the hell out of the judge. 'For goodness' sake, Mr Lee,' he said. 'Are you suggesting that Mr Kennedy was merely helping an elderly lady to cross the road . . . at *knife* point?'

Kevan got three years.

'I'll have a go at it with a sponge,' Karen says, picking at the stain with a nail. 'Could make all the difference between prison and community service.'

'Perhaps,' he agrees. 'Stranger things have happened lately.'

The strangest thing of all was the speed with which the Birds conceded the fight for their mother's money. Both Alvin and Trevor Poll expected them to scrap to the bitter end. 'When you've got their kind of dough, there's no such thing as a lost cause,' the solicitor opined. But a short while after Jeremy Bird was charged, the claim on the estate was dropped. Probate ran its course and, even after costs and inheritance tax, Alvin and Karen found themselves considerably richer than they were before.

The first thing Alvin did was to write fresh cheques to the five charities that Louise Bird was about to favour on the day she was mugged.

Which made barely a dent.

So they paid off their mortgage arrears.

And their mortgage.

And Alvin finally got the gears fixed on his bike.

And he got brand-new bicycles for Shannon, Annie and Sid.

And a Lambretta for Mercedes.

And he bought a new television.

It was so big that it wouldn't actually fit in the living room.

But strangely, the solution to that problem lay just around the corner and six miles up the road. The Birds moved out of Beresford House, which gave Alvin a choice of four living rooms, in any one of which a 52-inch plasma-screen television seems self-effacingly titchy.

That Jeremy Bird and his family moved out without a whimper seemed for a time the most bizarre turn of events. But it fell into place when Alvin heard that as soon as Jeremy Bird was charged, his wife hired a first-rate lawyer and initiated divorce. While he licked his wounds in his Mayfair flat, she calculated that since he didn't actually own it, Beresford House could form no part of a settlement. She moved out – Jeremy Bird owns three houses, plus the W1 apartment – and now the former Miss United Kingdom is catching the last rays of the Provençal summer and handling the dissolution of her marriage via fax and email. And Alvin at last twigged what her game was; that leaving her husband's nemesis with vacant possession of his family home was her final act of punishment.

If things had turned out differently, if, rather than Jeremy Bird, Alvin had been the one to end with the guilty verdict, he *firmly* believes that Karen would not have made him pay so dearly for fucking up. But that's Alvin for you.

'Shall we do it?' he asked Karen when Poll informed him that he now had free run of a neogothic mansion. And a trout lake.

'Move in?' she replied. 'Why the hell wouldn't we?'

'All that space, though . . .'

'I'm sure we'll find a way of filling it, angel.'

Mary *Jaaay!*

At the bottom of the staircase . . .

It's one of those that showily cleave in two halfway up.

At the bottom of the staircase Alvin hops back as the stabilisers on Sid's bike threaten to lop off his toes. He's racing to catch up with Annie, who is disappearing through the doorway that leads to the dining room. More of a dining hall – like Alvin and Karen's shoes in the dressing-room cubbyholes, their tiny gate-legged table didn't have a hope of filling it.

He follows the cyclists.

The room is buzzing, though the only dining taking place involves crisps, Tango and baby milk. Chenil Shakespeare sits against a panelled wall, holding a bottle to Kanye Pharrell's mouth. He's bigger than when Alvin first cradled him in a single hand, but he would still fit into a Start-rite shoebox. In the far corner Shannon is with Roland Goffe and Curtis Young who are hunched over Louise Bird's Macintosh. Alvin has no idea what they're doing, but he trusts it isn't porn. Debbie Coates, Kelly Hendricks and Aaliyah Pratt sit on chairs in the centre of the room. Beside them are Jackie Farrow and Jimi Becker – Becker of the famous party – two more Wood Hill kids who almost slipped into Alvin's orbit in ILD. Despite its inaccessibility, Beresford House has become a drop-in centre for his former charges, as well as for their mates.

Ajab, a wiry Indian boy, hovers around Curtis. He's not Wood Hill and Alvin doesn't know him. But he's spent enough time around teenagers to know a walking pharmacy when he sees one. He's keeping a close eye on Ajab. His gothic mansion turning into a five-star crack house isn't part of the dream.

Annie and Sid join Debbie, Kelly, Aaliyah, Jackie and Jimi, who are bobbing their heads rhythmically. In front of them – surrounded by amps, mics, guitars on stands, keyboards on flimsy trestles, a drum kit, cables snaking and tangling across the parquet floor – sits Jamie McGreevy, his bum perched on a tall stool, a scuffed Gibson acoustic perched on his thigh. He hasn't had an audience as rapt as this since 1986, and probably not even then. This is Jamie Unplugged . . .

He is the lover man
The everyone's brother man
She's gotta let him in her heart
But she is queen of mean
Too wrapped up in how she's seen
She'll miss the train when he departs

. . . Or perhaps Unhinged.

The song is new and while the tune is strong, the lyrics are distinctly iffy. *Queen of mean*? Someone he met in *Sugar* magazine? But Alvin has no need to wonder who the train-riding boy is. There is a giveaway plastered across the guitar's soundboard. The old sticker – the one that proclaimed IF IT AIN'T STIFF IT AIN'T WORTH A FUCK – has been covered by a sparkly new one, one that commands the reader to SMILE because JESUS LOVES YOU.

It happened two months ago, Jamie's road-to-Damascus moment, though actually it was on the motorway to Birmingham. It was when his can't-fail ring tones venture inevitably went belly up, leaving several people – but mostly Colin Stanislavski – measurably poorer and extremely angry. Jamie did a runner, taking flight on a coach to the Midlands. That was when he discovered the Good News. Christ, apparently, sat on the seat beside him. 'He was *there*, Alv, I *swear*,' Jamie exulted. 'He reached out to me just past Newport Pagnell services and I let him in, man.'

And for two months he has remained firm. Easily beating his conversion to Buddhism (ten days), his rigorous attempt to get to grips with the central tenets of Islam (less than twenty-four hours) and his devotion to Scientology (fifteen minutes tops). Perhaps this is the real thing. Whatever, the new Jesus-Jamie is non-drinking, non-drugging and non-scamming.

Annie arrives at Alvin's side as Jamie reprises the chorus. By now Alvin is bobbing his head along with the rest of them because the tune really is insidiously hooky. 'You like the song?' he asks her.

She ignores him. Her eyes are screwed up in concentration as she studies Jamie's fingers on the frets. 'F . . . C . . . B . . . A . . .' she whispers.

'That's brilliant, sweetheart,' Alvin coos. 'You really know your chords.'

'F, C, B, A!' she snaps, annoyed with her father now.

'Yeeeees?'

'"Sk8er *Boi*"!'

Alvin shakes his head, baffled.

'Avril *Thing*! That's her *song*! "Sk8er Boi"! It's spelled with an *eight*. F, C, B, A is the *chords*!'

At least Jamie has moved on, thinks Alvin resignedly; at least he's no longer nicking tunes from Brian Wilson, Ray Davies and (once) Mozart. He's up with the times, raiding the catalogues of twenty-first-century pop minxes.

Jamie contrives a fade-out to a ripple of approval from all except Annie. Alvin feels he can't be too picky because – although he's slightly unsettled by God's omnipresence in his friend – if it weren't for Jamie's rudely energetic presence, The Project might never have got off the ground.

Not that it's flying exactly. And not that it was ever something that Alvin planned – a few weeks ago it wasn't even a project with a lowercase p. It just kind of *happened*.

Like so: Curtis and Roland were helping Karen and Alvin to move in – not that there was much to move. 'What shall we do with these?' Curtis asked. He was talking about the two amplifiers, the cased bass guitar and the two-thirds of a drum kit that had been in Alvin's tiny garden shed, covered with dust sheets, untouched for the best part of a decade. 'Stick them over there for now,' Alvin replied, pointing towards the dining hall. Five minutes later he jumped at the sound of a throbbing E string. Someone – Roland – was attacking his Fender American Vintage '57 Precision Bass and – so bloody what that it had been gathering mildew in a shed for years? – it aroused aggressively protective feelings that he hadn't experienced since stumbling across eight-year-old Mercedes being bullied. When he reached the dining hall he found that Roland wasn't being unkind to the instrument and before he knew it he was playing it himself – for the first time in what seemed like, oh . . .

For ever.

That was when the Pied Piper effect kicked in.

All to do with the magnetic properties of music. Jimi Becker turned up one day with a cheap Stratocaster copy and, shortly after, Jamie arrived with the genuine article, plus his Sinclavier. And again, before Alvin knew it, Beresford House had been transformed into a sort of commune for wannabe musos; an English version of the château where the Stones hung out one legendary summer recording *Exile on Main Street*. Less musically competent, perhaps, and minus the industrial quantities of heroin – though maybe Ajab is doing something about that. *Keep a very close eye*, Alvin tells himself.

The turning point from bumbling summer-long jam into Project with a cap P was provided by Wood Hill's Girl Least Likely To – Chenil Shakespeare. One day she arrived with Kanye

Pharrell – and, it has to be said, probably a litre of Woodpecker inside her – parted her hair curtains and opened her mouth. All present – and more than likely the birds in the trees outside – were almost literally blown away.

'Mary *Jaaay*!' Debbie exclaimed.

'Dusty bloody Springfield!' Alvin gasped.

'Janis effing Joplin!' Jamie raved.

Yes, the girl can *sing*.

The only problem remains her crippling shyness. Plying her with fortifying flagons of cider isn't a responsible option, but luckily Alvin has discovered a solution in Kelly and Aaliyah. They can't hold a tune too convincingly, but they possess a quality that, these days, is more valuable still; they *look* as if they can. Stick microphones in their hands and it's like throwing a switch: suddenly Kelly and Aaliyah have the diva aura of pop stars. Put Chenil in between them and they act as props, wedging her tight, giving her no place to run and nothing to do but open her gob and sing.

As soon as they discovered Chenil's gift, it dawned on Alvin that they should do this properly.

'We should do this properly,' he announced to Jamie and Karen.

'*Yeah,*' Jamie enthused, 'lay down a demo and get it to the labels.'

'No, no, *this*.' Alvin swept his arms outwards, gesturing at his manor house filled with council-estate youth. 'Look at them. *Listen* to them. I've never seen these kids so committed to anything. Not to anything that didn't come with a jail term at least.'

Karen looked at him warily.

'What are we gonna do when the summer's over?' he continued. 'Just let them drift off? How could any of them afford the gear or the rehearsal space? We've got this place, we've got money to invest in equipment. We should make this somewhere they can come to learn how to play and record, compose . . .'

He trailed off as Karen's eyebrows arced upwards.

'Well, I told you we'd find a way of filling the space,' she said at last. 'I think it's a brilliant idea.'

And so The Project was born. Enough gear has been bought to make Beresford House seem like a rich man's Abbey Road. Builders have begun the job of converting the estate's redundant stable block into rehearsal and studio space. Until that is ready, the dining hall will have to do.

If it all sounds a bit dreamlike – a bit like something in a Cliff Richard film; *let's do a show and let's do it right here* – well, the venture hasn't been problem-free. Alvin has had his reputation to contend with. The cloud under which he departed Wood Hill hasn't entirely dispersed, though he has moved on from being the local pervert. Now he's the rich pervert in the big house – a bit like Michael Jackson, though he has yet to build the theme park. The gossip led to resistance from parents reluctant to let their children hang out with the rich pervert in the big house. Most of it was fomented by Debbie's mum.

'You could do what Jacko did,' Karen suggested. 'You know, go see her . . . with a Cartier watch.'

Alvin did go to see her, though when he waited nervously on her doorstep he wished he'd brought a peace offering – a Timex at least. In the event, it went better than he'd expected. Her qualified welcome was down to the fact that some weeks earlier Alvin had decided not to help the police with their assault case against her boyfriend – enough was enough, he'd decided – and as a result they'd dropped the charges. Maddie Coates gave him grudging thanks and a cup of tea for that. And she agreed to let her daughter come out to Beresford House – no sleepovers though; not that any were in the pipeline.

Alvin wonders if she is impressed by the progress Debbie has made on the drums, or at least by the fact that while she has been at Beresford House she hasn't once been caught shoplifting.

And Jamie hasn't relieved any more suckers of their life savings. He has been too busy writing. Alvin – in between teaching Roland the bass – has been helping, steering him clear of the more blatant rip-offs, though somehow the Avril Lavigne copy slipped under his radar.

Now they have a clutch of songs that don't sound like anything else – at least like nothing in living memory – that don't have *overtly* Christian lyrics and that Alvin and Jamie, with the aid of Curtis's nascent wizardry with Apple Macs, are attempting to lend a modishly urban sound.

'Get a load of this, Alv,' Jamie says, putting down his guitar and fumbling with the mouse on a Mac set up beside his Sinclavier.

Nothing happens.

He clicks pointlessly with the mouse, then tosses it aside angrily.

'Curt, why can't I get this effing tape to play?' he calls.

'It ain't on tape, man,' Curtis yells from the far side of the room without looking round. 'It's *digital*.'

'You know what he's on about?' Jamie says to Alvin.

'Everything's digital now,' Alvin explains. 'We don't use tape any –'

'Whatever, we need some grown-up help here. I mean, the kid's doing his best, but look at all this.' He gestures at the cables snaking and tangling across the floor like a spectacular linguine disaster and at the lumps of hardware, some of it still in boxes, other pieces stacked up and glowing with tiny esoteric lights. 'What does it all *do*?' he asks helplessly.

Who knows? Alvin has spent several tens of thousands of Louise Bird's pounds on studio ware, but he could have been sold a satellite launch system for all the sense it makes. Curtis *is* doing his best, but he faces a virtually sheer learning curve.

'You're right, Jamie, we could do with some help,' Alvin says. 'Someone with a keen analytical mind, a superb grasp of detail.'

'We need someone who can tell me where to stick these effing jacks,' Jamie says, holding up a bunch of plugs in need of homes.

'I've had a thought,' Alvin says.

'What?'

'This bloke . . . Used to be a wiz with traffic lights.'

'*Traffic* lights . . . ? Whatever, call him, get him in. But right now I wanna play you this tune.' Jamie scrabbles with the mouse again but still nothing happens. '*Curtis!* Help!' he yells.

Curtis saunters across the hall, takes a desultory look at the computer monitor, flicks at the mouse, clicks and . . . lift-off.

The room is shaken to its exposed oak beams by the most thrilling bass line Alvin has ever thrummed. Eight bars in a brand-new sound kicks in . . .

Chenil singing with the passion of a drunken gypsy king about the redemptive power of love (and *honestly*, you would only know she's singing about Our Saviour Jesus Christ if you were really, *really* listening for it).

As one, the room looks at her. Only Kanye Pharrell seems unimpressed. No one so much as flinches for a full one hundred and ninety-seven seconds, the length of the track.

As soon as it fades, bodies snap back to life. Jamie and Alvin look on as Chenil is mobbed by Debbie, Kelly and Aaliyah, and then by everyone else.

'You put the vocal on, then,' Alvin says to his partner.

'Yeah, while you were out playing at Caretaker Willy. Bitchin', huh?' Although out of respect for Jesus, Jamie has dramatically curbed his cursing, he has managed to insinuate some street-level Curtisisms into his vocabulary.

'It . . . is . . . totally . . . bitchin',' Alvin can only agree.

'Perfect juxtaposition of voice and rhythm track . . .'

Correct context? *Check*. No rogue N? *Check*.

'. . . I reckon we've nailed that one right in the oxlymoron.'

Something that, over the years, Alvin has learned to accept about Jamie McGreevy: it's *always* swings and roundabouts; lose Buddha, gain Jesus; and just as you've got used to life without junxtaposition . . .

'I could hear that in the kitchen,' says Karen who has appeared at Alvin's side. 'It was astonishing.'

'It's as good as the old days, babe,' Jamie says.

'Well, I wasn't around for your old days, guys, but I'd guess that this is even better. You need to get this in front of some A & R people.'

Jamie and Alvin look at one another – maybe she's right.

'You've found an absolute gem in that girl,' Karen continues. 'When I worked at the studio, Teena Marie came in for a session. I was never a soul girl, but she left me gasping for breath. I'd never heard anything like it. Chenil is almost as good and she's only sixteen.'

'The Lord gave her the gift,' Jamie says. 'Let's praise him for that.'

'Sod him. Let's praise Alvin,' Karen says, snaking an arm around her boyfriend's waist. 'If he hadn't stuck by her all these years, who knows where she'd be now? Possibly dead on a toilet floor; certainly not behind a mic giving us all great big bloody goosebumps.'

Alvin looks at his feet, suddenly feeling as bashful as Chenil.

But whatever his part in it, Alvin *knows* that he has just been witness to one of life's tiny moments of specialness; the sort of moment that *does* raise sizeable goosebumps; that defies adequate description; that only leaves the describer with *Look, you just had to be there, right?*

And luckily he was.

George, the patron saint of England (and also, for your information, of butchers, boy scouts and genital herpes)

A little later, Alvin is still feeling euphoric, though egg, chips and three noisy children are helping to draw him earthwards. It's dinner time *chez* Karen and Alvin. The family now eats at a kitchen table large enough to seat a rugby team, their wives and the club mascot.

'They're FOXES!' Sid shrieks at Annie, who's ten feet away at the far end of the table. 'You HAVE to shoot them or they eat the CATS.'

'We don't have any *cats*, poo bum,' his sister sneers.

'Bet there was cats. Bet the foxes EATED them!' Sid's eyes are rimmed with tears. 'Dad*dee*, can we get a gun . . . *pleeease*?'

'Shut up, *murderer*,' Shannon spits.

'Give him a break, Shannon,' Alvin says. 'He's only four. And sorry, Sid, but we're not getting a gun.'

The tears spill down Sid's cheeks now and Alvin puts an arm around his shoulder. 'I'll get you one of those water blaster things,' he says.

'Won't kill foxes,' Sid whimpers.

'No, but it'll make them really wet. Foxes *hate* water.'

Shotgun Sid, Karen calls him. Alvin doesn't know what to make of his son's new and urgent need to kill stuff – anything, basically, with fur, feathers or fishy scales. The most plausible explanation is the fresh country air; perhaps there's something in it.

The kitchen door creaks open and Curtis pokes his head through the gap. He looks sheepish because he knows he's out of bounds. Karen has been remarkably amenable about having her new home overrun by mostly undisciplined teenagers. Her one stipulation has been that the east wing, their quarters which include the kitchen, stays off limits.

However, she doesn't look too pissed off now. 'Hi, Curtis,' she says. 'I thought you'd gone back to town.'

'Sorry,' he mutters. 'I was just doing the website and that.'

The website: another of Alvin's schemes. Lynette Moorhouse mentioned that she wanted to set up an online forum for transsexuals. Alvin mentioned that he happened to know a wiz at computers. 'Are you *mad*?' Donna Hutton shrieked. 'It's like getting a Palestinian to build an air raid shelter for an Israeli.' She's convinced he'll booby-trap the site with lady-boy pop-ups or some such. But Alvin is prepared to trust him and – after all the flowers and the free burger that didn't give her dysentery – so too is Lynette.

'What's up?' Alvin asks Curtis because clearly something is.

'I found something, yeah? You'd better look at it.'

'What is it?'

'Like these two letters . . . One of 'em's to you.'

Alvin, Karen and Curtis stoop over the iMac while Curtis clicks on a Word file. A white page fills the screen and Curtis stands back as Karen and Alvin read. *Dear Mr Lee,* it starts, *You will almost certainly have no idea who I am, but I wanted to write and express my thanks to you.*

'I've seen this,' Alvin says. 'It was on there when I went to Louise Bird's flat. It was the thing she must have been writing when she . . . died.'

But this time the letter doesn't halt abruptly, mid-sentence. It continues all the way to the bottom of the screen.

'I don't get it,' he says. 'I thought she hadn't written all this. Or she'd lost it. Hadn't saved it or whatever.'

'She hadn't, right? You know, saved it and that,' Curtis explains.

'So how did you find it?' Karen asks.

'Nothing ever gets lost, yeah? There's this cache thing. On the hard drive. I mean, you think it's lost or trashed or whatever, but it's still there. On the cache thing.' Curtis looks at his audience and sees that he lost them at the first *cache*. 'Anyway, I managed to find it.'

'You're a bloody genius,' Alvin says admiringly.

Curtis looks at him awkwardly. 'You'd better read the letter, man.'

So Alvin does.

Dear Mr Lee,

You will almost certainly have no idea who I am, but I wanted to write and express my thanks to you. I am the lady that you found being attacked by a vicious mugger. Your intervention was an act of unimaginable bravery.

Not only that, but during the attack I sensed that you are one of the silent majority, among whom I am proud to include myself. I knew immediately that I had come across a true fellow when I heard you call my attacker 'scum'.

'Did I call him that?' Alvin says out loud. His stomach is lurching; it senses trouble ahead.

It is a cause of immense sadness to me that in this damnable age of political correctness, we can no longer freely express ourselves on an issue that is leading to the disintegration of civilised society. You were so right, Mr Lee. That boy is scum, as are all of his kind. It is a truth too few are prepared to acknowledge. The black man is not like us. He is lazy, corrupt and dissolute. Allowing the Negro into this country remains the gravest mistake our nation has ever committed.

'The heinous old witch,' Karen gasps.

'She thought I was a *racist* . . .'

Karen puts her hand on Alvin's arm.

'I'm *not*.'

'Of course you're not,' she says.

'I'm *not* a bloody racist.'

'I thought that's what she was getting at,' Curtis mumbles as he watches Alvin and Karen deconstruct the letter for him.

'I'm not a racist, Curtis. I didn't call him scum. Jesus, what did I say?'

'It doesn't matter,' Karen soothes. 'We know you're not racist. The old bat was loopy – as in loopy like Hitler, but also as in senile. It doesn't *matter*.'

'It *does*.' Alvin is sounding desperate now. 'What the hell did I say?'

'Please, Alvin, no one thinks you're racist,' Karen insists. 'Well, apart from one nutty old lady. Who's dead. So *literally* no one in the world has you down as racist. Now, Curtis, can we finish this letter?'

They've read to the bottom of the screen. Curtis scrolls the document on.

Sadly, too many of our fellow whites have been less fortunate than was I in finding a saviour from the black scourge. I will remain indebted to you for the rest of my life. By way of recompense, I have named you in my will. You deserve what-

ever I can leave you and I will rest at peace in the knowledge that my estate has been left to a man who embodies the integrity and chivalry of St George.

Yours in gratitude,

'Jesus . . .' Alvin whimpers, lost for anything further to say.

'Nazi bloody nutcase,' Karen says. 'I suppose we'll discover she was chairwoman of the British National Party next.'

'Er . . . is that what BNP stands for?' Curtis asks. 'You know, like them Nazi skinhead lot?'

'Yes . . . Why?'

'Man, I feel really bad about telling you this.'

'Telling us what?' Karen asks.

'That was the other letter I found. It was to them. She was sending them a cheque for, like, half a million quid.'

Would it help if I told you?

'C'mon, Alvin, you did your best for him.'

'*Six* months.'

'Look, he's already got three years for the mugging, so he probably won't even notice.'

'But six months doesn't seem fair. He did the right thing. It was him who turned Bird in – no one else.'

Alvin and Karen are sitting on a bench in the Crown Court's wide central corridor, drinking coffee from plastic cups. Court traffic – clerks, solicitors, barristers, the accused and their victims – bustles past them.

'Look at it this way,' Karen says. 'He did better than Bird.'

'Yeah, *four* years. That's heavy. Did you see him in the dock?'

'Yes. *Jesus*, he's *ugly*.'

'No, did you see how he looked? So . . . pathetic.'

'For Christ's sake, tell me you're not feeling sorry for him . . . *Tell* me.'

Alvin can't look at her because, well, sorry is exactly what he's feeling.

They are interrupted by a cough. They look up to see the other Karen. Kelis – now walking – is at her side, tugging hard on a harness as if she can sense that this is the place where people are sent down for extended chunks of their lives and SHE WANTS NO PART OF IT.

'Hi Karen,' Alvin says, turning to his own Karen. 'Karen, this is Karen, Kevan's mum.'

His Karen stands up and extends a hand. 'Hi . . . I'm sorry about your son. Six months . . .'

'That was bloody harsh,' Alvin says, standing as well.

Karen Nash shrugs. 'I look at it like this: me and Kelis have got the flat to ourselves for three years anyway, so . . .' The thought seems of scant consolation. 'I just wanted to say thanks,' she says, pulling herself together. 'You didn't have to say all that in there, not after what he did . . . It was really kind.'

'Honestly, it was the least I could do,' Alvin says with a shrug of his own. 'I'm just sorry it didn't make a difference.'

'You did your best, yeah?' Karen Nash looks at him, her face sad, but her eyes oozing warmth. 'I'd better be off. Kelis wants her dinner.'

As she scoops up her daughter, Alvin's Karen prods him with her elbow.

'There's something else,' he says. 'Something we want to give you.'

He reaches into his jacket pocket and takes out a folded cheque. He hands it to Karen Nash. She opens it out and stares at it with frank amazement.

'Twenty *grand*,' she says eventually.

'It's just a thank-you,' Alvin explains, 'for what you did for me. You know, for making Kevan go back to the police.'

'I can't accept this,' she says quietly.

'You have to,' Alvin insists. 'I want you to.'

'*We* want you to,' Alvin's Karen says. 'If you hadn't done what you did, Alvin would be going to prison now.'

'Thank you . . . It's really, really kind of you . . . But . . . I just can't take it.'

She pushes the cheque into Alvin's hand.

He shoves it right back.

'Please take it,' he says.

'I *can't*.'

'I insist,' he insists. 'It's what you deserve ... And it's not charity, if that's what you're thinking.'

'It's not that,' she says. She seems embarrassed now. 'It's 'cause ... Just that ... You know ... I haven't got a bank account.'

'That went well,' Karen says breezily as she watches the other Karen bundle Kelis through the doors leading to freedom. 'We not only made someone better off, but we also persuaded her to join the twenty-first century via the banking system. Now she can drown in credit card applications like the rest of us ... So why are you still looking so glum?'

But Alvin doesn't answer. He is staring straight ahead ...

'Alvin?'

... At a teenage girl dressed in a sober black suit. She is returning Alvin's stare with an intense glare of her own. Alvin remembers the last time he saw her. Then she looked at him with glib indifference before brushing past him to get to her perky little Peugeot – her jewel-like eyes carried none of the jet-black loathing they're filled with now.

'Who's she?' Karen asks, a vestige of suspicion in her voice.

'His daughter.'

'I thought she'd gone to France with her mum.'

'She must have come back. To support her dad.'

The two-way stare is broken by a gaggle of robed and wigged barristers. When they move on, the girl is no longer there. But her work is done, its impact still visible in the haunted look on Alvin's face.

'Don't do this to yourself, angel,' Karen urges, knowing *exactly* what he is doing to himself. 'It's not your fault. It's her father she should be blaming. He got exactly what he deserved. He's a bastard. End of story.'

'But ...'

'But *what*?'

'Yes, he's a bastard, but . . . he's also a dad. And he fucks up like all of us do. He's just . . . *human*. Not Darth Vader or some pantomime villain. I know what you're gonna say, but it'd really make me feel better if –'

'Please, *no*. Don't go there,' Karen pleads, knowing *exactly* where he's going. 'We've done our good deed for the day. I was happy to give something to Kevan's mum. She deserves it. But *him?*'

'Just something . . . a little bit. If we gave some of it back to him, just to show there're no hard feelings . . . I've never felt like it was my – *our* money anyway. He's lost everything.'

'He's lost his wife and temporary use of his six cars, but only through his own greedy stupidity. His daughter's clearly standing by him. And he's still *loaded*. When he comes out of jail he'll still have his fortune – far, far more than we've got. Besides, his mother didn't want him to have it. She left it to *you*.'

'His *mother*,' Alvin says. 'She also gave half a bloody million to the BN-bloody-P. How do you think that makes me feel?'

'OK, OK, bad point. I shouldn't have mentioned his mum. Look, think about what you're saying. Giving him money is just mad. If you feel bad, write him a nice letter or something . . .'

But she can see she's barely making a dent in his armour-plated conscience. Time for a different tack.

'Would it help if I told you he's a chip off the old block?' she asks.

'How do you mean?'

'Like mother like son kind of thing.'

'What are you talking about?'

'Would it make a difference if I told you he's been bankrolling British fascists for years?'

'Has he?'

'Would it help if I told you that all the progress the BNP has been making in the elections – all those town councillors they've got in places like Barking and wherever – is down to Jeremy Bird and his loot?'

'Really? Well, yes, of course it would make a diff— Hang on, how did you find out?'

'Er . . .'

'It was Curtis, wasn't it? He found something on the Net, didn't he?'

'Well, he was obviously devastated by what he found out yesterday. You wouldn't blame him if he did a bit of snooping, would you?'

'The bastard – Not Curtis, *Bird* . . .'

'You can never *truly* tell with people, can you?'

'. . . financing the neo-Nazis. The utter *bastard*.'

'C'mon,' Karen says, seizing the moment by grabbing his arm and dragging him towards the revolving doors and the High Street beyond. 'I know what'll make you feel better.'

'Where are we going?'

'Trust me, I know what I'm doing.'

One Flew into the Cuckoo*s Nest

Jonathan Craig steers his father's car slowly up the long drive. He's nervous – as scared as he was on his first day at Wood Hill . . . That seems like a long time ago. The *first* most terrifying day of his life. Which was followed by ninety-seven more. Then he quit. Life didn't exactly get better after that, but at least he didn't have to go to Wood Hill any more.

And today it starts all over again.

But today is going to be different.

Today he's got Alvin.

Alvin Lee is amazing, Jonathan has decided. 'He's practically a saint,' his mother tells him repeatedly and he doesn't disagree. Actually, he goes further. Alvin Lee *is* a saint. Who else has *ever* taken so much time to get to know him? His mother maybe, but even she doesn't know him like Alvin does. And who else has helped him get back onto his feet after his terrible accident?

OK, his mum has helped.

And his therapist. The new one. The old one had to go. He asked too many questions. The new one is a proper psychiatrist. He gives him pills and they help a lot – the ones to help him sleep, the others for the pain in his hip and for his headaches, the yellow ones that . . . What do they do? Help him to wake up happy, face the world with confidence.

But mostly Alvin has helped. Alvin has got him this far. Ready to face . . . *young* people again. He isn't quite sure what he wants him to do. Something to do with wires and plugs. They're making music up there and they can't make it properly until they sort out what plugs in where. Whatever, it requires a Keen Analytical Mind and a Superb Grasp of Detail. That's what Alvin said. And he has both of those things – someone he used to work with once told him.

He's scared all right, but he's ready for this. In his bag he's got his electrical tools and his ear defenders . . . Just in case the noise gets a bit much. They look just like professional studio headphones, so no one will be able to tell. He's got his pills as well, the yellow ones. His beanie hat too. His mum thinks it looks silly, but he likes it and when he pulls it down it covers up quite a lot of the rash.

He's ready.

Let's rock 'n' roll.

He drives around the house and stops the car outside a ramshackle building set to the rear. It looks like an old stable or something. There's a skip outside and lots of other builders' stuff stacked up – bricks and whatever. But there are no builders today because it's Saturday. But someone is working. A young person. He's painting a big mural on the end of the building. It's a montage sort of picture of guitars and drums and someone who looks a bit like Madonna. Or maybe one of the Spice Girls. It's hard to tell because it's a bit abstract. It's very good though. Bright and colourful.

Jonathan sits in the car and watches the painter for a bit. He recognises him. He's from Wood Hill. Jonathan remembers him. He wasn't one of the difficult ones. In fact, he never said a word. He's Romanian, you see.

Jonathan gets out of the car and the boy looks at him.

Jonathan waves. And smiles.

Then he sets off for the house.

He is ready to rock.

Like, two grand. For a telescope

Mercedes, nude, sweaty, slumps back onto the slatted pine bench. 'This is *brilliant*. I never knew we had this.'

'Neither did we until about a week ago,' says Karen, whose equally nude body also glistens with sweat.

Not being strictly mother and daughter, they seem to be qualmless about sprawling naked in front of one another.

'Whoo!' gasps Mercedes.

'*Whoo!*' Karen agrees.

They're in the sauna. The sauna is in the cellar at Beresford House. Alvin found it when Sid and Annie went missing for a couple of hours one afternoon. They'd turned it into their secret den, complete with teddies, dolls and a selection of Tupperware. Despite a certain amount of resistance, Karen and Alvin reclaimed it as the family sauna.

'So, how's uni?' Karen asks.

'Oh, you know . . . Cool.'

Mercedes is a fresher now, home for the weekend. She's only as far away as central London, but she chose to live in a hall of residence in Bloomsbury rather than commute from the family mansion (with its family sauna). She's at University College reading Astronomy.

Astronomy! How the hell did that happen? Karen was surprised that she chose university at all – what, with unprecedented access to funding for not one but several gap years. Then that she chose astronomy . . . Karen had supposed she would go for something more right-on and voguish – a BA in Animal Rights, say, with a module called The Meanings of Evil: A Relative Study of Battery Farming and the Holocaust.

It's her first weekend at home. Karen expected her to turn up with the traditional student bundle of washing. And maybe a telescope. But all she had were cigarettes and a mobile phone.

Karen and Mercedes aren't alone in the sauna. Flat out on a bench on the other side of the room is Lynette Moorhouse, snoring quietly. She fell asleep almost as soon as she lay down. She's permanently exhausted these days, stressed from her new job as Wood Hill's head of humanities. She wasn't the front-runner for the post. But she gave a terrific interview and her path was eased when Colin Stanislavski, the short-odds favourite, inexplicably took his name from the shortlist. She never found out why he pulled out. It was strange, though. One minute he was up for it, the next – after a brief meeting with Chadwick – he was professing complete apathy . . . Very odd. There was talk of a compromising photograph, but she dismissed it. Wood Hill has always been a hotbed of gossip. She'd seen one career too many destroyed by it to want Stainslavski to become another victim, however much she disliked him.

Some days she wishes he'd got the job. It's not easy running a teaching department the size of a small African republic – and the fact that she is now Donna's boss has added friction to their relationship – but she's making a decent fist of it. By the time Friday comes, though, she's wasted and most weekends she bolts for Beresford House – a country house hotel for one.

'Aren't you gagging to have a look?' Mercedes asks.

'No, not particularly,' Karen replies.

'But she used to have a willy. And *balls*. Don't you wanna see what they did with it all?'

'No, I don't. And be quiet. She might hear you.'

'She's dead to the world, man. I'm gonna have a quick peek.'

Mercedes leans forward and plucks at the corner of the towel that covers Lynette.

'Stop it, Mercedes,' Karen commands. 'Stop it right now or I'll wake her.'

'Spoilsport,' Mercedes says, dropping the towel and sitting back down beside Karen. They recline in silence for a while, listening to the steady thump of bass and drums that travels slightly menacingly through the structure of the elderly building.

'What do you think of what they're doing up there?' Karen asks.

'What, Alvin's *Fame Academy*? You know, it's . . . cool.'

Which – given Mercedes's usual sneeriness towards her father's waifs and strays – translates as *totally fucking amazing*.

'As long as he doesn't go and spoil it by sticking them on something lame like *Top of the Pops*,' she qualifies.

'Of course,' Karen agrees. 'I mean, the charts, success . . . *phooey*.'

'*Exactly*, man.' Mercedes is still at the pre-irony stage, then. 'Who's the new weirdo up there?'

'Which one?' Karen asks.

'The guy with the Prozac grin and the rash all over his face.'

'He's called Jonathan. He's helping sort the equipment out. He used to be big in traffic lights or something.'

'Never heard of them.'

'It's not a band. The things at road junctions.'

'Figures. He looks a right trainspotter. And he's a gimp.'

'Don't be so cruel. He smashed his hip in a fall. He's going to walk like that for the rest of his life.'

'What did he fall off?'

'I don't know. Alvin won't say. He's very . . . *protective* of him.'

'God, him and his losers . . . By the way, he told me about Jeremy Bird being head Nazi or whatever.'

Karen doesn't respond, but closes her eyes, feigning a doze.

'Fucking incredible, huh?' Mercedes prods. 'Do you think they used to have parties in this place? You know, all dolled up in jackboots and swastikas?'

Karen's eyes close tighter, turning the doze into a Lynette-like sleep.

'How did you find out?' Mercedes asks. 'I mean, the old guy kept it pretty quiet, didn't he? Wouldn't've been good for business, I s'pose.'

Karen considers adding a snore.

'What, did you find a secret stash of papers hidden behind a secret panel or something? I mean, a place like this *must* have secret panels.'

'I didn't exactly find out,' Karen says at last.

'You what?'

'Your dad . . .' She leans in close to Mercedes and drops her voice to a whisper, all the while keeping her eye on Lynette for signs of movement. 'Yesterday he went off on one of his . . . One of his flights of saintliness.'

'Shit,' Mercedes says, perhaps beginning to glimpse the picture.

'He felt sorry for Jeremy Bird. Wanted to give him money.'

'*Idiot*, man.'

'*Shh*, keep your voice down . . . Anyway, I was desperate and came up with the BNP thing – it was kind of instant; a bit of improv.'

'You made it up? You *lied*?'

'Not *lied* exactly. I just posed the question. All I said was would it *help* if I said Jeremy Bird is a monster right-winger . . . I didn't actually *say* he is. I let your dad's imagination do the rest.'

'Man, Karen, you are . . . *wicked*.'

Karen thinks it's a compliment, though she can never tell with Mercedes. 'You're not going to tell him, are you?' she asks.

'And watch him give all our dosh to that ugly twat? I'm not stupid.'

'No, I know you're not,' Karen says. 'Thanks.'

'Anyway, he can't keep giving it away,' Mercedes adds. 'Not to strangers. I need to hit him for, like, two grand.'

'Two grand?'

'For a telescope.'

'Oh.'

'I really *need* one. And you can spend a lot more than two grand on one, you know.'

'I bet you can,' Karen says, thinking maybe of multi-million-pound mountaintop observatories. 'Look, don't worry, I'm sure it'll be OK. In fact, you might want to go for a slightly more expensive model.'

'Really?'

'It's an investment. In his daughter's future. He'll understand.'

'Cool. If you think so,' Mercedes says.

They steam in silence for a few minutes.

'So, what are your plans for Christmas?' Karen asks. 'You going to your mum's or sticking around with us?'

'That's *ages* away. Hadn't thought about it. Why?'

'Yesterday, after your dad's saint-attack, I had a little panic attack of my own. I could see all the money disappearing on . . . *causes*.'

'Man,' Mercedes gasps, fully in the picture now.

'I had this nightmare vision. Six months from now. He's giving our last twenty quid to a donkey sanctuary.'

'Maaan.'

'You don't want to know what he's spent on recording equipment.'

'That why you want me to get a more expensive telescope?'

'Every pound he spends on you is a pound he can't give away to –'

'Donkeys?'

'Don't get me wrong, Mercedes. I'm all for donkeys. But I'm

also quite pro *us* lot feeling a little benefit. Anyway, yesterday afternoon – in a *panic* – I dragged Alvin into a travel agent.'

'A travel agent?'

'And booked St Lucia.'

'St *Lucia*?'

'Two weeks at Christmas. All inclusive. A private villa in the hotel grounds. With our own plunge pool.'

'A *plunge* pool?'

'Flying business both ways.'

'*Jeez!*'

'Interested?' Karen asks, though she knows she had her at *travel agent*.

'St Lucia's got these, like, *awe*some night skies,' the astronomy student says. 'No ambient light pollution, you see?'

'You'll want to bring your telescope, then.'

e

Matt Beaumont

e is a tapestry of insincerity, backstabbing and bare-faced bitchiness – just everyday office politics.

Meet:

- a CEO with an MBA from the Joseph Stalin School of Management
- a director who is a genius, if only in his own head
- creatives with remarkable brains, if only in their trousers
- a copywriter with the two things no adwoman should ever show – underarm hair and a conscience
- secretaries who drip honey and spit cyanide
- the sad git in accounts

Consisting entirely of e-mails, *e* spends a week in the company of Miller Shanks, an advertising agency embarked upon the quest to land Coca-Cola – the account they would sell their collective grandmothers in a car boot sale to acquire. This is one pitch that nobody will ever forget . . .

'Depicts the Machiavellian scheming and summary sackings of the ad world in withering detail and with no shortage of dead-eye wit'
The Times

'Groundbreaking . . . an internet-enabled *Clarissa* for the 21st century'
Evening Standard

ISBN-13: 978 0 00 710068 2
ISBN-10: 0 00 710068 X

Staying Alive

Matt Beaumont

Murray's gone mad. He's started telling the truth at work. He's borrowed a stack of cash from a man with a gun, a speech impediment and no grasp whatsoever of APR. He's also taking drugs and – God help him – he's started dancing. Badly. To trance. And now he's on the run with a human version of Muttley and a teenage girl called Fish.

Which is strange, because a few weeks ago Murray didn't even burn the candle at one end. But when doctors tell him he has only months to live, he gives his boring old self the boot, relaunches a new improved Murray and falls in love with a passion he didn't know was in him.

His old self, of course, would tell him he's digging his own grave. But he'll be needing one of those soon anyway, won't he?

'Beaumont is an unflaggingly funny writer with a great facility for teetering on the edge of credibility and coming down on the correct side' *Guardian*

'Rip-roaringly funny...full of colourful characters and cinematic scenes...A brilliant read' *Heat*

ISBN-13: 978 0 00 716703 6
ISBN-10: 0 00 716703 2

Lightning Source UK Ltd.
Milton Keynes UK
28 October 2010

162068UK00001B/93/P

9 780007 335176